Joe Joyce is t the three
historical spy history/
biography of the Guinnesses and a critically acclaimed play,
The Tower, about James Joyce and Oliver St John Gogarty.
He is co-author with Peter Murtagh of *The Boss*, the classic
account of Charles Haughey in power, and *Blind Justice*,
about a miscarriage of justice in the 1970s. He has worked
as a journalist for *The Irish Times*, *The Guardian*, and Reuters
News Agency.

www.joejoyce.ie

Irish
Authors

Also by Joe Joyce

Fiction
Echobeat
Echoland
The Trigger Man
Off the Record

Non-Fiction
*The Guinnesses: The Untold Story of
Ireland's Most Successful Family*
Blind Justice (with Peter Murtagh)
The Boss: Charles J Haughey in Government
(with Peter Murtagh)

Plays
The Tower

www.joejoyce.ie

ECHOWAVE

Joe Joyce

NEW ISLAND

ECHOWAVE
First published in 2015 by Liberties Press
This edition published in 2017 by
New Island Books
16 Priory Office Park
Stillorgan
Co. Dublin
Ireland

www.newisland.ie

Copyright © Joe Joyce, 2017

The Author asserts his moral rights in accordance with the provisions
of the Copyright and Related Rights Act, 2000.

Print ISBN: 978-1-84840-649-0
Epub ISBN: 978-1-84840-650-6
Mobi ISBN: 978-1-84840-651-3

All rights reserved. The material in this publication is protected by
copyright law. Except as may be permitted by law, no part of the material may be reproduced (including by storage in a retrieval system)
or transmitted in any form or by any means; adapted; rented or lent
without the written permission of the copyright owner.

A CIP catalogue record for this book is available from the British
Library.

Typeset by JVR Creative India
Cover Design by Anna Morrison

New Island received financial assistance from The Arts Council (*An
Chomhairle Ealaíon*), 70 Merrion Square, Dublin 2, Ireland.

New Island Books is a member of Publishing Ireland.

MIX
Paper from
responsible sources
FSC
www.fsc.org   FSC® C013056

Printed and bound in Great Britain by
TJ International Ltd, Padstow, Cornwall

Prologue

A glint of light was the first he noticed. It was there one moment in the clear blue sky over the Atlantic, and it was gone the next so that he wasn't sure he had really seen it at all.

He was sitting on the ground against the crude concrete wall of the lookout post on the clifftop at Renvyle peninsula, sipping a mug of tea and feeling the warmth of the sun on his left. Ahead of him was the edge of Inishboffin and then the empty Atlantic, a deeper blue than the sky. From up here the surface of the ocean looked smooth, brushed here and there by a gentle breeze. Waves broke on the cove beneath the cliff, shuffling the shingle, and the breeze smoothed the long grass back from the edge of the headland.

He kept his eyes on the spot where he thought he had seen the glint of light, and then a speck appeared and he watched it grow bigger. Heading east-north-east, he thought automatically. One of the British patrols, going home to their base in Lough Erne, across the border in the North. Cutting the corner again, he gave a grim smile.

Under a secret agreement between the governments in Dublin and London, they were allowed to fly across the narrow strip of neutral Ireland that divided their base from the ocean. Known as the 'Donegal corridor', it saved the RAF patrols a lot of time and extended their range into the

Atlantic killing ground where German U-boats and British supply convoys from North America battled daily.

As the speck grew larger, though, it didn't look like one of their Catalina seaplanes: the shape was wrong.

He pushed himself up against the rough wall, tossed the dregs of his tea to one side, and exchanged the mug for the binoculars on the ledge inside the door of the tiny hut. He found the growing speck and focused the glasses on it. It was coming at an angle that made it difficult to identify, offering neither a head-on nor a clear side view. Definitely not a Catalina or any other seaplane: no floats underneath. He began to mentally tick off all the other possibilities, the British Liberators and the German Condors, all the usual belligerent air traffic that travelled the west coast of Ireland daily.

It wasn't any of them. It was a shape he wasn't used to, and he lowered the binoculars and glanced at the chart of fighter and bomber shapes on the wall. It didn't look like any of them.

He raised the binoculars again and tracked the plane as it approach the hump of Achill Island. Its silver fuselage had no camouflage and no markings that he could see. It occurred to him as it crossed the coast that it was gliding: something about its flight path. He listened as he watched, but he could hear nothing above the wind sighing through the grass and the rhythm of the waves on the shingle.

It's not going to make wherever it's heading for, he thought. He checked his watch as it continued inland, dipping from his sight behind the cone of Croagh Patrick. He went back into the hut and began entering the details in his logbook, but stopped after a moment and picked up the telephone. Headquarters would want to know about this immediately.

One

Paul Duggan lay on the bunk, wanting to die. Around him, the small metal box of the cabin vibrated and throbbed and shuddered and lurched as the coaster rose and dropped into the trough of another wave. The air was foetid with diesel fumes and the vomit in the bottom of the metal bucket that he held on the floor with an outstretched hand like a life-line.

He had nothing left to throw up. He had felt queasy on the crossing from Dublin to Holyhead, but had recovered while they unloaded their cargo of butter and cheese and took on coal for Lisbon. And waited for the navicert which would allow them safe passage through the British blockade. He thought he had got his sea legs as they headed south through the placid Irish Sea, sitting on deck in the summer sunshine, feeling the warm breeze, trying to relax into the motion of the ship. Then they had rounded Carnsore Point and headed west along the south coast of Ireland until the land fell behind beyond Mizen Head. They continued into the full force of the Atlantic until they reached twelve degrees longitude and swung south along the approved course for Portugal, just outside the British 'sink on sight' zone in the Bay of Biscay.

He wasn't sure how long he'd been in the bunk now and was beyond caring. Night was only distinguished from day by the arrival and snores of his cabin-mate, Jenkins, in the top bunk.

The door crashed open and Jenkins came in and held his nose. 'Get up,' he ordered. 'Captain wants everyone on deck.'

Duggan shook his head, the single movement exhausting him.

Jenkins took Duggan's bucket in one hand and grabbed his arm with the other. He was strong, a lifetime sailor in his mid-forties, twice Duggan's age. 'There's a Jerry bomber taking a look at us.' He pulled Duggan up like he was lifting a limp doll. 'Captain wants us ready to abandon ship if the fucker starts shooting.'

I don't care, Duggan thought as Jenkins pulled him along, bouncing off the narrow walls. Jenkins pushed him up a gangway on to the deck beside the bridge. The sunlight made him blink and the wind made him struggle for breath. He steadied himself against the wall of the bridge, holding on to the lever handle of another door, and looked around.

There was nothing to see, only water. It rose in leisurely swells that blocked out the horizon ahead and passed by in long languorous troughs behind. The plane came into view around the stern, flying low, and angled into a tight bank a couple of hundred yards away. He could see the black Luftwaffe cross on the fuselage and the swastika on the tail fin, and could make out the gondola with the forward gunner, in front of the bomb bay. A Focke-Wulf Condor, he thought, easily recognisable from its gondola.

The plane held its circle and Duggan made his way around the bridge, holding on to anything that would steady him, as it went by the bow, almost hidden behind a wave. The first mate was in front of the bridge, signalling with an Aldis lamp as soon as it came back into sight. Jenkins stood beside him, watching.

'What's he signalling?' Duggan asked, his interest in life reviving.

'Spelling out "Eire", Jenkins said. 'In case the fucker can't see it on the sides of the ship. Or doesn't know what the tricolour is.'

They watched the Condor continue its circle. It seemed to be climbing but it was hard to tell, as their horizon shifted up and down with the ocean and the ship's movement. Then the Condor levelled out and flew straight towards them.

He's attacking, Duggan thought, holding his breath, aware of their complete vulnerability. He could see the Perspex front of the gunner's gondola coming straight for them and knew there was a heavy machine gun there which could cut them in half in one burst.

The first mate sent a stream of curses at it as he signalled furiously with his lamp. Jenkins disappeared around the side of the bridge and instinct made Duggan turn to follow him, but he lost his footing and fell heavily on to the metal deck.

The plane swept over them, briefly blocking out the sun, its four engines thundering off the deck.

Jenkins bunched up the back of Duggan's heavy sweater and pulled him to his feet. 'You all right?' he asked.

Duggan nodded, rubbing his right shoulder where he'd fallen.

'That's one big fucker,' Jenkins said as they watched the plane climb away to the north. 'Wonder where he's off to.'

Continuing his patrol, Duggan could have told him. From Bordeaux up the west coast of Ireland to Stavanger in Norway, looking for British convoys. He had read enough daily reports from the lookout stations on the west coast to know the pattern. But he said nothing. No one on board, apart from the captain, knew he was in military intelligence. Or his real name. And the captain didn't know that, only knew him as Sean McCarthy.

Jenkins and other crewmen had probed for information during the first part of the voyage, when he had still been able to answer. Had he ever been to sea before? What part of the country was he from? Was he going on from Lisbon to America? Would he be coming back with them?

Duggan parried most of questions, telling the truth when it fitted with his cover. He hadn't been to sea before. He was from the west. No, he wasn't heading for America. Yes, he'd be coming back with them.

That had surprised Jenkins a little. So, Duggan had concluded, they've had one-way passengers before. Probably IRA men on the run, hoping to get to America. Or maybe Germany. Interesting, he'd thought, wondering if his superiors in G2 knew that this was one of the IRA's escape routes. But that was before he'd become really seasick and lost interest in his job, his mission, the war, remaining alive.

But the Condor scare and the fresh air had begun to revive him. The captain called down to him from the bridge and he pulled himself up the steps by the railing, not trusting his weak legs. The captain held out a mug of tea as Duggan entered and grabbed at a sturdy-looking knob to steady himself. Duggan shook his head.

'Take it.' The captain proffered the cup. 'It'll help.'

Duggan took the cup and sipped a little tea. The captain offered him a Jacob's ginger nut biscuit from a tin. Duggan shook his head again and regretted the movement as the ship lurched over the crest of another swell and a wave of dizziness hit him.

'It'll help too,' the captain said, oblivious to the movement. 'Seriously. I brought them for you.'

Duggan took the biscuit and bit into it.

'A hot drink and a bit of ginger works wonders,' the captain said, looking to the helmsman for confirmation. 'Settles the stomach.' The helmsman nodded with a knowing grin.

Duggan drank some more tea and felt its heat begin to calm his stomach. He leaned back against the wall, spread his legs to steady himself and dunked the hard biscuit into the tea.

'Keep your eyes on the horizon,' the captain added.

'What horizon?' Duggan grunted as the ship headed down into another trough.

'See,' the captain laughed. 'You're better already. Have another biscuit.'

It was true: he felt a little better. He reached for another biscuit and kept his eyes on the horizon as the bow cut at an angle through the crest of another swell. 'Do they always pretend they're going to attack?' he asked.

'Some of them,' the captain shrugged. 'Like to give us a bit of a fright now and then. And sometimes they do attack. You never know.'

'They don't recognise our neutrality?'

The captain shrugged again. 'Sometimes they do. Sometimes they don't. Seems to be up to the crew. How trigger-happy they are. We've been lucky so far. But we've lost some good friends.'

The ship rose on another swell and Duggan scanned the horizon. There was nothing on the ocean, just more swells as far as the eye could see. Overhead, white clouds scudded eastwards at speed, across the azure sky. There were no signs of life: no birds, no ships, no aircraft.

Duggan became aware again of the small vessel's vulnerability. It was another world out here from the investigations and diplomatic to-ing and fro-ing that followed the occasional attack on neutral Ireland's ships by German planes or U-boats. A different world from the reports and explanations he'd seen cross G2's desks. The crew mistook the Irish tricolour for the French one in bad light. They couldn't identify the ship. The ship ignored radio signals to identify herself. To heave to. The error is regretted. Compensation will be paid.

Standing in front of the bridge later at the captain's sug-gestion – it was the centre of the ship, he'd said, its most stable point – Duggan was conscious of how different it was from a desk at headquarters. How exposed the ships and their crews were to the vagaries of the moment. To a gunner with an itchy finger, to a snap decision by a pilot that a vessel wasn't what she appeared to be, to a submarine with a dirty periscope that couldn't make out clearly the flag on her side in heavy seas.

His seasickness was fading, but it was replaced now by another hollow feeling in his stomach. Ever since the war had started nearly two years earlier, he'd wondered how he would fare under fire if and when it came to Ireland. Now he knew. This was the first time he'd faced a gun that could have spat bullets at him at the pressure of a finger. And he'd tried to turn and run. And fallen in an ignominious heap on the deck.

The temperature rose as they moved south. The tension on board eased once they reached the relative safety of neutral Portugal's territorial waters. Even the ship seemed more relaxed, running with the Atlantic swell towards land, happy, as the captain put it, that it was once again in sight of a coast: it was never intended to be ocean-going, he told Duggan, to sail beyond sight of land.

Duggan felt well enough to shave off his week-long beard, and his gaunt cheeks began to colour again in the sunshine. He had hardly eaten during the voyage and reckoned he'd lost at least half a stone. He spent all his time on deck, not trusting himself to go below except to sleep, but he was well enough to read *Bones of Contention*, a collection of Frank O'Connor's short stories. The book was a handy defence against conversations, and against questions he didn't want to answer. Everybody left him alone: nobody suggested that he act out his cover by doing some work.

The vague outline of the coast sharpened into hills and fields and then settled into the outline of Lisbon as they entered the mouth of the Tagus and passed by the tower of Belém. Red-roofed buildings, their walls ochre and white, seemed piled on one another to create hills and valleys interspersed with church spires and domes. The summer sun was dropping into the ocean behind them, buttering the mellow colours of the city with its warm southern light. The sea breeze was blowing the smoke from the ship's funnel ahead of them like a pointer.

They followed it upriver, past a queue of ships at anchor facing the ocean and past busy quays with all their berths occupied. They anchored in the river beyond a large waterfront square, and the ship slowly swung around to face back the way it had come. Duggan and a few of the crew, their work finished and ocean-going sweaters discarded, leaned on the starboard rails, waiting. The docks were busy with the whine of crane engines and the clanging of their metal buckets on concrete and steel plate. Overhead, the blue of the sky had deepened and shadows had etched in some of the valleys on shore. The air was still hot and heavy.

'That's our spot,' Jenkins said, pointing to a similar-sized vessel with a crane swinging a bag-like container over its deck. 'We'll be in before nightfall. You coming ashore with us?'

'Sure,' Duggan said. 'Where are you going?'

'Antonio's place. You ever heard of it?'

'No,' Duggan lied. He'd been told about it at the briefing. It was where the contact was always made with the sailor he was replacing on this trip, the sailor they'd caught smuggling a message for the German spy Hermann Goertz. Though neither politics nor spying was the sailor's main interest. Smuggling was, which was why he was quick to cooperate with G2's plan to have Duggan replace him on this voyage. 'What is it?'

'A dive,' one of the other sailors laughed.

'Won't stop you joining the band, will it?' Jenkins shot back at him. 'Disgracing the nation with your attempt at singing.' He dropped his cigarette butt into the oil-slicked water and pushed back from the railing. 'Come on. Get ready.'

Duggan didn't move, in no hurry to go back to the cabin. He inhaled the warm air and closed his eyes, listening to the busy noises, feeling the ship still moving through the Atlantic swell. He felt the heat envelop him and sweat begin to build up under his collar in spite of the breeze off the water.

He was still there an hour later when they hauled anchor and edged into the berth as the other vessel left it. It was flying a flag he didn't recognise, and he made out the name '*Famagusta*' on its rusty stern as it went by. As soon as they tied up, the gangway was lowered and a port official came on board while a harbour policeman took up position beside it. He watched a boxy lorry roll by, its cargo hidden under a tarpaulin.

The captain and the Portuguese official emerged from the bridge after a while and shook hands at the gangway. The captain joined Duggan at the railing as they watched the officials depart.

'Busy place these days.' The captain stood upright, his hands resting on the railing, as though he was still on the bridge, in command. 'The crossroads of the world now. Been here before?'

'No.' Duggan had never been out of Ireland until now. 'It's hot.'

The captain laughed. 'It'll get a lot hotter than this in another month or more.' He paused. 'It can be a dangerous place. But I presume you know that. That they warned you to be careful.'

Duggan nodded, though he hadn't been given any information about specific dangers, just that Lisbon was a nest of spies and conspiracies, real and imagined.

'Be careful of anything you bring back on board,' the captain added.

'What do you mean?' Duggan asked in surprise.

'Make sure it is what you think it is. There have been bombs hidden in stuff people thought was just merchandise they were bringing home.'

'Really?'

'So the Brits say. There've been a couple of cases. Not just aimed at their own sailors, they say. At neutrals too.'

'I'm not planning on doing any smuggling,' Duggan said.

'Well if there's anything you want to bring back, I'd appreciate it if you'd tell me about it.'

'Sure.'

'There's a lot of cigarettes to be had here. And everything else.' The captain tapped the railings as though he was finished sending a message. 'I have to go and report to the British now.'

'Why?'

'Condition of the navicert,' the captain said. 'And inform them of the delivery of their coal. As well as listen to the usual instructions about where we're allowed to go in Lisbon.'

'How can they limit our movements here?' Duggan demanded, surprised, and aware that that might be a problem.

The captain shrugged. 'They can't. But they warn that certain areas are dominated by the Germans and are out of bounds. I wouldn't worry about it. Stick with the lads and you'll be all right.'

'How long will we be here?'

'Three days. Our wheat has already arrived from America so there shouldn't be any delays. They like to get us in and out as quick as possible these days. They're so busy.' The captain turned away, hesitated, turned back to Duggan and pointed inland to the east. 'In case nobody warns you,' he said. 'You should know that the girls in the red-light district over there are in the pay of the Germans. Supplement their income by picking up information. And trying to set up fellows like you.'

'Thanks,' Duggan muttered, not sure what to say.

'Not that I'd know anything about it.' The captain rubbed out an invisible spot on the deck with his shoe in embarrassment. 'It's what the Brits say. If you can believe them.'

Two

The middle-aged man looked up from the sink behind the bar as the door opened and the group of Irishmen came through. A broad smile crossed his face and he shouted '*Olá*, Paddy!' and grabbed a dishcloth to dry his hands.

'Antonio.' Jenkins pumped his outstretched hand. 'We're back again.'

Antonio raised a finger and concentrated for a moment. 'Safe and sound,' he said, remembering the learned phrase.

'And thirsty,' one of the other sailors interjected.

Duggan looked around the bar as Antonio lined up five small glasses and filled them from a bottle of rum. It was larger than he'd expected, dim after the brightness of the street lights outside, and infused with the pungent smell of strong tobacco. There were a couple of old men playing some kind of board game, watched by two others. In an alcove to one side, a young man picked at a guitar so slowly that the tune, if there was one, collapsed into individual notes. A morose middle-aged woman sat on the chair beside him, their backs to the wall.

He turned his attention to the rest of the room, trying to spot the contact. Nobody looked likely. Most of the men were in work clothes, probably dockers. There were a few women among them, wives or girlfriends, he thought, except for one – who could have been one of those the captain had warned him about.

'Get that into you,' Jenkins said, nudging him in the ribs.

'I feel drunk already,' Duggan said. He could still feel the rolling of the ship, though he knew he was on firm ground.

'You haven't seen anything yet.'

The night wore on, shots of rum alternating with glasses of beer. The guitar player picked up the pieces of his tune and the morose woman sang a sad song in a strong alto voice that seemed at odds with her frail frame. At some point, one of the sailors joined the guitar player and sang 'Boolavogue', slowing the pathos of its last verse into a maudlin wail.

Duggan woke up the next morning thinking that he was back at sea in the heaviest of the Atlantic rollers, until he realised that it wasn't the cabin that was vibrating, but the pulse of pain in his head. It took him another while to realise that all the noise was not within his brain. Some of it came from outside, where the cargo of coal was being shovelled into the crane bucket, hoisted ashore and tipped tumbling on to a truck.

He made his way to the galley, where the cook glanced at him and busied himself preparing something. Duggan sat down and the smell of fried eggs from an unwashed pan made him nauseous.

The cook put a glass in front of him full of some yellowish concoction streaked with red and black. 'For the hangover,' the cook said.

Duggan shook his head.

'Get it into you,' the cook said, standing over him, arms folded. 'It'll do the job.'

Duggan took a sip of the glutinous liquid and almost threw up.

'Not like that,' the cook ordered. 'Knock it back, quick as you can.'

Duggan closed his eyes and tried to pour the liquid down his throat without tasting it. He held his breath to keep it down. 'What's in it?'

'Raw egg and a few things.' The cook turned back to his counter.

'How do I get to Antonio's?'

'Not a good idea.' The cook shot him a look over his shoulder.

'I left my lighter there last night,' Duggan lied.

The cook gave him a suspicious look, then sighed and took a sheet of brown wrapping paper from a drawer, tore it in half and sketched a rough map. 'Don't be tempted by the hair of the dog,' he wagged a finger at him. 'You'll pay for it when we go back to sea.'

On deck, the sun blinded him and the humid heat covered him like a physical presence, sapping his energy. He squinted his way down the gangway and past the lorry being loaded with coal. The grinding and clanging of the crane was more bearable in the open air.

He made his way up a succession of narrow streets, where the four-storey buildings shut out the sun and the morning air had not yet been heated to the level on the open quayside. Some of the houses were covered in faded blue and white tiles, plaster peeled from others, and washing was draped on balconies and along walls on pulley systems. Two women talked across the street from first-floor balconies and a bent old man went slowly and painfully up a set of narrow steps. He rounded a corner into another street and stepped back in surprise as a small tram went by, its iron wheels screeching against the downhill bend.

He found the bar without difficulty, and bent down to enter its low door. He crossed to the counter and asked the woman there for a coffee. She gave him a tiny cup and a glass of water. He took them back to a table near the door where the light was slightly stronger. Two old men who could have been the same ones from the previous night were playing a board game at the same table. Another man was half hidden behind a newspaper, a coffee cup in front of him and a cigarette burning on a tin ashtray.

Duggan sat down, took out a packet of Gold Flake, lit one and left the yellow box open, standing upright on the table in the agreed signal. He sipped the muddy coffee, tasting the grinds on his tongue, and took a drink of water. It has to be the man with the newspaper, he thought, unrolling the sleeve of his shirt to wipe the sweat off his forehead.

The bar was silent except for the clicking of the pieces in the board game and the turning of a page in the newspaper. Occasional shouts of greeting and rapid bursts of conversation came from outside. A radio played music somewhere in the distance.

Duggan finished the cigarette and was beginning to worry that the contact wouldn't happen today, when a man ducked in, stopped inside the door and looked around. He was wearing a loose-fitting grey suit with a faint pinstripe and wide lapels, and a grey hat.

'Ah,' he said, glancing at the cigarette packet and quoting its advertisement. 'Gold Flake satisfy! I haven't had one for some time.'

'Please try one,' Duggan replied.

'Only if you'll try one of my American ones.' The man took a packet of Lucky Strikes from his jacket and shook one out.

'I'd like to,' Duggan said, and took the cigarette, completing the ritual.

The man sat down and put his hat on the table. He was in his thirties, lightly tanned and with dark eyes that seemed to view his surroundings with amusement. His black hair was parted in the middle, and he brushed it back with both hands to smooth out the mark of the hat. He looked like a film star and was aware of it. 'I'm Strasser,' he said, taking one of the Gold Flakes.

'Sean McCarthy,' Duggan said, flicking his lighter for the two cigarettes and wishing that he could stop sweating. He hoped Strasser didn't interpret this as nervousness or, worse, lying. Strasser didn't look like he had climbed any hills to get there.

'Where's Dermot?' Strasser raised a hand to catch the attention of the woman behind the bar and pointed at Duggan's coffee.

'He didn't come this time.'

'He's well?' Strasser turned back to Duggan, giving him his full attention.

'He's fine.' Duggan held his stare. 'It was decided that I should come. So we could make direct contact. Avoid any misunderstandings.'

'I wasn't aware of any misunderstandings.'

'Just in case. Speed things up.'

The woman came with a coffee and a glass of water on a tray. '*Obrigado, senhora*,' Strasser gave her a bright smile. He put half a spoon of sugar in his coffee and stirred it. 'And you are?' His English was good: the only hint of a German accent was in the precision with which he pronounced words.

'A captain on the headquarters staff of the Irish Republican Army.'

Strasser sipped his coffee. 'You can prove this?'

Duggan nodded and took a drag on his cigarette, taking his time. 'I have a message from Dr Goertz.'

Strasser's eyes widened in an uncontrolled gesture of surprise which belied his verbal 'Who?'

Duggan gave him a faint smile and said nothing. He knew that Strasser had been the conduit for messages to and from Hermann Goertz, carried by the sailor whose place he had taken on this voyage.

Strasser tapped his Gold Flake twice on the ashtray. 'Dr Goertz is no longer a free man,' he said in a flat voice. Goertz had been arrested by the Irish police with the help of G2 some months earlier and had been interned.

'We think he was betrayed.'

'By whom?' Strasser made no secret of his interest.

'An opportunist criminal type. We'll let you know when our investigation is complete.'

'That's your message?'

Duggan glanced around at the sudden noise behind him of a chair being scraped back, and he watched the man who'd been reading the newspaper go over to the counter and say something in Portuguese to the woman. She laughed and leant her elbows on the counter and they began a conversation.

'No.' Duggan took a small envelope from his back pocket and passed it across the table. Strasser put it into his inside pocket in a fluid movement. 'What is that?' he asked.

'A message from Dr Goertz,' Duggan said, playing his trump card. 'In code.'

'What does it say?'

'Dr Goertz hasn't shared the code with us.'

'And Dermot is still free?'

'Yes,' Duggan nodded. 'He's not one of ours.'

'Just an opportunist.' Strasser gave him a hint of a smile.

'They have their uses.' Duggan shrugged. 'He's a sailor and small-time smuggler.'

'He'll be back again?'

'On the next voyage.'

Strasser nodded in satisfaction. 'Good. He's an uncomplicated man. There's a lot to be said for uncomplicated men these days, wouldn't you say?'

Duggan gave a non-committal shrug, as if such concerns were of no interest to him.

Strasser stubbed out his cigarette and shook his head. 'I think their advertisements lie,' he said. 'Gold Flake does not satisfy.'

'I'm not sure about this either.' Duggan inhaled some smoke from the Lucky Strike and blew it out. 'A bit too sweet for my taste. Lacks bite.'

'Just like Americans,' Strasser smiled. 'Soft. Without conviction. You've met Dr Goertz?'

'No.'

'How did you get this message from him?'

'We've had long experience in getting things in and out of Free State jails. Of being treated like criminals in our own land. Unfortunately.'

Strasser stared at him for a moment, as if he was deciding something. Duggan held his stare. Strasser reached for his hat, stood up, and dropped some coins on the table. 'That'll cover the coffees,' he said. 'Same time tomorrow.'

Duggan nodded and waited until Strasser was gone a few minutes before releasing a deep breath. So far, so good, he thought, closing the Gold Flake packet and taking a cigarette case from his pocket. He lit a Sweet Afton and held in the familiar smoke for a moment and realised he had stopped sweating. Tomorrow would tell whether they'd succeeded. Whether there were any hidden tripwires in Goertz's code that they hadn't detected and that would tell the Germans that the message was not really from him.

He found a tram stop on the side of a steep hill, wondered how the tram's wheels could grip the iron rails, and waited. The cook's hangover cure was working: he was feeling better. The sun was beginning to edge down into the street and the temperature was rising. The only sounds were the distant cranes and metal-on-metal bangs from the unseen port. On the narrow footpath opposite him, two elderly women in long black dresses made their way slowly up the hill with flat wicker trays on their heads, carrying something he couldn't make out.

The single-decker tram ground to a halt and he got on. It was crowded and he grabbed a strap suspended from the ceiling to hold on to as it set off down the hill, clattering and screeching around the tight bends. All the windows were pushed up as far as they would go, but the heat was oppressive and he was conscious of the growing patch of sweat under his extended arm. At last, the tram came to the bottom of the hills and ran alongside Praça do Comércio and the breeze ruffled his shirt. He wished he could lower his head enough to feel it on his face.

The tram twisted into the small square of Largo Corpo Santo and he got off and stood for a moment looking at the church across the cobbled road from the stop. Now for the trickier job, he thought, spying on my own government. He took a deep breath, crossed to the double wooden doors flanked by flat white columns, and pushed on one side.

The church was smaller than he had expected, an octagonal building of uneven sides that was almost circular. He genuflected and sat into the last pew and looked around. After the glare of the sun the church was restful and cool, the air scented with a mixture of old incense and candle wax. The windows were small, high over the altar area and at the top of a small dome over the body of the church. The altar was flanked by two alcoves, one with a statue of the Virgin Mary, the other with one of St Patrick standing on a bed of fat snakes. Above him, the church's provenance was confirmed by a harp and, surprisingly, a crown. A shawled woman was lighting a votive candle at a rack by the altar rails.

The church had once been the centre of an Irish college that trained Catholic priests for Ireland during the Penal Laws of the seventeenth and eighteenth centuries, like the better-known colleges in France and Spain. The college was long gone, but the church was still run by Irish priests of the Dominican Order and now catered for the English-speaking Catholic population in Lisbon.

A sacristan in a black soutane appeared at the side of the altar, and Duggan made his way up the aisle and waited at the altar rails until he caught his attention.

'I'd like to see Father Alphonsus, please,' Duggan said when the man came down the altar steps to him.

'Are you a member of the congregation?' He spoke English with a strong accent.

'No. I just arrived from Dublin yesterday.'

'A sailor?'

Duggan nodded.

'Confessions are tomorrow evening,' the sacristan said, assuming he was in search of absolution.

'I'm not looking for confession,' Duggan said. 'I'd like to see Father Alphonsus about a private matter. It's important.'

'Does he know you?'

Duggan shook his head. 'I've been sent from Dublin to see him.'

The sacristan gave him a searching look, then said, 'He's not here.'

'When will he be back?'

'After lunch.'

'I'll come back then.'

'I'll tell him your name?'

'Sean McCarthy,' Duggan said.

'And the business you have with him?'

'It's confidential. A government matter.'

The sacristan dismissed him with a slow nod that implied that he didn't believe this shirted young man had any connection with officialdom.

Duggan wandered back along Rua do Arsenal, past some sort of naval building with barred windows and sailors standing guard at its entrance, to the seaside square again, where the full force of the sun made him narrow his eyes. He turned left up Rua Áurea, crossing to the shaded side of the street, and followed the lines of black and white cobbled stones north as if they were tram tracks for pedestrians. The high buildings here were white and it was a different world from the narrow streets of Alfama, where he'd met Strasser. Shops and banks lined the ground level and he went by the vaguely religious tower of the Santa Justa *elevador* up to the streets of Bairro Alto and stopped further on under a shop awning to consult the directions in his notebook.

He came out into Praça de Rossio, where the pavement cafés were full of well-dressed people and the air was filled with the buzz of business. He crossed into the centre of the square, the wave patterns of its black-and-white cobble-stones a reminder of his seasickness, and circled around the parked cars and fountains and the column to Pedro IV. He left the square by the horseshoe-shaped doors to the railway station, passed into Praça dos Restauradores and went by the Eden cinema. Two huge posters hung on the upper floors, one advertising a film called *Os Fugitivos da Guiana*. He recognised the names of Clark Gable and Joan Crawford.

On Avenida da Liberdade, he crossed over to the median and meandered among flower beds with a profusion of red, orange and purple flowers whose names he didn't know. They scented the hot air, battling the exhaust fumes of the cars and vans on either side. Ahead, he spotted a young woman sitting on a bench and thought for a heart-leaping moment that it was Gerda. Her profile was similar, her black hair rested on her shoulders and she was wearing a tight-waisted floral dress. She turned his way and their eyes passed and then she glanced back at him involuntarily, caught by the intensity of his gaze, before looking away again. He turned away in confusion, crossed the roadway to the buildings on one side and came to a post office.

On a whim he went in and bought a black-and-white postcard of Praça de Rossio and wrote on the back of it, 'Thinking of you. As always. P.' He addressed it to her American name, apartment number and street in New York, and queued to buy a stamp, smiling to himself at how intrigued she'd be to get a card from him in Lisbon.

Farther up the avenue he took a seat at an outdoor café and ordered sardines off the menu of the day, and a Sagres beer. A copy of *Diário de Lisboa* lay on his table, bound by a cane frame, and he leafed through it, understanding little but able to follow the war through the headlines. Something was happening in Syria, where he knew the British were fighting the French; Roosevelt had responded in some way to the German sinking in the south Atlantic of the merchant ship *Robin Moor*. He came to the small ads and some in German caught his eye. 'Diamond ring for sale, contact Frau M at Hotel Metropole'. 'Gold and silver jewellery at special price, room 38, Palazzia Hotel, Estoril'. There were others in French, offering similar wares. Refugees running out of money while they waited for exit visas and a ship to some part of the Americas.

It was like the captain had said, he thought. Lisbon is now the crossroads of the world and anything can be bought.

The church of Corpo Santo was empty when he returned. He sat into the first pew and waited for a moment, wondering how much he should tell the priest. As little as possible, his superior, Commandant George McClure, had said. But use your own judgment. As much as you have to tell him to get the information we want. Which, Duggan thought, was no help at all now that he had to decide how to handle the conversation.

His thoughts wandered instead to Gerda: I shouldn't have sent that card, he told himself. It could get her into trouble. There were probably lots of people in New York with friends in Lisbon at the moment, many of them Jewish refugees from the German-occupied areas of the Continent waiting or hoping for passage to America. But Gerda probably didn't want to be known as Jewish in New York either. Not if her new name, Grace Matthews, was anything to go by.

It was too late now to retrieve the postcard though.

The flames of the slender votive candles stirred in an unfelt breeze and the sacristan appeared to one side of the altar and indicated with a nod of his head that Duggan should follow him. They went through the wood-panelled sacristy, its atmosphere of quiet reverence familiar to Duggan from his days as an altar boy, and continued through an echoing corridor into the building behind. The sacristan opened a pointed wooden door and showed him into a room with the air of a transient waiting room, its air cold in spite of the outside temperature and heavy with the smell of polish.

'Wait,' the sacristan said again and left, closing the door behind him with a heavy click.

The room was panelled with dark wood and had a painting of a wistful-looking figure in a black cape and white habit over the empty fireplace. St Dominic, Duggan presumed. There were four straight-backed wooden chairs around a small table of some dark hardwood.

The door opened and an elderly monk wearing a white habit came in. 'Father Alphonsus,' he said, holding out his hand, making the gesture as much an enquiry as a handshake.

'Sean McCarthy.'

The priest pointed to the table and they took seats opposite each other. His head was bald on top and fringed with grey hair. It looked like it could have been a tonsure, but Duggan decided it was probably natural. His face had the ruddy look of an Irish countryman.

'A confidential matter, you said?' he prompted.

'I work for the Irish government,' Duggan began.

'You're a diplomat?' the priest interrupted with surprise, replicating the sacristan's glance at Duggan's casual clothes.

Duggan shook his head. 'I've come from Dublin to make some private enquiries into something that happened here a couple of months ago. It's a sensitive matter and we hope you may be able to help us. And that we can rely on your discretion.'

The priest gave him no encouragement, a hint of perplexity on his poker face.

Duggan took a mental breath and proceeded to lay his cards on the table. 'It's in connection with the visit of the Minister for the Coordination of Defensive Measures, Mr Aiken, here a few months ago. As you know, he was on his way to America to meet President Roosevelt. Unfortunately, a report of something Mr Aiken was supposed to have said here preceded him and made his mission more difficult. We'd like to find out exactly what the truth is and hope you can help us counter any false impressions that may have arisen.'

Which was one way of putting it, Duggan thought, surprising himself with his own civil-service-style circumlocution. What had happened was actually a complete disaster: a shouting match between Roosevelt and Aiken after Roosevelt's accusation that Aiken had told people in Lisbon that Ireland wouldn't mind if Germany won the war, that this could even solve a lot of outstanding problems. The meeting had ended with the president, in a fury, pulling the cloth from the table being set for his lunch, scattering cutlery on the floor. Aiken had failed to get the American arms he had sought and official relations between Ireland and the US had sunk to a frigid low.

'I don't see how I can help you,' Father Alphonsus said.

'You hosted the lunch at which Mr Aiken spoke about the war and our neutrality.'

Father Alphonsus nodded. 'I'm sure Mr Aiken can tell you what he said.'

'Of course,' Duggan agreed immediately. 'But we're trying to work out how what he said may have been misinterpreted. May have led someone to get the wrong impression.'

'Are you a policeman?'

'No, no,' Duggan said in surprise.

'A reporter?'

'No. I work for the government. My job is simply to try and find out how such an important misunderstanding could have arisen. You can appreciate how serious this could be for a small neutral country like us and our relations with a powerful country like America. We want to correct the record and make sure something like this doesn't happen again.' And find out who had sabotaged Aiken's mission.

'Who exactly do you work for?'

'A research group. We look into things for government departments.'

'Do you have any identity papers?'

Duggan handed him the passport in McCarthy's name. Father Alphonsus looked at the photograph of Duggan and examined his face. 'It says you're a sailor,' he said, raising a quizzical eyebrow.

'Because I came by ship,' Duggan said with confidence, as if that was the most obvious explanation possible. 'I'm here in a completely unofficial capacity. The government decided to make enquiries in this way rather than have someone from the Madrid legation come over and make the matter formal. Our Portuguese friends and other legations don't need to know about our enquiries.' Nor did anyone in Dublin outside of G2.

Father Alphonsus gave a heavy sigh and said nothing for a moment. 'I don't see how I can help you.'

'Perhaps you could just tell me about the lunch,' Duggan prompted, relieved that he was still talking to him.

The priest shrugged. 'We don't have many visits from members of the government, so it seemed appropriate that we should do something to mark the occasion. And Mr Aiken found himself at something of a loose end here when the Clipper to New York was delayed by the weather for a few days. So we invited the Irish community here, and some of our Portuguese friends, to meet him over lunch. That's all there was to it.'

'How many were there altogether?'

'I can't remember the exact number. About twenty-five. There were some last-minute cancellations.'

'All Irish or Portuguese?'

'I couldn't say with certainty. There's an Irish woman here married to a Spaniard: members of our congregation. There may be others married to people of other nationalities, like that. I wouldn't know who all the Portuguese are related to.'

'The Portuguese people?' Duggan hesitated. 'Who were they?'

'Friends of ours.' The priest waved an airy hand. 'People who attend the church. Benefactors. Some who have connections with Ireland of one kind or another. Personal, business.'

'Were there any outsiders? People you wouldn't have known normally?'

'I don't know what you mean.'

'I mean people who wouldn't normally attend your church functions or religious events.'

'No.' The priest shook his head slowly. 'It wasn't a public event. Just our usual circle of friends.'

'No representatives of other governments?'

'Lord, no, nothing like that.'

'Representatives of the Portuguese government?'

'Not as such. Some of our Portuguese friends work for the government. But they wouldn't have been here in that capacity.'

'Or representatives of any other governments?'

'Certainly not.'

Duggan sighed inwardly. The priest was willing to talk, but not to say anything. I'm not going to get anywhere with him, he thought. But I may as well keep going anyway. 'And Mr Aiken made a speech?'

'Not so much a speech. He said a few words. It was all very informal.'

'What did he say?'

'I'm sure he can tell you that himself,' Father Alphonsus shot back.

'He's still in America actually,' Duggan said. 'But I'm just trying to get a sense of the occasion. And how things might have come to be misinterpreted.'

'It was all very straightforward. He's a very straightforward man, as I'm sure you know. He talked about the Step Together campaign to improve the country's defences. To keep the country united, avoid divisions.' The priest closed his eyes, as though thinking back. 'About the problems of the blockade, how Ireland was the most blockaded country in Europe. The difficulties of getting supplies and maintaining neutrality. The pressures the country was coming under from the British. And how our great strength was the unity of the country behind the government policy.' He opened his eyes and tapped his fingers on the table as though he were hearing the marching tune in his head. 'Like the words of the song, "steady boys and step together".'

'And did he say anything about the outcome of the war? Who Ireland would like to see emerge victorious?'

Father Alphonsus stared at him in silence for a moment. Duggan held his gaze, thinking, Yes, he did, as the moment stretched into several seconds.

'I'd say he maintained a strict neutrality all round,' the priest said at last.

'Did he go into the pros and cons about both sides?' Duggan persisted. 'From Ireland's point of view?'

Father Alphonsus shook his head. 'He was talking about Ireland all the time. About the problems she faces with the blockade. The difficulties of getting supplies.'

'The British blockade?'

'They're the ones cutting back supplies to the country, aren't they?'

'They are,' Duggan agreed, wondering how far Aiken had gone in explaining the background. That the British squeeze on Irish supplies was a deliberate punishment for Ireland's refusal to give her access to her western ports to help protect the supply convoys from the US and Canada. And the first stage in a plan which ultimately provided for invasion and the seizure of the ports.

'I'm sure any fair-minded person would agree that he stuck to a strictly neutral line.'

'Were there questions afterwards?'

'No, no. It wasn't like that. All very informal. Though there was applause when he finished,' the priest added, as if he was finally revealing something. 'I imagine people found it very informative. And were very supportive of the Irish position. The Portuguese understand it very well. They're in the same boat.'

'Neutrality is very hard to maintain against major powers,' Duggan offered.

'It certainly is,' Father Alphonsus said, appearing to relax. 'I told Mr Aiken afterwards that Mr de Valera should come here and meet Dr Salazar. They have a lot in common, you know. Two great men facing the same problems in the face of much stronger powers who care nothing for the rights of small nations. They'd have a lot to talk about. And, I dare say, could even learn from each other.'

'What did he think?'

'Oh, he thought it was an excellent idea. But he said there were practical difficulties, and even dangers, in travelling at the moment. The country couldn't afford to lose the chief at such an important juncture in its history.'

'True enough,' Duggan agreed. 'How long have you been here?'

'Twenty-seven years come September,' Father Alphonsus said. 'It was a different place for a priest then, and our role here was more like a mission to the Portuguese, who were under the thumb of a fiercely anti-religious government. But we were able to give back to them some of what they'd given to us during the penal times. Keep the religious flame alive.'

He pushed his chair back and stood up.

'Thank you for seeing me,' Duggan said, following his lead.

The priest stopped on his way to the door. 'Mr de Valera could do worse than talk to Dr Salazar about other matters too. Like his *Estado Novo*, the "New State". It could be a worthy model for the new Ireland too. The same values. *Deus, Pátria e Família*. Like Marshal Pétain is providing for France now. Instead of the liberty, fraternity, equality that has caused them so much trouble.'

'I've heard that suggested,' Duggan said. He was aware of occasional speeches or letters to newspapers extolling the Portuguese example of Catholicism and family and rural values. A spiritual way between the anti-religion dictatorships of Hitler and Stalin on the one hand and the hedonistic materialism of the English and American democracies on the other.

'That's something you might do a little research into while you're here,' Father Alphonsus said. 'And you might suggest to the people you work for that Ireland open a legation here. Keep in touch with developments.'

'I'll pass that on,' Duggan said, and followed him along the corridor. Father Alphonsus stopped in the sacristy as if another thought had just struck him. 'It might be worth your while having a talk with Senhora Figueras,' he said. 'Maisie O'Gorman, that was.'

'She was there? At the lunch?'

'She was, of course. And her husband. And I think they met Mr Aiken again later. After his meeting with Dr Salazar.'

'Yes, I'd love to meet her.'

'You know Lapa?' Father Alphonsus opened a drawer, took out a sheet of paper and produced a pen from inside his habit. He wrote an address on it.

'I don't know Lisbon.'

'It's not too far from here.' He handed the address to Duggan. 'Anyone will direct you.'

'And who is Senhora … ?'

'Figueras. She came here as a governess to the family in the twenties. And ended up marrying one of the cousins. They're all very well off. Involved in banking and shipping. You should have a talk with her.'

'Thank you,' Duggan said, suspecting he was being set up for a lecture about the attractions of Salazar's *Estado Novo*.

Three

The ancient taxi made an ominous rattling noise and slowed to a walking pace as it climbed the hill to the address in Lapa. It threatened to stall as the driver turned into the steep street named on the sheet of paper Duggan had given him. The driver stopped with an apologetic shrug and pointed to the street name and the address on the paper. Duggan nodded in agreement, regretting the movement as it sent a pang of pain through his head, and paid him. It had been another long night in Antonio's and there had been no sign of the cook and his hangover remedy as he had left the ship this morning.

He had taken the taxi to avoid arriving in a lather of sweat, but sweat broke out on his back as he climbed the hill in the morning heat, squinting against the hard sunlight. He stopped after a few minutes to rest and looked back down at the view over the Tagus, trying to make out the ship from the jumble of vessels along the river's wharves. The sun was beating down from a cloudless sky, its heat seeming to increase by the moment.

He carried on and the hill levelled out and he came to the house, a double-fronted three-storey building. The sun bounced off its walls, turning their faded ochre almost white. The ground-floor windows were covered with grilles whose bars formed delicate circles, and patches of plaster were beginning to flake up near the roof. He pressed the large bell beside the door.

It was opened by a small old woman wearing a white apron over a black dress. '*Senhora Figueras por favor?*' he asked, using up half his Portuguese.

She said something as she stepped back and let him enter, but he had no idea what it was.

The hall was wide and long and dark after the daylight outside. The woman motioned to him to stay there, and went away. He felt the drop in temperature and waited for his eyes to adjust to the gloom. A few moments later a door closed somewhere and he heard high heels clicking on the hard floor before another woman came into view.

She was about forty and had bright red hair and a freckled face. She wore a yellow dress with flowers which matched her hair and walked with a bouncy stride that made the dress swing from side to side.

'Senhora Figueras,' he said. 'I'm … '

'Maisie.' She put her hand out with a mischievous smile. 'And you're Father Alphonsus's mystery man.'

'I wouldn't say that.' Duggan smiled, shaking her cool hand.

'He thinks you're a spy,' she said, tilting her head to one side, a question in her blue eyes.

'A spy?' Duggan stepped backwards with a surprised laugh.

'What else?' She gave an exaggerated shrug. 'Everybody in Lisbon thinks everybody's a spy these days. And you know what?'

'What?' he took the prompt.

She lowered her voice. 'They're right.'

She turned away and he followed her down the corridor and into a room which opened through French windows into a small internal courtyard with an elaborate pattern of black and white tiles. In the centre was a small fountain splashing a soothing trickle of water into a stone bowl. She waved at a chair facing the window. 'Would you like some Russian tea?'

'I don't think I've ever had Russian tea.'

'It's either that or gin,' she said, sitting down opposite him, her back to the light. 'The only things you can drink in this heat.'

'Oh, no. Not gin,' he said.

She gave him a knowing smile and picked up a hand bell from the small table between them and gave it a shake. The old woman appeared immediately and Maisie gave their order in Portuguese. 'So.' She leaned back in her chair and folded her arms. 'Tell me your secrets.'

'They're not very interesting,' Duggan offered. 'I'm a civil servant in Dublin. Working for the government.'

She inclined her head to one side again, whether in scepticism or encouragement he could not tell. Her features were in shadow against the sunshine in the courtyard: it was less intense in there, imprisoned and tamed by the surrounding walls.

'I'm trying to find out why some misunderstandings have arisen in America about Mr Aiken's visit here.'

'You want to know what the general got up to while he was here?' she said, with a delighted tone. 'You're spying on General Aiken.'

'Oh God no,' Duggan said quickly, wishing his brain would function, so that he could bat away her banter. Interesting, though, he thought, that she referred to Aiken as 'General', his title from the anti-treaty IRA and the civil war. Showed where her sympathies lay. 'Nothing like that.'

'So what's it like?'

Duggan was saved from having to say more by the return of the old woman with a silver tray and two glasses. She served the tea from a pot with a long spout, pouring it on top of a slice of lemon, and left.

'Let it cool a moment,' Maisie warned as Duggan went to taste the tea. 'Do you have any Irish cigarettes by any chance?'

'Yes.' Duggan got out his cigarette case and offered her one. 'Sweet Afton.'

'Ah, perfect,' she sighed. 'I don't much like their cigarettes here. But I have to smoke them these days. The sacrifices one has to make.' She gave a light laugh, mocking herself. From what Duggan had seen of Lisbon's bright lights, there weren't too many sacrifices required in Portugal.

'How long have you been here?' He leaned across the table to light her cigarette, taking advantage of the opening to change the subject.

'I thought *I* was asking the questions.' She propped her right elbow on her other hand, holding the cigarette upright by her face. 'Nearly fifteen years. Just after the old republic fell.' She took a thoughtful drag, as if remembering.

'The old republic was a mess and things got better after it was overthrown. Even better again since Dr Salazar came in with the New State. Keeping us out of the war, just like Mr de Valera with you. He and the general had a good chat about that. You know they met?'

Duggan nodded.

'Compared notes about the dreadful blockade that the British are imposing. Dr Salazar told him that the neutrals were paying for this war. It's terrible that England and America are trying to starve us into submission just because we won't get involved in the killing.'

Duggan took a cautious sip of his tea. Aiken didn't make any secret of his views while in Lisbon, he thought. He wondered how much she knew of Britain's plans to force Ireland to get involved in the war through the use of its Atlantic ports. Unless she was talking about Portugal. 'You mean Ireland?' he prompted.

She nodded. 'And Portugal. Being friends with the British hasn't done them a lot of good. But Dr Salazar won't make the mistake they made of getting involved in the last war. He won't be fooled into getting involved in this one.'

Duggan was aware that Portugal had fought with Britain and France in the First World War, but he wasn't altogether clear what she was alluding to.

'You know the British offered some of Portugal's colonies to the Germans during the last war?' she asked rhetorically. 'Behind their backs. Nice friends. But we're used to them and their devious ways, aren't we?'

'We are,' he nodded. 'You met the general at the lunch with the Dominicans?'

'I did. And again after that. He came around here one afternoon while he was waiting for the weather to clear. He sat where you are, had some Russian tea.'

'Did he like it?' Duggan sipped at his glass.

'I don't think he'll be introducing a new tea fashion to Dundalk,' she smiled.

'So you had a chat about everything?' Duggan knew now that he was in unexplored territory, even dangerous territory. On the one hand, he knew little of what his political masters in Dublin had been told of what Aiken had done and said in Lisbon. On the other, there was every chance that news of him questioning people here about Aiken would get back to the minister. He cursed Commandant McClure for his vague order – was it even an order? – to see if he could find out who had told the Americans about what Aiken had said in Lisbon. Or even *if* he had said it.

Masquerading as an IRA agent with the Germans was the main objective of his mission, and the one that held obvious dangers. But this other enquiry could yet cause more difficulties. And his only protection was his false name, which wouldn't stand up to much political investigation.

'We certainly had,' she agreed. 'The general doesn't mince his words.'

'What we're anxious to find out,' Duggan said, deciding to narrow the discussion for his own protection, to get back to issues that he could defend if necessary, 'is how some misunderstandings got to America about what he said at the Dominicans.'

'What misunderstandings?'

'They say he said he wanted Germany to win the war.'

'Did he?' she leaned forward to stub out her cigarette, leaving a generous broken butt in the marble ashtray.

'Well, I don't know,' Duggan said, smiling at her as she looked up at him. 'I wasn't there.'

'What does he say?'

'I think he says he didn't.'

'You think?'

'As far as I know. He's still in America.'

'What does it matter what he said?'

'It matters because it might get in the way of achieving his aim of getting the American supplies that we need. President Roosevelt is not inclined to give help to anyone who supports Germany.'

'He didn't say he supported Germany.'

'They say he said he didn't mind who won the war.'

'Isn't that what being neutral means?'

'It's not what President Roosevelt means by neutrality. He's certainly not neutral about who he wants to win.'

'Huh.' She gave a dismissive snort. 'As if the British are fighting for democracy. They only want to keep their empire.'

'The problem is that we mightn't get the arms we need to defend ourselves and our neutrality if the president thinks we're sympathetic to the wrong side.'

'You're not going to get them from Roosevelt anyway,' she said in a confidential tone. 'Dr Salazar told the general that. He won't give you any arms unless you join the British. That's what he told Dr Salazar.'

'What President Roosevelt told Dr Salazar?' Duggan repeated, to be sure he was hearing her correctly.

Maisie nodded. 'The doctor told the general that the Americans were trying to force all the neutrals to do their fighting for them. Using economic warfare to force them to give up their own neutrality while the Americans hold on to theirs. He told the general that he was wasting his time going to Washington. That was the gist of it. Of their chat.'

And Salazar was right, Duggan thought, as he put out his cigarette. It wasn't public knowledge because of the tight newspaper censorship at home, but Aiken hadn't got any arms. His visit to Washington *had* been a waste of time. Worse, it had left relations with the Americans in a state of near hostility. 'It seems like the well had been poisoned before the general ever got to Washington,' he said.

'Well, you know who did that?'

'Who?'

'The British. As usual.'

'Were any of them at the Dominicans' lunch?'

'They didn't need to be there,' she said. 'They had their lackey.'

'Who's that?'

'Maud Browne.' She sat back in her chair as if she had made the decisive move in a game of chess.

'Who's she?'

'Senhora Ferro. A Castle Catholic. From Dublin. Married to a bigwig in the foreign ministry here, Agostinho Ferro. A West Brit like herself. They're bosom friends with the British ambassador and all the rest of them. At all their embassy cocktail parties, the king's birthday and all the rest of it.'

'Was he there too?'

'Of course,' she said, as if that was obvious. 'They're great supporters of the church. Go to Mass in Corpo Santo every Sunday. Give to all the appeals. Get invited to everything.'

Duggan finished his tea. Maisie, who had hardly touched hers, watched him replace his empty glass. 'Stay for lunch,' she said.

'I can't,' he said, surprised. 'I'd love to. But I've got to meet someone.'

'Interrogating another innocent woman?'

'Are there innocent women in Lisbon?'

She gave a dirty chuckle. 'Tell me if you find one.'

'I'll keep an eye out.'

'Tomorrow, then.'

He shook his head with regret. 'My ship's sailing in the morning.'

'The story of my life.' She laughed lightly as she stood up. 'Anyway' – she held out her hand and he took it – 'Maud's your spy.'

He nodded. 'Thanks for the tea and the talk.'

She let go of his hand and led him to the corridor. 'You should get the government to open a legation here. Then you wouldn't have to ask questions like that. You'd know the answers already. The lie of the land.'

'Father Alphonsus said the same thing.'

She opened the hall door to the searing sunlight. 'Maybe they'll give you a job here.'

'I'll bring you some Afton if they do.'

'I'll expect a constant supply.' She raised a hand in a fluttering farewell and closed the door.

Duggan set off down the hill, hoping to come across a number 28 tram, which would take him back to Alfama. It seemed that Aiken had left some hostages to fortune in

Lisbon, whatever he had said. But, if Maisie's account of his talk with Salazar was correct, it wouldn't have made any difference anyway. The Americans were not going to sell any arms to neutrals.

He came out beside the basilica at Estrela, saw the tram stop in the middle of the road in front of the park and joined a short queue. A small tram came up the hill, going the wrong direction for him. It seemed to heave itself slowly over the brow and then glide towards them, almost dainty on its narrow wheels. He glanced at his watch and relaxed: there was plenty of time for his appointment in Antonio's with Strasser.

A tram marked 'M. Moniz' arrived. He found a single seat free on the right-hand side and it headed downhill at speed, creating a cooling breeze through the open windows. He wondered about Maisie and her flirting. Was she just a bored housewife, or something else? Was everybody in Lisbon a spy, as she said? If so, who could she be working for?

She'd obviously spoken to Father Alphonsus before he arrived. She had known what he wanted, and had an answer ready. Which was probably Father Alphonsus's answer as well, though he didn't want to be the one to give him Maud Browne's name. Whether her information was true was another matter. There was clearly no love lost between the two women. Rivals in some way, for all he knew. Maybe rival husbands or just rivals in Irish terms, from different classes, geographical areas, political backgrounds. Even if she was right about Maud Browne, he couldn't see how G2 or the Irish diplomats in the United States could use it to their advantage. Blaming the Brits without some kind of definitive proof wouldn't change Roosevelt's mind. Even with definitive proof, it probably wouldn't lead to an American change of heart. But proof could be useful to have anyway.

The tram slowed as it went down the hill into Praça Luis Camões. It let off some passengers there and then took another downward plunge, towards the river. It levelled out through Baixa and began to climb into Alfama. You should be more worried about Strasser, Duggan told himself. There was every possibility that the Germans would turn nasty if they realised that he wasn't who he pretended to be. But there was no reason why they should. Unless there was a tripwire in Goertz's code that G2 hadn't been aware of.

Sweat was beginning to break out on his forehead again by the time he walked up the final steep hill to Antonio's pub. He stopped outside for a moment to catch his breath and then ducked under the low door. Three of the crewmen from his ship were at the bar, including the cook. One saw him and said something to the others with a knowing laugh. Duggan ignored them and walked over to Strasser, who was sitting in the alcove, looking displeased.

'Am I late?' Duggan sat down opposite him.

'Do they know who you are?' Strasser flicked his eyes towards the bar without moving his head. He looked the same as the previous day: the same suit, the same hat on the table beside a small coffee cup.

'No.'

'Who do they think you are?'

'A smuggler.' Duggan shrugged and took out his cigarette case. 'Who do they think you are?'

'Dermot's supplier,' Strasser said, accepting a cigarette from Duggan's proffered case.

'And I'm Dermot's stand-in.'

Strasser flicked a silver lighter and held it out for Duggan to light his cigarette. 'Your message was very interesting.'

Duggan said nothing, picking a stray shred of tobacco from his lip.

'You don't know what it said?'

Duggan shook his head. 'I told you. Dr Goertz hasn't shared the code with us.'

'He wants a radio and arrangements for the reception and transmission of messages.'

'OK.'

'A strange request from a man in prison, don't you think?'

Duggan shrugged, looking bewildered. 'What does he want to do with it?'

'He doesn't want it for himself. He wants you people to have it, to be the conduit between us and him and other agents he says he has put in place.'

'OK,' Duggan said again, as if he was absorbing this information for the first time.

'You think he can run agents from a prison cell?'

'We have a very good communications system with people in there. It's been there a long time, as I told you before. And Dr Goertz has a lot of friends in Ireland. People were very impressed with him.'

'Were you?'

'I never had the chance to meet him,' Duggan said truthfully. Although he had been closely involved in the search for Goertz, he hadn't come face to face with him. 'He usually dealt with army-council members.'

Strasser pushed his untouched cup away. 'You know the Metropole Hotel in Rossio Square?'

'I'll find it.'

'Be there at five o'clock this afternoon. On the terrace.'

'OK.'

'And you'll want the usual things? For your friends?' He gave a faint nod towards the bar.

'Yes, please.'

'Anything in particular?'

'Whatever is usual. Cigarettes, tea, coffee.'

'We don't do tea. English cigarettes or American?'

'English are probably better.'

Strasser stood up, took his hat and put it on his head in one fluid movement, and walked out. Duggan wandered over to the bar, smiling with relief. I've done it, he thought. They've fallen for it. One of the crew slapped him on the shoulder and told him to have a drink.

'No thanks. I need your cure,' he said to the cook.

'Fuck that,' the cook said, already drunk, or maybe still drunk from the night before. 'Hair of the dog.'

Duggan inserted himself between Jenkins and the others and said in a low voice, 'Is there any problem getting stuff on board?'

Jenkins shook his head. 'They don't care. They'll let you walk in with anything you like. As long as it's not too big.'

'No, you can't bring her back with you,' one of the other crewmen laughed.

'Bring back anything you want as long as it's not the pox,' the cook added.

Duggan got a tram running along by the docks to Belém and got off just before a huge prow-shaped wooden monument to Portuguese explorers. He'd gone back to the post office, found Agostinho Ferro, Maud Browne's husband, in the phone book and checked the address against a street directory. The afternoon was heavy with heat, though there was a suggestion of a breeze from the sea, and the streets were relatively empty. It occurred to him that now might not be the best moment to call on anyone: siesta time. But he was running out of time.

The house was inland and uphill, in its own grounds and behind a high wall. Ferro was obviously very senior in the foreign ministry, or came from a rich family, or both. Duggan opened a metal side gate, crossed the tiled patio to the double hall door and rang the bell. It was opened by a middle-aged man in a butler's uniform, who looked him up and down.

'I'm from Ireland,' Duggan said in English, hoping he'd understand. 'I'd like to see Senhora Ferro please.'

The man said one word, which Duggan assumed meant 'wait', and closed the door. He stood still, looking back at the profusion of flowers lining the inside of the perimeter wall, catching their scents on the slight breeze. It was silent here, no sound rising from the river below or from the neighbourhood, whether because most activity had paused for siesta or because of the secluded location.

He was beginning to wonder if the one Portuguese word had been a curt dismissal when the door reopened and the butler indicated that he could come in. He showed Duggan into a small, functional room just inside the door, furnished only with two leather couches facing each other across a marble-topped coffee table. Left alone again, Duggan looked out the window at a short stretch of well-tended lawn at the side of the house.

Maud Browne was in her fifties, tall and thin, with a sharp-featured face and tightly curled hair beginning to go grey. She was wearing a salmon-coloured blouse, a single-strand necklace of grey pearls and a white linen skirt. She stepped into the room and gave him an enquiring look.

He went into his routine, telling her he was doing a report on Aiken's visit to Lisbon for the government.

'You wish to talk to my husband?' she asked, confused.

'No,' he said, adapting his approach to what he sensed was going to be a more difficult interview. 'I'm talking to people who met Mr Aiken when he was here. Like at the lunch at the Dominican church. I've been speaking to Father Alphonsus and am compiling a report on how the visit went down.'

'I don't see what I can tell you.' Her accent was posh Dublin, neither Irish nor English, and she held him in an unblinking stare. 'Mr Kearney was here from the Madrid legation and the minister had a man with him from the High Commission in London. I'm sure they've reported adequately on events.'

'Yes, they have.' Duggan held her stare. 'But I'm more concerned with how the people he met found his explanation of Ireland's neutrality. Whether he explained the policy well, the reasons for it, and the impression it created. The government is very concerned about having its policy understood properly.'

She folded her arms and thought about that for a moment. 'If by properly you mean clearly, I would say Mr Aiken certainly did that. He made it absolutely clear that Ireland will not get involved under any circumstances, unless attacked by a belligerent. Not even if the partition question was resolved and the country was united.'

Duggan nodded. Aiken hadn't pulled any punches, but nobody would have expected him to.

'I thought his assertion that Ireland's involvement could mean the complete destruction of the Irish race was somewhat overwrought,' she added.

'He said that?' Duggan injected a note of surprise into his voice as a prompt.

'Yes. It was unnecessarily melodramatic. I don't see the Irish race being wiped out by this or any other war. Do you?'

'It has been suggested by several senior government members,' he said, dodging the question.

She shook her head dismissively. 'It's a silly statement. They should find some better reasons if they don't want to stand with the other democracies.'

'The vast majority of people support neutrality.'

'Indeed,' she conceded. 'That is a better reason. But Mr Aiken made it clear that his government will not help Britain in any circumstance. In fact, to listen to him, you'd think that

Britain was the aggressor, and deliberately trying to starve Ireland through its blockade. No mention of the German blockade and the fact that their submarines are sinking so much shipping. Which is bringing supplies to Ireland as well as England.'

Duggan nodded, as if he agreed. She clearly hadn't been impressed with Aiken and his defence of neutrality, but did that mean she was the source of Roosevelt's accusations? 'Was he critical of Germany too?'

'Not that you'd notice,' she retorted. 'He seemed to equate neutrality with a lack of interest the outcome. As though a Nazi victory would make no difference to Ireland, or perhaps even be to its benefit.'

'He said that?'

'In effect,' she said. 'Which is a very short-sighted way of looking at things. Portugal is neutral too, but there's no doubt about whom Dr Salazar would like to see emerge victorious.'

'I gather he and Mr Aiken had a good meeting.'

'I wouldn't know anything about that,' she said, closing off this avenue of enquiry. 'I don't think I can tell you anything further.'

'Thank you for talking to me.'

She led him to the hall door and said goodbye.

Four

Duggan found a free table at the back of the Metropole Hotel's terrace on Praça do Rossio and sank into the wicker seat. He was ten minutes early for the meeting. The terrace was beginning to fill up in the cool of the afternoon. At the table next to him there was an elderly couple with their two adult daughters, all dressed in dark clothes, ignoring their surroundings, and lost in their own thoughts. Refugees, he decided, from a colder place.

He scanned the rest of the tables again. There was no sign of Strasser. Under a table at the front, a small boy was brushing the shoes of a businessman who was reading a newspaper and ignoring him. When he finished, the boy moved to the next table, where the man shooed him away with a wave of his hand. The boy ignored him and set about brushing the man's shoes.

Strasser passed by on the sunlit pavement. He didn't look at the terrace and Duggan watched him continue down the path until he disappeared. The waiter brought Duggan coffee, and a moment later his eye caught a tall, straight-backed man with a suitcase threading his way through the tables. He was wearing a generous-sized lightweight suit and a panama hat. He approached Duggan's table, sat down on the free chair with a sigh of relief and placed the suitcase on the ground between them.

'*Bin ich zu spät?*' he asked, taking off his hat and fanning himself with it, as if he had just completed a long, hot journey, although he gave no sign of being overheated.

'Sorry?' Duggan said, pretending not to understand German. He glanced around as if confused by the man's arrival. There was no sign of Strasser.

'I'm late?' the German repeated in English.

'No.' Duggan glanced at his watch. It was a minute past five o'clock. 'I don't think so. My watch is a little fast.'

'You're Sean?'

Duggan nodded.

'How do you like Lisbon?'

'It's hot.'

'Your first time?' The man gave a light laugh and looked around for a waiter.

'Yes,' Duggan said.

A waiter came and the man ordered a bottle of Sagres Branca and placed his hat on the table. He had a round, tanned face, sandy hair that was beginning to recede a little, and startling blue eyes. Duggan put his age in the mid-forties or more.

'We are very disappointed,' the German said, turning his gaze on Duggan.

'What?'

'You people talk a lot and do nothing.'

Duggan didn't have to feign surprise.

'You promise lots of things. Intelligence. Sabotage.' The man held him in his stare. 'But we receive no meaningful intelligence and have heard of no sabotage.'

'Did you not get our reports on Belfast?' Duggan countered. 'On the bombing of the shipyards?'

'I have seen nothing.'

'A report was prepared for you about the effects of the damage, and suggesting other targets.' Duggan had seen the

IRA's report, found in a Special Branch raid on a house. It had included a map of the damaged areas and a request that the Luftwaffe keep its bombs away from the marked Catholic areas of Belfast. 'You didn't get it?'

The man avoided the question again. 'What did it say?'

'I don't remember all the details. The first raid was most successful in hitting the docks. The Easter Tuesday raid was a disaster for your cause, killing too many people and missing some big targets, like the British aircraft carrier that was there for repairs.'

'What aircraft carrier?'

'*Ark Royal*,' Duggan said, aware that he had told him something to snag his interest.

'Why didn't you tell us beforehand?'

'You didn't get the message?'

The waiter arrived with a bottle of Sagres and a slender glass. Duggan opened his cigarette case and offered the man one while they waited for the waiter to half-fill the glass with the blonde beer. The man shook his head. Duggan lit his cigarette, thinking that the IRA had no means of communication with the Germans. Which was what G2 suspected, and his mission was partly intended to confirm. That was why the man kept dodging the question. Unless he was trying to trap Duggan into revealing his ignorance.

'We need a secure way of sending messages,' Duggan said when the waiter had left.

The German sampled the beer, put the glass down, and turned his amused eyes on Duggan again. 'I thought you couldn't read the code.'

'Herr Strasser told me what was in it,' Duggan said, holding his stare. 'But it doesn't surprise me that Dr Goertz has come to that conclusion.'

'What about the sabotage you promised?'

Duggan sighed. 'That's more difficult at the moment. You know that most of our best men have been interned?'

The German gave a slight nod.

'More every day. About four hundred of them now. We're under attack non-stop from the Free State Special Branch, so it's very difficult to mount operations at the moment.'

'You must move forward,' the man said, with an impatient shake of his head. 'Don't allow your enemies to decide your actions.'

'Easier said than done, when they've got all the power on their side.'

'Why are you fighting them anyway? Why don't you join forces with them? You both want to free Ireland from the British Empire, don't you?'

'Because they don't really. They've sold out. Accepted partition.'

The man shrugged, losing interest in the nuances of Irish politics, and topped up his glass with the remainder of the beer. 'How is Dr Goertz? You've seen him?'

Duggan shook his head. 'That's not possible. But we can get messages to him. And from him.'

'He's being treated well?'

'I think so. There are people in the puppet government who know he's not an enemy of Ireland.'

'How long does it take to get a message to him?'

'A few days. Sometimes a week. It depends.'

'There's a message there for him.' He glanced down at the suitcase. 'With the radio and all the information you need to make contact. *Und die anderen Dinge, die Sie gefragt.*'

'What?' Duggan gave him a puzzled look.

'The other things you asked for.' The German gave him a half-smile.

'Thanks,' Duggan said, wondering why he kept throwing in German phrases. A test or a trap? But there was no way he could know that Duggan spoke German.

'It's important we get a reply from Dr Goertz as soon as possible,' he said, finishing his beer.

'It will take longer to get a reply back from him,' Duggan said. 'Maybe up to two weeks from the time we get the message to him.'

'How long will it take you to get back to Ireland?'

'A week or more. From tomorrow.'

'We will expect Dr Goertz's reply in three weeks.' The German stood up and put on his hat.

'Who will I tell my superiors I met?' Duggan asked.

'A courier.' The man smiled down at him. 'Who made you pay for his beer.'

Jenkins had been right. The security men at the docks paid no attention to the brown suitcase in his hand as he showed his passport and told them the name of his ship.

Jenkins was on deck and tossed something to him as he stepped on board. 'Remember what that is?' he said as Duggan caught the orange with his free hand.

'Haven't a clue,' Duggan said. 'I'm too young to have ever seen one before.'

'Too young to be drinking then,' Jenkins laughed, eyeing the suitcase. 'All set for another session tonight?'

'Game ball,' Duggan lied.

He went down to his cabin and placed the suitcase with care on his bunk. That seemed to have gone well: the Germans had given him a radio and, even better, a message for Hermann Goertz. Which would allow G2 to set up a conversation with the Abwehr, so they would know what interested the Germans in Ireland and be able to control what information went back to Berlin. Unless – he tossed the orange from one hand to the other as he looked at the suitcase – they're just playing us along.

He lobbed the orange on to the pillow, took a deep breath and held it as he released one catch on the case. Nothing happened. He released the other catch and tipped the lid back with one finger.

There was a package wrapped in khaki canvas in the centre, padded around the sides of the case with packets of cigarettes and brown paper bags. He took out one of the bags and looked into it, knowing from the smell what it was before he saw the roasted coffee beans. He checked a few more bags at random and then took out the cigarettes. Packets of Player's and Gold Flake in cardboard sleeves. He tipped the five packs out of one sleeve and opened one at random. It only contained cigarettes.

He lifted out the canvas package, turned it over on the bunk and unwrapped it. A pair of headphones was wrapped neatly around the receiver, and a transmitter key around the other part. On top was an envelope, a separate sheet of paper with two wavelengths – numbered '1' and '2'– and a note saying 'Tuesday and Thursday 1835 hours plus 1 hour 45 mins alternative'. The envelope wasn't sealed and he took out two sheets of paper with blocks of typed letters in neat rows. It didn't mean anything to him: as he had told the German, he couldn't read Goertz's code.

He packed everything back into the case, wondering if he should call back to Maisie O'Gorman with a pack of the cigarettes. He decided against it and closed the case.

He took the case with him back on deck. Jenkins was still there, watching two dock workers guide a cargo of small wooden boxes down into the forward hold. The dockers had a rope each and were straining against them as they steadied the boxes dangling from a crane.

'The last of it,' Jenkins said, nodding at the cargo as it disappeared into the hold. 'Wine. Wonder who that's for?'

'Not for us anyway.'

Jenkins grunted his agreement and cast a sly eye at the suitcase. 'You've been shopping.'

'Hard to resist it here.'

'If you brought a bit of money you could make a lot more of it.'

'Is the captain around?'

'On the bridge.'

Duggan climbed up to the bridge, where the captain was reading a book. He looked up, glanced at the suitcase and gave Duggan an enquiring look.

'Can you put this somewhere safe?' Duggan asked.

'Is it what you think it is?' The captain left his book upside down on the windscreen ledge.

'I've checked it,' Duggan nodded. 'I'll show you, if you like.'

'No need. As long as you're sure.'

'I'm sure.'

'Leave it there,' the captain said, indicating the back wall of the bridge. 'I'll look after it.'

'Thanks.' Duggan put the case where he was told. 'They're finishing loading the cargo.'

'We'll be sailing with the morning ebb tide.' The captain gave him a slight smile. 'About half five. Don't forget to be back on board before then.'

The increased vibrations and engine noise woke Duggan, and he knew they were about to get under way. He curled up in the bunk and tried to go back to sleep but the throbbing prevented it. He turned on to his back and tried to figure out how much of the noise was in his head and how much in the metal cabin. He had tried to pace himself in Antonio's the night before, spacing his drinks as much as possible and leaving while the party was still in full swing, but he'd still been pretty drunk staggering back to the ship. Most of the throbbing was from the cabin, he decided, but his mouth was dry and he felt very thirsty.

Jenkins wasn't in his bunk and there was no sign he had ever been there. He must have stayed up all night, Duggan thought, must be still drunk, doing whatever he had to do on deck as they cast off. His watch showed it was nearly six o'clock. So he'd got nearly four hours' sleep. He put his feet on the floor and felt the vibrations. The prospect of days of seasickness stretched out before him.

Not this time, he decided, getting dressed quickly and making his way to the galley. 'You need the cure?' the cook asked, looking up from a frying pan in which he was turning over some rashers.

'No. Just thirsty.'

The cook poured tea into a large mug, added milk and three heaped spoons of sugar without asking, and handed it to him. 'Want some breakfast?'

'No, thanks.' Duggan took the tea, made his way to the stern and sat on one of the mooring bollards. Lisbon was already beginning to dissolve into an undistinguishable mass of buildings, backlit now by the sun climbing up over the hills behind it. The ship's wake was a broad, straight path on the calm sea but the early morning air was spoiled by the stink of diesel fumes.

He sipped the sweet tea and watched an optimistic gull circle behind them, waiting for them to dump some waste overboard. His first visit abroad had given him a taste for more. And a greater sense of a city at peace, all lit up and far enough away not to fear accidental bombs from incompetent navigators or confused bomber crews. Was that how Gerda found New York? he wondered. A safe haven where normal life went on, far distant from global politics and war?

He lit a cigarette, the first and always the best of the day, and thought about what he had accomplished. He had carried out his main mission successfully, set up contact with the Germans, and found out enough about his other task to know that Frank Aiken had made compromising comments in Lisbon. It was doubtful that he had actually said that he wanted Germany to win the war, but he had been clear enough about his desire that Britain shouldn't win outright to allow someone to make that claim. And to make it difficult to refute, even if it was not strictly accurate. The ship ran with the tide and he walked around the deck, cautiously testing his sea legs.

In the days that followed, he relaxed as if he was on a cruise, sitting with his back to the wheelhouse, finishing the Frank O'Connor short stories, chatting with the crew members who now accepted him as one of their group after the drunken nights in the bar, and sometimes just lying back and looking at the cloudless sky as the ship rose and fell with the slow swells.

The only sign of the war was a distant plume of black smoke away to the east, in the Bay of Biscay, on their second day out. 'God be good to the poor souls,' one of the crew muttered as they stood and watched it for a little while. It was difficult to believe that danger could be lurking unseen beneath the waves or appear out of the blue sky with scarcely a moment's notice.

On their third day out, a Sunday, the captain appeared in front of him as he sat on the deck in his usual position. Duggan was reading the Maurice Walsh novel he had borrowed from the captain in return for the Frank O'Connor stories. 'Have you heard the news?' the captain asked.

Duggan looked up and shaded his eyes against the sun.

'The Germans have invaded Russia,' the captain said.

Duggan stared at him, and neither man said anything for a moment.

'Crossed the border at four this morning,' the captain added then. 'On a thousand-mile front, they say.'

'Jesus,' Duggan swore, thinking that that was almost beyond imagining. But it means we're safe for the moment, he thought. The Germans can't open two fronts at the one time if one is on that scale. Which means they can't invade England or Ireland at the moment. Until they finish with the Russians. And then there will be no stopping them.

'That'll put the cat among the pigeons,' the captain added.

'How do you mean?'

'They're fighting the communists now. A lot of people weren't happy that they were aligning themselves with the communists.'

Duggan nodded, aware that many people in Ireland were wary of the Nazis because of Hitler's alliance with Stalin and their opposition to religion. 'You think it'll make more people support Germany?' he asked.

'Could do,' the captain said. 'People'd like to see the communists beaten after all they've done to the Church.'

'Herr Hitler isn't too keen on religion either,' Duggan offered.

'True enough. But he hasn't persecuted priests like the communists.'

It was an opportunity for the British too, Duggan was thinking, to open up another front on the Continent, maybe try and get a foothold back in France. But they were too weak to take it. Still, it should help them in the Middle East, maybe divert German forces away from there if the Russians put up a fight.

'Anyhow,' the captain shrugged, a confirmation of the irrelevance of their opinions. 'You enjoying the book?'

'Yes,' said Duggan, picking it up. 'More than halfway through it already.'

'There's another of his in my cabin if you want it.'

'I will at the rate I'm going. You like the O'Connor stories?'

'Remind me of some people I know,' the captain nodded. 'But I'm rationing myself to one a day now. Keep me going till we get home.'

The Fastnet lighthouse came into view that night, and the following day they saw the south-west coast of Ireland and kept it within sight as they steamed eastwards. The days were still bright and the sky blue, but the temperature had dropped, and Duggan now sat with a sweater on and sheltered at the sunny side of the wheelhouse from a cooler north-westerly breeze. As they went by the Waterford coast, he took a spare pair of binoculars and joined the lookout on the bridge scanning the waters ahead for mines drifting landwards from the British minefield in the Western Approaches. He saw nothing.

A British Hudson circled them once as they passed the Tuskar Rock in the Irish Sea, waggled its wings, and continued its patrol.

They followed two trawlers towards the Welsh coast and into Milford Haven. They kept going towards Pembroke, past the RAF flying-boat station, where a huge Sunderland wallowed at anchor like an obese bird, and edged towards a dock. 'Bloody waste of diesel this,' Jenkins said as he waited to cast a mooring line ashore. 'Having to come in here every time.'

Duggan watched a gang of workmen shovelling gravel into a bomb crater farther down the quay, as the ship sidled in and was tied up. A car pulled up beside the ship and two men got out and stood there, waiting. As soon as the gangway was put ashore they climbed on board and went to the bridge. A few minutes later the captain's voice on the tannoy ordered all hands on deck. Jenkins muttered a curse.

'What?' Duggan asked. 'Is this usual?'

Jenkins shook his head. 'Just a formality about the navicert usually. Captain talks to them.'

'To those guys?'

Jenkins shook his head again. 'Naval types usually.'

Half a dozen of the crew gathered on deck and the captain led the wheel-man and the two newcomers down from the bridge to join them. 'Is this everybody?' one of the men demanded.

'The chief engineer and one of his lads are still in the engine room,' the captain said. 'They're busy, closing down turbines.'

Two uniformed policemen stepped on deck and stood on either side of the gangway like sentinels. The plainclothes men walked around the loose group of crewmen, inspecting each one. When they had finished, one pointed at Duggan and said, 'You. Come with us.'

'What's this about?' the captain demanded as Duggan stepped forward.

'Not your concern, captain,' the man retorted.

'But I can't afford to wait here,' the captain protested. 'We've got perishables on board.'

'No reason for you to wait. You can be on your way as soon as you clear the navicert with the naval authorities.'

'I have to wait for my crew,' the captain said.

'You can't afford to wait that long,' the second man said. He took Duggan by the elbow and led him over to the uniformed policemen.

'Where are you taking him?' the captain demanded.

'Where's his cabin?' the first man responded.

The captain paused as if he was going to argue, but then decided against it. 'Show him,' he said in a quiet voice to Jenkins.

One of the policemen indicated to Duggan that he should come with them, and he followed them down the gangway, wondering what this was all about. It certainly wasn't part of the plan.

The policemen put him in the back of their patrol car and drove towards the gates to the docks.

'Will we show him the sights?' the driver asked his colleague as he stopped at the junction.

'Aye, do that, Jack,' the passenger replied. 'Let him see what his friends have been up to.'

The driver turned right and then took a left, and the damaged houses began to increase in number.

So that's it, Duggan thought. They think I'm in the IRA; they've fallen for my cover story. Someone in Lisbon must have tipped them off. But who? That woman, Maud Browne, the one who probably told them about Aiken and his lack of enthusiasm for a British victory. But why would she have assumed that he was in the IRA? She mightn't have accepted his claim that he worked for the government but there was no reason why she should have jumped to the conclusion that he was an IRA agent. Unless she didn't see or care about the distinction between the government and the IRA. All rebels to her.

Or it could have been the Germans. Or one of the crew.

'There's Laws Street on the left now,' the passenger was saying, like a tour guide. 'The McKensies and the Reynolds used to live there. And here's Gwyther Street.' The driver turned into it. 'That's where the Bazels lived and the Dunns and Mrs Lenham. Before they were all killed.'

'And the young Lenham lad,' the driver added. 'Only an infant.'

'Aye,' the passenger chorused. 'Eighteen months.'

Duggan watched the passing houses, noting how some of the ruins looked new, not yet weathered or tidied up, still bearing the signs of quick searches and freshly burned timbers. He'd seen similar scenes in Dublin only a month earlier, on the North Strand, and even remembered the names of some of the dead: the Browne family, three children and their parents and granny; and the Fitzpatricks, another extended family of infants, parents and grandparents. He said nothing.

They turned left at the end of the road, then right again and reached the police station. The policemen led him into a room and told him to empty his pockets. He did so, taking out his passport, cigarette case, lighter, some coins, including a few Portuguese escudos, and a set of keys.

'That's it?' the driver said, sounding disappointed, as the other policeman opened the passport. They were both middle-aged and had sing-song Welsh accents. They seemed almost happy to be dealing with him. Better than dealing with the aftermath of bombing raids, Duggan decided.

'And the watch,' the driver ordered.

Duggan opened the catch and put it on the table.

'Occupation,' the other policeman intoned, reading the passport. 'Bomber.'

The driver gave a harsh laugh. 'But really?'

'Able seaman.'

'He's no seaman.' The other policeman started to search Duggan, patting him down. 'I've seen enough seamen in my time to know that. You can smell them.' He unbuckled Duggan's belt, standing up close to him, and pulled it free. 'You don't smell like any seaman I've ever met.'

'Take out your shoelaces,' the driver ordered him.

After Duggan had done so, the other policeman pushed him towards the door. 'Can I take my cigarettes?' Duggan asked.

The driver snapped open the cigarette case and shook his head. 'Looks like an offensive weapon to me.'

'Give him one,' the other policeman suggested. 'It might be a while before those *gentlemen* are ready for him.'

The driver let Duggan pick an Afton from the case. He reached for the lighter.

'Oh no you don't.' The driver knocked Duggan's arm away. He picked up the lighter and flicked it to light Duggan's cigarette.

They led him down stone stairs to the basement and into a narrow cell and locked the door. Duggan sat on the bunk bed, a solid piece of wood attached to the wall and covered with a grey blanket, and leaned back against the cold stone wall. He inhaled a little smoke, trying to make the cigarette last, while he pondered this turn of events.

The only people who thought he was in the IRA were the two Germans he had met. Could one of them be a double agent? Or could they be British agents pretending to be Germans? The radio the second German had given him was of British make, but that didn't necessarily mean anything. The Germans probably had plenty of them since the fall of France. And if they were British agents, wouldn't they want to compromise the IRA by giving it a German-made transmitter?

The other possibility was that one of the crewmen had fingered him. They didn't know who he really was, but he'd picked up one or two hints that some of them suspected he was an IRA man, probably on an arms-buying mission. He considered each of them, but none was an obvious suspect. Which left Maud Browne as the most likely informant. Clearly, she was pro-British and most likely to have informed them about him, though it still wasn't clear to him why she should have assumed he was in the IRA.

He could feel the heat of the cigarette on his fingers as the butt burned down lower than usual. He held it between the nails of his thumb and forefinger to get a last drag, and then dropped it on the stone floor and ground it out with a loose shoe. He waited.

Five

The long midsummer twilight was finally fading into night when they came for him. Duggan had moved the pillow to the other end of the bunk so he could lie down looking at the small semi-circular window high up on the wall. It was barred and looked out on ground level. An occasional pair of feet passed by and, once, a car's wheel.

'The *gentlemen* are ready for you now,' the policeman said when he opened the door, once again dragging out the word as if it was some kind of joke.

Duggan's stomach rumbled as he dropped his legs to the floor and stood up. He reckoned it was about eleven o'clock or maybe later, and he'd had nothing to eat in the seven or so hours since he'd been detained. They went upstairs to a nondescript interview room with a pitted wooden table and a chair on either side. One of the Special Branch men from the ship was sitting at the table, and the other was leaning against the wall behind the second chair. Duggan's passport lay on the centre of the table, as if it had been placed with as much care as a centrepiece.

The seated one indicated the chair opposite him and Duggan sat down. They stared at each other in silence, each waiting for the other to speak first. The Branch man was in his early thirties, of military age, but, Duggan assumed, exempt from service because of his job. He had a lean face, short dark hair cut in military fashion, and intelligent brown eyes.

The Branch man took out a cigarette, lit it, leaned back in his chair and blew smoke at the bulb in the upturned-saucer-style light-shade above the table. Duggan bit his lip against his craving for a cigarette, which was more insistent than his hunger.

'Don't you want to know why you're here?' the detective asked at last, directing another plume of smoke at the light.

'Why am I here?'

'Because you've been consorting with the enemy, conspiring against His Majesty's government, and planning acts of war against the realm.'

Duggan almost laughed at the overblown rhetoric but restricted himself to an incredulous, 'What?'

'Sorry.' The Branch man gave a fake smile. 'Your style is more bicycle bombs aimed at pensioners coming out of post offices, isn't it?'

Duggan shook his head.

'What were you doing in Lisbon?'

'Working on the ship.'

'There wasn't much work to be done while you were in port.'

'Did a bit of drinking ashore. A bit of sightseeing.'

'And what sights did you see?'

Duggan shrugged. 'A bit of Lisbon. The squares. Main avenues.'

'Never had the pleasure myself. Nice city, is it?'

'Seemed nice. What I saw of it.'

'How would you compare it to other cities?'

'I haven't seen any other cities.'

'This was your first time,' the Branch man said, nodding as if this was a revelation to him. 'And why did you pick Lisbon for your first foray abroad?'

'That's where the ship was going. The ship that took me on as a deckhand.'

'So you'd just go anywhere? Wherever the urge took you?'

'I signed up with the one that'd take me. There aren't that many jobs in Ireland.'

'So it was your first time at sea?'

Duggan nodded. They don't know anything, he thought, haven't found the transmitter. But they could be just toying with me. Waiting to get down to the real business once they've lulled me into a false sense of security.

'Did you like it? Fall in love with the sailor's life?'

Duggan shook his head. 'I was seasick half the time.'

'So you won't be going again?'

'No.'

'Going back to what you did before?'

'Yes.'

'Which was what?'

'Farming.'

'You're a farmer?'

Duggan nodded.

'Who wanted to be a sailor?'

'I thought I'd give it a try.'

'And you've tried it and had enough of it?'

Duggan nodded again.

'What were you doing in Lisbon?'

'Waiting for the ship to load.'

'And having a chat with your German friends?'

'I don't have any German friends.'

'Oh, I understand,' the Branch man said, tipping the ash from his cigarette with a delicate touch against the side of the metal ashtray. 'They're not friends. Your German masters.'

Duggan shook his head, looking confused. 'I don't know any Germans.'

'Who were those Germans you were talking to then?'

'What Germans?'

'The ones you met.'

'I didn't meet any Germans.'

'Who did you think they were?'

'Who?'

'The people you met.'

'The people in the bar? I don't know. Just people in a bar.'

'What bar was that?'

'Place called Antonio's.'

'Where?'

'I don't know the name of the street.'

The Branch man sat back and shook his head as though he was disappointed. 'You don't know anything.'

'I don't know why I'm here.'

'Because you're a member of the so-called Irish Republican Army,' the detective said, widening his eyes in mock surprise. 'A "volunteer". Isn't that what you call yourselves?'

'I'm not a member of anything,' Duggan said.

'You a Roman Catholic?'

Duggan nodded.

'So you're a member of something.'

'I'm not in the IRA.'

'So why were you meeting those Germans?'

'What Germans?' Duggan held his breath inwardly, aware that he was inviting them to call his bluff and reveal more of what they knew. But he wanted to know what they knew. Who had told them about an IRA man visiting Lisbon and being on board his ship?

'The ones you said you met in the bar. What was it called? Antonio's?'

They really know nothing, Duggan thought. They're just fishing. 'I didn't say that.'

'Yes you did. You confessed to meeting German agents in a bar in Lisbon.' The detective looked over Duggan's shoulder at his colleague. 'You heard him, didn't you?'

'Clear as a bell, Sergeant,' the detective behind him said. 'He confessed.'

'I did not.' Duggan knew what they were doing and it strengthened his resolve not to give in to them. They were playing policemen's tricks, stringing together a collection of phrases into a confession. The kind of thing that had sent many an innocent Irishman to prison for years in this country. Even to the gallows. 'There might've been Germans in the bar for all I know. That's all.'

The detective brushed his words aside with his cigarette hand. 'We'll move on.' He leaned forward to stub out his cigarette. 'What did the German agents want?'

'I didn't meet any Germans.'

'A little sabotage? In England? Ulster? Where?'

'I didn't meet any Germans.' Duggan adopted a sullen tone.

'Maybe it was just a little information?'

'I didn't meet any Germans.'

'Harmless stuff, like the weather. Everybody in Ireland talks about the weather, don't they?'

Duggan said nothing.

'Maybe it was the other way round,' the detective said, sounding surprised at his own versatility. 'You were asking *them* for something? A little help?'

'I didn't meet any Germans.'

'A few guns? Bombs?'

'Bicycles,' the detective behind Duggan sniggered.

The detective doing the questioning gave Duggan an inquisitive look. Duggan stared back at him and said, 'I didn't meet any Germans.'

The detective picked up Duggan's passport and flicked through it for a moment. 'Citizen of Ireland,' he read with a short laugh. 'And Mr de Valera wants us to afford you every protection and assistance.'

He closed the passport and tapped its hard edge on the table to underline his words. 'Never mind this little piece of Eire theatrics. Let's be clear about the situation here, McCarthy. The law says you are a subject of His Majesty the King. And you have confessed to conspiring with the King's enemies in the middle of a war. You know what that means?' He paused. 'What happens to British subjects who assist the enemy in wartime?'

'I didn't meet any Germans,' Duggan muttered.

'You should think carefully about your predicament. Sleep on it, in a manner of speaking. And decide what's best for you. It will go easier for you if you tell us all about your German contacts. It's even possible that you could be released. If you give us your full cooperation.'

'Is my ship still here?' Duggan asked.

'It's long gone. You're on your own.'

Duggan dropped his chin on to his chest. The detective stood up and nodded to his colleague, who opened the door and called to the policeman. 'If there's a raid tonight,' he told the policeman when he came, 'take him down to the docks and give him a ringside seat. Handcuff him to something solid out in the open.'

The window of the cell had been blocked by a blackout shutter on the outside, and a feeble bulb lit the interior. 'Can I have something to eat?' Duggan asked, as the policeman stood back to let him enter. The policeman was the one who had been the passenger in the patrol car. He looked at Duggan for a moment and then nodded.

Duggan lay down on the bed while he waited, thinking back over the interrogation. They had reason to suspect he was in the IRA, but they had no specific information about his meetings with the Germans. So who would have tipped them off? None of the Irish people he met in Lisbon knew about his cover story of being in the IRA or about his contacts with the Germans. Some of the crew suspected him of IRA connections and had seen him with Strasser in the pub. So information from any of them could fit with what the Special Branch men knew.

He closed his eyes and hoped the Branch man had been telling the truth when he'd said the ship was long gone. That meant it should be back in Dublin by morning at the latest, and the captain would tell G2 what had happened. He was drifting off to sleep when the policeman came back with a mug of tea and a plate with two thinly buttered slices of bread. He handed them to Duggan without comment and left.

The tea was weak and had too much milk and no sugar, but it tasted great. The bread wasn't as grey as he was used to in Dublin and went a surprising distance towards quelling his hunger. The policeman returned a little later, handed him a cigarette and lit it for him with his own confiscated lighter.

'Thanks,' Duggan said with feeling as he inhaled, 'I really appreciate that.'

'Don't smoke myself. But the missus would go without food sooner than pass up a cigarette.'

'I know how she feels.' Duggan nodded. 'What time is it?'

The policeman hesitated a moment. 'Just after midnight. The end of my shift.'

'Thanks for the food and for this,' Duggan raised the cigarette.

As soon as he had finished his cigarette, he lay down again, rolled himself into the blanket and fell into a shallow and uneasy sleep, half wakening several times.

A roaring noise brought him fully awake, and he braced himself against the explosive blast, thinking of rolling off the bunk and under it.

No blast came, but the sound of engines grew and grew, and then began to fade into the distance. He realised it was probably a Sunderland flying boat taking off. Which meant it was probably first light, about four o'clock in the morning. The bulb was still lit and the blackout shutter gave no sign of daylight from outside. He waited until the engine noise faded completely and then he turned over and tried to go back to sleep.

It seemed like it was only seconds later that the cell door opened and someone shook him by the shoulder and shouted, 'Up! Get up!' He dropped his feet to the floor and stood up, unsteady with sleep. The policeman was a new one, middle-aged like his colleagues of the previous day. He caught Duggan by the shoulder and pushed him out the door, making no secret of his hostility.

They went upstairs again and Duggan caught a glimpse of grainy daylight from a room with an unshuttered window as they walked to the interview room. The light was still on there, the window blacked out. The second detective was seated at the table this time, a notebook open in front of him. His sergeant was lounging against the wall with his hands in his pockets: he yawned as Duggan entered and sat at the table.

'You're a lucky bastard,' the detective at the table said. 'Your friends didn't come last night.'

Duggan rubbed the sleep from his eyes.

'So you had a good night's sleep. You thought about what the sergeant said?'

'I didn't meet any Germans,' Duggan said.

'Good. That's the way you want to play it.' He took a pencil from his inside pocket. 'Name?'

'Sean McCarthy.'

'Rank?'

'Deckhand.'

'Your IRA rank? You chaps love playing soldiers, giving yourselves ranks, don't you?'

'I'm not in the IRA.'

The detective studied him for a moment, his head to one side. 'I'll put you down as a major.' He wrote in his notebook. 'What unit?'

'I'm not in the IRA.'

'The Dublin Brigade. That sound right?' The detective looked at his superior for confirmation. 'Right.' He wrote in the notebook again. 'And you entered the United Kingdom illegally.'

'No I didn't,' Duggan said.

'Where's your travel permit?'

'You know how I came to be here.'

'Yes, you were masquerading as a deckhand on a vessel and jumped ship when it came into port to present its navicert.' He wrote in the notebook again. 'And your mission?'

Duggan stared at him, saying nothing.

'Sabotage,' the detective said, nodding to himself. 'And the collection of information of use to the enemy. Where were you planning to bomb?' He waited for an answer and then said: 'Suspect refused to divulge the specific target of his mission.' He wrote for a moment. 'Suspect also refused to name his co-conspirators in the UK.' He looked up from his notebook. 'Can't say fairer than that, can I? That'll go down well with your commanders. Get you a medal. Posthumously.'

Duggan sighed and rested his arms on the table, his hands joined. His eyes were growing heavy again and he wanted to close them and go back to sleep.

'I don't think he's taking this seriously, sergeant.'

Duggan felt hands tighten on his shoulders from behind and shake him violently. 'He's paying attention now,' the sergeant said.

The detective lit a cigarette and pulled the ashtray closer to himself. He leaned back in his chair as though he was taking a break. 'You're not giving me much help,' he said.

'I didn't meet any Germans,' Duggan said, deciding to stick to this denial and thwart their transparent efforts to twist everything he said into an incriminating statement.

'Pity,' the detective muttered, almost to himself. He smoked in silence for a while, concentrating on the cigarette, then lunged across the table and grabbed Duggan's hand. The sergeant reached around him at the same time, grabbed his other arm and twisted it behind the back of the chair, imprisoning him against the upright. Duggan tried automatically to pull his hand free but the detective had a firm grip on his fingers, pulling them forward so that his arm was stretched out.

'That's no farmer's hand,' the detective said, using his cigarette as a pointer. He moved the burning tip of the cigarette closer to Duggan's palm. 'You're no more a farmer than a sailor.'

Duggan braced himself, feeling the heat of the cigarette grow as it approached and hovered over his palm.

'Not a bomber's hand either,' the detective said with surprise, and looked at the sergeant while letting his cigarette move closer to Duggan's hand. 'What we have here, Sergeant, is one of the officer class. One of those who orders ignorant Paddies to carry around weeping gelignite and kill innocent people if they don't kill themselves first.'

Duggan was transfixed by the cigarette and moved his thumb away from where it had been protecting his palm as the burning coal almost touched it. 'I'm a farmer,' he heard himself say.

The detective took his time withdrawing the cigarette and then inhaled a last drag. He released Duggan's hand and stubbed out the butt in the ashtray. The sergeant released Duggan other's arm.

'What kind of farmer?' the detective asked, as if they were continuing a casual chat.

'Mixed,' Duggan shrugged.

'What does that mean?'

'A few cattle and sheep. A bit of tillage.'

'What do you do with them?'

'Which? The bullocks or the hoggets or the wethers?'

The detective stared at him, not knowing what he was talking about. Duggan stared back, happy to have made a small point after giving in and answering their questions. 'Where's this farm?' the detective demanded.

'In the west. Galway.'

'And why did they order you to leave it?'

'No one ordered me to leave it.'

'You just decided to go off to Lisbon and say hello to the Germans.'

'I was bored. I thought I'd like to try the sea.'

'In the middle of a war?' the detective said, with a disbelieving laugh.

'Ireland is neutral.'

'Stabbing us in the back, you mean.'

'Making its own decisions.'

The detective gave a slight smile of victory. 'So a farmer who's interested in politics.'

'I'm not interested in politics.'

'You just told us you were.'

'No, I didn't,' Duggan parried, feeling drained. He was tired and hungry and knew this could go on for hours. Or even days, if they had held the ship, or if something happened to it on its way to Dublin. Stop, he told himself, reining in his imagination. I can tell them right now who I am, ask them to contact the Irish High Commission in London, and put an end to it. But a stubborn streak said, No, I'm not going to abandon my cover story until I'm ordered to. Not to the bloody British.

'You were looking for adventure?'

'Something like that.'

'Why didn't you come here and join the forces?'

'I didn't want to be a soldier.'

'You could've been a sailor. In the Royal Navy.'

'I don't want to fight anyone.'

'But you wanted to go off to sea,' the detective said, shaking his head. 'With ships being sunk every day. You think a jury's going to believe that?'

When the hostile policeman took him back to the cell, he found a mug of cold tea and two slices of cold toast on a tray. He sipped at the tea after stirring the settled milk on its surface with his finger, then ate the soggy toast and lay down. He was about to drift off when the policeman banged on the cell door, opened it, and took the tray away.

'Can I have one of my cigarettes, please?'

The policeman ignored him and left. He was drifting off again when noise outside the window brought him back to consciousness. Someone removed the blackout shutter and the cell light was clicked off. He couldn't tell what the day was like from the limited view. He fell asleep again and woke feeling exhausted and disorientated. Nothing had changed in the cell.

He put his hands under his head and tried to relax, imagining that he was back in his parents' house, sick in bed for the day, bored and restless. The only diversion was the occasional shadow passing by the window and a car wheel which blocked the light for a while until it moved away again. This is stupid, he thought. What am I trying to prove?

But he knew, deep down, what he was trying to prove. It wasn't just about being stubborn, of maintaining his cover until his superiors released him from it. Or trying to figure out why the detectives thought he was in the IRA. Or of standing up to the British, as his father had done during the War of Independence. It was about proving to himself that he could take the pressure. About the endless doubt since the war began about how he'd perform if called upon to actually fight an invader, about how he'd behave when things got rough.

You're just wasting everyone's time, including your own, he told himself. There are more important things to be getting on with than indulging your own insecurities.

He decided to admit who he was at the next interrogation, but nobody came for him and the day dragged by. He was sure it must be evening when the policeman came with his midday meal: two slices of spam with a boiled potato covered by some kind of watery gravy. The policeman acted as if he didn't exist when Duggan asked him what time it was.

'Tell the Special Branch men I want to talk to them,' he said when the policeman came back for the tray.

The policeman gave no sign that he had heard anything.

When he had left, Duggan walked the three paces up and down the cell for a time, trying without success to ignore his craving for nicotine. Then he dropped to the floor and did press-ups without counting until it became too much of an effort to raise himself. He flopped on to the bed, feeling better for the exercise but still craving a cigarette. He decided irritably that they could all fuck off, he wasn't going to tell them anything after all.

He dozed off again and was woken by the door opening. A man stood there as Duggan sat up.

'Captain Duggan,' the man said with an English accent. He was middle-aged, short and stout, and wore an open raincoat over a dark suit. He held out his hand. 'Tom Hopkins.'

Duggan stood up and shook his hand, and Hopkins motioned to him to go ahead of him, out of the cell and up the stairs to the station's day room. The hostile police-man and a colleague whom Duggan hadn't seen before were there. His possessions were on a table against the wall, including his kitbag, which they had brought from the ship.

'Is that everything?' Hopkins asked him.

Duggan gave it a cursory glance and nodded.

'You want to change, clean up?'

'No,' Duggan said, strapping on his watch. It was just before four o'clock. 'I'm fine.'

Hopkins gave him a wry look. 'Suit yourself.' He turned to the policemen. 'Thanks for looking after him.'

Outside, Duggan took a deep breath of the warm air. The sun was shining but there were puffy clouds in the sky and there was a light sprinkle of recent rain on the roadway. Hopkins led him over to a black Rover saloon and they sat in.

'Mind if I smoke?' Duggan asked.

'Go ahead,' Hopkins said, and shook his head when Duggan offered him a cigarette. Hopkins watched him light one and inhale the smoke deeply. 'They give you a hard time?'

'No.'

'Why didn't you tell them to contact us?'

Duggan assumed 'us' was MI5, which had a close rela-tionship with G2. 'Not up to me,' he said, shrugging, feeling light-headed from the sudden rush of nicotine.

Hopkins continued to watch him as he contemplated that answer, then shook his head and started the car. 'We're on the same side this time, you know,' he said.

'I know.' Duggan nodded, making his light-headedness worse. He wasn't always convinced, though. 'Where are we going?'

'Holyhead,' Hopkins said, driving off. 'A long drive, I'm afraid. You know the Fishguard mailboat was sunk the week before last?'

'No,' Duggan said, looking at him. 'What happened?'

'German bomber hit it bang on, amidships. Destroyed the bridge, killed most of the crew and some passengers. A few miles offshore.'

'Which shore?' Duggan asked, remembering how vulnerable he had felt when the patrolling Condor had passed over them.

'This side. I don't know all the details. I think it was on its way over from Ireland.'

They were already in the countryside, with hardly any traffic on the road. Hopkins drove fast with one languid hand on the steering wheel.

'You away for long?'

'A few weeks,' Duggan said vaguely.

'In Lisbon?'

'Only there for a few days,' Duggan said, aware that Hopkins was continuing the Special Branch men's interrogation in a friendlier environment. 'A couple of weeks coming and going.'

'A quiet passage?'

'Very quiet, especially on the way back. Hardly saw any signs of the war. A plane or two.'

'Ours or theirs?'

'One of each.' Duggan wound down his window to toss out his cigarette. The countryside looked familiar, lush in its midsummer green, little different from that on the other side of the Irish Sea. Lots of crops in well-tended fields, not many cattle, he noted. 'On separate occasions. On patrol.'

'They left you alone?'

Duggan nodded. 'Had a look at us. And continued about their business.'

They swept past a hay cart drawn by a horse and slowed through a small town of grey stone houses. Hopkins seemed to know where he was going, although there were no direction signs anywhere.

'What's happening in Russia?' Duggan asked when they were back on the open road, passing through a valley between two verdant hills.

'Another *blitzkrieg*. The Jerries are cutting through them like a knife through butter. They say they've advanced a couple of hundred miles already. It'll be over in a couple of months.'

'Jesus,' Duggan sighed. A thousand-mile front, advancing hundreds of miles in a week or so. It was almost impossible to imagine the scale of that operation. And if the Germans could do that, what could they do to Ireland's puny defences?

'Indeed,' Hopkins nodded. 'But it's given us breathing space. You know they were massing troops in Norway last month?'

Duggan shook his head. He hadn't heard that.

'It looked like they were preparing to invade the east coast. But it turned out to be a feint, to confuse Stalin about their intentions.'

'But when they're finished with the Russians … ' Duggan let the thought hang. 'What'll Churchill do then?'

'Pray,' Hopkins said, flashing him a humourless grin. 'Pray that the Americans come in.'

'Make peace?'

'Can't see Winston doing that.'

'Somebody else then?'

'Possible,' Hopkins nodded.

They came up behind a convoy of empty military trucks and remained silent as they leapfrogged them on short straights, the car accelerating fast and with no sound of engine strain. Shortly afterwards, they went down the narrow hill to the bridge over the River Teifi at Cardigan and veered left around the old castle and up the hill on the other side, through what looked to Duggan like the main street.

'Would you explain your neutrality to me?' Hopkins asked when they were clear of the town, sounding like he genuinely wanted to know. 'Why you are persisting with it?'

Duggan did his best to explain it. It was proof of independence, a way of avoiding internal conflict between those who supported the Allies and the Axis, and the only practical way of protecting Ireland's citizens in the absence of a meaningful military force.

'But we will give you protection,' Hopkins said.

'You have your hands full protecting your own people,' Duggan offered diplomatically. 'What can you spare for us?'

Hopkins conceded the point with a nod. 'You know,' he said, 'if we go down, you'll go down too.'

'Yes, I know,' Duggan agreed. There was no way Ireland could hold out on its own against a German invasion. Which wouldn't even be necessary if Britain was overrun: Germany could simply dictate what it wanted to happen in Ireland under its 'New Europe' policies.

'And the Nazis are not noted for their care of the citizens of conquered countries,' Hopkins added.

Duggan almost smiled at the delicacy with which Hopkins put it, thinking of Gerda's regular outbursts against their viciousness towards the Jews in Austria. And of Aiken's speech in Lisbon, in which he might or might not have suggested that a German victory would not be an unthinkable outcome of the war.

'You agree with this neutrality?'

'I'm only a soldier,' Duggan said, deflecting the probe, wondering if Hopkins was sounding him out as a possible agent. 'Ours not to wonder why.'

Hopkins gave him a sympathetic nod.

* * *

They stopped in Aberystwyth at a three-storey hotel on the seafront and got out. 'I'll go and check if they have food for us,' Hopkins said. Duggan stretched himself and looked across the road at the promenade. There were a few people strolling by or sitting on benches, faces raised to the sun. Beyond them, the sea in the half-moon bay looked very calm, and a gentle breeze blew inshore.

'Turning into an old salt already,' Hopkins said in an amused tone when he returned. 'Wishing you were back on the ocean wave.'

'No thanks,' Duggan said. 'I've had enough of that.' So, he thought, the Special Branch detectives had reported to him on their interrogation.

A matronly woman gave him a disapproving look as he followed Hopkins into a low-ceilinged dining room and she showed them to a table by the window. The only other occupants were an elderly couple at another window table.

'Scrambled eggs on toast,' the woman said to Duggan. 'Is that all right for you too?'

'That would be lovely.'

Duggan excused himself and went in search of the toilet when she had gone. He realised why she had given him that look as soon as he caught his image in the mottled mirror. He was unshaven, his left eye was bloodshot, and the healthy looking tan he had acquired on board the ship seemed to have vanished. His shirt was rumpled and he looked like he had slept in his clothes. Quite a contrast with the nattily dressed Hopkins.

When he returned to the table, Hopkins was watching two young women swinging a small boy between them on the promenade.

The woman came with their plates and a pot of tea on a tray. She kept her distance from Duggan, as if he might be contagious, stretching to place his plate in front of him.

'What was that about?' Duggan asked when she left.

'Probably thinks you're a deserter,' Hopkins said. 'And I'm your long-suffering guardian bringing you back to your unit.'

Duggan laughed and tasted the egg: it was grainy and metallic, unlike any egg he had ever tasted before. Hopkins caught his grimace and pushed the salt across the table. 'That'll help,' he said.

'What is it?' Duggan pointed at the egg.

'Reconstituted egg powder. You still have fresh eggs in Ireland?'

'I think so,' Duggan nodded. He had never given the matter any thought. Food was good in the army.

'Lot to be said for neutrality.' Hopkins poured cups of tea for both of them. 'You could add that to your arguments for neutrality. Real eggs.'

Duggan glanced at him but there was no edge to his voice or his demeanour. He didn't seem to resent Ireland's position, just accepted it as it was. Which was a surprise to Duggan, who had followed the often bitter attacks on Eire in the English papers. When they had finished their tea, Duggan lit a cigarette.

'You running out of those in Eire?' Hopkins asked.

'Don't think so,' Duggan said, thinking of the packets of cigarettes that presumably were waiting for him, along with the wireless, in Dublin. 'Not yet anyway.'

'Going short here. Some shops won't sell them to women any more.'

'Why?'

'Say they should be kept for men. Some will only sell them to men in the Services.'

Duggan wondered what G2 would do with the ciga-rettes, which had been a cover for his other activities, so that he could produce them if he had to persuade any of the other crewmen that he was just a small-time smuggler. Like their colleague whom he had replaced on the voyage.

'What did you think of Fritz Wiedermeyer?' Hopkins asked in the same casual tone.

'Who?'

'The man you were talking to in the Metropole Hotel,' Hopkins said, and added, 'in Lisbon,' as though Duggan regularly met Germans in Metropole hotels in many cities.

'That was his name?' There was no point denying it, Duggan decided. So they were the ones who told Special Branch about me. Got the police to pick me up. But didn't share all their information about my meetings in Lisbon. Interesting but not surprising, he thought. It was the same in Dublin between G2 and the Garda Special Branch.

Hopkins nodded. 'What did he call himself?'

'He didn't. I even asked him his name, but he didn't tell me. Said he was just a courier.'

Hopkins laughed without humour. 'Good old Fritz. Long time since he was a messenger boy.'

'You know him?'

'Haven't had the pleasure in person. But our paths have crossed.'

'You've been in Lisbon?'

Hopkins confirmed, with a slow flick of his eyelids, that he had. 'Fritz is a long-time Abwehr man. Probably second in command in Lisbon to von Karstorff.'

Duggan widened his own eyes in surprise. Why would such a high-up Abwehr man want to deliver a transmitter in person to the IRA? Hermann Goertz must be really important to them.

Hopkins nodded, confirming what he was thinking. 'I don't suppose you'd like to share your conversation with him?' he smiled.

Duggan widened his hands in a gesture of regret. 'Sorry,' he said. 'Not up to me.'

'Ours not to reason why.'

'And hope we don't have to follow up with the next line.'

'Do and die,' Hopkins nodded. 'Hopefully not.'

'It was nothing to do with this side of the water,' Duggan offered after a moment. 'Internal matters.'

Hopkins nodded as if he understood. 'I'll send you Fritz's file,' he said. 'If you're going back again, I can fill you in on their other people as well.'

'Doubt if I will be.' Duggan paused, then decided to go ahead. Since they were trading information. 'Did you ever come across one who calls himself "Strasser". Don't know his first name.'

'Strasser?' Hopkins repeated the name as if he was tasting it. He shook his head.

'Or Maud Browne?' Duggan enquired.

'She's one of theirs?' Hopkins asked in surprise.

'No, no,' Duggan said. 'I just wondered if you'd ever met her when you were there.'

Hopkins shook his head slowly, as if he was thinking.

'She's a presence on the diplomatic circuit, I think,' Duggan added, watching his reactions.

'English?'

'Irish.'

'I didn't have the pleasure of mixing with the diplomatic set either,' Hopkins said. 'I was only a visiting fireman.'

Duggan decided it would be overstepping an invisible line to ask what fires he had been in Lisbon to extinguish. But he was reasonably sure that Hopkins had never heard of Maud Browne before. Which was not too surprising, even if she was acting as a British agent. In that event she'd be working with MI6, and they probably didn't tell MI5 everything. If she had passed on information about Aiken's comments, it was much more likely to have been through the diplomatic circuit: gossip over cocktails. And if she was indeed an MI6 agent, word might filter back through Hopkins that the Irish knew about her. And might stop her telling tales about Irish matters.

Daylight had faded into a midsummer half-dark by the time they had crossed the Menai Bridge into Anglesea and dipped down into Holyhead. The town was blacked out, but the outline of two funnels was visible in the harbour beyond the bulk of the embarkation shed. Smoke was rising almost straight up from one of them.

Hopkins circled down to the harbour, the Rover's restricted headlights making little impact on the half-light, and parked behind the shed. Before they got out, Hopkins took a small notebook from an inside pocket, wrote a phone number on a page, tore it out and gave it to Duggan. 'If you ever want to check anything in a hurry,' he said. 'Cut through the formal structures.'

Duggan looked at the London number, folded the sheet, and put it in his pocket. 'You have to go back to London now?' he asked.

'In the morning.'

Duggan took his kitbag from the back seat and followed Hopkins to a door into the shed, away from the official entrance. Inside, Hopkins showed something to a policeman and they cut through corridors that bypassed the ticket and travel-permit checks and the customs hall. They came out on the quayside beside the *Cambria*.

Hopkins stopped beside the gangway, shook Duggan's hand, and said: 'One of your people will meet you on the other side. Safe journey.'

'Thanks,' Duggan said, and walked aboard the blacked-out ship.

He decided to stay on deck and found a bench on the port side near the stern and lay down on it, using his kit-bag as a pillow. He opened his cigarette case and saw that he had only two left and debated whether to have one. He didn't have any English money on him so couldn't buy any more on board. I'll have one when we get going, he thought.

He dozed for a while until the ship began to rumble as the engines picked up power and it moved away from the quay and steamed towards the mouth of the harbour. He stood up and leaned on the rails and listened to the swish of the water and felt a cool breeze break the balmy night air as the mailboat picked up speed. A few others had come on deck and also watched in silence as they slid out of the harbour and the dark coast of Wales passed by. With no lights visible, it looked like an uninhabited land.

He smoked his second-last cigarette and let his memory flick back and forth at random over everything that had happened. Lisbon already seemed like a long time ago. and the questions had mounted up.

Why did this Fritz Wiedermeyer get involved in what they thought was an IRA request for a radio? Was Maisie O'Gorman as simply flirtatious as she appeared? What had happened to the Rosslare mailboat? What did Aiken really say in Lisbon? Why did MI5 send Hopkins to act as my personal chauffeur? Couldn't they have just let me go and left it to the High Commission in London to get me back to Ireland? Why did Wiedermeyer meet me in such a public place? Did the Germans want the Brits to pick me up? If so, why? Because they thought I was an IRA man? Or because they thought I was a plant?

The passing waves offered no answers to any of his questions, and he smoked the cigarette down as far as he could before flicking the butt overboard and watching the pinprick of fire being swept back and disappearing. He returned to his bench, lay down, and wasn't aware of anything until he was woken by the sound of a bottle rolling down the wooden deck and banging into steel.

He sat up and saw that there was a group of men sitting in a half-circle on the deck nearby, bottles of Guinness in their hands, empties rolling around them in tune with the boat's motion. He stood up, feeling groggy, stretched himself and leaned on the railing. The sky had lightened and the sun was about to break over the horizon, off to their left. He smoked his last cigarette and watched the sunshine settle on to the ship, washing over the funnels and then the bridge as the sun rose and the Irish coast came into view, a series of small humps. They passed by the Kish lightship and he let out a deep breath, relieved to be home.

Six

Captain Bill Sullivan was waiting, in uniform, on the quayside when the *Cambria* berthed at St Michael's wharf in Dun Laoghaire harbour. 'Jaysus,' he said when Duggan stepped off the gangway behind the group of navvies, 'they gave you the third degree.'

'Not really,' Duggan yawned. 'Haven't slept much in the last couple of nights.'

'You look like shit.'

'Sorry for getting you up so early.'

Duggan followed him into the disembarkation area and around the passport and travel-permit checkers after Sullivan flashed his identity card at them.

'Not so fast,' a middle-aged customs officer called as they went by a queue of people having their bags examined at a table.

Sullivan showed him his ID but the customs officer ignored him and told Duggan to put his kitbag on the table. 'Fuck's sake,' Sullivan muttered as the customs officer took his time rooting through the dirty clothes. When he'd finished, he chalked a mark on the bag and let Duggan take it back. 'World's full of little Hitlers these days,' Sullivan said, loudly enough for the customs officer to hear him as they walked away.

They went by the waiting train, its idling engine chugging bursts of steam, out of the terminal, by a line of horse-drawn cabs and up to where Sullivan had parked the car. 'You wouldn't have any fags on you?' Duggan asked as they sat into the unmarked Ford Prefect. Sullivan was an occasional smoker, usually of Duggan's cigarettes.

Sullivan unbuttoned his tunic pocket and handed him a blue packet of Player's.

'Buying the strong ones now,' Duggan said in surprise, as he helped himself to one and offered the open packet to Sullivan.

Sullivan shook his head. 'That's one of yours,' he said. 'The ones you were smuggling.'

Duggan inhaled a lungful of smoke and felt light-headed from the stronger hit of nicotine on an empty stomach as they drove up Marine Road and turned right into George's Street at the church. There was no sign of life anywhere; all the shops were shuttered and there was no traffic on the road. The sun was up now, brightening everything with the fresh promise of a new day.

'How did you get yourself arrested?' Sullivan asked.

'Good question,' Duggan said.

They usually worked on separate operations, but they shared an office, so each inevitably picked up details of what the other was up to. And Sullivan was in charge of G2's interrogation of Hermann Goertz, so he knew that Duggan had been carrying a message to the Abwehr that was supposed to have come from the German spy. He knew nothing about Duggan's attempts to check up on Frank Aiken's doings in Lisbon.

'The boss was very worried about you,' Sullivan said, giving him a sardonic grin. It was a regular complaint of his that their immediate superior, Commandant McClure, favoured Duggan over him, giving him the more interesting jobs and treating him more as an equal. 'Afraid they'd hurt you.'

Duggan ignored the jibe. 'You got the transmitter?'

'And the fags and the coffee.' Sullivan sped down the road into Blackrock village, giving a wide berth to a wobbly cyclist who looked like he was on his way home from a hard night's drinking. 'I didn't know you were doing a little smuggling on the side.'

'And the message for Goertz?'

Sullivan nodded. 'Hasn't been decoded yet. Dr Hayes wasn't available yesterday.' Richard Hayes, the head of the National Library, was their unofficial cryptographer, and the man who had broken the code used by Goertz.

'How is Hermann?'

'Can't shut the fucker up,' Sullivan sighed. He'd been delighted at first to be given the task of interrogating Goertz after his capture at the end of a long pursuit, but his interest was beginning to fade.

'Anything interesting?'

'Just repeating the same old stuff at this stage. I'm Ireland's best friend. Working night and day to protect your neutrality. Germany loves Ireland,' Sullivan mimicked. 'And moaning about the shower of unreliable fuckers in the IRA.'

'All good news,' Duggan laughed.

Sullivan nodded. 'And there's another love letter for you.'

'You got it?'

'In the office.'

'How did you get this American penfriend anyway?'

'Can't tell you,' Duggan said. They had already had this sparring conversation several times. Sullivan knew nothing of his relationship with Gerda Meier, or even that she was his correspondent.

'Which reminds me. Your smart-arse Special Branch friend was looking for you.'

'For what?'

'Talking his usual shite. Worried about your morals. Wanted to make sure you weren't eating meat on Fridays. Going to confession every week.'

'You didn't tell him where I was?'

'Told him I didn't know where you were. And cared less.'

A milkman was pouring milk into a jug for a uniformed maid outside a large house on Merrion Road, and there were more signs of life as they neared the city centre. Sullivan slowed as the traffic light at the corner of Merrion Square and Clare Street turned red, and glanced to either side to make sure there was nothing coming. He continued without stopping.

There was no pointsman on duty at O'Connell Bridge yet and Sullivan turned on to Bachelors Walk and drove down by the Liffey. The sunshine followed them westwards, mellowing the faded red brickwork of the buildings, which was broken only by the rebuilt facade of the Four Courts. They turned into Collins Barracks and one sentry saluted while another raised the barrier and Sullivan drove under the archway into the parade ground and parked on the right in front of the mess.

Sullivan stayed in the car as Duggan got out. 'You not going back to bed?' Duggan leaned down to ask through the open door.

'No point,' Sullivan said. 'I'll go into the office. Get an early start on the daily report.'

Duggan went upstairs to his room, opened the door with his key, and tossed his kitbag on the floor at the end of the iron bed. It was spartan but the window was open an inch, so it didn't have the air of a room that hadn't been occupied for six weeks. Somebody has been using it, he thought, but that wasn't unusual: visiting officers were accommodated in any available rooms.

He sat on the side of the bed, unlaced his shoes, pushed each one off with the other foot and lay down. He fell asleep while still thinking he should get undressed.

Commandant McClure was sitting behind his desk in the Red House, the headquarters of G2, the inevitable cigarette in his ashtray producing a thin column of smoke, which divided into a victory sign as it climbed towards the ceiling. 'Well,' he said, sitting back with a smile as Duggan entered after a casual knock. 'You got more than you bargained for.'

'A little,' Duggan agreed.

'Tell me all,' McClure said, pointing at the chair opposite him.

Duggan told him everything that had happened, in chronological order, knowing that he'd want to hear how things had developed. McClure listened with few interruptions and jotted an occasional note on a pad. 'So Mr Aiken wasn't being very diplomatic,' he said, circling a couple of words on the pad when Duggan had finished. 'But then he never is. Our friend in External Affairs has been up in a heap about the whole American trip. It's turned into something of a disaster.'

'They won't give us any arms.'

'Worse than that,' said McClure, shaking his head. 'They've made it fairly clear that they'll support the British if Churchill decides he has to seize our ports.'

'Jesus,' Duggan said.

The pressure over the ports seemed to be ratcheting up inexorably. Churchill had a bee in his bonnet about them, was determined to get them back and was being restrained by his military advisers, who didn't think that seizing and securing them would be worth the effort. And by fears of how a British invasion of Ireland would be perceived in America, where the isolationists were still very strong, probably in a majority in spite of President Roosevelt's determined anti-Nazi stance. If the British knew the Yanks wouldn't object ...

'I don't know why Mr de Valera sent him in the first place,' McClure was saying. 'It never looked like a good idea.'

'Maybe he thought the Americans needed to hear some straight talking.' Duggan thought of his uncle, Timmy Monaghan, a government backbencher and a supporter of Aiken. Like him, Timmy was convinced that Britain was Ireland's main enemy, and that Churchill was spoiling for a rerun of the War of Independence, in which Timmy had fought alongside Duggan's father.

'Time and place for everything,' McClure muttered as he tapped another line in his notes with his pen. 'You believe this fellow Hopkins?'

'About Fritz Wiedermeyer?'

McClure nodded.

'MI5 knew I'd met some German and had me taken off the ship in Pembroke. Somebody tipped them off, or one of their people saw me. If the German's as senior as Hopkins says, that'd make sense. They're probably watching each other's men over there.'

'But why was a senior Abwehr agent interested in a low-level IRA man?' McClure asked, something in his tone making the question rhetorical as he reached for a file on top of a pile on the right-hand side of his desk. 'And the answer is here.' McClure waved the folder, put it on his desk and opened it. 'The message he gave you for Goertz. Dr Hayes has started decoding it, and it may explain his interest. Nothing to do with the IRA as such.'

Duggan could see the rows of letters in blocks of four as McClure shuffled a couple of pages of shiny photocopies and came to a foolscap worksheet with a jumble of notes on it. He sat back, ignoring the file.

'An American Flying Fortress crashed in Mayo a month or so ago,' he said. 'It had no markings on it. No armaments on board. All the crew in civvies. So, technically, it was a civilian aircraft and, anyway, not even from a belligerent country. Seems it ran out of fuel on its way to England.' McClure paused to light a cigarette and tossed one to Duggan. 'The co-pilot was killed, pilot and navigator injured but not seriously. Walking wounded. They were taken to a hospital in Castlebar and the American legation took over looking after them and so on. Asked that they be allowed to continue their journey to England with the co-pilot's body. And asked that the wreckage be salvaged and taken to the North. Which is what happened.'

McClure stretched out a finger to tap the file in front of him. 'Wiedermeyer's message to Goertz is about this plane.'

Duggan gave a low whistle. 'Was the crash in the papers?'

McClure shook his head. 'No. It was censored. And it gets more interesting. His message says that the plane was carrying a secret new American bombsight.'

'Was it?'

'First we've heard of it.'

'So how did the Germans know about it?' Duggan asked.

McClure stared back at him, letting the question hang in the air.

'They've got another spy here? Apart from Goertz?'

'Don't think so,' McClure said, stirring himself and standing up. 'If they had, and if that person could have told them about the bombsight, they wouldn't need to enlist Goertz's help to try and find it.'

'Find it?' Duggan repeated. 'It's missing?'

McClure nodded.

'How could they know that? That it was on board and that it's missing.'

'The sixty-four-thousand-dollar question,' McClure said, beginning to pace back and forth from his desk to the window, leaving a trail of smoke that doubled back on itself as he moved. The afternoon sky was a bright blue outside but this side of the building was in the shade. 'We don't even know if it's true. If there was anything like that on board.'

'Can't we ask the Americans?' Even as he said it, Duggan knew that that wasn't a good idea: they'd want to know immediately how G2 had heard about the bombsight.

'We already asked them what was on board and they assured us there was nothing of significance. No armaments and so on.'

'Is a bombsight an armament?'

'Clearly not if you don't want it to be.'

Duggan stood up as well, trying to tease out his jumbled thoughts. 'Couldn't we ask the Americans if anything is missing?'

McClure gave a short laugh. 'Lots of things were missing. It was carrying supplies for their London legation. Food. Drink. Cigarettes. Paper. Typewriter ribbons. Office stuff. Things in short supply in England.'

Duggan nodded his understanding. 'How long did it take to secure the site?'

'Long enough for most of the supplies to have disappeared. Some of the paper was left.'

McClure stopped behind his desk to stub out his cigarette. 'We need to look back over everything to do with that plane. See what might have happened to what was on board and figure out how the Germans know about it.'

'Use the transmitter to ask them for more information,' Duggan suggested.

'Perhaps. We need to set it up first. But I'd like to know a lot more about this before we ask the Germans or the Americans anything. Especially in the current state of our relations with the Americans. We're floundering around in the dark at the moment.'

Duggan sat down at his desk and looked at the pile of files and documents. On top was a report about the crash of the

Flying Fortress, which he put to one side. He sifted quickly through the rest, realising how most things resolved themselves unaided if they were left alone long enough. There were four letters: three from his mother and one from Gerda. His mother's gave his full rank and army headquarters as the address; Gerda's had no rank and said 'The Red House, Infirmary Road, Dublin'. He smiled again at the thought of some American post office sorter thinking what a quaint Irish address it was; the red house as distinct from the green house or the blue house. And what if there were two red houses on the road,? Would one be the first red house?

'How is she?' Sullivan interrupted his reverie from his spot at the other end of the table which served as their desk.

'My mother? I'll tell you as soon as I open them.'

'Your girlfriend.'

'Why do you assume it's from a woman?' Duggan turned over the envelope, where the sender's address said 'G. Matthews'. '"G" is for Gearoid.'

'Bollocks,' Sullivan laughed. 'That's a woman's writing.'

'You a handwriting expert now?'

'I know a woman's writing when I see it.'

'I'll tell him he'd better change it.' Duggan put the letters aside. 'People are getting the wrong idea about him.'

'We've set the date,' Sullivan said.

'For the wedding?' Duggan asked in surprise. Sullivan had been engaged to be married to Carmel since the beginning of the year but had never seemed in a hurry to get to the altar.

'September sixth.'

'Congratulations.'

'Her father's not well. She wants to do it sooner rather than later, in case.'

'Is he in hospital?'

Sullivan shook his head and shrugged. 'Give me one of those cigarettes I gave you.'

Duggan tossed the packet of Player's down the table and skated his lighter after it.

'What are you going to do with them?' Sullivan sent the packet skimming back along the table.

'The cigarettes? Forgot to ask the boss what we should do with them. Where are they anyway?'

Sullivan pointed over Duggan's shoulder to where the coat stand was. Duggan turned and saw the suitcase Wiedermeyer had given him in the corner. He picked it up, put it on the table and snapped open the catches. The radio equipment was gone but the cartons of cigarettes and bags of coffee were still there.

'A guy from Signals took the radio,' Sullivan said. 'They're setting it up in a house in Greystones. Waiting for you to come back before sending a first message.'

'Why Greystones?'

'Because it's full of West Brits.' Sullivan gave him a crooked smile. 'It'll confuse the real Brits if they locate it and think some of their supporters are talking to the Jerries.'

Duggan counted the cartons of cigarettes but had no idea how many more had gone missing. One sleeve of Player's was already missing most of its packs. He shrugged to himself and put a packet in his pocket.

He cleared a space on the table in front of him for the big Royal typewriter. He put two sheets of carbon paper between three pages of blank foolscap, rolled them into the typewriter's platen and loosened its lock to straighten them. It took him more than two hours to write his report on his visit to Lisbon, his meetings with the Germans, his detention at Pembroke and his conversations with the MI5 man who called himself Tom Hopkins. He did not try to interpret or speculate, just described each conversation and event. As

McClure had instructed him, he made no mention of his efforts to find out what Frank Aiken had told people there.

When he had finished, he tipped the typewriter up on its end, read through the document and initialled each of the copies. Sullivan had disappeared, and he stood by the window for a bit, stretching himself. It was a lovely long summer's evening out there, the sky bright blue, but shadows were beginning to lengthen and stretch out from the Red House.

He opened Gerda's envelope and caught a faint trace of perfume as he took out the flimsy air-mail paper. He took his time reading it, leaning against the wall by the window and hearing her voice behind the words as she described the daily tedium of her job in an insurance company's typing pool, the friendships she'd made with two other girls, and their progress, or lack of it, in getting an apartment to share. She signed off with 'missing you' followed by a neat drawing of a heart with an arrow through it and a 'G'.

He read it again, trying to visualise her life there, but his only real images of New York came from films and were usually black and white and involved gangsters and crime. He smiled at the thought of her surprise when she got his postcard from Lisbon and checked the date on the letter again. She wouldn't have received it when she wrote but she should have got it by now.

He read through his mother's letters, the usual catalogue of local news, more deaths than births or marriages. His father had put the car up on blocks, refusing his brother-in-law Timmy's offer of a few cans of petrol from Timmy's private store, and they were now using the pony and trap to get to town. One of his school friends was trying to get a travel permit to go to England after running away from the construction corps because of the bad conditions on the bogs, where they lived and worked cutting turf.

Good luck to him with that, Duggan thought, aware of rumours that Sean Lemass, the minister in charge of supplies, was thinking of banning emigration by all able-bodied men, and cutting their dole to force them to work at whatever he wanted done. He went back to his desk, put down the typewriter and wrote to his mother, apologising for the long silence. He'd been on manoeuvres, he told her: his parents didn't know he'd been out of the country.

When he'd finished, he opened the file on the Flying Fortress crash. The first report was from LOP 55, the lookout post at Renvyle point which had first sighted the unmarked plane crossing the coast a few days after he had left for Lisbon. It was followed by a Garda report describing the crash site, interviews with the pilot in hospital and a final report on the operation to remove the wreckage, which had taken a couple of days.

The plane had left from Washington and had had to divert northwards around a thunderstorm in its intended flight path. That, and a possible slow leak in a fuel line, had left it running out of fuel as it approached the Irish coast. The pilot had tried to land it on what looked like a flat area just north of a lake, and it had come down on a bog, skidded on its belly for nearly half a mile and crashed into a small wood. Wreckage had been found all along the landing area – bits of wings and engines – and the main part of the fuselage was in the wood.

The report listed the names of the crew and their injuries but without any ranks, except for the pilot. He was referred to as 'Captain', but whether that was a military rank or his position in charge of the aircraft wasn't clear.

The final document was an internal G2 report on the removal of the wreckage, signed with the initials 'L.A.' Liam Anderson. Shit, Duggan thought, of all the people who might have gone down there. Anderson was a captain on the British desk with whom Duggan had had several run-ins in the past, when there had been an overlap between the German and British desks. But there was nothing for it but to talk to him.

He found Anderson in his office listening to a joke, and waited for the punchline to ask if he could have a word with him.

'What are you fellows doing these days?' Anderson retorted in his strong northern accent. 'Nothing for you to do since the Germans turned their attention to Russia.'

'I wanted to ask you about the Flying Fortress crash in Mayo.'

Anderson gave him a suspicious eye. 'You trying to muscle in on our area?'

'There might be a German angle to it.'

'What?' Anderson said, making no secret of his scepticism.

'That's what we're trying to find out.'

'I didn't see any Germans there. Unless they were very well disguised as Americans.'

'Were there Americans there? Among the people from the North?'

Anderson tipped his chair on to its back legs and looked up at Duggan. 'Just what the fuck are you up to?'

'I'm not sure. We've come across a hint that the Germans might be interested in this plane and we're trying to figure out why that might be.'

'Just want to see how it works,' Anderson said with dismissive certainty.

'Could be,' Duggan agreed. 'But they know they're not in a position to send a military expert down there to look at it. And they probably know it's not there any more.'

'How would they know that?'

'People talk to their legation all the time,' Duggan shrugged. 'Tell them things.'

Anderson turned to his colleague. 'They're just chasing gossip,' Anderson said of Duggan and the German desk. 'Nothing better to be doing.'

'Tell me about what was on board,' Duggan persisted.

'Ah,' Anderson laughed. 'You just want a cigar. Why didn't you say?'

'If you're giving them away.'

'Ah, I only got the one. I was much too late getting there. But from what I heard, all of Mayo's smoking the finest Cuban cigars. After having caviar for breakfast, dinner and tea. And sipping Jim Beam instead of poteen.'

'There was a lot of that on board?'

'Tons of it. Stuff that had never been seen in Mayo before. They didn't know whether to eat it raw, boil it, bake it or stuff it in a chicken. The Americans know how to look after their legations. Place in London must be a gourmet's paradise.'

'And it was all gone by the time you got there?'

Anderson nodded. 'That bog is an out-of-the-way place. And the locals weren't in any hurry to notify anyone.'

'What about the crew?'

'They looked after them all right. The co-pilot was dead when they found him, and they took the other two to hospital by horse and cart. But it was a good twelve hours before the guards got there, next morning by the time the LDF was mobilised to protect the site.'

'And there was nothing left by then.'

'No caviar anyway.'

'What about equipment? Was it carrying any?'

'What do you mean, equipment?'

'Was it carrying anything else apart from food and drink?'

'Some office stuff. There were bits of that lying around.'

'Nothing else?'

'Nothing else I heard of.'

'No weapons?'

Anderson shook his head. 'Not even a pistol. The turrets were all empty and I don't think anyone around there could have removed and disappeared seven heavy-calibre machine guns that fast. Have you ever seen one of those? A Flying Fortress?'

Duggan shook his head.

'One big bastard of a plane.'

'No mention of documents on board?' Duggan asked, to throw him off the scent. 'A diplomatic bag? Anything like that?'

'No. There were a couple of Americans there from the legation when they started the salvage job. That tall fellow with the Swedish name, the intelligence guy … '

'Max Linqvist.'

Anderson nodded. 'And the first secretary.'

'You talk to them?'

'Had a word with Linqvist. Asked him if they were as well fed in the Dublin legation as in London. He denied it, said he was only there to see what he could pick up too.'

'Did he stick around for long?'

'A couple of hours.'

'That's all?' Duggan couldn't keep the surprise out of his voice. If the Germans' information was correct, surely Linqvist would have been trying to find out what had happened to a missing secret bombsight. 'He was only there for a few hours altogether?'

'Far as I know.' Anderson gave him a sharp look again. 'He didn't seem half as concerned about it as you. First secretary thanked us for our help with the crew and getting the plane away.'

'Who took it away?'

'An RAF team from Castle Archdale,' Anderson said, referring to the flying-boat base just across the border on

Lough Erne, which sent Catalina patrols out into the Atlantic by the Donegal corridor.

'Any Americans among them?'

'You're very interested in Americans all of a sudden,' Anderson noted.

'Just trying to figure out what was going on there.'

'Obvious,' Anderson said. 'They were delivering one of these planes to the Brits. Part of the lend-lease thing. And took the opportunity to supply their London legation with goodies at the same time.'

'You're probably right,' Duggan conceded. 'You know what rumours and gossip are like these days.'

'Of course the Jerries'd like to have a look inside it if they could.'

Duggan nodded. 'Thanks for your help,' he said, and headed for the door.

'Keep me in the loop,' Anderson called after him.

'Sure thing,' Duggan lied.

Seven

Duggan picked up the phone and asked the switchboard to put him through to Dublin Castle. While he waited, he glanced at the front-page headlines in the *Irish Times*. The US was promising aid to Russia; the Germans and Russians were making contradictory claims of success on the battlefields; the Trade Union Bill banning strikes had been denounced as 'dictatorship' in the Dáil; a stockbroker was being questioned about missing money in Cork Bankruptcy Court. A small headline down the page caught his eye as the switchboard in Dublin Castle answered.

He asked for Garda Peter Gifford in the Special Detective Unit and read the report as he waited. Mr Frank Aiken, it said, was on his way home from America and expected to arrive at the weekend or early the following week, via Lisbon.

'My prayers are answered,' Gifford said in his ear. 'They've released you from the stockade. The general's batman changed his story.'

'Something like that,' Duggan laughed. 'Can we meet?'

'The batman's gone back to his first story?'

'Much worse than that.'

'I can't wait. The Dolphin in half an hour?'

Duggan replaced the receiver and read the two-sentence story about Aiken's return again. What if he stops off in Lisbon for a few days, he wondered, and meets the women or priest I talked to? They'd be sure to mention the man from Dublin who'd been asking about his previous visit. Which would put the cat among the pigeons. It wouldn't take Aiken long to find out who Sean McCarthy really was.

He shrugged as he left the office. There was no point worrying about it. He didn't doubt that Commandant McClure would stand by him if necessary. But he had no idea where the original idea of checking on Aiken had come from. From External Affairs, if he had to guess. Not from anyone in the defence forces. But he had no illusions about what would happen if Aiken made a stink about it. That's what soldiers were for. To make themselves a target in order to find the enemy.

The day was clammy and overcast. The tide was out and the Liffey had been reduced to little more than a dribble by weeks of drought. The stink from the grey ooze enveloped the quays as he cycled along, trying not to breathe through his nose. He crossed over Father Mathew Bridge in the hope that the smell might be less on the south side, but the windless air was just as bad on Merchant's Quay as he went by Adam and Eve's church. The bells from one of the churches in the area pealed out eleven times as he turned into Parliament Street and swung left into Essex Street.

There was a line of cars parked outside the Dolphin Hotel and a queue of horse-drawn cabs at the back of the Clarence Hotel opposite. Duggan found a lamp post, chained his bicycle to it and walked back to the hotel. The entrance hall was busy with men and women dressed up for a day at the Curragh races, the men with soft hats and binoculars hanging from their shoulders, the women with furs draped around theirs.

'It'll be a bit of a squeeze,' one man was saying to another as Duggan tried to make his way behind them, 'but we'll fit you in.'

'I can get the special from Kingsbridge at a quarter to one,' the other protested.

'No you won't,' the first man said. 'You're not going on the train. You'll come in the car with us.'

Duggan checked the bars off to the left, but most were busy with people drinking and talking with a slightly manic edge. He found Gifford at the end of the curved counter of the lunch bar. It was silent and empty, apart from a couple of men intently examining the racing pages of newspapers. Gifford had two glasses of red lemonade in front of him on the marble counter. He pushed one in front of Duggan as he sat on the stool next to him.

'Not the smartest place to meet on the day that's in it,' Gifford said.

'You pick up any tips on the way in?'

'There was a fellow whispering "Easy Chair" to another in the jacks.'

'Worth a shilling each way?'

'For all I know he was talking about furniture, not the Derby.'

'Back to square one then.'

'Or it could be the tide that leads on to fortune.' Gifford dropped his voice although there was no one near them. 'You were away?'

Duggan gave him a slight nod of confirmation and took a sip of the lemonade.

'Moscow?'

'What?' Duggan laughed in surprise.

'Trouble follows wherever you go,' Gifford said. 'So I reckoned Herr Hitler heard you were in Moscow talking to Comrade Stalin and decided, "Enough of this pact, I can't trust that Bolshie bastard any more. Look at the company he's keeping now."'

Duggan said under his breath, 'Lisbon.'

'Really?' Gifford gave a low whistle. 'And was your mission a success?'

Duggan twisted one hand from side to side in a yes-and-no gesture. 'Time will tell.'

'You can tell me. So what is it? The secret of Fatima? That's obviously what you were after.'

Duggan took out a cigarette and lit it, taking his time inhaling. 'The Irish will inherit the earth.'

'Tell us something we didn't know.'

'But only when everyone else is finished with it,' Duggan exhaled.

Gifford nodded his head in mock seriousness. 'We truly are a most unfortunate country.'

'What's new with you?' Duggan asked, knowing that Gifford wouldn't press him to say anything about his mission in Lisbon and trusting him to keep the fact of it to himself. Gifford already knew enough secrets about him to land him in serious trouble several times over.

'Nothing much,' Gifford said. 'I proposed to Sinead.'

'That's nothing?' Duggan said in surprise. Gifford and Sinead had been going out for a year and surreptitiously living together for half that time at weekends, when she pretended to go down the country to her family. 'Congratulations.'

'She turned me down.'

'What? I don't believe you.'

'"Don't be daft," she said in that lovely culchie accent. "Don't you know there's a war on?"'

'You're pulling my leg,' Duggan said, although he could hear Sinead saying exactly that.

'Seems she took to heart some of your incoherent ramblings in which you mentioned something about the

Germans executing all secret policemen when they take over here. Said she didn't want to be a widow.'

'It's all off?'

'Not so fast, you,' Gifford smiled at him. 'Nothing has changed. I've just saved myself a lot of trouble over a wedding. And I can go on getting some sleep during the week when she goes back to her digs.'

'You knew she'd say no,' Duggan realised, with a touch of admiration.

Gifford gave him a mock bow with a hand on his chest. 'You have to be up early in the morning to keep a step ahead of these women. You meet any *señoritas* or whatever they call them in Portugal?'

'No.'

'Still in touch with what-you-may-call-her?'

'Grace. Yes.'

'It's not going to work,' Gifford said in a sad tone. 'Absence is one thing. Distance is another kettle of fish, as they say.'

'We'll see.'

'So it's not woman trouble this time,' Gifford said, switching to cheerful. 'You had me worried for a minute that it was some Portuguese *señorita* on her way over here with a tommy gun in one hand and a message from the Blessed Virgin in the other.'

'No, it's more mundane,' Duggan said, stabbing the butt of his cigarette at the ashtray. 'The black market.'

'The black market?' Gifford switched to his version of a country accent. 'And what would you be wanting with the likes of that when you're guaranteed three square meals a day and have all the petrol you'd be needing for swanning around the country?'

'Your lads haven't come across an upsurge of American stuff for sale by any chance?'

Joe Joyce

'Our lads have no more interest in the black market than your average housewife,' Gifford said, with deliberate ambiguity, of his Special Branch colleagues. 'But the detective branch is another matter entirely. Some of them have too close an interest in it. If you follow my drift.'

Duggan nodded. He had come across hints before that some detectives were involved in the city's thriving black market. 'Could you keep an eye out for an increase in American cigarettes, booze, food?'

'And why would we be interested in another neutral's spare produce?'

Duggan told him about the crash of the Flying Fortress and its cargo. 'I'd like to find out who's selling this stuff. Have a word with them.'

'You want to buy some?'

Duggan checked over his shoulder. There was only one man left in the bar, his pencil poised over the paper in indecision, and no sign of a barman. He told Gifford about the possible missing bombsight but not of how G2 had heard of it. 'Somebody must have it, even if they don't know what it is. There's a chance it's been offered to the black-marketeers.'

'If it's not in a bog hole in Mayo.'

'That's possible.'

'I doubt if any of that stuff has reached the city's black market,' Gifford offered. 'The culchies have probably drunk and smoked it all themselves.'

'That's possible, too.' Duggan drained his lemonade. 'Remember our black-market friend Benny Reilly? Is he still about?'

'Saw him a week or two ago. On a horse and cart in Dawson Street. Gave me a dirty look as if it was my fault he was reduced to that.'

'Is he still at it?'

'Is the Pope still saying his prayers?'

'He hasn't been pulled in again?' Duggan had used Reilly for information before, effectively promising him immunity from arrest if he provided it. Which he had.

'Not that I know of.'

'I thought they were cracking down on the black market.'

'They blow hot and cold about it,' Gifford shrugged. 'All those cars outside aren't doctors on calls, are they? The powers that be have to make noises about the evils of the black market to reassure those that can't afford to use it. But they're afraid of a revolution if they try and stop those who can afford it from getting their tea and petrol.'

'Has Reilly still got that place in North Lotts?'

'Want to go see?'

Some of the cars were moving off, packed, as Gifford and Duggan left the hotel and walked along Essex Street and Temple Bar and under Merchant's Arch. Duggan wheeled his bicycle up and down the steps and over the hump of the Ha'penny Bridge while Gifford held his nose. The tide was beginning to creep up the river, smoothing over the mud, and everybody on the streets seemed to move lethargically under the dirty white sky.

They turned into a laneway before they reached O'Connell Bridge and then into North Lotts, a stretch of lock-up workshops and stores. 'I think we're in luck,' Gifford said. Halfway down, there was a horse and cart outside an open door.

Benny Reilly, a wiry middle-aged man, was carrying out a small armchair and putting it alongside other bits of furniture on the dray as they approached. He saw them as he turned back to the shed, and stopped, his shoulders drooping in an unconscious gesture of dismay.

'Mr Reilly,' Gifford said, with an air of bonhomie. 'Good to see you engaged in honest toil.'

'Lads,' Reilly said without enthusiasm, his eyes on Duggan.

'Could we pick your brains about something?' Duggan asked.

Reilly glanced up and down the lane. There was nobody about: sounds of hammering and sawing came from a nearby workshop. He indicated with his head and they followed him inside. In the centre of the stone floor was a matching arm-chair, some kitchen chairs on top of a scrubbed deal table, a coal scuttle, and a fireside set and brass fender.

'Moving house?' Gifford enquired.

'Not myself.' Reilly took a half-smoked cigarette from behind his ear and lit it. 'Haulage job.'

'I appreciate your help in the past,' Duggan said. 'And no pressure this time. Just wondering if there's been an increase of American things on the market recently.'

'What things?'

'Whiskey, cigars, exotic food.'

Reilly inhaled deeply and screwed up his face as if the smoke was painful. 'No,' he shook his head several times. 'No.'

'Is there usually American drink and so on around?'

'There wouldn't be much of that these days.'

'None around at the moment?'

'Not that I've heard.'

'Any American office equipment? Typewriters? Ribbons?'

Reilly shook his head again.

'Optical equipment?'

'Optical equipment?' Reilly repeated in a surprised tone. 'Like what?'

'Things with lenses in them,' Duggan said vaguely, not knowing what a bombsight looked like. 'Like microscopes or something.'

'Microscopes?' Reilly gave him a look that questioned his sanity.

'That sort of thing.'

'Who'd buy that?' Reilly asked himself, wondering whether there was a market he'd overlooked. 'Where would American stuff come from?'

'Same place as the films,' Gifford interjected.

'Just following up on some rumours I heard,' Duggan said.

'Ask his friends in the Castle,' Reilly said, inclining his head towards Gifford while still looking at Duggan.

'Now, now,' Gifford said. 'Don't be cheeky.'

'They're the fellows who could tell you all about the black market. I don't know why you're asking me.'

'Because you're a man who keeps his ear to the ground.' Duggan gave him a wan smile. 'Thanks anyway.'

As they left, Duggan said: 'Sounds like Benny might even have gone legit.'

'Driven out by the competition,' Gifford said, with a touch of bitterness. 'If he has.'

'From the detective branch? Is nobody doing anything about that?'

'They're going to have to clean it up. It's getting out of hand.'

Gifford stopped when they got back to Bachelors Walk and put his hand out. 'Gimme a shilling,' he said. 'And we'll go each way on Easy Chair. That had to be a sign back there.'

'What?' Duggan laughed. 'Benny putting easy chairs on his cart?'

'Too many coincidences,' Gifford said. 'Got to be an omen. Third time lucky.'

Duggan leaned against the crossbar of his bicycle as he rooted in his pockets and found a shilling.

'Make it a half-crown,' Gifford said.

'It wasn't that big a sign.'

'A sign's a sign. Can't be ignored.'

Duggan took out a handful of change and handed him another shilling and a sixpenny piece.

'See you back in the Dolphin later for a juicy steak with the winnings,' Gifford said, giving him a wink and a one-fingered salute, and heading towards O'Connell Street.

Duggan cycled back along the quays between the unused tramlines, taking his time but still arriving at the Red House in a sweat from the humid air. Sullivan was picking at his typewriter in their office. 'How's Herr Dr Goertz today?' Duggan asked, as he draped his jacket over the back of his own chair. Sullivan had been to see Goertz around the corner in Arbour Hill Prison earlier.

'Chatty as usual,' Sullivan said. 'But I don't know if it solves our problem.' He held up a sheaf of photocopies from beside his typewriter. 'The full transcript of the Germans' message to him. It looks like there's a confirmation code in there.'

'Fuck,' Duggan said with feeling, as he took the pages and scanned the clean copy of the decoded message. He noted in passing that the missing bombsight was called a 'Norden', but his attention quickly leapt to the last line. '*Alles ist gut in Mannheim.*'

'Bollocks,' Duggan said, slapping the papers back down on the table. The trip to Lisbon had been a waste of time, the whole operation a failure. 'All's well in Mannheim' was clearly an identity phrase to which they did not have the required response. And without it, the Germans would know that Duggan was not in touch with Goertz at all, that the radio they had given him was compromised, and that the Sean McCarthy they'd met was probably an enemy agent.

'All's not lost, the boss says.'

'Why not?' Duggan threw his hands in the air. 'They'll know it's not from Goertz as soon as we send them the return message.'

'He thinks they might be bluffing.'

'Why would they be bluffing?'

'He didn't explain his thinking to me,' Sullivan said, shrugging. 'Just told me to ask Goertz a couple of questions, like 'Do you miss Mannheim?' and note his demeanour as well as the answers.'

'And?' Duggan prompted.

'And,' Sullivan pointed at what he had just typed and read from it, 'he replied, "I've never been in Mannheim." Subject seemed surprised by the question. I said, "I thought you had friends or relations there." Subject replied, "No. Where did you get that idea?"'

Duggan sat back against the side of the table and folded his arms. 'How did he seemed surprised? Surprised that you knew about Mannheim? Or surprised because he doesn't know Mannheim or anyone there?'

'Surprised at why I mentioned Mannheim,' Sullivan said. 'My first reaction was that he doesn't know about any password system using Mannheim.'

Duggan gave that a moment's thought. 'Maybe the commandant's right,' he said. 'Is he upstairs?'

'Far as I know.'

Duggan took the stairs two at a time. 'The very man,' McClure said, looking up from something he was writing. 'Take a look at this.'

Duggan took the proffered sheet and read carefully through McClure's neat German script. It said the message had been received and understood. Their Irish friends would investigate and report back, but the communication channels could be slow. It ended with '*Alles ist gut hier.*'

'You think their code is a bluff?'

'Better than a fifty-fifty chance,' McClure said, picking up his cigarette from the ashtray. 'Look at it this way. By his own admission, Goertz hasn't been able to communicate directly with them since he lost his radio when he arrived here. They probably had a time-limited recognition confirmation, but it was never used, and that time is long past. And if they really had a confirmation sequence, wouldn't they have used it first to establish contact, without mentioning anything about the bombsight? And Sullivan says Goertz seemed genuinely surprised at why anyone would mention Mannheim to him.'

'He just told me.'

'But you're not convinced?'

'There's a lot of presumptions there.'

'What do you suggest we do?'

Duggan shrugged, on the spot. 'Send word to them that the operation was aborted by Sean McCarthy's arrest in Pembroke. And that the British seized the radio equipment. And try to set up another meeting in Lisbon.'

McClure gave him one of his long stares and slowly broke into a crooked smile. 'That might be a good fallback position. Let's play it my way for the moment. And if it appears that they don't believe they're communicating with Goertz, we can switch to your story. Let them think it was the British who were trying to fool them.'

'Could be a dangerous game.'

'Aren't they all these days?' McClure said, taking back his written message. 'We'll get this coded and you can take it out to Greystones this evening and have it transmitted. Getting anywhere with the missing bombsight?'

'Nowhere yet. Other than wondering if it really exists. That plane seemed to be full of food and drink.'

McClure pulled another file out of the teetering pile on the left of his desk. 'Have a word with Commandant

Flood in the Air Corps. He might know something about this bombsight. The RAF invited him up to Aldergrove recently. Showed him some of their secret equipment, some radio-detection thing that can see planes long before they come into view. His report,' McClure handed over the file, 'doesn't say anything about bombsights, but he might have heard some casual chat in the mess about the Flying Fortress.'

Duggan stopped at the door as he was about to leave. 'I see Mr Aiken is on his way home. I hope he doesn't do the rounds in Lisbon again.'

McClure took a moment to interpret what he had heard. 'Don't worry,' he said. 'He can't wait to get home, apparently.'

Duggan went down the stairs, half reassured, but knowing that it would only take a moment's conversation between Aiken and one of the people he had met to land him back in the infantry. At best.

Shops were winding up their canopies and offices were emptying as Duggan made his way across South King Street, on to Stephen's Green and on up Harcourt Street to the station. He tied up his bicycle, bought an *Evening Herald* from a newsboy, went up the steps into the station and queued to buy a return ticket to Greystones.

He made it to the platform just in time and found a seat across the aisle from four businessmen, who had already resumed their twice-daily poker game. The headlines had the Minister for Supplies warning that the worst was yet to come, that people had to prepare themselves for greater shortages and the danger of a breakdown of order. The government might not be able to maintain control, he had said.

There were the usual conflicting claims by the Germans and Russians of breakthroughs and successful counter-attacks, and the Press Association's unnamed military correspondent suggested that it might take the Germans longer than the predicted month to defeat the Soviet Union. It could take between six weeks and two months.

Only a respite, Duggan thought as the train stopped at Milltown and then built up steam to cross the Nine Arches Viaduct and sped through open fields to Dundrum. That's why the government was making such warnings. Trying to shake people out of their complacency. In spite of the bombing of the North Strand and some other incidents, the war seemed to be moving further away. And all the false alarms of the previous years had created a dangerous sense of security that neutrality was enough to protect them. If the German *blitzkrieg* worked again in the east, that would change very fast.

The pot of silver coins in the poker game opposite Duggan grew as two players raised each other and the tension somehow spread across the aisle. Everyone in the vicinity watched in silence as one man studied his cards again, then pushed two shilling pieces into the pot and said, 'See you. And raise you another shilling.'

The man opposite him flicked a two-shilling piece forward without bothering to look at his cards. 'Another bob,' he said.

The first man took a deep breath in through his nose and examined his cards again as if he might find something different. He sighed and pushed forward another two-shilling piece. 'Up again,' he said.

The train stopped at Dundrum station and one of the men opposite Duggan waited until the last moment to see the outcome before having to hurry off without knowing who had won. As the train shuddered and began to move again, the second man gave a confident smile and said, 'Why stop now?' as he flicked another two-shilling piece into the pot.

'Ah,' the first man said, 'I don't want to bankrupt you. See you.'

The second man turned up his cards. 'Ace-high straight,' he said.

'Four tens,' the first man said with an apologetic smile.

'Jaysus,' one of the other players breathed as the first man scooped his winnings towards himself with a cupped hand.

Nicely played, Duggan thought, going back to his paper. The winner had raised the stakes by appearing uncertain, confirming the other man's belief in the strength of his own hand. It was a salutary reminder of how you could lose while thinking you held all the right cards. Thinking of winning and losing, he remembered the bet on the Derby as the train slowed into Foxrock station and passed the siding for Leopardstown racecourse and the deserted stand beyond. The 'Stop Press' box on the back page of the *Herald* had the result of the 3.25 and the 3.55 Derby from the Curragh. Easy Chair wasn't in the first three.

So much for signs and omens, Duggan thought.

The businessmen were still playing their cards when the train reached Greystones and they packed up and got off without a word. Duggan followed them across the footbridge and out of the station, where the two who had played for the big pot headed together across the road into the Burnaby. The other two turned right towards the town.

'That's one hand Harry won't be telling Mabel about,' one said to the other.

'He can afford it,' the other said. 'You know he made a killing on the market last week?'

Duggan veered off to the right, crossed the railway line and knocked on the door of a terraced house. It was opened by a man in his thirties in an open shirt and trousers. Duggan identified himself and the man said he was Sergeant O'Neill.

'All set?'

'All set, sir.'

Duggan followed O'Neill up the bare stairs, their footsteps reverberating through the empty house, and into a bedroom at the back. The transmitter was on a trestle table, with a chair in front of it, and an aerial was strung across the room. Its dial and valves were already lit up.

'Anything from them?'

'Not a peep,' O'Neill said.

Duggan gave him the page of code and checked his watch. It was almost the time slot he'd been given for transmission. 'Whenever you're ready,' he said.

O'Neill unfolded the chair, sat down, put on the headphones and began tapping the call sign. Duggan stood back against the wall beside the small window and watched. O'Neill finished and waited, then repeated the call sign. After several tries, he shifted one of the earphones off his right ear and said, 'No response so far.'

'Is it a good evening for transmitting?'

O'Neill nodded while sending his call sign again. 'Pretty good. Not too much interference yet. It'll get worse as the night draws in.'

'Will they be able to tell where the signal's coming from?'

'The British?'

'The Germans.'

'Depends how badly they want to know. How much effort they put into triangulating it.'

'And they'll be able to tell it's from here? Greystones?'

'In theory, but in practice – I doubt it.' His fingers tapped away as if they had a mind of their own. 'The British keep complaining about radio signals from Ireland but they can't tell us exactly where they're coming from, and they're a lot closer to us. North of Dublin is all they can say.'

'But the Germans would be able to tell it's from Ireland?'

'If they really wanted to know.' He raised a finger, put the earphone back in place, and then raised a thumb. 'You want me to send?'

Duggan nodded and O'Neill straightened the page of code with his left hand and began transmitting the stream of letters with his right. The play, as McClure called it, was on.

Eight

Duggan felt the wind in his hair and heard an unbroken chorus of birdsong as he freewheeled down the hill after leaving the main road to Naas. Around him, the bushes, heavy with foliage, nearly enclosed the narrow road, revealing only glimpses of fields of wheat and corn as he sped by. He caught a sweet whiff of newly mown hay before he saw the shorn meadow, a rare enough sight these days. He slowed down, swung his leg over the saddle and coasted up to the sentry at the Air Corps' headquarters.

'Captain Duggan from headquarters to see Commandant Flood.'

'He said to send you around to the hangar, sir,' the sentry said, pointing around to the side. 'The one on the left.'

Duggan followed the roadway up a line of Nissen huts and past an anti-aircraft unit, its Bofors 50-millimetre cannon pointed at the sky to the east. Two Gloster Gladiator biplane fighters were parked in front of one of the hangers, facing the grass runway sloping up to the south-west towards Saggart. A twin-engined Avro Anson patrol aircraft was being refuelled by a tanker in front of the other hangar. Another anti-aircraft gun pointed up from an emplacement in the centre of the field, and he could see concrete machine-gun positions around the perimeter of the field.

Duggan parked his bicycle and went into the hangar on the left and followed the whine of a mechanical saw cutting through metal towards the back. A group of men in fatigues were gathered around a Hurricane fighter with one wing, no cowling and a blackened gap where the engine should have been. The RAF markings were clear along its muddied and scorched side. A man in full uniform was standing a little apart, watching the mechanics with his arms folded and a scowl.

Duggan approached, saluted formally and identified himself.

Commandant Flood glanced at him and then turned back to continue scowling at the mechanics grappling with the engine on the floor.

'You read my report?' he asked.

'Yes, sir.'

'There's nothing more to tell you. I told Commandant McClure you were wasting your time coming out here.'

'We were hoping, sir, that you might have heard something about the American Flying Fortress crash.'

'There was nothing to hear about it. They thanked me for our help in having it returned across the border. That was all.'

'Was there any mention of a missing bombsight?'

'I just told you, Captain,' Flood said, turning the full force of his glare on Duggan, 'there was no mention of anything to do with the plane. Besides,' he seemed to remember something, 'that aircraft was not fitted out as a military plane.'

'The bombsight was part of the cargo, sir.'

'Why would it be carrying a bombsight as cargo?'

'We understand it was a newly developed bombsight. Something called a Norden.'

Flood turned his attention back to the mechanics working on the Hurricane.

'And we were hoping you might be able to tell us something about it,' Duggan ventured, not sure whether he had been dismissed or not.

'Tell you what about it?' Commandant Flood turned back to him. 'It's a secret bombsight developed by the Americans. How would I know anything about it?'

'You've heard of it,' Duggan said, making it a statement rather than a question. He had probably heard something about it on his visit north, Duggan thought, but hadn't mentioned it in his report and wasn't going to admit it now. 'We'd like to know what it might look like, how big it might be, what it would weigh.'

'Why?'

'Because we believe there was one on board the Flying Fortress and it has gone missing. Somebody in this country probably has it.'

'Fat lot of good it'll do them.'

'We'd like to find it.'

'Why?' Flood repeated. 'What use would it be to us? We don't want to bomb anyone.' He waved his hand around the hangar, at all the bits and pieces of airframes and engines and other assorted equipment. 'We've our hands full trying to put together a fighter or two from crashed planes.'

'We have reason to believe the Germans are interested in getting their hands on it, sir.'

Comprehension dawned on Flood's face and he nodded, turned and walked away. Duggan wasn't sure whether the interview was over or not, but after a moment's hesitation, he followed Flood. The commandant marched over to the other side of the hangar, to an area of shelving and workbenches, as one engine started up outside, followed by a second. They built to a roar and then throttled back to idle. Flood walked along the bench until he found what he was looking for: a dented, grey, irregular-shaped box with two big dials on its side. 'Bombsight from a Heinkel,' he said, pulling it forward to the edge of the bench.

It was about eighteen inches high and a foot across. Duggan lifted it up and reckoned it was three or four stone-weight: not something that would be carried about easily, but transportable. 'The dials set the altitude and wind speed,' Flood said, and pointed to an eyepiece on the top, 'and the bombardier looks through there and the machine calculates when to release the bombs.'

'Would the American one be about the same size?'

The commandant shrugged. 'Can't be much bigger. They have to take it to a special storage vault at the airfield every time they land, so the bombardier has to be able to carry it without too much difficulty.' He paused. 'They say there's a thermite grenade built into it, so it's destroyed if the aircraft crashes. Turns it into a lump of molten metal.'

'Could that have happened in the Flying Fortress?' Duggan asked, looking at him in surprise.

'There was no bombsight in situ,' Flood said with a hint of impatience. 'There was no bombardier on board. And no lumps of molten metal found in the nose, for that matter.'

Duggan finished his examination of the German bomb-sight and thanked the commandant for his help, but Flood seemed more eager to talk now. 'What makes you think there was a Norden on board?' he asked.

'Sorry, sir. I'm not sure I'm at liberty to say. I can ask Commandant McClure to … '

Flood cut him short with a wave of his hand. 'No need. The Americans treat the Norden as the ace up their sleeve if they get involved. The card that'd win the war for them.'

'Really?'

'So they say,' the commandant said, nodding, without specifying who 'they' were. Duggan assumed 'they' were some RAF people with whom he'd had a drink or two. He had clearly had a chat with somebody who knew something about the Norden sight.

'They haven't given it to the British?'

'I don't think so. They could have been sending them one to have a look at,' Flood said, pausing as the engine noise from outside grew into a crescendo again and then faded as the plane went down the runway. 'In return for a look at the British radio-detection system. A trade of secret equipment.'

'That'd make sense,' Duggan agreed. But what made more sense to him now was why the Germans would want to see this war-winning piece of equipment that the Americans were taking such measures to keep out of their hands. Why they might seize on any chance to get one, even risking a dubious radio connection with a captured agent. And why a senior Abwehr officer would involve himself with what he thought was a low-level Irish republican.

'I was wondering why the RAF showed you their secret radio-detection system,' Duggan continued, seizing the opportunity of Flood's talkativeness to satisfy his own curiosity.

'I think they wanted to impress on us that they have things to counter the Germans' superior manpower,' the commandant said, indicating that he had pondered the same question. 'That they have a secret weapon or two as well.'

Duggan thanked him again and turned to go.

'I don't need to remind you, Captain, of the sensitivity of all that information,' the commandant said.

'No, sir, of course not.'

'We need to find it,' Duggan said, concluding his report on his visit to the Air Corps. 'Make sure it doesn't get into the Germans' hands. It'd upset the Americans if their secret bombsight got from here to Berlin.'

'That doesn't bear thinking about in the current climate,' Commandant McClure agreed. 'Of course, they haven't asked for our help. Haven't even told us that the thing was on this plane.'

'Still.'

'Exactly,' McClure said.

They both knew that would be seen by the Americans as no excuse and would probably be taken by them as confirmation that Ireland was not just a base for German intelligence, but was in cahoots with them. The consequences would be serious.

'Why do you think they haven't asked for our help?' McClure mused, indicating that he was in a thinking-aloud mood, ready to tease out the implications of what they knew. And what they didn't know.

'Because they don't trust us,' Duggan offered. 'After Mr Aiken's comments in Lisbon.'

'Because they're afraid that word would filter through to the Germans about the sight.'

'But it already has.'

'Which raises the big question,' McClure concluded. 'How did the Germans in Lisbon know about this cargo on a crashed plane in Ireland?'

They both fell silent, thinking about the options.

'One,' McClure raised a finger, 'there's a German agent at large about whom we know nothing. Two,' he put up a second finger, 'information somehow came from someone on the ground to the German legation and they passed it on through their transmitter. Or, three, the information came from abroad, probably from a German agent in the US itself.'

Duggan nodded his agreement.

'I don't think "one" is likely,' McClure went on. ' "Two" does not seem likely either: for one thing, the British haven't complained recently about any transmissions from the German legation, and we know how quick they are to do that. And if someone told the German legation about it, they'd probably know how to find it and wouldn't be asking for Goertz's help. The most likely is "three", that some of their agents in the US heard about it.'

'Do the Americans know that the Germans know about it?' Duggan asked. 'Maybe we should tell them. Build up some credit with them.'

McClure closed his eyes and a pained expression crossed his face as if he had a sudden headache. 'Then we'd be under pressure to find it fast,' he said, without opening his eyes. 'It'd be better if we found it first, then told them and handed it back.'

'That's what I was thinking,' Duggan said, and told him of the plan he had worked out on his cycle back along the Naas road to the Red House.

'Why do you want to bring Gifford with you?' McClure asked when he had finished.

'Because he can tap into the local guards and their information. And use his powers of arrest if need be.'

'He knows all about the bombsight already?'

'Not all.'

'And he will keep the information to himself?'

'He always has in the past,' Duggan said. Much more than McClure realised.

'OK,' McClure said.

Bill Sullivan had a map of the north side of Dublin city laid out on the table and was marking arrows in pencil on it when Duggan returned to their office. 'You involved in this?' he asked, scratching his head with the pencil and casting his hand over the map.

Manoeuvres involving the local defence forces were planned for the weekend, with the LDF acting as the Blue

Army, defending the city from the regular army, which would act as the Red Army, attacking from the north. It was no secret who the Red Army was meant to be, a reminder to the British, and the Germans, that Ireland was ready to fight any invader.

'Got to go down the country,' Duggan smiled.

'Fuck's sake,' Sullivan said, scratching his head with renewed vigour. 'Off on your holliers again.'

Duggan put a call through to Garda Peter Gifford at Dublin Castle. 'I've been slapping myself on the wrist all morning,' Gifford said, without any preliminaries. 'The clue was staring us in the face. In the name.'

'What clue?'

'Easy Chair,' Gifford said. 'If you were a horse and your owner called you "Easy Chair", what would you do?'

'You have a point,' Duggan said. He'd already forgotten about the previous day's Derby and their loss of half a crown each.

'Exactly,' Gifford went on. 'You'd lie back with your feet up and rest yourself. But there's no need to give out to me. I've already had words with myself for failing to follow the proper procedure on how to find the guilty man. Chapter One of the policeman's manual. Does his name fit the crime?'

'And Easy Chair didn't fit in the winner's enclosure.'

'You're a quick learner today,' Gifford said in Duggan's ear, as Sullivan gave him a quizzical glance.

'You busy for the next couple of days?' Duggan asked.

'Only doing penance for my failure to follow proper procedures.'

'We want your help on something. Down the country.'

'That sounds suitably penitential.'

'A request for you to assist us is on its way to your superiors.'

'Their sorrow to be without me for a few days will be a trauma to behold. Heart-rending.'

'They'll get over it.'

Duggan put down the phone, smiling to himself, and took up the suitcase he had brought back from Lisbon and placed it on his desk.

'You're bringing your boyfriend down the country with you,' Sullivan said with exaggerated horror. 'You know that's illegal.'

'Only if we go beyond looking into each other's eyes.'

'Jaysus.' Sullivan shuddered. 'You're getting as bad as him.'

'Speaking of boyfriends,' Duggan said, pausing with his thumbs on the suitcase catches, 'is Carmel's friend Breda still seeing that fellow from the American legation? Max Linqvist?'

'Seeing him?' Sullivan snorted. 'She's practically devouring him. It's disgusting the way she fawns over him. Wouldn't surprise me if she was doing something illegal with him too.'

'Tut tut,' Duggan laughed.

'You still sore at how she leapt on him instead of you?'

'Not at all.'

'As a matter of fact,' Sullivan said, pointing his pencil at Duggan as he remembered something, 'he was asking about you recently.'

'Linqvist?'

'Said he hadn't seen you around. Wondering if you'd been transferred.'

'When was this?'

'A couple of weeks after you went off on your cruise.' Sullivan paused as a thought struck him.

After the Flying Fortress crash, Duggan thought. 'Has he ever mentioned me before?'

'No.'

I don't like the sound of it, Duggan decided. Linqvist looking for me could only mean one thing. That he wants to call in a favour. Which probably means that he wants to know if we've got the Norden sight. To which there was an easy answer, if Linqvist left it at that. But he probably wouldn't.

'I didn't know you were pals,' Sullivan was saying.

'We're not,' Duggan shrugged. 'I've come across him once or twice. What exactly did he say?'

Sullivan closed his eyes and visualised the scene. 'We were waiting for the girls to come back from the ladies'. And he just asked if you'd been transferred. Said he hadn't seen you for a while. I thought he was just making conversation. That Breda had probably told him she was supposed to be on a blind date with you when she met him.'

McClure hasn't shown him the contents of the message to Goertz and told him about the missing bombsight, Duggan realised. Otherwise Sullivan would have tied Linqvist's query to the plane crash. McClure was like that: kept everything in separate compartments.

'You should come out with us all some night,' Sullivan said.

'And watch Breda fawning over him?' Duggan retorted. He had no wish to meet Linqvist, knowing what would follow. There was no such thing as simply doing someone a good turn in this world, he knew. And Linqvist had done him a good turn in helping Gerda go to America. For which he would expect payment sooner or later. And it looked like sooner. 'No thanks.'

Sullivan glanced up with a triumphant smile. 'So you're still sore over missing your chance there.'

An orderly came in and handed Duggan a letter.

'Maybe your American friend is a man after all,' Sullivan said, noting the American stamps on the envelope. 'What did you say his name was? Does your smart-arse friend in the Castle know about him?'

'Enough of that.' Duggan snapped open the suitcase he'd got in Lisbon and threw back the lid. 'Do you want another packet of fags before I take this away?'

'Yeah. Why not?'

'Player's or Gold Flake?'

'What's the difference?'

'Gold Flake's not as strong.'

'One of them then.'

Duggan slid open one of the cartons of Gold Flake and tossed a packet to him. 'What are you going to do with the rest?' Sullivan asked as he caught it.

'Put them on the black market.'

'Yeah, but really?'

'Really,' Duggan said, closing the suitcase, sitting down behind it and opening Gerda's letter.

'You are in your shite,' Sullivan muttered, going back to his map.

Duggan read the letter slowly, smiling as she confirmed in a roundabout way that she'd received his postcard from Lisbon. She was going to Long Island with one of her work colleagues for a few days, she wrote, but didn't have the time off, or the money, to travel to exotic places like some people she knew.

Nine

'What's that song about the west being asleep or something?' Peter Gifford asked as they crossed the hump bridge over the River Shannon at Termonbarry and passed through the village.

'You mean "The West's Awake".' Duggan launched into the last verse for him:

> And if, when all a vigil keep,
> The West's asleep! the West's asleep!
> Alas! and well may Erin weep
> That Connacht lies in slumber deep.
> But, hark! a voice like thunder spake,
> The West's awake! the West's awake!
> Sing, Oh! hurrah! let England quake,
> We'll watch till death for Erin's sake.

'Jaysus,' Gifford said when Duggan had finished with a flourish. 'I'm quaking, never mind England.'

The countryside was bright and green under a high blue sky dotted with puffs of cotton-wool clouds that barely interrupted the sunshine as they floated by with serene disregard. The road twisted and turned between opaque bushes, its high camber tilting the car to the left. There was no motor traffic to slow their progress as they sped past carts hauled by plodding horses and over-burdened donkeys. Everyone gave them an automatic salute, curiosity in their gazes after the two young men flying by in the Ford Prefect.

Gifford looked at the road map spread across his knees. 'How long more?'

'What are you?' Duggan glanced at him. 'Ten years old?'

'I'd no idea there was so much of it. Culchie land. It goes on and on forever.'

'Good to broaden your horizons. Haven't you been out of Dublin before?'

'Course I have!' Gifford said in an outraged tone. 'I've been to Howth. And Bray.'

'Seriously? Have you never been down the country before?'

'Not this far out,' Gifford said, like a swimmer who'd gone farther than ever before from the shore. 'Or down. Or whatever you call it.'

'Don't worry. They won't eat you.'

'But what do they do out here? Down here?'

'Same as they do in the city. Work and drink and chase women. Haven't you ever asked Sinead what she does when she goes home?'

'What?' Gifford straightened himself in the seat as if he was shocked. 'You think she chases women?'

'You never know.'

'She says she helps her mother milk the cow, collect eggs, catch up on all the local back-biting and avoid being mauled by old bachelor farmers with horny hands in the local dance hall. You think she's trying to deceive me?'

Duggan shook his head. 'Sounds accurate enough to me.'

'No wonder you all run away to the city,' Gifford sighed.

'Ah, it's not that bad,' Duggan said as they swept down a hill and the countryside opened out before them like a quilt of irregular patches in shades of green, broken by the dull gold of fields of corn. 'Look at that.'

'What?'

'The view.'

'Where are all the people?'

'They're there. Keeping an eye on your every move.'

'You mean we can't see them but they're watching us?'

'Probably lining us up in their sights now,' Duggan said.

'You're a bad bastard, trying to frighten an innocent city lad.'

'Getting my own back for that half-crown you lost me on the Derby.'

'Are all culchies such sore losers?'

'We never forget a bad turn.'

As they came into Swinford, they passed a trotting pony and trap carrying a man and woman dressed up for a visit to town. The main street seemed to be in hiding from the sun: canopies darkened the shop windows and striped blinds protected hall doors. A large dog was curled up on the sunny side of the road, unconcerned by a donkey and cart that made its way around him and forced Duggan to come to a halt until it had finished its manoeuvre.

'Not too far now,' Duggan said when they had left the town a few miles behind. 'Time to switch to the other map.'

'Yes, sir.' Gifford folded up the road map, tossed it on to the back seat and reached behind for the Ordnance Survey map. He unfolded it, looked at it for a moment, then turned it around the other way. 'Can't make head or tail of this.'

'Can you find that road on the left we just passed?'

'I can't even see the road we're on.'

Duggan slowed to a stop near a gate with a small struc-ture behind it. A whiff of cow dung came through the open windows as he propped the map against the steering wheel and studied it for a moment. 'Second next turn on the left,

I think.' He traced the route from where he thought they were with a finger and handed the map back to Gifford. As he drove off again, they waved to a young boy hanging over the gate, his feet on a slanted board. He watched them with a solemn expression and didn't wave back.

Duggan drove slowly, watching for a gap in the hedges which would indicate a turn-off. He wasn't sure if the road they wanted would warrant a signpost in normal times, but there were no signposts now anyway: they had all been taken down as an invasion precaution. It seemed to take an age to find it.

'This is a road?' Gifford asked, with an air of incredulity, as they turned into it. It was just the width of the car, two tracks of beaten-down earth with grass running between them.

'Just like Grafton Street or one of those,' Duggan laughed, winding up his window quickly as an overhanging bush brushed against the side of the bonnet.

Gifford copied his action on his side. 'What if we run into another car down here?'

'There won't be any cars down here unless they're up to no good.'

'Just like us.'

'Exactly.'

They continued on for more than a mile and then turned into a track on the right and the bushes fell away and the land flattened out into a bog. The track was dry turf mould, compacted and rutted by cart wheels. Small clamps of greying turf, left over from the previous year, stood here and there by its side. Gifford viewed it all with amazement. 'This is it?' he asked.

'This is it.'

They kept going, slowly, the car jolting over holes covered roughly with branches across them, until the track was suddenly cut by a wide ditch a foot deep. Duggan stopped and turned off the engine and they got out in the silence. The ditch ran in both directions from the road, widening and deepening as it stretched away to the left, cutting through the heather, bog holes and small footings of turf, and into a distant wood.

'Jesus,' Gifford breathed.

Duggan imagined the pilot picking this piece of flat purple-and-brown earth for a crash landing. He must have kept the wheels up – or maybe hadn't been able to lower them – and landed on the plane's belly. And it had slid along here. 'They were lucky,' he said as he lit a cigarette, tasting the extra bite the fresh air gave the smoke. The bog had absorbed some of the impact, yielding more easily to the plane's weight and energy than hard ground would have.

Gifford turned in a slow circle, feeling for the first time the sensation of standing on top of the world created by the flatness of the bog and the enormous dome of the open sky above them. Small birds twittered and hopped about and little tufts of bog cotton stood up here and there on their long stems, like white lights wavering above the heather. A couple of swallows swooped and dived high above, in one-sided dogfights with flies. A few hundred yards away, a man and a woman were bent over small heaps of turf they were building. When Gifford turned back to him, Duggan was already walking towards the couple.

Gifford caught up with him as he hopped across an old bog cutting and they continued together across the springy ground.

'Don't fall into a bog hole,' Duggan said as they went by the edge of a black pool, flicking his half-finished cigarette into the water. Insects skated along its still surface. 'They're bottomless.'

'And full of bodies.'

'Probably.'

When they came up to the couple, Duggan said, 'God bless the work,' and the man and woman straightened up and wiped their foreheads with the backs of their hands. They looked to be in their thirties, wearing old clothes, the woman a purple dress with a faded floral design, the man a collarless shirt and braces holding up grubby tweed trousers.

'Great day for it.' Duggan nodded at the piles of turf they were building out of the smaller footings.

''Tis,' the man said. 'Great year for the turf.'

'We were just having a look at where the plane came down,' Duggan offered.

'Destroyed a good few turf banks,' the man nodded. 'Not to mention what had already been cut.'

'I can see that,' Duggan agreed. 'Did you happen to see it yourselves?'

'No, no,' the man said. The woman stretched her shoulders and neck, the backs of her hands on her hips. 'We don't live around here. We're from the next parish.'

'Who'd be the nearest house to here?'

'I wouldn't know that now. You'd have to ask someone from the area.'

Duggan nodded as if the man had actually told him something. 'Does the road go around to the wood over there?' He indicated with his head where the Flying Fortress had ended up.

'It does,' the man said, giving the lie to his professed lack of local knowledge. 'Just follow it round for a mile or so.'

'Thanks,' Duggan said. 'Tough on the people who've lost their turf.'

'They'll feel it in the winter. But they say the Americans are going to pay compensation.'

'Your bank escaped anyway.'

'It did,' the man said, giving him a rueful look. 'But it might've been easier on the back if it hadn't. And we'd got the compensation.'

'That's true,' Duggan grinned back. 'But there mightn't be any turf or coal to be bought this winter.'

'There's always things to be bought by them that has the money.'

They left the couple and headed back to the car.

'So, Sherlock,' Gifford said, 'what'd you learn from that?'

'Fuck all,' Duggan admitted.

'I'm disappointed. I thought all that meaningless culchie chatter meant something.'

'Sometimes it does, sometimes it doesn't.'

'That's deep,' Gifford snorted. 'As bottomless as your bog holes.'

It took a seven-point turn to get the car facing back towards the road and they drove along it for well over a mile until they came to the wood that bordered the bog. Duggan pulled in to a gateway where the ground was badly cut up with what looked like tractor tracks. They followed the tracks on foot through the trees, noting where some smaller trees had been chopped down to make way for them, until they came to where the Flying Fortress had ended up.

The air was still, the leaves on the undamaged trees unmoving, as if the wood and everything in it was holding its breath. To one side, they could see where the plane had burst into the trees from the bog like an angry fist. Some trees were toppled, branches were torn off others, and the ground was churned up, roots exposed and left dangling in mid-air. Bits of Plexiglass glinted in the raw earth and smears of silver paint were cut into trunks. Small fragments of metal were scattered about with bits of wood on what had been a carpet of moss.

They walked around separately in silence and came together at a large oak tree, its lower branches sheared off and a deep gash cut in its trunk about ten feet up. Duggan looked at Gifford and shook his head. Gifford nodded, silent for once.

Back in the car, Duggan reversed on to the road, turned back the way they had come and drove up to a two-storey farmhouse they had passed earlier. A sheepdog announced them, barking furiously while carefully keeping its distance as they got out and went to the hall door. It was opened by a middle-aged woman in a wrap-around housecoat.

'Sorry to bother you, ma'am,' Duggan said. 'We were wondering if you could tell us anything about the plane that crashed in the wood?'

She looked from one to the other, her round face closing, and back to Duggan again. 'I wouldn't know anything about that,' she said.

'Did you hear the crash?'

'Are you from the papers?' She glanced from Duggan to Gifford again.

'No, ma'am,' Duggan said. 'We're from the Forestry Department.'

'What's the Forestry got to do with it? That's a private wood.'

'Is it your wood?'

She shook her head in an unconvincing denial.

'We just happened to be in the area and thought we'd take a look at it. To see what kind of damage an air crash can do to the trees.'

'I didn't want to see it,' she said with a little shiver. 'I haven't gone in there. You'd have to talk to himself about it.'

'Is he around?'

'No, he's gone for the day. Helping his brother with the hay.'

'He must've been one of the first to get there.'

'He's not the better of it yet. The poor man, the one that was dead, was a terrible sight. And the others didn't look much better.'

'How did they manage to get them out of there?'

'It took a lot of work,' she said. 'Gerry was the first there, but he had to wait for help before they could get the poor lads out. A terrible sight.'

'They did a great job.'

'One of the men had a little diesel left for his tractor and they brought them to hospital on the trailer.'

'Probably saved the lives of the other two,' Duggan nodded.

'You seem to know a lot about it,' the woman said, narrowing her eyes.

'Just what I've heard around,' Duggan shrugged. 'It was a good thing it didn't explode anyway.'

'It might as well have. There were bits of it all over the place. The bog as well.'

'But they've taken it all away now. Nothing left but the damaged trees.'

'They were at it for days. Coming and going with big trucks.'

'Who were they?'

'I wouldn't know. I wasn't talking to any of them.'

Gifford swore when they got back into the car. 'If I hear another of these rambling culchie conversations I might pull out my gun and put a bullet in someone's brain.'

'Not mine, I hope,' Duggan said as he started the engine.

'Probably my own.'

'Patience,' Duggan suggested. 'You need to be more patient.'

'I need to talk to people who can answer a question without asking one. Where to now?'

'We'll have a word with the LDF lieutenant who was in charge of the guard.'

They stopped outside the man's school, a small two-roomed building near a crossroads. There was one house nearby and no other buildings. Gifford got out and looked around. 'Where do the children come from?' They could hear some of them reciting a multiplication table through the open window of one of the rooms. In the silence after the children finished, they could hear the hoarse double call of a corncrake from a nearby field.

'Around here.'

They waited, leaning against the hot bonnet of the car, until they heard a rousing chorus of 'Clare's Dragoons' and a small group of boys came bursting out of the door with yells and a tattered football. The boys were followed by girls, who disappeared down the roads in more sedate groups. A little later a middle-aged woman and a tall, thin young man emerged. He locked the door and handed the woman the key, and they came down the path.

'Lieutenant Ganly?' Duggan asked as they approached.

The man stopped and said, 'See you tomorrow' to the woman as she kept going, with a nod to Duggan and Gifford.

'I'm Captain Paul Duggan from army headquarters in Dublin.'

'Yes, sir.'

Ganly looked like he wasn't sure whether he should salute or not. He was in his mid-twenties and his thinness and long narrow face made him look taller than he actually was.

'Paul.' Duggan put out his hand.

'Tommy.' Ganly shook it.

'I wanted a word with you about the Flying Fortress.'

'There was another man here from headquarters at the time.'

'Captain Anderson.'

Ganly nodded and a slight smile broke his serious look. 'We had a good night in the local pub. He's a good singer. A great voice.'

Duggan nodded as if he knew that, although he hadn't. 'What did you find when you got there?'

Ganly took a deep breath and blew it out. 'It was the day after we were mobilised and got there. So the crew was gone but all the wreckage was still there. I've never seen anything like it. That plane was huge and the wreckage was ... ' He shook his head. 'I don't know how anyone came out of it alive. It was just mangled.'

Duggan held out his open cigarette case and lit cigarettes for both of them. Shouts from the field beside the school, where two long sticks stood upright as more-or-less-straight goalposts, reached an angry crescendo. Ganly turned to them and shouted, 'Hey!' The shouting subsided.

'There were strips of metal torn off the sides, rolled up like paper,' Ganly said, turning his attention back to Duggan. 'The side of the cockpit where the co-pilot had been was smashed almost flat against a big oak tree. He hadn't a chance. There was a wing that had cut through some saplings and then broken up against some trees. One of the engines was half buried in the ground. Enormous things.' He inhaled deeply. 'I don't know how the whole thing ever got off the ground at all.'

'What about the cargo?'

'There was still some stuff scattered around when we got there. Broken bottles of whiskey. And some boxes that had burst open and scattered tins of food. Some mashed-up cartons of cigarettes. You couldn't smoke them.'

'I've heard about all that stuff. Did you see any boxes of equipment?'

'There was a broken-up typewriter,' Ganly said, exhaling another lungful of smoke as he thought. 'Somebody mentioned typewriter ribbons too, but I didn't see them.'

'Any mechanical equipment? Optical equipment?'

Ganly shook his head. 'Not when we were there. To be honest, a lot of stuff had gone before we got there. Even when we did arrive, there were lots of treasure hunters on the bog, mostly young lads. But we'd been told only to guard the plane. We didn't have the numbers to cordon off the bog area.'

'Sure,' Duggan nodded. 'The plane itself was the most important thing.'

'This equipment you're looking for? Was this what the Yank was after as well?'

'What Yank?' Duggan asked, although he knew the answer.

'A fellow from the American legation in Dublin. The cultural attaché.'

'Did he tell you what he was looking for?'

'A bombsight.'

Duggan covered up his surprise that Linqvist would have admitted what he was looking for. But that made it more likely that word had circulated back to the German legation, explaining how the man he had met in Lisbon knew about it. 'He was telling everybody that?'

Ganly nodded. 'Said there'd be a reward for anyone who found it.'

'How much?'

Ganly gave a slight smile. 'He didn't put a figure on it. Dollars, he said. A reward in dollars.'

'Did he say why they wanted it back?'

'It was an expensive thing. But no use to anyone else. And they were afraid the finder might dump it because he wouldn't be able to use it for anything, or even sell it.'

Duggan dropped his cigarette on the gravel at the edge of the road and buried it with the toe of his shoe. 'Anyone flashing dollars around recently?'

'Not that I heard of.'

'Anybody emigrating to America all of a sudden?' Duggan asked, thinking of Gerda.

'Don't know of anyone yet,' Ganly said, following Duggan's example, dropping his cigarette butt on the ground and rubbing it out with his foot. 'He only offered it last week.'

'Last week?' Duggan asked in surprise. So that couldn't explain how the Germans in Lisbon knew about it after all.

'He was down fishing in Lough Conn and just dropped by on his way. Had a load of fishing gear in the car and an old man with him.'

'The American Minister? Mr Gray?'

'I don't know who he was. I was in town and dropped into Curley's for a pint, and they'd just been there. On their way back to Dublin after staying in one of the big houses near the lake for a few days' fishing. They said.'

'And that's when he offered the reward?'

'The locals were all talking about it after they'd left. One of them asked me what a bombsight looked like. As if I'd know.'

'Do you think someone has it?'

Ganly shrugged. 'If they have, they're not going to tell anyone till they get the dollars. And maybe not then.'

'So where does that leave us?' Gifford asked as they drove away, passing two of the young footballers dragging their feet through the dust at the side of the road. 'Snookered,' he said, answering his own question. 'Nobody's going to give you the yoke for a few packets of fags and a few bags of coffee when they can sell it for mighty dollars.'

Duggan gave a dejected nod of agreement. It had seemed like a workable plan. He'd thought that whatever people found and didn't want for themselves would have found its way to the local black-marketeers. Who might have been happy to trade something like the bombsight for things that were easier to sell. But Linqvist's reward had changed everything.

'I don't understand it,' Duggan said. 'This Norden bombsight is a big military secret. And here are the Americans telling everybody in Mayo about it.'

They drove in silence for a moment, each with an elbow resting on an open window, the wind from the car's momentum ruffling their rolled-up shirt sleeves. 'A bluff,' Gifford said at last. 'That's what it is. So nobody thinks it's really important. Just a big enough deal that they're willing to pay a few dollars to get it back. For convenience's sake.'

'Seems a strange way to carry on with your military secrets.' At least, Duggan thought, G2 could now ask the Americans about the missing sight without having to explain how they knew about it.

'Typical Americans,' Gifford said. 'What is it now since the crash? A month or more. They haven't been able to find it. So they offer to buy it. It's the way they think. That the dollar can buy anything.'

And it'll probably work, Duggan acknowledged silently. They'll get their bombsight back. And we can tell the Germans what happened without lying or compromising anything. Build up credit for their supposed link with the IRA. And keep that operation on track. See what they want next from their friends.

'What's so amusing?' Gifford demanded.

'What?'

'Why've you got a dirty little smile on your face?'

'I have?'

'I know.' Gifford raised a finger. 'You're thinking about claiming the reward and running off to America to be with Gerda. Or whatever she calls herself now.'

'Grace.' Duggan's smile broadened at the thought. Gifford was the only one who really knew about his relationship with Gerda. 'All we have to do is find the bombsight.'

'Why didn't you say so?' Gifford demanded with mock impatience. 'I was wondering what we were doing down here, having conversations as meandering as the roads. It'll be no problem at all with the mighty brainpower of the Garda Síochána behind us.'

'And beat the mighty dollar to it.'

'To the nearest barracks.' Gifford pointed down the road.

'Isn't there a section of your handbook about finding things under Americans' noses?'

Gifford slapped himself on the forehead. 'Chapter Twelve, Section Eight, Subsection B Fourteen. I'd almost forgotten.'

'You're getting old.' Duggan speeded up.

The afternoon was beginning to turn dull as a high covering of wispy white clouds crept over from the west, steadily blotting out the light-blue ink of the sky. They came to another crossroads and stopped while Duggan consulted the map.

'Have you thought about going to America?' Gifford asked when they got going again.

'Maybe when the war's over.'

'She mightn't wait that long.'

'I can't go before that,' Duggan said, shaking his head, remembering Gerda once saying to him that this war would never end.

'Maybe it won't last that long,' Gifford said, switching tack as if he was responding to Duggan's thoughts. 'Could end very quickly once the Jerries finish with the Rooskies.'

'How about you? Would you go to America?'

'Me?' Gifford sat back against the door in a physical rejection of the idea. 'God, no. People are expected to work there.'

'They say it's a great place for people who can live off their wits.'

'No, thanks. Americans are too earnest for my liking.'

'Maybe Hollywood or somewhere like that. That'd suit you.'

'You think I could be a cowboy?'

'You've already got the six-gun.'

'True enough,' Gifford said, reaching under his seat and pulling out his shoulder holster and revolver. He took out the gun, spun the cylinder and pointed it out the side window, resting on his left arm. 'Maybe we should shoot a few rabbits while we're here.'

'You wouldn't hit a barn door with that thing.'

'Just as well barn doors aren't the bad guys,' Gifford said, withdrawing the gun as they overtook a woman on a bicycle and putting it back in its holster under the seat.

They arrived in a small village, no more than a straggle of houses, a shop and a pub. A church stood at the end, with a cemetery on one side and the priest's house on the other. Opposite it was the Garda station, a two-storey building with the police shield over the porch. A sturdy bicycle lay against the weathered white pebble-dash of the wall.

They went in through the open door and found themselves in the empty day room. Posters were tacked to a noticeboard warning farmers about the penalties for failing to till more than an eighth of their land, and encouraging young men to join the construction corps and older men to join the local security force. A chair scraped on a wooden floor in an adjoining room and a middle-aged sergeant came in, buttoning his tunic around his generous stomach.

Gifford introduced himself, handing over his warrant card. The sergeant studied it and sat down behind a desk in a captain's chair. 'And you are?' He looked at Duggan.

'Paul Duggan.'

The sergeant gave him a hard look, then decided not to pursue his suspicions. 'To what do we owe this honour?' he asked Gifford in an unhurried voice. He had a ruddy round face and his fair hair was stretched over his balding head.

'A bombsight,' Gifford said, getting straight to the point.

A slow smile spread across the sergeant's face. 'Ye're here to join the treasure hunt.'

Gifford returned his smile. 'That's it, Sergeant.'

'The Castle's in need of a few dollars, is it?'

'Who doesn't need a few dollars these days, Sarge? But there are more important things at stake.'

'Is that so?'

'The honour of the force. We think the Garda Síochána should find this thing before the Americans. Can't have them wandering round our ranch, picking up whatever they want.'

'The honour of the force?' The sergeant settled back in his chair and put his hands in his trouser pockets, as if he was relaxing into an evening's entertainment.

'That's it.'

'Ye wouldn't be after the dollars yourselves, would ye?'

'Oh, no, no. Not at all. Our minds are on higher things.'

'I can imagine that all right. Young bucks like ye. And how do ye propose to find this thing?'

'With your help, Sarge.'

'And will I get a few of the dollars too?'

'You'll get something much more valuable. A share in the honour.'

'A share in the honour,' the sergeant repeated, wrinkling up his forehead in amusement. 'Fancy that.'

'The crowning moment of your career.'

The sergeant gave a delighted laugh. 'Gifford?' he mused. 'What sort of a name is that?'

'Just mine, Sarge. That's all I know.'

'And Duggan. Where are you from?'

'He came down in the last shower,' Gifford said. 'Don't mind him.'

The sergeant gave a nod of sympathy as if he understood Duggan's affliction. 'I can't say I've met any Branch boys like ye before. They're always rushing about in a hurry. Wanting everything they want an hour ago.'

'Imagine having to work with them every day,' Gifford sighed. 'It's a penance.'

'How do you put up with it?'

'I offer it up. For the honour of the force.'

The sergeant gave him a wry smile, a recognition of a kindred spirit. 'So how can I help ye?'

'Tell us where the bombsight is,' Gifford said in an innocent tone, as if he was asking for directions to the next village.

'I'm beginning to think it's in one of the bog holes over beyond. Fell in during the accident or thrown in by someone who didn't want it.'

'That'd be a pity.'

'Indeed, it would.' The sergeant took his hands out of his pockets and opened a drawer in front of him. He took out two sheets of paper and tossed them on to the desk.

Gifford picked them up and handed one to Duggan. Both were fold-out diagrams apparently torn from a manual. They showed the wiring of two pieces of electrical equipment. One said 'Fig 4-40 Bombsight Wiring Diagram'; the other said 'Figure 5-57 Wiring Diagram (G1048A)'. The first one had parts marked 'Telescope Motor', 'Gyro' and 'Automatic Release Switch'. The second had fewer descriptions but also mentioned a gyro and motor; Duggan recognised electrical symbols for switches, resistors and earths.

Gifford gave the sergeant an admiring look. 'I knew all we had to do was ask,' he said.

'If it was only as easy as that,' the sergeant replied. 'These were handed in by an honest citizen, one of the rescue workers. Found them in the woods. Thought they might be important.'

Duggan was about to ask if other parts of the manual had been found too, but decided to stay silent, not to interrupt the rapport Gifford had established with the sergeant. At least, he thought, these diagrams prove that the Norden sight was on board the Flying Fortress.

'That's it, is it?' the sergeant asked.

Gifford looked at Duggan, who nodded. 'He doesn't say much but he's a whizz with the pen and ink,' Gifford told the sergeant. 'A real scholar.'

'I was thinking of giving them to the blacksmith,' the sergeant said in a lazy drawl. 'There were some men sitting round the forge the other day watching him shoe a horse and asking if he'd be able to make a bombsight they could give the Yanks.'

Duggan grinned, imagining the smithy hammering out a bombsight on his anvil, sparks flying in all directions.

'The same man can turn rods of iron into very delicate flowers and things,' the sergeant said to him, addressing him directly. 'You'd be amazed.'

'But would it fool the Yanks?' Gifford asked, shaking his head as if he was giving the question serious consideration.

The sergeant put his palms flat on the desk and raised himself to his feet. 'There's a place called Curley's in the town. Pub and general merchant. Very scrupulous about the coupons and sticking to the official prices. He might be able to help ye.'

Gifford pursed his lips. 'Would you be able to talk to him for us?'

'It's important, is it?' The sergeant glanced from Gifford to Duggan.

'It's important,' Duggan said. 'Part of a bigger picture to do with neutrality.'

'It might be best if I had a word with him myself then,' the sergeant nodded. 'Give me a few minutes to change my clothes. I wouldn't want to go into another man's territory in uniform.'

They waited as the sergeant's heavy footsteps climbed a stairs and crossed a room above. Duggan gave Gifford a thumbsup and they had a short conversation under their breath. Then Duggan went over to the noticeboard and read the poster about compulsory tillage, which warned that farmers who didn't comply could have their land confiscated. Gifford sat against the edge of the sergeant's desk and contemplated his feet stretched out in front of him.

The sergeant returned in a dark suit that looked like his Sunday best. 'Right,' he said, straightening his jacket around his neck. 'Ye can follow me into the town and ye go and pull into the church and say a few prayers and I'll come and talk to ye when I'm finished.'

'Ah,' Gifford coughed as if he had something delicate to say, 'we can offer a little reward of our own. If you think it's appropriate and it would help.'

The sergeant gave him a questioning look.

'A thousand cigarettes. Give or take. Player's and Gold Flakes. And a few bags of coffee. They go together nicely, a coffee and a fag.'

The sergeant gave a nod that didn't signal approval or disapproval. 'We'll see how it goes,' he said. 'He's a decent man, like I said. People started coming to him with surpluses they had of this or that and trading them for whatever they wanted. He found himself with a stockroom full of all sorts of things that he never intended dealing in. He's not a black-marketeer. Just a decent man who can't say no to any-one. Always ready to help out anyone who needs a bit extra for a wake or a wedding.'

'You think he has the bombsight?'

'I couldn't tell you. But he might have come across some-thing.'

The sergeant pulled the door behind them and went down the side of the house while they got back into their Prefect. He emerged a few minutes later in a dusty black Morris 8 and drove back down through the village the way they'd come.

'That was a lucky stroke,' Duggan said as he followed the Morris at a distance.

'Nothing lucky about it,' Gifford said in an airy tone. 'I told you all we had to do was tap into the great living brain that is the Garda Síochána.'

'We could've run into a sergeant like your boss.' Gifford's sergeant was an impatient, humourless and occasionally violent man who had no time for Gifford or what he called 'fucking-about fripperies'.

'I bet this is a peaceful area,' Gifford said, examining the few cattle and sheep grazing the passing fields. 'And he's good at keeping it that way. His main problem is probably stopping people killing themselves out of boredom.'

They followed the Morris into the town and overtook it as the sergeant parked on the main street. Duggan circled through the few streets until he came to a large church and pulled into its empty car park. They sat there for a moment and then Gifford opened his door. 'We better go and pray,' he said.

At the door of the church Duggan stopped. 'I'm going to have a smoke,' he said. He lit a cigarette and walked slowly around the building. There were houses on either side and green fields behind it. A dog barked somewhere, a woman called out to a child in an exasperated voice, and the metal wheels of a cart rumbled on a road. The small-town sounds of a somnolent summer afternoon.

He finished the cigarette in two slow circuits and went into the church. Gifford was sitting in the second-last row, his head bowed and his arms folded as though he was deep in contemplation or sleep. Duggan slid in beside him. There was no one else in the church: its silence seemed to send the few noises of the town even further into the distance. Gifford gave no sign that he was aware of Duggan's presence. We should start looking for somewhere to spend the night, Duggan thought. If we're lucky, the sergeant's contact will lead us on to someone else who might have the sight. But we could be chasing our tails around here for days yet.

He had sunk into a semi-comatose state when solid footsteps behind them sounded on the tiled floor. The sergeant genuflected with his right hand on the edge of the seat and stepped into the pew, a faint whiff of whiskey on his breath. A brown sack hung heavily from his left hand and he swung it around between them as they made way for it on the seat.

Duggan gave him a look of surprise and the sergeant gave him a big grin and a wink. Gifford opened the mouth of the sack and pulled it down around a cardboard box. On the side was stencilled a big black arrow pointing upwards and some words. One jumped out at Duggan in capital letters: 'BOMBSIGHT'. The duct tape sealing the top of the box had been sliced open and he pulled back the lids. Inside was a new bombsight, black and neatly efficient-looking. In the centre was an eyepiece over a lens, on the right a half circle of metal calibrated in numbers; on the left a piece of heavy tape kept it from moving about.

Duggan turned to the sergeant and said in a low voice, 'Thanks, that's great.'

The sergeant took two bars of Hershey's chocolate from his jacket pocket and gave them one each. 'I told him I couldn't have another drink because I had two young lads waiting outside,' he whispered. 'So he gave me these for ye. Thought ye were schoolboys.'

'A decent man,' Gifford said, nodding, opening his bar and taking a bite. He made a face and held up the bar to examine it, as if somebody had played a dirty trick on him.

Duggan stood up and lifted the bag, feeling the weight of the bombsight.

'There's a bit of weight to it,' the sergeant whispered. He stopped in the porch and added in a normal voice, 'he's got two wakes coming up now. Another old man died out the country this morning. He could do with a few more cigarettes.'

'Sure,' Duggan said, leading them to the Prefect. He opened the boot, took out the suitcase and hefted the bag in. 'Thanks again for all your help. And thank him for us.'

'You'll be mentioned in dispatches,' Gifford added, shaking the sergeant's hand.

'But no details.' The sergeant gave him a steely look.

'No details,' Gifford agreed, and looked to Duggan.

'No details,' Duggan nodded, handing the suitcase to the sergeant.

'Ye going back to Dublin now, boys?'

'We are,' Gifford said, looking at Duggan, who nodded.

'Safe home,' the sergeant said as they got in the car. 'The crowning moment of my career.' He shook his head in wonder and gave them an amused smiled.

'This is it, Sarge,' Gifford smiled back before he slammed his door.

The sergeant walked away with an added bounce to his step, swinging the suitcase like a young man embarking on an exciting new life.

Ten

Duggan walked into Commandant McClure's office with the brown sack and let it rest carefully on the floor. McClure eased himself up behind his desk. He glanced at the sack and then back at Duggan's triumphant face. 'Is that what I think it is?' He didn't sound delighted.

'It is,' Duggan said, and gave him a concise report on what had happened in Mayo.

'Strange,' McClure said, letting out a long breath and squatting down beside the box to have a look at the bombsight. He turned the box around to read the serial number and other information stencilled on the side. 'This is a Norden?'

'I assume so.' Duggan handed him the wiring diagrams and explained where they had come from.

'Send them out to the Air Corps.' McClure straightened up. 'Ask them what bombsight they are. Don't mention the Norden.'

McClure went back behind his desk, took two cigarettes from his pack and tossed one to Duggan. 'Strange,' he repeated when he had lit his own. 'Why would the Americans tell everybody about the Norden?'

'It's not a secret, in one sense.' Duggan lit his own cigarette, outlining his own conclusions. He had given a

154

lot of thought to the question but had no definite answer. 'Everybody seems to know they have this secret bombsight called the Norden. The secret seems to lie in keeping it in the box, not showing it to anyone.'

'That's one way of putting it,' McClure said, giving him a lopsided grin. 'So why was it on this plane?'

'They were going to give it to the British.'

'Probably,' McClure nodded.

'Do we give it back to them? Now that everybody knows they're looking for it?'

McClure waved his cigarette hand back and forth, creating a non-committal trail of smoke. 'Let's think about that. There's no hurry now that we know it hasn't fallen into the wrong hands.'

'And what do we tell the Germans?'

'That the Americans are offering a reward. And that you're doing your utmost to find it.'

'Could get interesting if they make a better offer,' Duggan suggested, half seriously.

McClure gave a decisive shake of his head. 'Not a good idea for small countries to play games with the military affairs of big ones.'

Duggan accepted the instruction with a nod. 'Have they responded to our first radio message?'

'Just a confirmation.'

'So I'll send them a message about the reward.'

'No hurry. Meanwhile, draw up the monthly report for External Affairs on German activities. We've got to go there this afternoon.'

'Anything new?'

McClure shook his head. 'German activity has eased off. No sign that they've been using their legation radio recently. Seems they've taken the government's protests about it on board.'

'Should we tell them about this?' Duggan pointed at the box.

'External Affairs? No. That's an operational detail. We could tell them about the Americans seeking it, and the fact that they hadn't told us it was missing. But don't put that in the report. We'll do that verbally if the opportunity arises.'

Duggan propped the *Irish Times* against his typewriter and read the headlines. Germany said it had captured Minsk and Lwow, and the Russians claimed to have beaten back a German-Finnish landing at Viborg, which had been part of an attempt to seize back the Karelian Isthmus in the Gulf of Finland. He flicked over the unfamiliar names, places which were just words in communiqués, of which he had no real knowledge. He didn't even know where they were. The US Secretary of the Navy was urging his country to clear U-boats from the Atlantic and secure the safety of supply convoys to Britain now that Germany's attention was elsewhere. The new ration of one egg per person per week had come into force in the North and in Britain.

'Hard at work,' Bill Sullivan said as he came in.

'Waiting for you,' Duggan tossed the paper to one side. 'Anything new from Herr Dr Goertz?'

'Bloody man's becoming a bore,' Sullivan said, sinking into his chair with a defeated air. 'Just repeating himself at this stage. Same stuff over and over again. You should go visit him. You might get something new.'

'No thanks,' Duggan said, rolling a sandwich of typing and carbon papers into his typewriter.

'When's he due his next visit from Henning Thomsen?' Duggan asked. Thomsen was the diplomat in the German legation who usually liaised with German nationals interned in Ireland.

'Any day now.'

'And we're ready for it?'

'Ready as we'll ever be.' Sullivan smirked. 'Our lad who can hear a pin drop at fifty yards is all set up.'

'And you're sure his German is good enough to understand their conversation?'

'He'll get the gist of it anyway.'

Would that be enough? Duggan wondered. They needed to know if Thomsen said anything which indicated that the Abwehr was trying to communicate with Goertz through the legation. The chances were that it wouldn't try, partly because of the difficulty of communicating with the legation, and partly because the German Minister had made clear his insistence on sticking to diplomatic formalities and his objection to being dragged into espionage. Still, it was a risk, and it could scupper their operation. 'Give me the file of daily reports,' he said.

Sullivan slid a buff folder of documents down the table. Duggan flicked through them, noting the number of incursions into Irish airspace by German aircraft, the occasional references to the country in Lord Haw-Haw's nightly broadcasts, and the reports of wreckage and bodies being washed up on the west coast, particularly in Donegal. He summarised the information in three succinct paragraphs and looked to Sullivan, who was now hidden behind the *Irish Press*.

'What'll I tell External Affairs about Goertz?'

'Tell them … ' Sullivan lowered his paper with a deflated look. 'Tell them he's continuing to cooperate but won't name names of his IRA contacts.'

'They don't care about that.'

'Or the names of others who provided him with information or safe houses.'

Duggan began typing but stopped as Sullivan added: 'Or the full details of his relations with the German legation.'

'What do you mean?'

'He's cagey about that. Complains that the German Minister wouldn't treat him as a representative of the Wehrmacht high command. Kept him at arm's length.'

Good, Duggan thought. So relations between them are not the best. 'Should we say he's not cooperating fully?'

'I wouldn't go that far,' Sullivan said, pondering the question. 'More a case of him not wanting to be too critical of them, I think.'

'Keeping his distance,' Duggan said to himself as he scrolled up the paper to reread what he had written. He shrugged and scrolled back down to the line he was on and modified the end of the sentence he had begun.

'Are you free this evening?' Sullivan folded his newspaper.

Duggan nodded as he finished typing and took the carbons from between the three sheets of typing paper.

'Carmel's cousin is down from Belfast and she'd like you to come to the Metropole with us.'

'No chance,' Duggan laughed. 'I'm not going on another of your blind dates.'

'It's not my idea. It's Carmel's.'

'That's what I mean. I'm not going on another of Carmel's blind dates.'

'Ah, come on. Doesn't mean anything. We'll have a few jars.'

'Did she ask you to ask me?'

Sullivan gave a vigorous nod. 'Yeah. She likes you.'

'And I like her too. But I'm not so keen on the way she keeps trying to fix me up with her friends.'

'It's not like that. It's only her cousin.'

'Why don't you ask Anderson? They could talk about Belfast or wherever he's from up there.'

'That prick,' Sullivan muttered. He had a visceral dislike of Captain Liam Anderson, which, unlike Duggan's antipathy towards him, was not based on anything more specific than his northern arrogance. As far as Duggan knew. 'I wouldn't let him near her.'

'You've met her?'

'You'll like her,' Sullivan nodded. 'She's good fun. Good looker too.'

'All right,' Duggan said, signing his name to the bottom of the top copy of his report. 'But tell Carmel not to get any ideas.'

'Sure,' Sullivan said with a relieved smile. 'She knows it's not like that. She knows about your American penfriend.'

The afternoon had brightened up, a warm breeze from the west breaking up the clouds and sending them scudding across the sky, their shadows drifting fast over the river and its quaysides. Duggan drove with McClure in the passenger seat. They crossed the Liffey after the Four Courts and went up under the bridge at Christchurch and around by St Patrick's Cathedral and into Kevin Street.

'Have you sent the message to the Germans?' McClure asked as they crossed the bottom of Harcourt Street into St Stephen's Green.

'Haven't had a chance to code it yet. I'll get it done when we go back, and get it out to the signals man in Greystones in time for tonight's transmission.'

'Good.' McClure pointed as they passed Newman House. 'Pull over there and park.'

Duggan did as instructed and stopped short of the new headquarters of the Department of External Affairs at Iveagh House. 'You heard about the representative of the Polish government in exile in England?' McClure asked as they got out, continuing without waiting for an answer. 'Got a cab from the mailboat and asked the driver to take him to Iveagh House. The cabbie took him to the Iveagh Hostel. Which was probably appropriate enough for a representative of a homeless government.'

Duggan laughed as they went up the steps under the portico and entered the marbled entrance hall, thinking it was a far cry from the hostel they had passed on nearby Bride Street. A porter took their names and spoke on a phone. 'You know where it is?' he asked McClure, who had been there the previous month when Duggan was in Lisbon.

McClure nodded and led Duggan up the grand staircase and around to the left when it divided in two. He caught Duggan's silent whistle at the luxury of the building and smiled his agreement. Their contact, Pól Ó Murchú, was in a small high-ceilinged room with doors leading in both directions, suggesting that it had previously been a passageway or anteroom when it was a Guinness home. His new surroundings hadn't changed his demeanour: he looked as troubled as usual, old beyond his forty-odd years.

'Gentlemen,' he nodded to them. 'Pull over a chair.'

They each took an upright chair from the wall opposite and brought them in front of his desk. It was beginning to pile as high with files as his old desk in Government Buildings. 'What do you have for me?'

'Not a lot, sir,' McClure said, laying Duggan's report on the desk facing him. 'The Germans have not been very busy in the past month.'

'Other things on their minds,' Ó Murchú said automatically as he scanned the page. 'Good.' He looked up. 'We've more than enough on our plate with our other friends.' He managed to make 'friends' sound more like the opposite of its usual meaning.

'The Americans?' McClure suggested, seeing his opening. 'It has come to our attention that they were less than forthcoming about their plane that crashed in Mayo some weeks ago.'

Ó Murchú said nothing but gave him a quizzical look. McClure told him about the Norden bombsight and that the Americans were now offering a reward for its recovery. 'We weren't made aware of any of this,' McClure concluded.

'Nor was I,' Ó Murchú replied to his unasked question. 'What do you make of it?'

'We're not sure what to make of it. This bombsight is said to be of great military significance. "The bomber will always get through",' he said, quoting the common phrase of the pre-war years, 'but can it hit its target? That's the question. And that's what the Norden bombsight allows it to do.'

'So it's important.'

'Yes, sir.'

'Do we assume it was on its way to England? That they were giving it to the English?'

'Yes, sir.'

'Could that plane have been on its way to the North?'

'That's possible. But they said it was en route to England. And most of its cargo seemed destined for their legation in London. Caviar and the like.'

Ó Murchú pursed his lips and gave the matter some thought. 'You know we've reason to believe that they've got some of their people in the North? Without as much as a by-your-leave from us.'

McClure nodded. Most of the reports of American activity around the docks in Derry had originated with G2, beginning with some information Duggan had come across six months earlier.

'It's extremely unhelpful in the current climate,' Ó Murchú sighed, as if it was a matter of personal discomfort. 'After Mr Aiken's visit to America. You know they've refused our request for arms? Offered to sell us a couple of ships but are now dragging their heels on that. It's impossible to categorise their attitude as friendly at the moment. It's anything but, in reality.'

Duggan wondered if the results of his enquiries into Aiken's comments in Lisbon had made their way to Ó Murchú's desk. It wouldn't surprise me, he thought. But there was no way he could ask anyone if it was true, not even McClure, in spite of their close working relationship. Things had to be kept in their own compartments.

'If I may speak frankly and, of course, confidentially, Mr Aiken's visit was not the success we'd hoped for. And Mr Dillon is only too happy to point that out. Of course he's playing Gray's game as usual,' Ó Murchú was saying of the opposition TD James Dillon.

Dillon had questioned the success of Aiken's mission, which the government was presenting as having deepened America's understanding of Ireland's neutrality. Dillon was known to be friendly with David Gray, the American Minister in Ireland, who made no secret of his opposition to Irish, and American, neutrality in the war against Hitler.

'That's by the by,' Ó Murchú said. 'We can prevent the newspapers going to town on it. But everything to do with the Americans must be handled with great care at the moment.'

'Yes, sir,' McClure said.

'We cannot afford any further misunderstandings with them,' Ó Murchú added. Yes, Duggan decided, he has been told what I found out in Lisbon. 'We are trying to make it clear to them in a friendly fashion that we have the right to make our own decisions on the war, but they don't want to listen. Mr Gray wants everyone involved and he's poisoning the well on us in Washington. So everything to do with them is to be handled with the utmost care.'

'Understood.'

'Is this bomb thing going to cause a problem?'

'No, sir. It's under control.'

'You have it?'

'Yes,' McClure admitted, unable to dodge the direct question.

'You're going to give it back to them?'

'Not immediately. We thought we'd try and work out why they're offering a reward for it first.'

'Because they want it back,' Ó Murchú said, giving him a bland look, stating what seemed obvious.

'Why they've gone public about a piece of secret military equipment,' McClure clarified. 'Why they're risking the German legation hearing about it. And putting two and two together. That they're giving it to the British.'

Ó Murchú took a deep breath, as if he was about to challenge what McClure had said. 'All right,' he exhaled. 'But be extra careful. Don't create any further misunderstandings. Don't cause an incident.'

'We'll be careful.'

'Thank you, gentlemen.' Ó Murchú dismissed them, adding as they replaced their chairs against the wall, 'At least we won't have to pretend to be best friends with the Americans on Friday. There's no Fourth of July garden party in the Phoenix Park this year.'

'Why not?' McClure asked in surprise.

'A diplomatic illness, perhaps,' Ó Murchú said with a wintry grimace. 'Mr Gray is going off to Adare to spend the day with some of his Ascendancy friends.'

'I've heard a lot about you,' Carmel's cousin Maura said as she shook Duggan's hand.

'All lies, if the information came from him,' Duggan smiled as he nodded towards Sullivan. They were standing in the lobby of the Metropole, where Duggan and Sullivan had been waiting for the two girls to arrive. The queue outside for the night's film, *This Man Is Dangerous* with James Mason, was being allowed into the box office by a uniformed commissionaire in groups of twenty or so.

'Oh, I don't know,' Maura said with a tilt to her head, as if appraising him. She had light brown hair raised up by a slide at each side, lively grey eyes, and slightly prominent teeth in a narrow face. 'It's all very complimentary.'

'Let's go on in,' Carmel suggested, as if there was a reason to hurry.

They followed her into the ballroom, where she stopped inside the door. The Phil Murtagh band was playing a lively tune but the dance floor was empty. Tables around the edges of the room were mostly occupied. 'There they are,' Carmel said, and set off across the dance floor towards the far corner.

Duggan caught sight of Max Linqvist's blonde hair. Linqvist was half-hidden behind a pillar, his arm around the shoulders of his girlfriend, Breda.

'You fucker,' Duggan muttered to Sullivan as they followed the girls.

'I didn't know they'd be here,' Sullivan muttered back, assuming Duggan's upset was caused by Breda's presence.

'Bollocks,' Duggan retorted. This is a set-up, he thought. Linqvist has organised it, whether Sullivan realised it or not. Which meant that he wanted something. And something he didn't want to go through the normal channels to get.

Linqvist and Breda were on their feet, being introduced to Maura, as Duggan and Sullivan arrived. 'And you know Paul,' Carmel said to Linqvist.

'We've met before.' Linqvist shook hands with Duggan. 'Good to see you again.'

'Paul,' Breda said as she gave Duggan a dazzling smile, took his hand in both of hers and gave him a peck on the cheek. 'I'm so glad you could come.'

They all sat down and ordered drinks from a waitress. Duggan concentrated on Maura, asking her how Belfast was.

'Nervous,' she said. 'Everybody's on edge waiting for the next raid.'

'Were you there during the last ones?'

'Aye. Two girls I was at school with were killed.'

'Friends of yours?'

'Not really. I just knew them from school.'

'It must have been terrible.'

'It was,' she said in a matter-of-fact voice. 'Seemed to go on for hours, bomb after bomb. And now we've got the Twelfth coming up.'

'Is that why you're here?'

'Took my holidays to get away for the two weeks.'

The band's singer, Peggy Dell, appeared on stage and began crooning 'Blue Moon' in a husky voice.

'My song,' Breda said, tugging at Linqvist's sleeve, interrupting his conversation with Sullivan. 'Dance, Max.'

Duggan watched her drag him on to the dance floor, thinking, He's much too distinctive to be a spy, working for the American State Department. He was more than six feet tall, and his height and bright blonde hair made him stand out wherever he was.

Maura was giving him an inquisitive look when he turned back to her. 'Would you like to dance?' he asked.

'Thought you'd never ask,' she replied.

She moved in close to him on the dance floor, her hair tickling his cheek. 'So you're in the Free State army too?' she said into his ear.

'I am.'

'Do you think you'll be doing any fighting?'

'I hope not.'

She leaned back to look him in the eye. 'That's a good answer.'

'Is it?'

'It means you're a smart man.'

'It could also mean I'm a coward.'

She shook her head, giving him a serious look. 'You should keep out of it down here if you can.'

'That's the intention.'

'It doesn't take many bombs to make people realise how full of shit the armchair generals are.'

He was taken aback by her language and the vehemence in her voice. He increased the pressure on her back, and she moved closer to him again. 'Let's not talk about that,' she said into his ear.

'No,' he agreed.

Instead, they talked about her job in a chemist's in Great Victoria Street, and where he came from, and that he'd never been to Belfast and how she'd had a holiday in Salthill before the war. Duggan began to enjoy the evening as it went on, dancing with Carmel and Breda as well, and relaxing in Maura's company.

He was in a mellow mood by the time the three of them went off to the ladies'. 'I hear you've been down the west,' he said to Linqvist, deciding to take the initiative. 'Fishing.'

'I was,' Linqvist said, offering him and Sullivan cigarettes from a packet of Lucky Strikes.

'Catch anything?' Duggan asked, flicking his lighter and leaning across the table to light Linqvist's and Sullivan's cigarettes.

'A few packs of these,' Linqvist said, holding up the cigarette packet with a lazy smile.

'I hear there were more than a few of them around. And booze and chocolate and even more exotic things.'

'There were. We only got our hands on a few before it was all whisked away to the London legation.'

'I'd been looking forward to the Independence Day party here this year,' Duggan said. 'But you're going fishing again with Mr Gray.'

'Not me. Not this time.' Linqvist gave him a languid grin. Sullivan watched them, aware that there was something going on beneath the surface of the conversation, but not knowing what. 'His driver's back. I was only standing in for him on the trip to Mayo.'

'Was it a success? The trip to Mayo?'

'He didn't catch anything. But he enjoyed himself.'

'Maybe he was using the wrong flies.'

'That's possible.' Linqvist leaned forward to tap the ash on his cigarette into the glass tray. 'I hear you were in Mayo yourself recently. Get any fishing in?'

'No.' Interesting, Duggan thought. How did he know that?

'What flies would you recommend?'

'I wouldn't know anything about flies.' Duggan tapped his cigarette against the ashtray. 'Never fished with any bait other than the basic. A worm.'

'A worm,' Linqvist repeated, nodding his head as if that was meaningful advice. 'A lot to be said for keeping it simple, I guess.'

The girls returned, looking satisfied with themselves. 'Have a good gossip?' Sullivan asked. Carmel swung her handbag at his chest and said, 'Mind your manners, you.' Everyone else laughed and they went back to dancing. After the national anthem, as they were leaving, Duggan and Linqvist found themselves side by side going down the stairs. 'How's Grace?' Linqvist asked in a quiet voice. 'You still in touch with her?'

'Yes,' Duggan said, knowing that Linqvist probably knew he was. And knowing, too, that the enquiry was a none-too-subtle reminder that he was in Linqvist's debt. 'She seems to like New York.'

'We should have a talk.'

'Yes,' Duggan said in a decisive tone, hoping to make it clear that there were things he wanted too.

'You know McDaid's in Harry Street? After the Holy Hour tomorrow?'

'Fine.'

Outside, Linqvist and Breda said goodbye to the others and crossed the street to the median, where his two-seater MG was parked alongside the rough concrete of the bomb shelter. Envious glances followed them from the crowd emerging from the Metropole as Linqvist accelerated away. Is he trying to be conspicuous, driving such a fancy car when few people had any petrol, never mind a sports car? Duggan wondered.

They waited for a horse-drawn growler and Sullivan gave the driver Carmel's address in Glasnevin as they got in. Duggan sat beside Maura, opposite Sullivan and Carmel, and they knocked shoulders as the carriage swayed over the cobblestones. It wasn't late, but the buses and trams had stopped running hours earlier and O'Connell Street was busy with couples heading home on foot from the cinemas. The night was almost balmy, a warm breeze coming through the open window, and the motion of the carriage and the clop-clop of the horse's hooves left them sleepy by the time they reached Carmel's house in Mobhi Road.

Inside, Carmel and Maura disappeared into the kitchen at the back of the house while Duggan and Sullivan stood in the front room, its air stale from lack of use.

'What was all that talk of fishing about?' Sullivan asked.

Duggan told him about the Norden bombsight and how Linqvist had been offering a reward for its recovery.

'Did we know that?'

'Not till I heard about it in Mayo.' Duggan took a deep breath. 'Did you tell Carmel I was down there?'

Sullivan nodded after a moment.

So that was how Linqvist knew, Duggan thought. 'And that I was in Lisbon?'

Sullivan nodded again.

'And she probably tells Breda everything.'

'And she tells Max,' Sullivan finished for him. 'Yeah. Fuck.'

'It doesn't matter,' Duggan assured him.

'You're not going to tell the boss, are you?'

'No, no. Course not.' Duggan paused as a thought occurred to him. 'But we could use it. You could tell her that we're very upset with Max and his friends. At the games they're playing behind our backs. While we've been straight with them.'

'Yeah,' Sullivan said with a slow smile. 'I'll do that.'

'Do what?' Carmel asked, pushing open the door with her elbow as she carried in a tray of tea things.

Sullivan tapped his nose and waved his finger at her. 'Curiosity killed the cat.'

'And information made him fat,' Maura said as she followed Carmel in with a plate of queen cakes.

'Or maybe it was the cakes,' Duggan said to her.

'You can only have one,' she shot back.

They continued their light-hearted banter as they had cups of tea and ate queen cakes. Afterwards, Sullivan and Carmel disappeared into the kitchen, leaving Duggan and Maura together on the couch in the unused room. They sat in silence, he very conscious of her closeness and tempted to move towards her, knowing she would respond if he did. It was unlikely he'd ever see Gerda again, not while the war lasted anyway. And who knew how long it would last? And how it would end? And what the world would be like afterwards?

'Listen,' he said, unsure what he was going to say and running his fingers down the back of her hand where it lay between them on the couch. 'I ... '

'I know,' she said, turning her hand over to entwine his fingers with hers. 'You have a mystery girlfriend. In America.'

'Mystery?' he said. 'How mystery?'

'Nobody's ever seen her,' she smiled, letting her head tilt sideways in a question mark.

'That was just the way things worked out. She wasn't here very long. I mean, I didn't know her for very long before she went away.'

'Must've been love at first sight then.'

'You're teasing me.'

'Aye. I'm sorry.' She moved towards him and kissed him on the lips.

Her presence was almost overwhelming: the press of her breast against his chest, the taste of her lips, the smell of her hair and the softness of her skin. He knew all he had to do was put his other arm around her and prolong the kiss. But he hesitated on the point of abandonment and she pulled back.

'Thank you for a lovely evening,' she said. 'I really enjoyed it.'

'Me too,' he said. 'I hope we'll meet again before you go home.'

'I'm sure we will.'

'If there's anything you want to see in Dublin, let me know.'

She went to the hall door with him, holding hands, and kissed him on the cheek as he left. He walked back to Phibsborough, still feeling her physical presence, and passed a couple entangled in each other in a doorway as he turned at Doyle's Corner towards the North Circular Road. He took his time, enjoying the warmth of the night, passing by the cattle market with its smells of the country, and wondering if Gerda was back from her holidays, if maybe she'd met some-one, had a holiday romance, if it was realistic to think they'd ever see each other again.

The sky was indigo in the east behind him, but lightened towards the west into an inky blue that presaged the coming dawn as the earth turned on its slow round.

Eleven

The phone rang and Duggan picked it up and gave his name. 'Commandant Flood for you,' the switchboard orderly said.

'Commandant,' Duggan said, unconsciously straightening up on the chair.

'That wiring diagram you sent us,' the Air Corps man said. 'Why was the writing in English?'

'Ah … ' Duggan hesitated, confused by the question and unable to formulate an answer.

'It's a German bombsight,' the commandant said in an accusatory tone, as if G2 had been trying to catch out the Air Corps by asking a trick question.

'I don't understand.'

'Neither do I. Why was it in English?'

'Because it came from an American manual.'

'Why would the Americans have a manual about the Heinkel bombsight?'

'I don't know, sir,' Duggan said, perplexed. 'Maybe it wasn't actually a manual.'

'What was it then?'

'I don't know, sir,' Duggan repeated. 'It was found in the wreckage of the Flying Fortress that crashed in Mayo.'

The commandant gave a harrumph, as if that was the final straw. 'Well, our lads say it's a drawing of the electrics in the bombsight I showed you the other day from the Heinkel.'

Duggan was about to say that maybe it was from an American report on German equipment, but Flood had hung up. Duggan tipped back his chair and put his feet up on the table and his hands in his trouser pockets. He had assumed the diagram was of the Norden bombsight, but there had been no reason to jump to that conclusion. The pages had not been in the box with the Norden – the obvious place for a manual. It could as easily have been an intelligence report on Luftwaffe equipment as anything else. Which suggested there might have been other interesting things on board the Flying Fortress.

He dropped his feet to the floor again and picked up the phone. He asked the switchboard to get him the Garda station in Mayo, where he and Gifford had met the sergeant.

'Boss wants you,' Sullivan said behind him as he came into the room. 'Got something for you.'

'What?'

'Didn't say.'

'Is it urgent?' Duggan nodded at the phone. 'I'm just waiting for a call.'

'Didn't sound urgent,' Sullivan said, yawning as he sat down at the end of his table.

'You stayed late at Carmel's?'

Sullivan nodded. 'You left in a hurry.'

'No, I didn't.'

'Without even saying goodbye.'

'I didn't want to interrupt you.'

'Anyway,' Sullivan said through another yawn. 'Maura took a shine to you for some reason.'

'You told me it wasn't going to be like that.'

'You know what Carmel's like,' Sullivan said in a fond tone. 'You might as well tell her not to breathe as tell her not to be match-making.'

The phone gave a single ring and the switch told him his call to Mayo was on the line.

'Ah, the young bucks,' the sergeant said when Duggan identified himself. 'Ye got back to the big smoke safely.'

'We did, thanks,' Duggan said. 'There was something I wanted to check with you.'

'Fire ahead.'

'That diagram you gave us. Was it part of something else? A bigger document?'

'I couldn't tell you. What I gave you was what was given to me. '

'Were there many other documents lying around after the crash?'

The sergeant took a deep breath as if he was thinking. 'There was all sorts of stuff lying around. There were some papers around all right. But nobody was paying them much attention. If you follow my meaning.'

'I do,' Duggan said, assuming he meant there was much more interest in the booty. 'Could you ask the man who gave them to you if he saw any other papers? Even better, if he has any others?'

'I can surely.'

'Thanks for all your help.'

'No bother at all. Have ye claimed the reward yet?'

'Not yet.'

'So the treasure hunt can go on,' the sergeant chuckled. 'There's still a few young lads taking a rare interest in the bog now and then. But it's tapering off.'

'Good for them to get some fresh air,' Duggan laughed.

'How's your Branch friend?' The sergeant seemed in no hurry to end the conversation.

'He's fine.'

'He hasn't been put back into uniform yet?'

'Not as far as I know.'

'He'd want to watch himself. I wouldn't be surprised to see him turn up some place down here one of the days, if he's not careful. Back in uniform in Belmullet or somewhere.'

'I'll warn him next time I see him.' Duggan smiled as he imagined Gifford's horror at being posted to some rural outpost. He'd never stay in the Garda Síochána if that happened.

He hung up and went in search of Captain Anderson on the British desk. He found him with his head in his hands, focused on a lengthy document he was reading.

'Can I interrupt you for a moment?' Duggan asked.

Anderson looked up at him, put a pencil on the page he was reading and closed the file over from the back so that whatever it said on the front was not visible. 'You were to keep me in the loop about that plane,' he said in an accusatory voice.

'That's why I'm here,' Duggan lied.

'Everybody knows about the American reward for a bombsight now.'

'There was no mention of it when you were down there with the salvage crew?'

'You think I was keeping it secret so I could claim the reward?' Anderson shot back.

'No,' Duggan said evenly, not interested in getting into an argument with him. 'You remember I told you my interest was in documents on the plane?'

'That's what took you down there?'

'I came across some documents that had been handed in to the guards,' Duggan said, ignoring the question.

'What kind of documents?'

Duggan paused, then decided there was no reason not to tell him. 'Wiring diagrams of German bombsights.'

'German bombsights,' Anderson repeated.

Duggan could see him trying to figure out what this meant, could see that the information had piqued his interest. 'Two pages of them, but no commentary, or any indication of what they were from.'

'You think it was part of something else?' Anderson said, thinking aloud. The hostile edge to his voice had disappeared.

'Looks like it. They're not the kind of thing you'd send somebody on their own. Not without a covering note, at the very least.'

Anderson nodded his head several times, opened the bottom drawer on his desk and took out a file. He flicked through the first couple of pages and stopped at a typed list. 'The inventory of everything they took away,' he said, running his finger down the list. Duggan glanced at it over his shoulder. It included parts of the aircraft that had broken away from the main wreckage, and then the boxes of supplies destined for the London legation.

Anderson's finger stopped and he tapped an item: 'One leather briefcase'.

'That was open,' Anderson said. 'Had details about the flight. Weather forecast. Route and so on. I assumed it was the pilot's. Briefing documents.'

He continued running his finger down to the end of the list.

'That's it,' he said, looking up at Duggan. 'Nothing that looks likely. Though Christ knows what had disappeared before we got there.'

'And none of the Americans or Brits asked about anything that was missing?'

'Not a word. There were jokes about parties in the locality. But not a mention of anything they wanted back.'

Duggan thanked him and was heading for the door when Anderson asked, 'What do you make of this reward?'

'I don't know what to make of it,' Duggan replied, turning back.

'Can't be much of a secret if they're telling everybody about it.'

'And why didn't they ask you about it when you were there?'

'They're up to something.'

'But what?'

'Fucked if I know,' Anderson shrugged. 'Keep me posted.'

'Will do.'

Commandant McClure was standing by the window, looking out at the sun-washed parking area, his chin propped in the heel of his left hand. He half turned as Duggan entered, after a cursory knock, and nodded towards his desk. 'Your German friends have responded to your message,' he said.

Duggan went behind the desk and looked at the open file lying on it. There was a sheet with blocks of letters on one side and the uncoded message in German on the other. An English translation was half hidden underneath, but Duggan read the German.

'We've set up an auction,' he said with a short laugh. The message told Hermann Goertz to get his friends to offer more than the Americans were willing to pay for the Norden bombsight. And to set up a bank account in the name of a trading company to pay whoever delivered it.

'Seems so,' McClure said.

'You don't think we should do it?' Duggan said, picking up the lack of enthusiasm in McClure's voice.

'It's dangerous,' McClure said, leaning back against the wall at the side of the window. 'We're getting into uncharted waters. In danger of becoming too closely involved in the affairs of the belligerents.'

'But the Americans aren't belligerents.'

'They are in all but name.' McClure reached over to his desk for a cigarette, and lit it. 'The real problem is we don't know what we're getting involved in.'

'We're setting up an IRA-German link so that we can monitor their activities,' Duggan reminded him.

'Yes. But we're now setting up an auction over secret American military equipment.'

'But we're not going to give it to the Germans at the end of the day,' Duggan protested, realising how disappointed he'd be if his visit to Lisbon turned out to have been a waste of time. 'And this is a golden opportunity to set up a money route from the Germans to the IRA, which we can control. And which they'll probably use to fund other activities here. Even other agents.'

McClure gave a couple of nods of weary agreement. 'What bothers me is how the Germans knew about the Norden bombsight in the first place. We didn't know about it. The Americans obviously knew. The British probably did. And whoever found it in Mayo. And the black-marketeer who ended up with it. So how did the Germans get to hear about it before we did?'

Duggan lit a Sweet Afton in the silence. McClure, as usual, had gone back to basics, to questions that Duggan had pushed to the back of his mind as he was carried along by developments.

'We can't overlook the possibility that there is a well-placed German agent operating here,' McClure continued. 'Someone who has penetrated the American legation or the British representative's office. Or even someone who has been more successful than Dr Goertz at infiltrating the IRA. And,' he leaned forward to tap the tip of the cigarette into the ashtray, 'not necessarily a German. Indeed, almost certainly not a German.'

Jesus, Duggan thought. That could mean that his whole Lisbon operation was compromised from the word go, that the Germans were simply playing him along. And were still doing it with the latest coded message. 'So we should close down the radio link?' he asked.

'Perhaps.' McClure gave him a wan smile. 'Or maybe I'm just in a paranoid mood today. Let's review everything we know about all this. All that's happened since you went to Lisbon.'

'Write a report on it?'

McClure shook his head. 'Just take a fresh look at it. In light of what we know now, and didn't know then.'

'Max Linqvist has contacted me,' Duggan said. 'Asked to meet this afternoon.'

'Good,' McClure said, cheering up, as though that was the best news he'd heard all week.

Duggan looked at his watch and slowed down, falling into position behind a woman on a bike whom he'd been about to overtake. There was no point getting to McDaid's before half three, when the Holy Hour ended and the pubs reopened. He cycled automatically, one hand on the handlebars, the other in his pocket, his thoughts far from the sunny quays and the drays going by, their iron wheels grinding on the road.

Why, he was wondering, did that Abwehr agent Wiedermeyer meet me in such a public place in Lisbon? Because he wanted me to be seen with him. But why? To let the British know that the Abwehr was dealing with the IRA. Why would they want the British to know that? Because they were not dealing with the IRA. Or, if Hermann Goertz was to be believed, because they had given up on the IRA as a waste of time, bogged down in internal rifts and incapable of doing anything useful for the German war effort. That was more likely. So why are they then going along with my IRA operation?

He stopped at O'Connell Bridge with one foot on the ground as the stream of traffic was held up by the garda on point duty. Pedestrians passed in front of him, the women in a blur of colour brought out by the sunshine. A bus went by behind them, followed by an open-topped tram with an advertisement saying 'I want Cadburys!' separating its decks. Which reminded him of Hershey bars and distracted him from his train of thought for a moment.

The traffic began to move again, and he took his left hand from his pocket to balance the bicycle. Then it struck him. The Germans wanted the British to know they were using the IRA, wanted them to think the relationship was more meaningful than it was. To be a thorn in the Brits' side and, as an added bonus, to disrupt Ireland's relations with Britain. Even to the point that it would become a factor in a British decision to reinvade Ireland. Which would bring the Wehrmacht to Ireland's defence. And turn the country into a battlefield, a bloody sideshow.

Maybe McClure's right, he thought as he went round by Trinity College, we should be very careful of playing games with these people. Maybe we should shut down the radio link. Simply not reply to the latest message. Plant a short news report in the newspapers about a guard at Arbour Hill Prison being questioned about carrying messages to and from an unnamed internee.

He went up Grafton Street, its shops shaded by their canopies. It wasn't a day for window shopping or for brooding about the war, he thought as he navigated around the few parked cars. He turned into Harry Street and chained his bicycle to a lamp post. Across the road, a Guinness dray waited in front of another pub as a burly man rolled wooden barrels off the edge to a colleague waiting to take them as they bounced off a thick sack of straw. He checked his watch and a small man with a flat cap preceded him to the door of McDaid's, stopped, hawked up some mucus, and spat it at the base of the wall.

Max Linqvist was already inside, sitting against the back wall, a cigarette smoking in the ashtray in front of him. 'What'll you have?' He made to get up.

'I'll get it,' Duggan said. 'I'm on my feet.'

'Glass of Guinness then,' Linqvist said, sinking back.

Duggan ordered two half-pints of Guinness and sat down on a stool opposite him.

'Good night last night,' Linqvist said.

Duggan nodded. 'I didn't see any sign of your sports car outside.'

'It's becoming a liability,' Linqvist groaned. 'Breda says it's too ostentatious. On the other hand, we've got to fly the flag. Live up to your expectations. You think we're all millionaires.'

'And film stars?'

'That what Grace says?'

'She doesn't say. But I think she's enjoying New York.'

'Glad to hear it. You think she'll come back?'

'I don't know,' Duggan said, though he knew she wouldn't.

'You ever think of going there?'

'Maybe after the war.' Why is everyone so interested in my love life? he wondered, tempted to ask Linqvist. But he refrained, not wanting to talk to him about Gerda and the circumstances under which she had gone to America.

The barman called to Duggan and he went back to the counter to collect the two glasses, and pay. The man who had preceded him into the pub was on a stool beside a partition and staring at the array of bottles behind the bar with the fixed devotion of a contemplative monk before an altar.

Linqvist raised the glass to Duggan with a 'Thanks' and took a sip. 'I'm only developing a true appreciation of Guinness now.' He put the glass back on the table between them. 'It's taken a while.'

'Like developing a taste for Hershey chocolate.'

'Like that,' Linqvist nodded, with a knowing grin. 'I thought we should have a talk.' He leant forward and stubbed out the cigarette carefully, as if he was trying to choose his words with equal care. From the length of the ash on the cigarette, it was clear that he had smoked hardly any of it. 'Our masters are on a collision course and it's not going to do either of our countries any good if it comes to a bust-up.'

Duggan took a drink of his stout, neither agreeing nor disagreeing.

'Your General Aiken did not make a favourable impression in Washington,' Linqvist continued. 'He couldn't have been more successful at irritating President Roosevelt if that was what he set out to do. Which I don't imagine it was.'

'Hardly.' Duggan offered his cigarette case, but Linqvist shook his head. Duggan lit a cigarette for himself.

'But that was the upshot. And my minister was so worried about it that he put pressure on people to make some ships and other aid available. You'll have noticed that that offer was not made to General Aiken but to the government here through the legation.'

Duggan hadn't been aware of the diplomatic niceties of the American offer of ships which had been elided with Aiken's visit in newspaper reports and presented as proof of the success of his efforts. 'I think some misunderstandings went to Washington ahead of Mr Aiken,' Duggan said. 'Made his visit more difficult even before he got there.'

'You mean Wild Bill?'

'Wild Bill?'

'Colonel Donovan.'

'Who exactly is he?' Duggan asked.

The newspapers sometimes referred to him as President Roosevelt's 'mystery man', who had visited a number of European countries earlier in the year. He had come to Dublin for a few hours, met the Taoiseach and some ministers, and left as suddenly as he had come. No information about the visit had filtered down to Duggan or to the public. Asked about the visit by reporters, Donovan had breezed past, saying he had to catch a plane and had no time to talk.

'President's special representative,' Linqvist said. He glanced from side to side and lowered his voice. 'About to be appointed coordinator of all intelligence. You know he was in Lisbon when General Aiken was there?'

Duggan shook his head. He hadn't known that.

'And that they had a talk?' Linqvist took another drink as Duggan shook his head again, making no attempt to cover the fact that this was news to him. So my enquiries about who reported Aiken's comments in Lisbon were also a waste of time, he was thinking. And he wondered if McClure knew about this meeting between Aiken and Donovan.

'I don't think Wild Bill was very happy with General Aiken's attitude,' Linqvist said. 'He made it clear to him that the only aggression Ireland was concerned about was British aggression. That it was the only country that had ever aggressed – if that's a word – Ireland.'

'That's why the president accused him of wanting a German victory?'

'There were other straws in the wind, too,' Linqvist said. 'All amounting to a big question mark over General Aiken's attitude. And he's Mr de Valera closest adviser, we're told.'

'I don't know about that,' Duggan said. He knew from his uncle Timmy, a government backbencher and fan of Aiken's, that he was not always enamoured by de Valera's stance towards the British.

'That's not true?'

'I wouldn't take it as a fact. Just because they're old comrades, I don't think it would be wise to assume that Mr de Valera relies on his advice. Or anyone else's, for that matter.'

'That's not the only thing that made the General's visit to Washington more difficult, as you put it,' Linqvist said, shaking a Lucky Strike from his packet and pausing to light it. 'You know that the anti-interventionists are very strong in America, have public opinion on their side. So the president has to move very cautiously with his anti-Nazi efforts. And he's not happy that the Irish-American section of his own party is on the anti-interventionist side because of Ireland's neutrality. Even to the extent of cooperating with the German American Bund who, of course, are also in favour of American neutrality. General Aiken spent most of his three months in the US arguing for neutrality, even appearing on a platform with Colonel Lindbergh, the Bund's greatest supporter.' He paused to inhale some smoke. 'Have you read Machiavelli?'

'Never felt the need,' Duggan said. 'I've got an uncle who's a politician.'

Linqvist smiled. '"He who is not your friend will demand your neutrality, whilst he who is your friend will entreat you to declare yourself with arms." That sums it up. The Germans want us both to stay neutral. Our friends don't. Your friends don't.'

'Our friends want us to commit suicide,' Duggan said.

'That's crazy,' Linqvist retorted. 'Mr de Valera says it. But does he believe it? You don't believe it. Nobody believes it.'

'It would leave a lot of Irish people dead. For nothing that will make any difference to the outcome of the war.'

'It would make a difference. Having the west-coast ports would make a big difference to the supply lines. Hasten the end to the war.'

'It'd make a hell of a bigger difference if America declared war on Germany.'

'You know there are reasons why we can't.'

'And you know there are reasons why we can't. Not least that you won't give us any weapons to defend ourselves.'

'Touché,' Linqvist said, spreading his hands in a gesture of surrender. 'Time for another drink, I think.'

Duggan finished his cigarette while Linqvist waited at the counter for the barman to pull two more half-pints. This wasn't at all what he had expected. He'd assumed Linqvist was going to remind him that he, Duggan, owed him a favour over Gerda and put pressure on him to help find the Norden bombsight. Or, worse, demand some other favour that would be impossible to provide without betraying somebody's trust or even his own oath of loyalty. So far, so good, at least on that front.

Linqvist put down the two glasses and resumed his place and continued as if there had been no interruption. 'We could argue our respective neutralities back and forth all night,' he said, 'and we'd both be right. But there's another element as well as General Aiken's activities in the US that is in danger of sending our relationship careering off the tracks. My minister, Mr Gray. Or rather your people's attitude towards him.'

Duggan had seen David Gray, the elderly American representative in Dublin, on a couple of occasions, social or ceremonial, but had never heard him speak. He knew, however, that Gray was seen as pro-British, too friendly with some of the landed families and some opposition figures, and too impatient with Ireland's neutrality.

'OK,' Linqvist said, as if Duggan had made a point, 'he's not the most diplomatic of diplomats. But it'd be a big mistake to dismiss his views because you don't like them. Or because you think he spends too much time with some West Britons. Or that he owes his position only to the fact that his wife and Mrs Roosevelt are family.

'He and the president are completely at one in their view of what this war is about. It's about the future of our democracies. It's not an arm-wrestle between rival empires, as some people here seem to think. The president has no interest, none, in maintaining the British Empire, and if our side wins you'll see that empire fade away. You can take anything Mr Gray says on these matters as if it came direct from the president's mouth.'

'Why are you telling me this?'

'Because I fear our bosses are not listening to each other any more. That they're digging themselves into entrenched positions which won't do either of our countries any good.'

'I don't see there's much I can do.'

'It's important that there are people in the system who can talk to each other like this,' Linqvist said, waving a hand to encompass their surroundings. 'Without all the protocol of formal meetings, notes, memorandums, demarches and all that diplomatic paraphernalia.'

'As we're speaking plainly,' Duggan said, 'you should know that our people are very upset at this reward you're offering for the recovery of the Norden bombsight.'

'That,' Linqvist sighed and took a drink from his glass. 'Yeah.' He put the glass back on the table. 'That was a fuck-up. Not our idea. An air-force general insisted on it.'

Duggan gave him a sceptical look.

'Yeah,' Linqvist repeated. 'I was down in Mayo with Mr Gray. We got a call from a Republican senator who'd been contacted by an air-force general from his state, complaining that we weren't making any effort to recover this secret weapon. So he insisted that we offer a reward to get it back as fast as possible. I know,' he held up a hand to stop Duggan saying what he thought he was thinking, 'stupid idea. But Mr Gray agreed, mainly to get this guy off the phone and off his back. So I did it.'

'Why didn't you tell us about it in the first place?'

'Because it was supposed to be a secret. The thing itself. And the fact that it was on that plane.'

'Was it going to the North?'

'No. To England. To show to someone there.'

'What's so secret about it?'

'Its accuracy. It can drop a bomb into a pickle barrel from ten thousand feet. Nobody else has anything as accurate as that. The British have given up trying to develop something similar and gone in for blanket-bombing instead. The Germans are playing the same game now, just trying to blitz English cities. Being able to put bombs where you want them to go is a big advantage. Damn thing cost a fortune to develop, apparently. A couple of hundred million dollars.'

'Have you got it back yet?' Duggan asked, thinking of the box in McClure's office: it didn't look like a hundred million dollars.

'What we've got is a switchboard going crazy. People telling us who might be hiding it and people wanting to know exactly how much the reward is before they say anything else.'

'How much is it?'

'You got it?'

'Depends on the reward,' Duggan laughed.

'Five hundred dollars.'

A hundred pounds or a bit more, Duggan thought. Not bad. 'Not enough,' he smiled. 'Aren't you worried the Germans are going to hear about it?'

'What Germans? You guys swear they're all locked up.'

'Their legation is bound to hear of it.'

'So what? They can't communicate with Berlin. Isn't that what you tell us?'

'As far as we know.'

'So they have a radio?'

'I don't honestly know for sure,' Duggan said, stretching the truth. G2 knew the Germans did have a radio transmitter in their legation but were using it sparingly after protests from the government. Still, it was a constant cause of complaint by the British, although they also had a radio transmitter in their offices – more than one.

'Another thing that bugs Mr Gray,' Linqvist said, as if he was running through a mental checklist. He's not acting on his own initiative here, Duggan thought. But then he had never expected that he was, wondering if Linqvist's superiors, whoever they were, knew about Gerda too. 'Your government's complaints about being blockaded by both sides. It's not just General Aiken who's been complaining about it, but Mr de Valera too.'

'The blockades are hitting us hard,' Duggan said, remembering what he'd been told about Aiken's meeting with the Portuguese dictator Salazar, in which they'd agreed that the neutrals were bearing the cost of the war because of the blockades.

'But they're not equal. The Germans have sunk some of your ships. The British haven't sunk any, have they? And they're carrying most of your supplies on their convoys.'

'But cutting back on them.'

'Because of their losses on the Atlantic. If they really blockaded Ireland, you'd be in a very bad way. The Germans aren't providing you with any supplies at all, are they? How would you have got to Lisbon if the British were blockading you completely?'

Duggan nodded, conceding the point. He forbore from adding that both the Luftwaffe and the RAF had taken a look at his ship and let them through, more interested in whether Linqvist was leading up to something about his visit to Lisbon.

But the American wasn't. 'It's a bugbear with him, with Mr Gray,' he said. 'The way your people carry on as if there was this equality between the belligerents in everything from their war aims to their treatment of Ireland.'

'It's the only way to be neutral.'

'President Roosevelt has found another way.'

'America's a long way away and it's very powerful. The Germans obviously don't want to draw you into the conflict.'

Linqvist took a long drink of his Guinness. 'As I say,' he put down the glass, 'we could argue about neutrality all day and neither of us would be wrong.'

'True enough,' Duggan said, finishing his drink as well. He took the electrical diagrams he had got in Mayo from his inside pocket and handed them across the table. 'You might want these back. Turned up in Mayo recently.'

Linqvist unfolded them, examined both sides of the sheets, and looked up. 'What are they?'

'I don't know,' Duggan said. 'Somebody found them near the crash site, apparently.'

Linqvist looked at them again and shrugged. 'Don't mean anything to me.'

'We thought it might be part of a manual. Maybe to do with your secret bombsight.'

'Could be.' Linqvist pursed his lips. 'Can I keep them?'

'Sure,' Duggan said, satisfied that he really knew no more about them than he himself did. Less, actually. If they were part of some missing intelligence report about German weapons systems, Linqvist certainly didn't know about it. Which meant they probably weren't.

'Thanks.' Linqvist folded the documents and put them in his pocket. 'Appreciate it.'

'This isn't going to improve Ó Murchú's or External Affairs' humour,' Commandant McClure said as he read quickly through Duggan's report on his conversation with Linqvist.

'It wasn't what I was expecting,' Duggan said. 'All politics.'

'Interesting.' McClure finished reading and dropped the

typed report on his desk. 'He doesn't seemed very pushed about his missing bombsight.'

'I brought up the bombsight, not him.'

'You believe his story about offering the reward?'

Duggan shrugged. 'It doesn't sound likely. But politicians don't always do things that are likely. Or even make sense.'

'You're speaking from experience,' McClure said, giving him a knowing grin.

Duggan nodded, wondering how much McClure knew about his dealings with his politician uncle. Not too much, he hoped. But that was all water under the bridge. In the past. His uncle Timmy had left him alone recently. Which was a surprise, but a welcome one.

'We better send a copy around to Mr Ó Murchú,' McClure said. 'He'll be intrigued that they're setting up another channel of communication. Intrigued, but not delighted.'

'I want to have a look at this again.' Duggan took the Norden bombsight box from the corner where it rested and turned it around to see the stencilled print on it. It said 'Unit Bombsight; Model M-9'; the space for a serial number was empty. There was no mention of Norden. Was an M-9 a Norden? Or was this some other bombsight? 'It doesn't say that this is a Norden.'

'What are you getting at?'

'Maybe it's not a Norden, but some kind of standard bombsight. And they're only pretending that it's the secret one.'

'Why would they do that?'

'I don't know,' Duggan admitted. 'But there's something funny about this whole business.'

McClure rubbed his eyes with his thumb and forefinger, pinching his nose. 'For all we know, an M-9 bombsight is a Norden. See if the Air Corps knows its technical description.'

'OK,' Duggan said, making for the door.

'Meanwhile,' McClure stopped him, 'open a bank account and tell your German friends how much the Yanks are offering for their bombsight.'

'We're going ahead with it?' Duggan asked in surprise.

'We are,' McClure said.

Duggan waited, but McClure offered nothing more. 'Any bank in particular?' he asked, in the hope of drawing him out.

'Any busy city-centre branch will do.'

Back in his own office, Duggan drafted a message in German for transmission, wondering about McClure's change of mind about going ahead with the deception. It's not a change of heart, he decided; it's a decision from higher up. He knew McClure well enough by now to know when he wasn't happy about something, and his whole demeanour said he was not happy about this. Which meant it was someone else's decision to continue with the Sean McCarthy mission.

He paused for a moment over the name on the bank account, deciding it should be something random but credible, and settled on Amárach Trading. He got the phone directory, looked up branches of the National Bank and picked one in Dame Street. He was almost finished coding the German message when the phone rang.

'Fancy a little action?' Garda Peter Gifford asked.

'What kind?'

'We're putting a posse together to chase down some baddies who're hiding some loot they got from a crashed plane.'

'From our crashed plane?'

'Uh-huh,' Gifford said. 'According to information received.'

'From anyone I know?'

'Uh-huh.'

Benny Reilly, the black-marketeeer they had visited,

Duggan thought, his interest quickening. 'Where?'

'The badlands outside town.'

'When?'

'An hour or so. After we've watered the horses.'

'Count me in.'

'Bring your own horse.'

Duggan hung up and took his Sean McCarthy passport from the drawer of his desk. He should have time to get to the bank and set up the account before meeting Gifford in Dublin Castle. He turned back at the door, reopened the drawer and took out his Webley revolver in its shoulder holster and a box of shells.

Twelve

Duggan drove fast to keep up with the convoy of Special Branch cars heading out through Donnybrook towards Bray. The road twisted and turned, the traffic of bicycles and carts and occasional cars and buses tailing off after they climbed up past the posh new houses of Mount Merrion and went through Stillorgan out into the countryside. Fields opened out on either side of the road, some with cattle swishing their tails to keep the flies away, others with ripening crops of oats and barley.

Duggan had no idea where they were going. Gifford had only had time to tell him 'Rathmichael' before the convoy had swept out of Dublin Castle, but Duggan had no idea where that was. Gifford's sergeant had snapped, 'You again,' when he'd seen Duggan, as if that was a bad omen, and had got into the front car, with Gifford driving. Two other cars with four detectives in each had followed them. Duggan had brought up the rear in his car.

A group of men lounging against a corner in Cabinteely watched them go by, their cigarettes paused in various stages of smoking. Just before Shankill, they turned right and went by some large houses half hidden behind heavy foliage among fields rising uphill. The last car of Branch men stopped at a gateway and Duggan overtook it as the detectives piled out and climbed the gate. The lead car stopped at the next gate-way and the second overtook it and turned into a laneway a little further on.

Duggan pulled in behind the lead car as one of the men in the back got out and opened a gate into a farmyard. He followed the car in and they all got out. In front of them was a large barn, one of its big doors open, sounds of movement coming from inside. The detectives all drew their revolvers, cocked the hammers. Duggan followed their example but left his hammer down.

'Police!' the sergeant shouted as they took up positions on both sides of the door. 'Identify yourself and come out.'

There was no response.

Away to the left, Duggan saw the detectives from the sec-ond car coming over a barbed-wire fence and beginning to run towards the back of the barn, dodging around cocks of golden hay. He assumed the men from the third car were moving in from the other side as well.

There was a shuffling sound from inside.

'Come on out,' the sergeant shouted again. 'This is the Gardaí.'

A horse neighed inside. One of the detectives laughed and another moved up to the open door and glanced inside. A moment later, he went in, leading with his revolver and shouting, 'Hello, anybody here?'

There was nobody there. They all went in and looked around. On one side there were three stalls, one occupied by the horse, which stared back at them over a half-door. Beside the stalls, a sidecar rested on its shafts, harnesses hung on the wall, and other agricultural implements were lined up. The other side of the barn was mainly empty, a scattering of hay on the ground indicating where the new hay was going to be when it was moved in from the fields.

They all put their guns away and began to look around.

One man climbed the ladder at the side of the stalls to see what was above them. He reappeared a moment later and shook his head to the sergeant. Another walked over the empty floor, kicking the thin layer of hay out of his way like a child walking through autumnal leaves. A third took up a stub-pronged hay fork, went into the unoccupied stalls and began to prod the floor through the straw.

Some of the other detectives arrived at the door and one of them shook his head to the sergeant, who turned to Gifford.

'Sorry, Sarge,' Gifford said, giving a helpless shrug. 'Fucker must've been lying.'

The sergeant gave him a murderous look and marched to the door as the others began to follow. One of them went over to the horse and patted its forehead. The horse stepped back, away from his touch. 'Hold on!' the detective shouted after the others, who were going out the open door. 'Did you hear that?'

'What?' the sergeant asked, stopping.

'The horse just stepped on wood. Sounded hollow.'

The sergeant turned back. 'Get him out of there,' he ordered.

The detective got a halter from the wall, put it over the horse's head, and led it into one of the other stalls. Another retrieved the hay fork and began to prod the straw where the horse had been, until he found the area that sounded hollow. He cleared away the dirty straw and revealed a trapdoor. He pulled it up and there was a ladder leading down into the dark.

'Torches,' the sergeant snapped. One of the men ran back to their car and returned a couple of minutes later with two torches. Three of the detectives descended into the hole and everyone waited. One of them popped his head back up and said, 'You got to see this, Sarge.'

The sergeant disappeared through the trapdoor. Duggan caught Gifford's eye and Gifford began whistling a vague tune. One of his colleagues punched him in the arm and said in a low voice, 'You've just avoided an almighty root up the arse from a size-twelve boot.' Gifford gave him an unconcerned grin.

A detective reappeared from the trapdoor and said to Gifford, 'He wants you.' He pointed at Duggan and added, 'You too.'

Duggan followed Gifford down the ladder, through a strong smell of horse manure and into a low-ceilinged area the size of a modest living room. In the centre was a table with an oil lamp. A detective had just lit it and was adjusting the wick. Around the walls were shelves that looked like those of a well-stocked shop, laden with bottles of whiskey and other spirits, stacked packs of cigarettes, sides of bacon, large bags of sugar and boxes of tea. On the table beside the oil lamp was a weighing scales with a couple of weights stacked beside it. Grains of sugar and tea lined the joins between the rough planks of the table.

'I don't see any machine guns,' the sergeant snapped at Gifford.

Gifford walked around, opening the tops of some sacks under the shelves.

'Well?' the sergeant demanded.

Gifford gave him his perplexed look and shook his head as if he couldn't understand what had happened.

'Who was this informant?'

'He wouldn't give his name,' Gifford said. 'Said he'd heard we were looking for some machine guns off an American plane and we should have a look here. In this barn.'

'What are these machine guns?' the sergeant asked, turning to Duggan.

'There's normally up to half a dozen on a Flying Fortress,' Duggan said, backing up Gifford with a statement of fact intended to deceive. 'But there was nothing there by the time we got to the crash scene. A whole lot of stuff had gone missing.' He caught sight of a couple of bottles of Jim Beam and went over to the shelf and took one off. 'Like this. Whiskey. Cigarettes. Exotic foods. As well as the weapons.' He began to walk around the room, examining the shelves more closely, and found two red cartons of Pall Mall cigarettes. 'Like these,' he pointed at the cigarettes. 'Looks like some of the stuff from the plane is definitely here.'

'But no guns.' The sergeant made it an accusation.

'Whoever owns this knows more about what came off that plane,' Duggan offered.

The sergeant gave an uninterested sigh and said to his other man, 'Get the locals up here to guard this place. And find out who owns it.' The detective nodded and went up the ladder. 'He didn't tell you that, did he?' the sergeant asked Gifford.

'No, Sarge. Just gave me directions here,' Gifford said. 'Very good directions.'

The sergeant reached for a bottle of Powers, pulled the cork out and took a swig of whiskey, glaring at Gifford and then at Duggan as if to dare them to say anything. Duggan turned away and began to walk around the room, examining the shelves in more detail and peering into the sacks of sugar and tea. It was unlikely anything was hidden in them, he thought: their contents were too valuable to be used just to conceal something else.

There was a jumble of rubbish thrown in a corner: strips of brown paper, bits of newspaper that had been used as wrapping, broken bits of wood from a box. Duggan sifted through it with his foot and caught sight of what he thought at first was a magazine. He bent down and pulled it out. What had caught his eye was a cartoon-style drawing of a man with a sledgehammer smashing what looked like an engine, causing springs and washers to fly off it. Then he realised that it was a picture of a man destroying the bombsight in McClure's office.

The page was headed 'Field Inspection and Care' and gave instructions for cleaning and maintaining the bomb-sight. He turned back some of the pages attached and found the cover. It said 'Bombardier's Information File' and was marked 'RESTRICTED'.

Duggan held it up and said, 'This is one of the things we've been looking for.' The sergeant looked less than impressed and took another swig from his bottle. Gifford gave him an aviator's thumbs up. Duggan went back to root-ing in the rubbish but found nothing else of interest.

'Out of here,' the sergeant said. 'We've got real work to be doing.'

He led them up into the barn, still carrying the bottle of whiskey. 'Locals on their way, Sarge,' one of his men said, eyeing the bottle. The sergeant handed it to him and it was passed around among a few of them.

Another detective came in the gate as they were about to get into their cars. 'This place belongs to an old fella called Mannion. He lives up the hill.'

'Pick him up,' the sergeant ordered.

'Bring him to the Castle?'

'No. Leave him with the locals.'

The detective dropped his voice. 'He's an uncle of one of the lads in the CDU.'

The sergeant stopped as he was about to open the front passenger door, and glowered across its roof at Gifford. 'Fuck,' he muttered.

Duggan read through the pages of the bombsight manual, trying to get his head around the complexities of drift knobs, dropping-rate angles and vertical-gyro settings. It didn't make a lot of sense to him, just added up to the fact that aiming a bomb from an aircraft was a difficult business involving a lot of computations to do with wind, speed, altitude and many other factors.

'You like machines,' Commandant McClure said over his shoulder.

Duggan looked up in surprise: he hadn't heard him enter the office. 'Up to a point. It's a complicated business, dropping a bomb into a pickle barrel. Whatever that is.'

'I'm sure it is,' McClure said, with a distinct lack of interest.

'I'm not entirely sure which is the secret part of the Norden,' Duggan said, still wrapped up in what he had been reading. 'We've got the optical unit but there's also a stabiliser and an aircraft control part. They all have to work together, but which is the most important? The secret bit?'

McClure shrugged. 'Let's go for a walk.'

Duggan followed him down the stairs, intrigued. He had already told McClure about the raid on the barn and the first interrogation of the farmer, who said the underground store belonged to his nephew in the Central Detective Unit in Dublin Castle and he knew nothing about its contents. Which had left his interrogators at a loss for further questions.

'You've certainly dropped some kind of bombshell into Dublin Castle,' McClure said as they left the Red House and went by a saluting sentry on to Infirmary Road. 'Left it in a right pickle. I got a call from a super wanting to know why they hadn't been informed about missing machine guns.'

Duggan waited for a reprimand as they crossed the street, went around the corner and headed into the Phoenix Park, McClure setting a fast pace as if they were on a route march. It was late afternoon but the sun was still high in the sky, holding the promise of another long, lazy summer evening.

Over to their left some women sat on the massive steps of the Wellington Monument while a group of small boys chased a football in herd-like fashion, their excited voices carrying on the still air. A cyclist came out of the park whistling, both hands in his pockets, sitting upright as if unconcerned with where the bicycle was taking him.

'It's all right,' McClure said. 'I fudged it, said there were sensitive military issues involved with this plane, and they needn't worry about machine guns being in anybody's hands. And thanked them for raiding the barn, which had produced important intelligence.'

'Thanks,' Duggan said.

'What they're really concerned about of course is the black-market operation running under their noses. They can't pretend they don't know about it any more.'

'No.'

'Was that why you and your Branch friend set it up?'

'No, no,' Duggan said in surprise. 'Not at all. We'd asked a black-marketeer who'd helped us before if anybody was offering American merchandise from the plane for sale.'

'And he saw the chance of wiping out some of his competitors?'

'Possibly,' Duggan admitted, as if the idea was new, though it had already occurred to him that that was exactly what Benny Reilly had done. 'But he did send us to the right place. There were things from the plane there.'

'True enough,' McClure said.

They marched on in silence, turning towards the entrance to the zoo. Two street traders outside it were offering chocolate bars to a couple with four children as they emerged. One of the children tried to hang back but his mother dragged him along.

'This bloody war,' McClure sighed, impervious to his surroundings. 'It doesn't get any easier. Nearly two years of it now and it gets more and more complicated.'

Duggan wasn't sure what he was talking about but said nothing. Although he worked closely with McClure, they had no relationship outside of G2. He knew that the McClures had had their second child, a daughter, in recent months, and was aware in a general way that the commandant had been more tired than usual. Sleepless nights, he had presumed.

'We're getting dragged into it more and more, farther and farther away from strict neutrality,' McClure continued. 'Maybe that's inevitable. And there may be good reasons for it. But it makes our situation increasingly precarious. The odds are still on a German victory and we're playing a dangerous game getting more involved with the British. Albeit under cover.'

McClure stopped at a bench facing down into the valley opposite the zoo and sat down. Duggan sat beside him and they lit cigarettes. Some couples were lying on the side of the hill and four young girls were putting on a private display of Irish dancing in the bandstand below them.

'The British know all about your Lisbon operation,' McClure said.

'How come?'

'We told them,' McClure sighed. 'We had to. They intercepted your radio message to the Germans about the American reward for the Norden. We're getting agitated about it.'

'They broke the Goertz code?'

'We'd given that to them last year when Dr Hayes broke it. So we've had to tell them what's going on.'

'Jesus,' Duggan said, trying to catch up with all the implications of this information. 'They know about the bank account I've set up? Everything?'

'Yes, but not everything,' McClure corrected him. 'They don't know we've got the Norden.'

'But they know the Germans know about it.'

McClure nodded.

'And they'll tell the Americans.'

'Maybe. Maybe not. Everybody likes to keep something up their sleeve.'

They smoked in silence for a moment. 'Anyway, they're very keen that we continue this link with the Germans,' McClure continued.

'Why?'

'For the same reasons we started it. To keep tabs on the Germans' relations with the IRA. And also as a conduit for feeding information to the Germans.'

'They want to use it for their own purposes?'

McClure nodded.

'Like what?'

'I don't know. They probably don't know. Don't have anything specific in mind at the moment.'

'And if the Germans find out we're feeding them British disinformation … ' Duggan let the thought hang like smoke in the still air.

'Yes,' McClure agreed with his unstated conclusion. 'It's risky,' he continued after a moment, 'but there's also a positive side to it. Our close relations with MI5 are a useful balance to some of their politicians' gut instincts. Given a free hand, Churchill would invade and grab the ports in the morning. It's only the military and the security services who're holding him back.'

'He'd have the blessing of the Americans,' Duggan nodded, thinking of his conversation with Linqvist.

'Exactly.' McClure inhaled deeply.

'So we're going to continue with the German operation.'

McClure gave an affirmative grunt.

'What'll we tell the British about the bombsight?'

'Nothing,' McClure said. 'None of their business. Anyway they're not very interested in it. Even dismissive of it.'

'They know about it?'

'They've heard about the American reward but think it's all a bit of a farce.'

'They've got it already?'

'Don't know if they've actually got it or if they've just seen it. But they're throwing cold water on its supposed accuracy. Which may be true, or may be sour grapes because it doesn't fit in with their blanket-bombing strategy.'

McClure dropped his cigarette butt on the grass in front of him and rubbed it into the ground with the toe of his shoe. 'The other thing I want you to do is to cultivate your relationship with Max Linqvist,' he said, still rubbing at the disintegrated end of the cigarette. 'He's obviously keen to open another channel of communications with us, and we should encourage it. For the same reason we keep open the channel with MI5. As a counter-weight to the formal diplomatic channels.'

'I presumed he was acting under his minister's orders.'

'Maybe, or maybe not. He works for the intelligence unit in the State Department and there's every chance he'll be moving to Colonel Donovan's new outfit.'

'What's that?'

'I don't know if it's got a name yet. But Donovan is being appointed coordinator of intelligence by Roosevelt and is setting up a central agency to coordinate all their different units. Probably including the likes of Linqvist.'

'OK,' Duggan said.

'Let him think you're sympathetic to the American position and that you're even prepared to give him some information if necessary.'

That would be even easier than McClure realised, Duggan thought, as Linqvist believes I owe him a big favour. 'Tell him we have the Norden?'

McClure nodded.

'And that the Germans know about it?'

McClure shook his head. He stood up and they continued on their round back to the Red House by the North Circular Road gate to the park. From the zoo came a series of high-pitched shrieks from some jungle animal. Duggan smiled to himself as they passed the Garda headquarters, imagining there was something similar going on in there as news of the raid on the barn went up the chain of command.

'I passed on your message,' Sullivan said when Duggan got back to his office.

'What message?'

Sullivan gave him a pitying look. 'The message you wanted delivered to Max,' he said, as if he was talking to someone on the edge of senility. 'Told Carmel we're very upset that he was holding back important information from us and then spreading it around among the culchies in Mayo.'

'That,' Duggan nodded. 'Thanks.' He'd already told Linqvist, but it was no harm letting him hear it again, and letting him think that he had another line into G2 through gossip from Carmel and Breda.

He sat down and continued reading the bombardier information file, but his mind was elsewhere. McClure clearly wasn't happy with the direction things were taking but was acting under orders. And I agree with him, he thought. It was dangerous to be collaborating too closely with the British. It did have its benefits, as McClure had said, but it would make the maintenance of neutrality much more difficult if the Germans found out. And there was every chance they would find out. How had they known about the Norden?

That was the unanswered question at the centre of this bombsight business that niggled away at him. They must have an agent or informant in a very sensitive position, he thought. It has to be someone in, or close to, the American legation. They were the only ones who knew what was on the Flying Fortress. So it has to be someone with access to their information. Which could only mean someone who works in their legation in the Phoenix Park, or maybe in their consulate in Merrion Square. Or someone who is very close to them.

One of David Gray's Anglo-Irish friends perhaps? Even one of his handful of Irish political confidants? That was unlikely. One of his Anglo-Irish friends was a better bet. It was no secret that some of the British upper classes had a soft spot for Hitler and the order he'd brought to Germany out of the chaos left by the competing political factions in the Weimar Republic. It was unlikely there were any of them in Ireland. Still, it might be worth looking more closely at Gray's associates. Though that was probably not an idea that would be welcomed upstairs.

He scratched his head with both hands in an unconscious attempt to clear his brain, and put the information file in the bottom drawer of his desk.

'When are you going dancing again?' he asked Sullivan.

'Oh, ho,' Sullivan shot back. 'You want another outing with Maura?'

Duggan gave him an embarrassed grin.

'A bird in the hand,' Sullivan chortled. 'Your American pen pal hasn't written in a while.'

'Fuck's sake,' Duggan shot back. 'Can't you answer a simple question?'

He was acutely conscious that the gaps between Gerda's letters had lengthened – as, to be fair, had the gaps between his. Perhaps their relationship wasn't strong enough to survive their separation. He didn't want it to be so but it might be inevitable. And it wasn't helped by the censors and the knowledge that their words were going to be read by faceless bureaucrats. And the fact that he couldn't tell her what he was really doing. Both of which had a dampening effect on any real communication.

'OK, OK,' Sullivan put his hands up in apology. 'Friday night, probably. You want to make it a foursome?'

'Thought it'd be a sixsome?'

'You have a problem with that?'

'No,' Duggan said. 'Not at all. That's fine with me.'

'I'll tell them,' Sullivan said, giving Duggan a shrewd look. 'They'll be delighted.'

Thirteen

Duggan parked the Ford Prefect on Bachelors Walk, just short of O'Connell Bridge and Gifford spotted him and heaved himself upright from the corner he had been lounging against. Duggan locked the car, joined him at the entrance to the laneway leading into North Lotts and looked him up and down.

'No visible marks,' he smiled.

'It's the invisible ones that hurt,' Gifford muttered as they turned into the laneway.

'They give you a hard time?'

'Accused me of allowing myself be manipulated by G2. Imagine the pain of that.'

'That's clearly beyond my imagination,' Duggan laughed.

'Trying to find someone to blame. Like to put it on you fellas if they could.'

'That's ridiculous,' Duggan retorted. 'What about the fella who had all the black-market stuff?'

'He's been suspended. Pending the investigation.'

'Good. They're doing something about it at last.'

'And there's talk of a new super being moved into CDU to clean it up.'

'They finished with you?'

'Gave me a fool's pardon,' Gifford said, sounding affronted.

'Saved you from a bollocking.'

'What about my self-respect?' Gifford shivered in the heavy atmosphere. The morning was cloudy and the air was dense with the stench from the low tide in the Liffey and a smell of smoke. 'To be manipulated by military intelligence. What greater insult could there be?'

'But you know you weren't,' Duggan smiled.

Gifford gave a theatrical sigh. 'My reward for trying to help you navigate the streets without tripping over your own feet.'

They turned into North Lotts, and the smell of smoke deepened. 'Jesus,' Duggan said as they approached the burnt-out shell of Benny Reilly's lock-up garage. The door was gone and the roof had fallen in, sheets of blackened galvanise lying lopsided on the burnt remains of a counter and on the floor. It smelled of burnt timber and petrol or oil and the amal-gam of tobacco and tea and other things that had gone up in smoke.

'Your lads know about this?' Duggan asked as they stared at the ruin.

Gifford shook his head, uncharacteristically silent. He turned around and saw someone watching them from the window of a small printworks on the other side of the lane. He went over and opened the wicket door and stepped inside. Duggan followed as Gifford asked the man what had happened.

'There was a fire,' the man said, as if he was giving them new information. He was standing beside a high Linotype machine and wiping his hands on a rag. An oilcan and a screwdriver lay on the concrete floor at his feet. 'In the mid-dle of the night,' he added.

'What caused it?'

'They didn't tell me. The blessing of God the whole row didn't go up. And that it didn't jump the lane.'

A neat job, Duggan thought. 'Was Benny here this morning?'

'Who?' The man finished wiping his hands and picked up his screwdriver and oilcan.

'Benny Reilly,' Gifford said.

'I didn't see him. He must've left a lamp lighting or something. A rat might've knocked it over.'

'Is that what the firemen said?' Duggan asked.

'They didn't tell me anything.'

They walked away in silence and turned into the lane back towards Bachelors Walk. 'I didn't tell them,' Gifford said in a quiet voice.

'I know you didn't,' Duggan nodded, no doubt in his mind that Gifford hadn't told his superiors that Benny was their informant. 'It is possible that it was an accident, as the man said.'

'Yeah, a rat,' Gifford said in a bitter tone. 'A whole squad of fucking rats.'

They sat into the car. Duggan paused as he was about to start the engine. 'We go and see if Benny's at home?'

'For what? To apologise to him?'

'To see what he knows,' Duggan said. 'He must have known what he was doing when he called you. He knew that barn was a store for the lads in the Castle. It's not like we forced his hand in any way.'

Gifford grunted his agreement.

'And they knew immediately it was him,' Duggan continued as he started the car. 'Didn't waste any time retaliating. There must be something going on between them. Some kind of war.'

'That's just what we need. Another war to add to all the other ones.'

'Benny might be in a more talkative mood now,' Duggan suggested. 'Offer some more information about his rivals, if nothing else.'

'There's that possibility,' Gifford agreed. 'Let's go see.'

Duggan drove across O'Connell Street and past the cinemas on Eden Quay and around the corner at Liberty Hall, keeping pace for a moment with a train crossing the loop line over the Liffey before passing under it. As they approached the North Strand, there were workmen on the roofs of some houses, replacing slates dislodged in the bombing six weeks earlier.

'Have you geniuses worked out what that was about?' Gifford asked Duggan as he watched a glazier fitting a new pane to a broken window.

'Probably an off-course bomber.'

'Nothing to do with the Dublin fire brigade going to help Belfast after the bombs there?'

'Anything's possible,' Duggan shrugged. He'd been at sea and in Lisbon while the bombing was investigated and didn't know much of the ins and outs of the debate about the Germans' motivation. Except that a factor in the Luftwaffe pilot's decision may have been that the city's anti-aircraft batteries had opened fire on the bomber. 'But it was probably a mistake.'

'Some mistake,' Gifford muttered. 'Kill twenty-eight or thirty people for nothing.'

Workmen were clearing piles of rubble from what had once been houses, on both sides of the road where a bomb had caused the most casualties. They were shovelling bricks and mortar into barrows and taking them to waiting carts. Men in hats stood in small groups watching them, and a group of boys played King of the Castle, pushing and pulling each other off another heap of rubble.

They followed a loaded cart slowly up to the brow of the bridge over the Royal Canal and overtook it on the other side.

'Sinead's pregnant,' Gifford said, without warning.

'Jesus,' Duggan breathed, without thinking.

'Unfortunately not,' Gifford said, with a flash of his usual self.

'Since when?' Duggan glanced at him as he overtook two cyclists.

'Not sure. Could be six weeks or more.'

'When did she tell you?'

'Last night.'

'Jesus,' Duggan repeated. Gifford had obviously had a tough twenty-four hours.

'Never rains but it pours.' Gifford gave him a light punch in the shoulder. 'Aren't you going to congratulate me?'

'Yeah. Of course. You're happy about it?'

'Well, the timing isn't ideal. Don't know whether he'll grow up speaking German or English. Or even Irish.'

'What about Sinead?'

'She's worried about her parents. They'll be upset. But the good thing is she doesn't live down there with them in culchie land.'

'You're going to get married?'

'Uh-huh. And guess who the best man's going to be?'

'Really?' Duggan laughed, slowing down on the Clontarf seafront to turn into one of the avenues running inland.

'Who else? We need someone with a shotgun.'

'I can borrow a Lee Enfield.'

'Doesn't have the same ring to it.'

'Give Sinead my congratulations. It's great news.'

'It is,' Gifford agreed. 'This way we get the deed done without any preliminaries.'

'Looks like the deed was done long ago.'

'The formalities then, if you must be pedantic.'

'How soon?'

'As soon as possible. Seems it'll take a few weeks.'

Duggan slowed again to turn right, into a twisting road of new houses, and tried to remember which one was Benny's. It turned out to be easy to identify: his battered white van was parked in the driveway.

A worn woman opened the door to them, and Duggan asked if Benny was in. The woman shook her head.

'Mrs Reilly, is it?' he asked.

She gave a brief nod.

'We're friends of his. Do you know when he'll be back?'

She shook her head again, seemingly determined not to say a word.

'OK,' Duggan said, admitting defeat. 'Tell him we called. We're very sorry about the fire at his place in town.'

She gave no sign that this was or was not news to her, or of any interest one way or the other.

'Thanks,' Duggan said.

Back in the car, Gifford said, 'I don't think we'll see Benny around these parts for a long time to come.'

'You think he's gone? Without the van?'

'If I was him, I'd be gone. Wouldn't you?'

'He has another place out in the country beyond Raheny.'

'Forget it,' Gifford advised. 'He's probably over the border by now. Waiting his chance to go to England. Having wiped out his own operation, along with the opposition's.'

'A Pyrrhic victory,' Duggan agreed.

He drove to the end of the road and circled back down to the seafront and headed towards the city centre.

'He'll be the most extraordinary baby,' Gifford said, as if their conversation about Sinead's pregnancy had not been interrupted. 'For one thing, he'll be born three months old. At least as far as his culchie grandparents are concerned.'

'He?' Duggan queried. 'Maybe he's a she.'

'He's not.'

'You're sure?'

'Sure I'm sure. When was I last wrong?'

'Yesterday,' Duggan reminded him.

'Oh fuck off,' Gifford retorted with mock anger. 'A technicality.'

'That what you told the sarge?'

'You know him. He doesn't do technicalities. Or subtleties.'

The office was empty and there was a letter from Gerda on his desk when he got back. He lit a cigarette and propped his feet up on the desk to read it. It was mainly a travelogue, describing her few days off on Long Island, and the temperature rising in New York and how she was looking forward to her first summer there. He read it twice, finished the cigarette, and straightened up at the desk to write back to her.

He told her about Gifford getting married, but not about Sinead's pregnancy: she had never met either of them but knew of his friendship with them. He was about to tell her that Bill Sullivan was getting married as well, but decided not to. She didn't know Sullivan either, and he didn't want her to think he had marriage on his mind, even if everyone around him suddenly seemed to be doing it.

He finished the letter with some more inconsequential comments, conscious as always that it was likely to be read by censors on both sides of the Atlantic, and careful to make no reference to his work. He put it in an envelope and addressed it and picked up the day's *Irish Times* and propped it against the typewriter. The main headline said that Murmansk had fallen to the Germans and the report said they were now moving on to Leningrad.

Duggan switched to a report about confusion in Washington following a speech by the Secretary of the Navy urging military action against Germany over attacks on American shipping, and President Roosevelt's comments that he still hoped America could stay out of the war. People were mystified about what was in the president's mind, a correspondent wrote. Was he preparing the people for war or was the secretary being insubordinate?

The answer to that was clear, Duggan thought. Roosevelt was preparing public opinion for entering the war.

He opened the paper and began reading an editorial predicting that many people would go cold during the coming winter because of the absence of English coal, even though the government had 30,000 men on the bogs cutting turf. And the coal shortage would mean cuts in electricity and gas as well.

'You busy tonight?' Sullivan asked as he returned from visiting Hermann Goertz in Arbour Hill prison, around the corner.

Duggan shook his head. He had nothing to do at the moment other than wait.

'The girls have changed their minds. They want to go out tonight instead of Friday.'

'Suits me fine.'

Sullivan glanced at the letters beside Duggan's typewriter. 'I hope you're not two-timing Maura,' he said as he went to his place at the end of the table.

'What do you mean?'

'You know what I mean. Carmel and she are very close. I don't want to get caught in some love triangle of yours.'

'A love triangle with letters,' Duggan laughed, wondering not for the first time whether Sullivan's fiancée was as intimately involved with all her friends' and relations' lives as he claimed.

'I hope you're not messing her about.'

'How am I messing her about?' Duggan asked, picking up his letter to Gerda. 'She knows about this. I told her.'

'I know, I know. But you know what women are like.'

'What are they like?'

'They get notions.'

'She thinks it's serious?' Duggan sounded incredulous. 'It's not like that.'

'I know,' Sullivan said, dropping his voice and glancing over Duggan's shoulder to make sure there was no one at the door. 'I know that it's Max you really want to see. You're just using her as an excuse.'

Duggan gave no sign that he was right or wrong.

'That's what I mean about messing her about,' Sullivan continued. 'She's reading something else into it.'

'She said that?'

'No. But that's what's going on in their heads. I know.'

Duggan sighed, knowing that Sullivan was probably right, but not knowing what was going on in his own head. He liked Maura and in other circumstances would certainly have been happy to go out with her. But it felt like he was being disloyal to Gerda. Even though he had no idea if that relationship was going anywhere. Or could go anywhere. Already their letters were becoming more distant, more for-mulaic. Like boats drifting farther apart on unseen currents.

'What do you think of him?' Duggan asked, steering the conversation back towards easier territory. 'Max?'

'He's all right,' Sullivan shrugged. 'Seems a straight guy. Good company.'

'He ever ask you anything about things in the office here?'

Sullivan shook his head.

'About me being in Lisbon?'

'No. That just came up in general conversation. Is he up to something?'

'It's his job to be up to something. But nothing out of the ordinary for a diplomat. As far as I know. Does he talk about the war? Politics?'

'No,' Sullivan said. 'It's purely social.'

'What do you know about his background?'

'He's from one of those states in the middle of America. Minnesota, I think. Second-generation American. His grand-parents went there from Sweden.'

'Both sets?'

'No,' Sullivan said, pausing as he search his memory. 'His mother's background is much more varied. Even some Irish blood there. Some Scandinavian too, I think. And maybe some German and even Indian.'

'He told you that?'

'It just came up one time in general conversation. Said he was a right mongrel.'

'Where was he before he came here?'

'In Washington. This is his first posting abroad.'

Duggan rolled a sheet of paper into his typewriter and started writing a brief note of what Sullivan had told him, stopping at the possibility of a German background. Can he be working both sides? he wondered. Someone had told the Germans about the Norden, and Linqvist had certainly known about the bombsight.

Sullivan watched Duggan for a few moments. 'You're investigating him?'

Duggan shook his head and turned to make sure there was no one behind him. 'He seems to want to talk to me. And we're just making it easy for us to meet. Don't mention it to anyone,' Duggan said, pointing at the ceiling. McClure occasionally lectured everybody about avoiding gossip in the office.

Sullivan nodded his understanding.

'How's Hermann?' Duggan asked him.

Sullivan muttered a curse. 'I'm only sorry you didn't get stuck with him.' Sullivan had been on hand at the German spy's arrest, although Duggan had done most of the work on the case. 'He's worse than a cracked record: the same thing over and over again.'

'And his meeting with Thomsen from the legation?'

'Interesting,' Sullivan said. 'They didn't seem to be too friendly. It was short and all very formal. "How are you?" "How are you being treated?" That sort of stuff. Our man with the ears got the impression there was no love lost between them.'

'That's good.' But not too surprising, Duggan thought. They already knew that relations between Goertz and the German legation were bad, he complaining about their lack of assistance and recognition of his role, and they not wanting to become embroiled in his spying activities, especially his relations with the IRA. 'Nothing that should concern us then?'

'Not a whisper.'

The Phil Murtagh band finished up the quickstep set with a flourish and they all drifted back to their table. 'Thirsty work,' Linqvist said. 'Time for another round.'

'I'll give you a hand,' Duggan offered.

They walked over to the mineral bar and joined the queue.

'We've got what you've been looking for,' Duggan said in a quiet voice as they waited.

'That was quick.' Linqvist glanced at him. 'Unless you've had it all along.'

'It's just been handed in. I'll drop it around to you tomorrow.'

'You want to claim the reward?' Linqvist smiled.

'No. But the Department of Defence might bill you for salvage, custody and delivery charges. Which will come to much more than the reward. How many millions did you say it was worth?'

'I didn't say what it was worth. I said what it cost.'

'Isn't it worth what it cost?'

'Is anything?' Linqvist laughed. 'It'll be a great help to your credit rating in certain quarters.'

'Seems our credit rating with the State Department needs all the help it can get.'

'Don't know if it'll help you there, but it'll help elsewhere.'

Duggan was about to ask where 'elsewhere' was, but they were at the counter. Linqvist ordered a collection of lemonades, oranges and Cidonas. They took three each back to the table.

'You offered to show me the sights,' Maura said to Duggan as they danced later. 'I'd love to drive up into the Wicklow Mountains.'

'There's not much driving going on now. No petrol.'

'Carmel says you have a car all the time.'

'Only for work.' So, Duggan thought, Sullivan's been bitching about me again. McClure's white-haired boy. Able to take a car whenever I want it. No questions asked.

'Oh,' she said, disappointed.

'We could go to Bray or Greystones on the train.'

'I've been there.'

They danced in silence. Peggy Dell was singing 'In Other Words, We're Through'. The lyrics about adding two and two made Duggan wonder if the drive to Wicklow had been some kind of test. I've obviously failed it if it was, he thought. Does that bother me? He didn't know.

'A friend of mine has just got engaged and I was thinking of taking them out to dinner to celebrate,' he said on the spur of the moment. 'Would you like to come along too?'

'When?'

'Nothing's arranged yet.'

'Yes,' she said, moving closer to him. 'I'd love to.'

Fourteen

McClure's office was empty when Duggan went to collect the Norden bombsight, and he debated for a moment whether he should take it without telling him. He was searching for a blank sheet of paper to leave a message when the commandant came in carrying a notepad. Duggan told him he was about to hand the Norden back to the Americans.

'OK,' McClure said. 'The Germans are transferring five hundred pounds into your bank account.'

'What?' Duggan said in surprise. 'How do you know?'

'The British.' McClure sat down and tossed his pad on to the desk. 'Money's not here yet. But the transfer has been ordered through their bank in Zurich.'

'How do they know that?'

'Must have a man in the bank.'

And why are they telling us? Duggan wondered. To impress us with their reach. And to show that they're willing to share information about this conduit to the Germans. That we're not just messengers. But involved in the deception. 'That's not good,' he said.

McClure gave him a quizzical eyebrow.

'They're muscling in on our operation. Turning it into a joint one.'

'It's already that,' McClure corrected him. 'In effect. But we can still close it down at any time. Have Sean McCarthy interned. Break the connection.'

'Five hundred pounds? That's more than two thousand dollars.'

'Exactly. They've obviously got something in mind other than trying to outbid the Americans for the Norden. And we'd like to know what.'

'But we're still giving this back to the Americans?' Duggan asked, pointing at the Norden's box, which he had left on the edge of the desk.

'Yes. And draft a message for the Germans telling them the Americans have got the bombsight back. That their reward paid off. And asking how the IRA can help them at the moment. Any specific intelligence or operational require-ments. Let's see what they're up to, now that this diversion is out of the way.'

Duggan returned to his office with the Norden and phoned the American legation. Linqvist wasn't there but he was told he'd be back in half an hour. He occupied the time writing a message for the Germans and then checked that Linqvist was there and told him he was on his way.

He drove into the Phoenix Park behind an army lorry loaded with turf, and followed it up the main road until it stopped where a huge clamp of turf was beginning to rise more than three feet from its foundation. The Dublin wits had already christened the broad road through the park 'the new bog road'. He continued on up to the Phoenix Monument and turned left into the gateway of the American legation.

He waited while a guard made a call and then told Duggan to follow the driveway up to the main house. Linqvist came out a side door as he parked and walked over to the car, his feet crunching on the gravel. Duggan wound down his window and said, 'There it is,' pointing at the box on the passenger seat.

Linqvist gave the box a cursory glance. 'You have time for a stroll?'

Duggan got out of the car and they walked along the front of the building and around its side, to the ornate gardens behind. The sun was shining but the shadows of passing clouds drifted over the green grass of the lawns and the parkland beyond and the distant Dublin Mountains were a haze of purple. Birds twittered in the hedges, the only sound breaking the silence apart from their footsteps on the path. They could have been in the countryside, miles from any urban area.

'A delicate situation has arisen,' Linqvist said at last.

They kept walking. Duggan said nothing, waiting for him to explain.

'You guys are too efficient,' Linqvist said with a laugh after another few steps. He took another two strides and then a deep breath. 'We were hoping that the Norden would find its way to the Germans.'

Duggan stopped by a manicured hedge and stared at him. Linqvist stopped as well and shrugged. 'I know,' he nodded. 'Our secret weapon. All that. But it's a complicated situation. And what I'm about to tell you is obviously top secret. I'm relying on your discretion.'

Duggan was too surprised to agree or disagree. He took out his cigarette case and automatically offered Linqvist one.

'Yeah, I'll try one,' Linqvist said, seeming glad of the respite. Whatever it is he's going to tell me, he's not happy to have to do it, Duggan thought as he lit their cigarettes. Linqvist inhaled deeply and coughed at the unaccustomed harshness of the Afton.

'People back home think we have this magic bombsight,' he said. 'Drop a bomb into a pickle barrel. Or down Adolf's chimney if we have to. And it's true that it is very accurate.

But only in test conditions. The RAF has tried it out in combat conditions, and it's a different story when you're being shot at and trying to take evasive action and your nerves are stretched to breaking point and all that.'

Duggan nodded. That was all simple enough, but not a reason to give it to the enemy.

'There's another aspect to it as well,' Linqvist said, taking a more cautious drag on his cigarette. 'The secret aspect. The Germans know all about the Norden. Have known about it since before the war started, we think. Thanks to a German who worked for Norden and gave them the original plans a couple of years back.'

'And they've made their own sights the same way,' Duggan said, remembering the Air Corps commandant's insistence that the diagram he had given him was from a Heinkel bombsight. The one he had shown him in his maintenance hangar. Though it didn't look anything like the device in the box on the front seat of his car.

'Yep,' Linqvist nodded. 'They based theirs on the same technology. But that was one of the early models. We've refined it as time's gone on. This one's said to be the latest and much-improved model.'

'And you want to give it to the Germans to show them that American know-how is getting better?' Duggan suggested with a sceptical look.

'Not quite. This particular one has been adapted in ways which should send them down some blind alleys if they try and adopt its changes.'

That makes some sort of sense, Duggan thought.

Linqvist took his time taking another drag and exhaled the smoke in a long stream, like a penitent preparing to confess all. 'That's not all,' he said. 'There's another reason why we want this to fall into their hands in the right way. To trap a German spy ring in the US.'

Numerous thoughts competed for attention in Duggan's brain. Tell me more, one insisted. You don't want to hear any of this, another said. It's sucking us into another complicated conspiracy. You know why he's telling you all this, the darkest one said. To blackmail you into doing something you won't want to do.

'The FBI has been tracking them for a while, building a case,' Linqvist was saying. 'They're mostly German-Americans, members of the Bund, and some others who've kept their heads down. But the Bureau's had difficulties tying them all together and getting a simple narrative that'll show their treachery and convince a jury of solid citizens.'

'Catch them sending the Norden to Germany,' Duggan said as another brick dropped into place. So that was how the Germans had known about the Norden going missing in Ireland before G2 had. They had been told by their American agents that it had been on its way to them on board the Flying Fortress that had crashed.

'Exactly,' Linqvist said. 'One of the crew on board the Flying Fortress was an FBI plant on the fringes of this group. And he'd told them he would smuggle it on to this milk run to England and hand it over to someone there who would take it on to Germany.'

'But it didn't get to England.'

'It ended up in a bog in Mayo.'

'So you've had to abort the operation.'

'The colonel doesn't approve of aborting,' Linqvist said. 'He believes in improvising.'

'Colonel Donovan?'

Linqvist nodded.

'You're working for his new organisation.' Duggan made it a half-question, half-statement.

Linqvist nodded again.

'Does it have a name?'

'Office of Strategic Services.'

'That doesn't mean anything in particular.'

'It's not meant to. It means anything you want it to mean. And the colonel's gung-ho to get going. Firing on all fronts.'

Duggan dropped his cigarette end on the ground and buried it in the gravel. A wisp of smoke emerged from between the pebbles and he watched it until it disappeared. A cloud passed between them and the sun, dulling their surroundings.

'What we want to do,' Linqvist said as he dropped his butt and copied Duggan's action, 'is to get the Norden to the IRA and for them to give it to the Germans.'

Duggan shook his head emphatically. 'My people will never agree to that.'

'Why not?'

'They won't have any truck with the IRA. Certainly won't help them do anything which might increase their credibility with the Germans.'

'Your people don't have to know about it.'

Duggan felt his stomach sink. Here it is at last, he thought. The return for the favour Linqvist had done for Gerda. It had been so long coming he had almost hoped it would never arrive. But he had always known that it would. He turned and began to walk back the way they had come.

Linqvist fell into step beside him. 'All you need to do is identify the right person to give it to. You can do it yourself or I can help.'

'I don't know the right person,' Duggan said. 'I don't have anything to do with them. Know nothing about them.'

'But you can find out.'

'Jesus, Max, it's not like they have a liaison officer for contact with the Germans.'

'Isn't it? I don't know. You know more than I do.'

'I'm sure your Office of Strategic Whatever won't have any difficulty making contact with the IRA. Here or in America.'

'We can't risk that,' Linqvist countered. 'We can't be seen to be involved in any way in getting it to the Germans. We have to appear to be doing our best to stop that happening.'

Duggan kept walking until they got back to the car. He opened the passenger door and stood back to let Linqvist take the Norden. Linqvist made no move to pick it up. 'Listen,' he sighed, 'I really don't want to do this but ... '

'Why don't you just send it on to England?' Duggan interrupted him. 'Give it to whoever was supposed to take it from there.'

'Can't,' Linqvist said. 'For one thing, they'll want to know how it got to them. For another, the contact there has switched sides. A hard-line communist who believed in the Hitler-Stalin pact. He was a German ally when the Flying Fortress left Washington but he's now Adolf's greatest enemy since he invaded Russia.'

Duggan shook his head.

'I had to pull a lot of strings to get Gerda Meier into the US,' Linqvist said with a touch of sorrow. 'For you.'

Duggan stared at him. He hadn't expected that. Hadn't expected that Linqvist would use Gerda herself as a pawn in this game. Had expected a more direct threat to himself. A threat to expose what had happened before Gerda left.

'She could be in trouble if anyone questioned the validity of her visa,' Linqvist added.

'You can't do that,' Duggan said. 'You can't have her sent back here.'

'She's Austrian,' Linqvist said.

Duggan resisted an urge to hit him. Deport a Jew to Austria, to 'Greater Germany'. The bastard.

Linqvist put his hand on the passenger door and pushed it just hard enough to close it without a bang. Duggan let it go.

'I'm sorry,' Linqvist said. 'Really, I am. But Wild Bill doesn't take no for an answer.'

He walked away.

Duggan stopped on his way back to the office, pulling on to the verge just beyond the growing clamp of turf on the park's main road, to calm his anger at Linqvist's threat to Gerda. Two men were up on the back of the army truck, tossing sods into the outline of the clamp, while two others on the ground built up its slanted side. He lit another cigarette and opened the window, letting in the sounds of the sods and the desultory chat of the turf workers.

It's a bluff, he thought. Linqvist or Colonel Donovan couldn't deport Gerda back to Austria. Couldn't send her back into the hands of the Nazis with all that was known about their treatment of the Jews. It'd kill her. Even the threat of being sent back could be enough to make her do something drastic. Even kill herself. Stop being overly dramatic, he told himself. But I know how much she hates them, hates everything German now. Even the language. 'Don't speak German to me again,' she ordered once.

It has to be a bluff.

But in this war the fates of individuals mattered little. Not at all when you thought about the blanket-bombing of civilians. What would one more death be among the many? It was only about one thing: winning. And doing whatever you thought had to be done to win. This case probably wasn't even about convicting some German spies in the US. It could be about staging a show trial to justify American entry into the war. Or at least take another step towards that end.

He rested his head on his hands on the steering wheel, the half-smoked cigarette sticking out between his fingers, and tried to get his thoughts in order. An elderly couple walked by, giving him a curious look.

He moved when the heat of the cigarette reached his fingers, tossed the butt out, and ignored a shout from someone at the clamp of turf about the danger of fire.

What to do? he wondered. He didn't know any current IRA men. But it wouldn't be a problem finding the best person to pass the Norden on to. Gifford would probably know off the top of his head. Or could find out with ease. And they could just give it to them. And no one would be the wiser.

But what if the guards then found it in one of their raids? And there was an almighty stink about it? Questions were asked of the Americans? And the Americans denied that they ever had it? And the finger came to rest on him? That was court-martial territory.

The other option was to report all that Linqvist had said. Except the blackmail threat, of course. His superiors knew nothing of how Gerda had gone to the US. They wouldn't agree to what Linqvist wanted. That would call his bluff. Which I can't afford to risk, he decided.

He closed his eyes and slumped back in the seat, letting his thoughts drift, listening to the workers behind him and the fast clip-clop of a passing trap and children's shouts in the distance. There was only one choice: he had to go back to Lisbon and deliver it himself.

He carried the Norden back into McClure's office and placed it on his desk. McClure leaned back in his chair, folded his arms, and waited for an explanation. Duggan gave it to him, telling him what Linqvist had said, without the threats.

'So this is a decoy duck.' McClure stared at the box when he had finished. 'Designed to lure some game into a trap.'

'Something like that,' Duggan agreed.

'And what did you tell him?'

'I told him we'd never agree to hand it over to the IRA.'

'And how did he think the Germans would get it from Ireland back to Germany? When our friend Dr Goertz, a seasoned spy, failed to find a way to get himself back there for the best part of a year.'

'He didn't say.'

'You didn't ask him?'

'I didn't think of that,' Duggan admitted. 'I was so taken aback by what he told me.'

'Probably on one of those U-boats they think pop up regularly in western bays,' McClure said with a tired voice. 'Fairy tales.'

'You think it's all a fairy tale?'

McClure raised his shoulders in a non-committal shrug and reached for his cigarettes. He tossed one to Duggan and they both lit their own. They smoked in silence for a bit.

'There's one way we can turn this to our advantage,' Duggan said, seizing the opportunity to outline the only way out of his dilemma that he could see. 'Sean McCarthy could give it to the Germans.'

McClure fixed him with an unblinking stare. 'Go back to Lisbon,' he said after a long moment's thought.

'Yes.'

'Too dangerous,' McClure said, shaking his head.

'Think about it,' Duggan said, trying to keep a touch of desperation out of his voice.

'I just have.'

'It's the best chance we'll ever have of convincing the Germans that the McCarthy link is genuine. That this link to the IRA can produce results. Get things done. Carry out whatever they want the IRA to do. Get them to trust us.'

'And what will they think when this German spy ring is rounded up and the Norden is Exhibit A for the prosecution?'

'They can't blame us,' Duggan argued, slipping into his McCarthy role. 'We didn't offer it to them in the first place.

They asked us to find it for them. And we did. That's all we did. It was their own people in America who were fooled. Who fooled them.'

McClure gave a half-nod, accepting the logic of what he was saying.

'And it puts us in the Americans' good books,' Duggan pressed his case. 'At least in the good books of this new ... ' he paused to remember the name, 'Office of Strategic Services that Colonel Donovan's setting up.'

'Linqvist is in it?'

'Yes. And it's in our interest to be friendly with them. To counteract the State Department and the diplomatic bad feeling that's grown up with Mr Aiken's visit.'

McClure raised his hands in a gesture meant to slow him down. 'We keep out of politics,' he warned.

'I know,' Duggan conceded. 'But it's just like our relationship with MI5. A counterweight to what the politicians are doing. You said it yourself.'

'It's very dangerous. We're still not sure the Germans have really bought the McCarthy story. Remember?'

Duggan nodded, noting how McClure had gone from describing it as 'too dangerous' to just 'very dangerous'.

'But they sent us the reward money,' Duggan said. 'A sure sign they have bought it.'

McClure sighed, indicating that he wasn't entirely convinced.

'We've put a lot of time and effort into setting up the German link,' Duggan said, pressing his advantage. He pointed at the ceiling, at their superiors' offices. 'And they want us to maintain it.'

'We don't have to do this to maintain it.'

'No, but we can copper-fasten it with this. Convince the Germans. Secure the link for our own purposes and for the British if they want to use it. And do the Americans a major favour at the same time.'

McClure reached for his ashtray to put out his cigarette. Duggan took a final drag of his and stubbed it out.

'OK,' McClure said. 'Do nothing for the moment. Think about whether you really want to do this. Then I'll put it to the powers that be.'

'It has to be done,' Duggan said with more truth than McClure knew.

'What are you so happy about?' Sullivan demanded when Duggan returned to their office.

'Me?' Duggan asked, unaware of the half smile of relief on his face. There was every chance that McClure would agree to his plan and ensure that Gerda was out of danger. 'It's a lovely sunny day.'

'Bollocks,' Sullivan retorted. 'What was that present I saw you carrying up to the boss's office?'

'Can't tell you,' Duggan said, sitting down at his place and unlocking the drawer of his desk. He took out the message he had prepared for transmission to the Germans. He was about to tear it up and drop it in the burn bag but hesitated. The deal wasn't done yet.

'I know very well what it was,' Sullivan said.

'What?' Duggan looked up with sudden interest.

'A chicken or two. A side of bacon. Couple of pounds of butter.'

'Shit. How did you know?'

'Sucking up to the boss again. And you wouldn't even take Maura for a drive in the country.'

'News travels fast. Does she tell Carmel everything I say?'

'I'd work on that assumption if I were you.'

'And Carmel tells you.'

'Not everything. I only hear the complaints.'

Duggan muttered a curse to himself. This is ridiculous, he thought. Do I want a relationship with someone like that,

who's going to gossip about everything we do? Do I want
to get sucked into Sullivan and his fiancée's circle? It didn't
seem to bother Linqvist, who was already part of it. But that's
another reason now that I don't want any part of it.

'Is it true about your Special Branch friend? He's getting
married?'

Duggan nodded.

'And I thought he was a homo, the way he carries on.'

'And you were wrong.'

'I'm not convinced.'

I can't take Maura to meet Gifford and Sinead, he
thought. Not if she's going to gossip about them, about the
pregnancy and everything. I can't not take her either. That
would cause all sorts of bad feeling.

'Word is that he's caused havoc with the black market,'
Sullivan went on. 'Upset the whole applecart. There's going
to be severe shortages of everything now.'

'Did Carmel tell you that too?'

'No, that's the gossip around town.' Sullivan missed the
edge of sarcasm in Duggan's voice.

'I don't think you can blame it on him. Blame it on the
people who were running the black market.'

'That's not the way things work.'

Duggan nodded, realising that Sullivan was right. Very
often it wasn't the wrongdoers who got the blame, but the
person who exposed them. When nobody wanted them
exposed, wanted the trouble of having to deal with them.
Or in this case, really wanted the safety valve of the black
market disrupted too much. If people couldn't supplement
the rations with a little more now and then, they might turn
hostile towards the powers that be.

Fifteen

'Are you all right?' Duggan asked when he got Gifford on the phone the next morning.

'As right as the day is long,' Gifford said in a cheerful voice.

'Seriously?'

'Well, the day isn't as long as it was a few weeks ago, but it's still long enough.'

'Is that the answer to my question? The dark nights are drawing in. Slowly.'

Gifford laughed. 'You guys think too much. Stretch the metaphors beyond the breaking point. Actually I was about to call you. A snippet of news you'll enjoy.'

'What?'

'Can't tell you over the phone, can I? Real news can only be imparted in person. Out of the side of the mouth. Over a drink.'

Duggan looked at his watch. 'I've time for a quick one.' McClure was at the weekly heads-of-sections meeting with the colonel in charge of G2, putting Duggan's plan to take the Norden to Lisbon to him, and they were due to go to External Affairs for a routine briefing after that.

'Perfect. The Dolphin. Fifteen minutes.'

Duggan debated taking the car – was this work? – but decided he needed some exercise. He cycled fast along the quays, overtaking other cyclists and slow-moving carts. The weather had broken and a seamless layer of grey clouds lay as heavy and dense as a sheet of blotting paper over the city, soaking up its energy. There was hardly any wind and the air was heavy with the smell of roasting malt from the Guinness brewery.

The hotel was quiet; no sign of race-goers today. Gifford was sitting in the lounge and a fresh-faced young waitress was putting two coffees on the table in front of him. 'Here he is now,' he said to her as Duggan approached, as though he had been telling her all about him. 'She's brought us the good stuff,' he added to Duggan. 'I told her you'd need something to stiffen you up.'

The waitress giggled and went away, and they had the lounge all to themselves.

'You'll have to stop that.' Duggan wagged a finger at him. 'Now that you're practically a married man.'

'But who'll brighten their days? You're not ready yet to assume duty, in spite of my best efforts.'

'So, tell me,' Duggan ordered. 'What's the news?'

Gifford tasted his coffee and licked his lips. 'This is good stuff. The stuff you brought back from your travels.'

'Come on,' Duggan said. 'Enough of the build-up.'

'That's it.'

'What's what?'

'The coffee.' Gifford pointed at his cup. 'Taste it. It's the coffee you brought back from Lisbon in your bag of tricks.'

Duggan laughed and dropped two level spoons of sugar into his cup and stirred it. He took a sip and said, 'No, it's not. I'd recognise my coffee anywhere.'

'It is.' Gifford gave him an earnest look. 'Seriously. Traced back from the black-marketeer in Mayo. Sold for premium prices to only the best places in Dublin.'

'Come off it.'

'I'm serious. This is part of what we handed over to that black-marketeer down there. Apparently there's no demand for real coffee in culchie land. All tea-drinkers.'

Duggan took another sip and gave Gifford his most sceptical look. Gifford made the sign of the cross on his chest and said, 'Cross my heart, hope to die.'

Duggan lit a cigarette and studied him for a moment and decided he was telling the truth. 'Why hasn't this place been raided for using black-market goods?'

'And where would the more refined guardians of the peace get a decent cup of coffee then?' Gifford leaned forward with a look of delight on his face. 'But that's not the best part. The best part is the sergeant we met down there who spun us that heart-warming story of the poor publican who couldn't stop himself doing favours for all the decent people of the parish. Remember?'

Duggan nodded.

'The publican was a fairy tale. The sergeant himself controls the black market. Runs everything down there.'

'Fuck's sake.' Duggan couldn't help laughing. 'Is the entire force involved in the black market?'

'Part of the service, you could say. Maintaining law and order by making sure the natives don't get restless if they can't get enough tea and sugar, and that their betters don't get crotchety from lack of caffeine and port.'

Duggan shook his head. 'So all that rigmarole about driving to the town and having us wait in the church while he went off to have a drink with his friendly publican was a charade.'

Gifford nodded. 'Probably had your bombsight thing in the boot of his car all along. Or in some store in the town.'

And acting the country cute whore, Duggan knew, playing with the 'young bucks' from Dublin who thought they were so smart. 'How'd you find out?'

'Part of the questions fired at me over Benny and the barn and all that. Somebody dragged out the report I'd done on our visit to Mayo and wanted to know why I'd commended the sergeant for his assistance with your enquiries. Somebody who already knew about his activities.'

'Have you got through all the questioning?'

'Oh, yeah,' Gifford said with a breezy air. 'Still persona non grata in some quarters. Have to avoid dark alleys and that sort of thing for a while. But fine otherwise.'

'No other repercussions?'

'Our lads don't have a lot of time for the guys in the detective branch. It's like … ' Gifford paused to work out the analogy and then began again. 'Everybody corporate must have an arsehole, and I'm their arsehole. They mightn't like it but they'll protect it because it's their own and they have to. Where would they be without it?'

Duggan laughed. 'I'll remember that. Garda Gifford finally confesses to being an arsehole.'

'A fair cop, your honour.' Gifford bowed his head in submission. 'Nothing but a humble arsehole.'

'Now that we've cleared that up, I was thinking of taking you and Sinead out for a celebratory meal,' Duggan said.

'She'd like that.'

'At the weekend?'

'I'll check with her. Should be all right.'

'OK if I bring someone too?'

'She's back?' Gifford widened his eyes in surprise. He knew the circumstances in which Gerda had left the country.

'No.'

'She's gone?'

'No.'

'She's neither here nor there?'

'I don't know. Something like that.'

'Jaysus, don't start that bewildering culchie talk.'

'She's still in America. But I really don't know whether it's on or off.'

'Distance doesn't make the heart grow fonder?'

'Distance just makes distance.'

'So she won't be coming out with us,' Gifford said with an air of disappointment. 'I'm still dying to meet her.'

'It's someone else.' Duggan told him about Maura.

'Ah, a holiday fling.'

'Something like that.'

'There you go again.'

'I'm confused.'

'That's only to be expected,' Gifford grinned. 'If you will work in that oxymoronic place. You should move to the Garda Síochána if you want a life of clarity.'

McClure sat into the passenger seat of the Prefect and Duggan started the car and drove out of army headquarters on to Infirmary Road. McClure had said nothing about the outcome of his meeting as they'd come downstairs, and Duggan had resisted the temptation to ask what the colonel had decided about him going back to Lisbon.

'Did Sullivan give you something on Goertz?' McClure asked as they leapfrogged all the other traffic. There was scarcely another motor vehicle in sight, only a small van which reminded Duggan of Benny's for a moment, until he realised it was a different make but the same colour and shape.

'It's in the file on the back seat.'

'And you did a summary of your conversation with Linqvist? The first one,' McClure added.

'It's there too.'

'Good.'

The silence stretched out as they crossed the Liffey after the Four Courts and went up the hill by Christchurch.

Duggan finally gave in as they went by St Patrick's Cathedral. 'What did he think?'

'He's still thinking about it,' McClure said, giving him a wan smile.

Duggan hid his disappointment. It wasn't a no but it was far from a yes.

'I put all the points you made to him,' McClure said as they turned into Kevin Street. 'And I put my reservations as well.'

Duggan's heart sank. The colonel was much more likely to take note of the commandant's views than those of a near-neophyte captain.

'I don't think we should try to play in the big league,' McClure expanded. 'We don't have the people, the experience or the range of the big players. The British have been at this a long time. The Germans too. The Americans are new to it but that may make them even more dangerous because they'll be impatient. It's not in our interest to get tangled up in their intrigues.'

Duggan said nothing. It was hard to argue with that.

'But,' McClure added, 'I've already been overruled about letting the British use our link to the Germans. In theory at least.'

Duggan waited for a couple of cyclists to pass on the other side of the road and then pulled across to park in front of the Department of External Affairs on Stephen's Green.

Pól Ó Murchú looked liked he had settled into his new surroundings, grown into the grandeur of the building. He was standing at the window when they were announced, staring at the heavy foliage of the trees in the park, his hands clasped behind his back. 'Gentlemen,' he said without turning around. 'Make yourselves comfortable.'

McClure placed the file of reports on the neat desk and they took the chairs in front of it. Ó Murchú continued to stare out the window for a few moments and then turned and took his seat. 'What do you have for me?'

'Reports are there, sir,' McClure said. 'No activity on the German front. We're still questioning Dr Goertz and he's being cooperative. There's no indication that they have any other agents here at present. There's also a fuller report of the approach we've had from Mr Linqvist, which I told you about.'

'Yes. The Americans,' Ó Murchú said. He opened the file and flicked to Duggan's report. He scanned it quickly and looked at Duggan. 'He approached you. Any idea why?'

'No, sir,' Duggan lied, surprised at the question. 'Our paths had crossed once or twice. And we'd met socially.'

'We've reason to believe that he's been transferred from the State Department to Colonel Donovan's new intelligence organisation,' McClure added.

'Ah, yes, Colonel Donovan,' Ó Murchú said, his tone implying disapproval, as if Donovan was a black sheep in a relative's family. 'What do you make of him? Of Mr Linqvist?'

'He seems anxious to explain their position to us,' Duggan said. 'To try and improve relations.'

'What does he say about his boss, Mr Gray?'

'That he's very close to President Roosevelt politically. They share the same views and he reports directly to the president. It's not just that he's related to the Roosevelts.'

'And about the way he carries on here?'

Duggan searched his memory. 'I don't think he's said anything about that, sir.'

'I trust you've been putting our position to him.'

'Yes, sir.'

'And is he receptive?'

'He appears to be.'

'Let's hope that he leaves the State Department's attitude behind him in his new organisation,' Ó Murchú sniffed.

'We're confident that this is a very useful channel of communication,' McClure offered. 'Especially as Colonel Donovan is also said to have the ear of the president.'

'You've taken over responsibility for the Americans now as well as for the Germans?' Ó Murchú asked.

'That's the way events have developed, but no formal decision has been taken.'

Ó Murchú flipped the file closed, as if to end the formal discussion. 'The Americans are still causing us more trouble than the belligerents,' he said. 'Dragging their heels about these two ships they promised to sell us. And were announced by the Taoiseach and Mr Aiken. And, for that matter, by President Roosevelt as well. But they keep putting up obstacles. We're not eligible for lend-lease because we're not fighting the Nazis. And the priority is to help those who are, and so on.

'We need those ships. The supply situation is becoming more and more critical. Not to mention the fact that questions will be asked if we don't get them soon, since the announcement was made by the highest levels.'

It'd be a stick for the opposition to beat the government with, Duggan knew, well aware of the political realities behind Ó Murchú's careful phrases. A handful of politicians had already questioned the official depiction of Aiken's visit to America as a success but their accusations had been snuffed out by denials and censorship. The ships were the only tangible evidence of the declared success, and failure to acquire them would undermine the official position.

'Happy with that?' McClure asked as they drove back to the office. 'External Affairs are on your side?'

'I don't think Mr Ó Murchú knows that,' Duggan smiled. But he was indeed happy with the outcome of the meeting. The instruction was clear: use Linqvist to try and get the ships released. And Duggan could now go back to him and offer to get the Norden to the Germans if Linqvist would use his new organisation's influence to speed up delivery of the ships.

'I'll put his views on the table,' McClure said, lighting a cigarette and opening his window.

'Thanks.'

McClure gave him a surprised look, catching the heart-felt relief behind Duggan's words. 'Why are you so keen to go back to Lisbon?'

'I'm not,' Duggan said, aware that he had piqued McClure's interest, maybe even raised a suspicion that there was more to this than met the eye. 'It's a nice city but … '

'But … ' McClure prompted.

'But I've no great desire to go back there. There's a lot of other cities I'd like to see first.'

'Like where?'

'Paris. Rome. Even London.'

'You haven't been to London?'

'No. Have you?'

'London, Paris, yes. And Berlin.'

'Which is best?' Duggan tried to keep the conversation away from awkward questions.

'That's easy,' McClure said. 'Paris. Hard to imagine what it's like now, under German occupation.'

'Maybe I could go and have a look,' Duggan said with a sly smile, his relief at having solved his problem making him almost as light-headed as a rush of nicotine.

'You'll have to wait till the war's over.'

Duggan found it difficult to concentrate, impatience at waiting for the colonel's go-ahead mixed with a sliver of nervousness that the colonel might take McClure's advice – although he was confident he wouldn't. As McClure had admitted, he was in a minority on this issue. Had been overruled already.

He tried to read the main news reports but his mind kept wandering. The French were seeking an end to the fighting with the British in the Middle East, as the British moved on Beirut, and had put armistice proposals to them through the US consul in Turkey. Paris must be a strange place at the moment, he thought, not quite at war, not being bombed like London and Berlin, not at peace either.

His thoughts jumped back to what he needed to do before going to Lisbon. If I'm going. Plan it out, he ordered himself. Think it all through.

He dropped the newspaper on the desk and walked around the office. Better not tell the Germans I'm bringing the Norden to Lisbon, he decided. If I do, the Brits will know about it too. They'll read the radio message. And there's no reason to let them know about it. So I need to draft a radio message that doesn't give anything away.

Should I contact that MI5 man in London, Tom Hopkins, the one who brought me to Holyhead? Might be no harm having a contact in Lisbon if things go wrong there.

He sat down at the typewriter and stared at a blank sheet of paper for a few moments, then typed a brief message to transmit to the Germans. 'Hope to make progress on your request in coming week,' it said. 'Further information will follow.'

He lit a cigarette and stared at the page. That'll do it, he decided. Something like that. Something that the Brits would read as stringing the Germans along. The Germans might even read it the same way but that wouldn't matter. And Linqvist. What do I tell him? He'll want to know who we're giving the Norden to, and how we'll make sure it gets to the Germans. Tell him the truth?

Is there a reason not to? There was every reason not to trust the fucker after his threat to Gerda.

He was still agonising about the nuts and bolts of the operation when McClure came in and looked over his shoulder at what he had typed. 'Jumping the gun,' he said.

'Just trying to tease things out,' Duggan said, his heart sinking. That sounded a little ominous. 'I assume we don't want the British to know about the Norden. If I take it to Lisbon.'

McClure propped himself against the desk. 'They want us to send the Germans a message,' he said.

'The British?'

McClure nodded. 'A message saying that they're increasing their garrison in the North. And that we're moving extra forces to our side of the border.'

Duggan gave him a quizzical look.

'Seems they want the Germans to think they're up to something on the western front. Maybe seizing the opportunity to occupy our ports while the Germans are focused on the eastern front.'

'You want me to send it?'

'You can tack your message on to the end of it. It'll look routine there.'

'Are they really building up their forces in the North?' Duggan asked, thinking this would be a good time for them to actually invade. When the Germans were preoccupied elsewhere and the Americans had given up any semblance of patience with Ireland's neutrality.

'Rotating some units,' McClure said. 'Which will mean a lot of activity on the roads around ports. If the Germans have anyone up there, they'll probably get wind of that. And we'll increase activities in the First Division area, which will probably come to the attention of the German legation.'

'So it'll all confirm our message.'

'That's it. Build up the credibility of your McCarthy character.'

'Don't really need this message to do that if we deliver the Norden to them.'

'But the British don't know about that.'

'They wouldn't be thinking of actually invading, would they?'

'They say not. They'd hardly be telling us if they were.' McClure gave a tired sigh. 'Unless it's a double bluff, of course.'

Duggan shook his head to clear it. Maybe McClure was right: they shouldn't be getting involved in the big boys' games. But he had his own reason for encouraging it, which trumped the general principle for the time being.

'And,' McClure straightened up, 'your visit to Lisbon has been approved. The ship's in port at the moment. Sailing tomorrow.'

'Tomorrow?' Duggan said, taken aback at the suddenness.

'You're in luck.' McClure gave him a faint smile. 'Another twenty-four hours and you'd have missed it. Would have had to wait till the middle of August. Try and get some commitment out of Linqvist about our new ships before you leave.'

Sixteen

Duggan was welcomed on board the ship with surprise. His former cabin-mate, Jenkins, stepped back in astonishment as he saw him step off the gangway. 'Jaysus,' he said, 'never thought I'd see you again in this life.'

'Can't get rid of a bad penny,' Duggan said, shaking his hard hand. 'It was all a mistake. Mistaken identity.'

'There's fellas who've spent their lives in jail over there because of mistaken identities,' Jenkins said, giving him a shrewd look, and casting his eyes over the large square package Duggan had with his kitbag and mentally reconfiguring all that he knew about Sean McCarthy.

'Hope I won't stink up your cabin this time,' Duggan said, to deflect any questions about his miraculous escape from the British police.

'Dermot's not coming?'

Duggan shook his head. The man he was replacing on the crew list hadn't been happy about the last-minute change of plan. A week at home with three small children had left him eager to get back to sea again. G2 had had to pay him for the missed voyage and remind him he could still face spying charges for the messages he had been carrying back and forth to Lisbon for Hermann Goertz before his capture. Not to mention his small-time smuggling operation, which was his ongoing payment from the Germans.

'We haven't got all day to stand around,' the captain called down from the edge of the bridge.

Jenkins went back to work and Duggan climbed up to the bridge and shook hands with the captain. 'Thanks for bringing me along again,' he said.

The captain accepted the thanks with a nod, though it was questionable whether he had a choice.

'They treat you all right over there?' the captain asked.

'It was okay.'

'Part of your mission?'

'Not quite,' Duggan smiled. 'But it worked out okay.' He touched the Norden box with his foot. 'Could you put this somewhere safe for me?'

'Not to be found?'

'Not to be found.'

The captain gave the box a practised look, assessing its size and shape for appropriate hiding places, and wondering what it might be. It looked like a butter box but he doubted that that described its contents.

The ship was tied up at the North Wall, high against the quayside on the full tide. Duggan stayed on the edge of the bridge as the vibrations from the engines increased, and the crew cast off and the vessel moved into the centre of the river. There were few ships in the port, all of them small, and the line of cranes on the quay stood idle. Across the river near the power station a couple of small fishing boats bobbed on the tide.

In the background, Duggan could hear the captain's instructions to the engine room as they went slowly by the port-control naval unit at Alexandra Basin and a small grey patrol boat with angled torpedo tubes on its deck, and then by the Poolbeg lighthouse, and picked up speed as the bay opened out before them. The day was overcast and a light mist was coming up, shrouding the heather and cliffs of Howth, but he stayed where he was, determined to avoid seasickness by remaining in the open as long as possible.

After a while the rain got heavier and the captain opened the door to the bridge to toss him a heavy oilskin. He put it on and left the hood down, letting the rain drench his hair and run down his face. Assuming he could avoid seasickness and that they didn't run into any trouble, he was looking forward to the voyage. It was a good opportunity to get away from the daily routine, and all he had to do was deliver the Norden. Which should make the Germans happy, and placate the Americans and, above all, nullify Linqvist's threat to Gerda's future in the US.

He had met Linqvist the previous afternoon, insisting this time that they meet in the Phoenix Park, outside of the legation, on neutral ground. They sat on the bench overlooking the bandstand, in the hollow where he and McClure had previously rested. Linqvist was his usual pleasant self, as if he had never threatened Gerda. Duggan explained the condition on which he would deliver the Norden to the Germans.

'I don't know anything about the sale of those ships,' Linqvist protested. 'Only what I've read in the papers. The commercial people are handling that.'

'It seems to be more political than commercial,' Duggan said. 'Somebody is blocking it for some reason, even though your president has approved it.'

'I'll ask my minister about it.'

'We don't want to know who's blocking it, or why. We want the blockage removed.'

'I'll see what I can do.'

'It's a condition of doing what you want us to do,' Duggan said. 'That the sale go through.'

'That may be a problem,' Linqvist said, looking concerned. 'Until I find out what's going on. I can't have it resolved until I know what it is.'

'We're not asking that you make enquiries,' Duggan repeated. 'We want the problem resolved. Surely Colonel Donovan can do that.'

Linqvist leaned back against the bench and stretched his legs out in front of him. 'None of this is personal,' he said after a moment, aware of Duggan's hostility.

'You made it personal,' Duggan said, staring down at the empty bandstand. There was nobody around. Even the zoo behind them seemed to be subdued by the dull weather.

'It was a personal favour I did you.'

'But you threatened her, not me.'

'It would've been all right if I'd threatened you?' Linqvist asked, a note of curiosity in his voice.

Duggan nodded. That's what he had expected all along. Nobody did any favours for nothing in this world, he knew.

'That's very chivalrous of you.'

'No, it's not,' Duggan snapped back. 'You could only threaten my career, but threatening to send a Jewish woman back to Austria endangers her very being.'

Linqvist studied his shoes, moving his toes up and down. 'I don't know,' he said. 'I don't necessarily accept everything the Zionists say about the Nazis.'

'If you'd heard her talk about it you'd know how she felt.'

'OK,' Linqvist conceded. 'I'll pull out all the stops. But I'm just a small cog in this machine. I can't guarantee anything.'

'It's all been approved at the highest levels. It just needs some heads lower down to be knocked together.'

'We should be able to do that,' Linqvist said. He didn't explain who 'we' was, but Duggan assumed he meant the Office of Strategic Services. 'I need to know how you're going to do this.'

Duggan was expecting the question. He and McClure had debated how much to tell Linqvist and decided the Americans would want to know everything about the delivery. Otherwise, they couldn't fill in their chain of evidence. 'I'll take it to Lisbon,' he said.

'You have a German contact there,' Linqvist said, nodding to himself at confirmation of what he had suspected.

'Yes.'

'A diplomat?'

'An Abwehr man. Fritz Wiedermeyer.'

The name meant nothing to Linqvist but it should ring some bells when he reported it back. If what Hopkins had told him about Wiedermeyer's status in the Abwehr in Lisbon was true – and he had no reason to doubt it.

'It's an internal security operation,' Duggan added, using the formula McClure and he had worked out to answer the next question the Americans would ask, whether Linqvist actually asked it or not. Why were the Irish in contact with a senior Abwehr man? 'Strictly limited to that. Nothing to do with the wider world.'

Linqvist filed the information away, linking it to the all-consuming Irish obsession with their internal politics. 'When will the delivery take place?'

'I can't say. As soon as possible.' Duggan didn't want to give him any details which would reveal how and when he was getting to Lisbon.

'You'll let me know when it's done?'

Duggan nodded.

'And I'll get working on your ships pronto,' Linqvist said.

They stood up and walked back to the roadway in silence. As they parted, Linqvist said, 'No hard feelings.'

'As long as there are no more threats like that.' Duggan gave him a hard stare.

'There won't be.' Linqvist held out his hand and Duggan shook it. 'We're both on the same side at heart. See you at the dances.'

No, you won't, Duggan had thought as he walked back to the office. He was going to extricate himself from that set, something made easier now by his imminent departure and the fact that Maura's holiday in Dublin was nearing an end. He had told Sullivan he had to go back to Lisbon suddenly, but not why, and asked him to give Maura his apologies. 'Tell her it's the army fucking us around as usual,' he suggested.

Sullivan nodded. It was always easy to blame the brass for their sudden and inexplicable decisions.

'And don't tell Linqvist anything about my movements,' Duggan added.

'No, I won't.' Sullivan sounded hurt at the suggestion.

'He knows I'm going to Lisbon but I don't want him to know how or when, or any details.'

'I can keep my mouth shut,' Sullivan retorted with a hint of anger.

'I know,' Duggan backed off. 'Sorry.'

Then he had phoned Gifford to tell him his invitation to a meal with Sinead would have to be postponed.

'Off on your holliers again,' Gifford sniffed. 'Hope you get the weather.'

'I always get the weather. Guaranteed.'

'Be careful,' Gifford said, picking up the coded message. 'Too much sun can be bad for culchies. Not used to it.'

'I'll stay in the shade.'

'Will you be back in time for the wedding?'

'Have you fixed the date?'

'August some time. Got to do it as soon as possible or she'll be too big to kneel at the altar rails. Embarrass the bridesmaid.'

'And shock the best man.'

'Can't have that,' Gifford snorted. 'Can't have you swooning as well.'

Duggan smiled at the image of them all swooning at the altar rails and the captain opened the door to the bridge and held out a mug of tea and said, 'Are you going to stand there the whole way to Lisbon?'

'Thanks,' Duggan said, taking the mug, stepping inside and opening the oilskin. 'Just trying to acclimatise myself. Get used to the ship.'

'I still have your Frank O'Connor book,' the captain said. 'Meant to send it back to you but never got round to it. It's down in the cabin if you want to come down with me.'

'No hurry,' Duggan said quickly. 'I'd prefer to stay up here for the moment.'

'It's not going anywhere. Bring anything interesting to read this time?'

'No. Didn't have time.'

'You can have a look at my little library. You might find something of interest.'

'Thanks, I'd like that. And if I can do anything useful … '

'You could help the lookout when we get near the minefield. Two sets of eyes are better than one.'

'Sure.' Duggan sipped at the tea, trying to let his body relax into the gentle roll of the ship and not brace himself against the unaccustomed movement.

'We had a few nervous moments outbound on the last voyage. Came close to a mine. Much too close. Drifted by to starboard, less than fifty yards away. Nothing much you can do in that situation. Can't swerve her like a car.'

'Cross your fingers and pray,' the helmsman said.

'Hold your course and hope for the best.'

Duggan stared ahead, scanning for bobbing mines. The surface of the sea was calm, moving in long, slow undulations the colour and texture of freshly poured concrete. Slight squalls ruffled it here and there and heavier showers pockmarked the surface. They had long passed the Kish lightship, Ireland had fallen behind, and nothing was visible ahead through the rain that drifted across their path in bands of greater and lesser density.

'With U-boats and destroyers and planes you have the chance that they will recognise your neutrality,' the captain said. 'But the mine doesn't care who you are. Totally random.'

'How do you cope with the constant tension?' Duggan asked.

'Make your peace with God,' the captain said. 'And leave it all in His hands.'

The helmsman kept his eyes on the sea ahead but Duggan had the impression he didn't share the captain's faith or fatalism. His earlier comment seemed, in retrospect, to have been a description of the captain's attitude rather than one he shared.

'We're bound for Milford Haven this time,' the captain said, as if the previous subject had been exhausted. 'For the navicert and the cargo of coal. I hope there won't be any problems there.' He raised a questioning eyebrow at Duggan behind the helmsman's back.

Duggan shook his head. There shouldn't be any problems for him. McClure and he had debated whether he should take up Hopkins's offer to provide more information about who was who in Lisbon. It would be useful but it could raise questions in British minds about what he was up to, and why there had been no indication in the radio messages of his impending visit. On the other hand, it might provide support for him if things went wrong. In the event, he hadn't had time to contact Hopkins. But there was no reason the British should question his presence on board the ship this time.

There was no hold-up in Milford Haven and they set sail with their new cargo, passing by the trawler moorings in the early dawn light the next morning. A thunderous noise rose up behind and Duggan, standing on deck, thought for a heart-fluttering moment that it was the rolling sound of a heavy bombing raid. But it was a Sunderland flying boat climbing from its base farther up the bay at Pembroke. It passed overhead, engines straining to heave its bulk into the sky, and headed out before them to patrol the Western Approaches.

The morning was overcast again but the cloud base was higher and the day was brighter. The rain had stopped and the air tasted fresh, away from the stench of burnt diesel from the funnel. Duggan had slept well but lightly, waking at the sound of increased activity as the crew rose and made ready to sail. He had got up too and eaten in the galley before the ship cast off, ready to resume his self-appointed position on deck before it got under way.

He scanned the sea ahead with binoculars as they sailed along the south coast of Ireland. They were north of the marked minefield, but they all knew that mines drifted. He saw nothing. There was no sign of any other shipping, only an occasional fishing boat closer to the coast. The radio room plugged the BBC news bulletin on to the bridge and he listened to its reports from the eastern front that the Russians were putting up stiffer resistance than the Germans had expected, even counter-attacking in some places. A German communiqué mentioned the Russians' unconventional methods, almost sounding like a complaint that they weren't playing fair and rolling over before the *blitzkrieg*, but didn't specify what they were.

Maybe that's why it's so quiet here, he thought. All their attention is on Russia. But he knew from the daily reports of the coast-watch stations that that wasn't true. Bodies and wreckage were still washing ashore regularly along the north-west coast: the battle for the Atlantic sea lanes was as fierce as ever.

The voyage continued without incident, the sea swell increasing as they moved out into the Atlantic. The weather held up, a steady south-westerly wind that slowed their progress and brought occasional bands of rain. Duggan felt fine and slowly began to move around the ship, with growing confidence that he had conquered his seasickness. He borrowed a Maurice Walsh novel from the captain's library and sat out some of the showers indoors, immersed in the story of Hugh Forbes and his battles against the Black and Tans during the War of Independence. In the evenings, he joined in a crew game of Twenty-Five, playing cards for pennies.

They turned south when they reached twelve degrees longitude, along the approved route for Lisbon. Two days later, as dusk was settling with the help of a murky mist, there was a shout from the lookout and everybody was called on deck.

'A submarine over there,' the captain said, pointing out to the west. 'Half a mile away or so.'

Duggan peered through the mist and fading light but could see nothing. The ship had its running lights on, floodlights illuminating the word 'Eire' and the tricolour on its side, further hindering their ability to see through the glow around them.

The captain handed Duggan the binoculars and he focused them but could see nothing. They only seemed to make the murk more opaque. Then, as a band of mist drifted away, he caught sight of the long grey shape low on the water. It was parallel to them, in complete darkness, no life visible. He tried to focus on its conning tower to see if there was anybody there but the mist thickened again and the image faded and disappeared.

'What's he doing?' he asked as he handed the binoculars back.

'Probably recharging his batteries,' the captain said, raising the glasses to his eyes. 'Using the bad visibility as an opportunity to surface.'

'I couldn't see any signs of life.'

'They're there all right. On the tower. But nobody near the gun. Far as I can see.'

'Still nothing on the open channel,' the radio officer's voice said through the deck's speaker.

They watched where they thought the U-boat was, waiting for a flash of gunfire from its cannon, and scanned the waters for the second of warning they'd get of a torpedo. Aware of their vulnerability. Aware that their only protection was their lights, which declared them a non-belligerent. And hoping that the submarine commander accepted that at face value.

The thumping of the engine felt like their own heartbeats as they watched and waited in silence as the U-boat headed north and the ship continued its steady course south.

'I think he's gone on his merry way,' the captain said at last, scanning the growing dark to the north-west. He tossed a bunch of keys to the cook. 'We could all do with a drink.'

They reached Lisbon with the dawn, coming in to the mouth of the Tagus on a full tide with a blinding sun rising in a clear blue sky before them. Everyone was up as they went by Cascais and the huge bulk of the now-familiar wooden memorial to the Portuguese explorers, facing the water like the prow of an enormous ship.

The port was busy, the contrast with Dublin all too obvious: Portugal was doing well out of this war. Among the cargo ships a long liner stood out, its name, *Serpa Pinto*, painted in huge white letters along its side, followed by the Portuguese flag and the word 'Portugal'. Some refugees are about to have their wishes come true, Duggan thought as they went by it. Finally escape this savage continent to the Americas or the Portuguese colonies in southern Africa or Asia.

They had to drop anchor in the middle of the estuary, awaiting their turn to get a berth. 'It's going to take hours,' the captain said in frustration, after talking to the port authorities by radio. 'Noon at the earliest. Probably later.'

Duggan propped himself against the cover of the forward hold and tried to finish the Maurice Walsh book. The sun blazed down, but the wind from the ocean kept the temperature bearable. He was too restless to concentrate. He walked around the deck as the ship swung slowly around its anchor with the turning tide. He was anxious to get on with his mission, thinking of what lay ahead, trying to make sure that nothing went wrong. The memory of the two stockbrokers playing cards on the train to Greystones came back to him. How the one player had been certain that his hand was unbeatable. And it would have been nine times out of ten – maybe more. The man had been confident of success until the cards were turned face up and he was beaten, fooled by his own confidence. Don't take anything for granted, he warned himself. Certainly not with the Germans. As McClure had said, they'd been at this game a lot longer than him.

It was late afternoon before they were given a berth and hauled anchor and manoeuvred into the quayside. Duggan watched the operation as they eased in between a

Greek-registered coaster and a larger Panama-registered ship which towered over them.

'Let me know when you want your package,' the captain said as he waited at the top of the gangway for the port officials to come on board.

'It'll be tomorrow at the earliest,' Duggan replied as they watched the uniformed officials approach. He moved away as they came up the gangway and the captain greeted one of them by name.

He had no idea how Strasser would know when the ship was in port. Probably tipped off by someone in Antonio's bar or, more likely, someone in the port offices. No doubt all the rival intelligence services kept an eye on the shipping traffic. But he'd have to spend the night drinking in Antonio's with the rest of the crew just in case.

Seventeen

Duggan made his way up the steep hill into Alfama. A small tram came screeching down around a bend, piercing his headache like chalk squealing on a blackboard. It'd been a late night in spite of his best intentions, which had all dissolved after a few rounds of drinks. He'd taken the cook's hangover cure, forcing it down his protesting throat. It was helping, but a dull headache lingered.

The day was hot. He kept to the shaded side of the streets but sweat was beginning to break out on his forehead from the hangover, the heat and the hill.

Antonio's was a cool and a pleasant contrast to the glaring sun. There was nobody there, only the same woman from before behind the bar. He ordered a coffee and sat down at a table with his back to the wall and a view of the open door and the bright cobbled street beyond.

He took sips of the coffee and the glass of water the woman had brought him, and lit an Afton from his cigarette case. He placed a packet of Gold Flake upright on the table in front of him in case Strasser wanted to go through the whole identification routine again.

Strasser arrived on the dot of eleven and paused in the doorway a moment to adjust his vision to the gloom. He looked around the room, his eyes sweeping over Duggan and then coming back to rest on him. He took off his hat and said, '*Bom dia senhora, um café, por favor,*' to the woman behind the bar as he walked over and sat down opposite Duggan.

'*Senhor* McCarthy,' he said. 'This is a surprise.' And not necessarily a pleasant one, his tone said.

'I brought something you wanted.' Duggan got straight to the point.

'What?'

'Something your people requested.'

Strasser gave him an irritated look but restrained himself. He lit a cigarette while the woman placed a coffee and a glass of water in front of him. He is in a bad mood, Duggan decided, not like the man I met before, who seemed to enjoy his job and find everything amusing. But his bad mood can't have anything to do with me, as he didn't know I'd be here.

'The something that your people requested by radio,' Duggan added, testing whether Strasser knew anything about the Norden. It was probable that he didn't. 'Your colleague knows about it.'

'Where's Dermot?' Strasser demanded. 'Why didn't he come?'

'Because we didn't want to trust this to a messenger,' Duggan said, deciding that Strasser knew nothing about the Norden. 'Your people implied that this was very important for your war effort. And you wanted it as soon as possible.'

'You didn't give him the supplies that we gave you the last time you were here.'

'What?' Duggan asked in surprise. 'He complained to you?'

Strasser nodded, as if it was a serious matter.

Duggan gave a short laugh at Dermot's nerve. 'I handed the cigarettes and coffee over to my quartermaster,' he said in a cold tone. 'I'm sure he put them to better use than Dermot would have.'

'Dermot is a trusted courier.'

Duggan shook his head dismissively. 'Dermot is a small-time smuggler. An opportunist. He has no interest in our struggle.'

'He's trusted by our agent.'

Duggan conceded the point with a nod. 'And a reliable messenger. But that is all. And Dr Goertz cannot get messages to him any more.'

'But you can?'

'Yes,' Duggan said. 'We can.'

'So you could still use Dermot as a messenger.'

'We don't need to. Now that we have a direct radio link.'

Strasser drank his coffee in one gulp and followed it with a deep drag on his cigarette. 'You will tell Dermot we don't need his services any more.'

Duggan hid his surprise. 'OK.'

'We can't go on giving him the supplies we've been giving him, as he is doing nothing in return since Herr Dr Goertz was arrested.'

'I'll explain the situation to him,' Duggan nodded.

Strasser picked up his hat. 'The Metropole Hotel at five o'clock. And if you're coming again, let us know in advance. No times or dates. We'll know when to come here.'

Duggan walked back down the hill, taking his time, thinking about the conversation. It wasn't at all what he had expected. Was it simply that Strasser had come to the meeting just to dismiss Dermot, tying up a loose end? That that was all he had on his mind? A bureaucratic problem? Why are we paying this man who no longer does anything for us? Possibly, he thought. Maybe it upset German sensibilities to pay him for doing nothing.

But the conversation unsettled him. Is there something else going on that I'm missing? What? He had no idea.

He stopped at a small square that overlooked the river and leaned on a railing, staring at the busy stretch of the port below, beneath the tiers of ochre roofs. Two ferries passed each other in midstream, crossing the river. Cranes dipped and rose and the distant crash of heavy materials pouring on to the backs of lorries carried up to where he stood.

We'll have to do something about Dermot, he thought. Can't allow him to come back here. He's obviously disgruntled over losing the booty I brought back. And will be even more pissed off when he finds out he's lost his extra income permanently, especially now that prices are likely to rise because of the clamp-down on the black market. So pissed off that he might even tell the Germans how G2 had blackmailed him and hijacked his route.

He continued down the hill, telling himself not to over-analyse the situation, not to read too much into every little thing. All was still on course to hand over the Norden to Wiedermeyer. What I really want to do in the meantime, he decided, is to go for a swim. To cool down.

He went back to the ship and got his swimming trunks and a towel and asked the captain where he should go.

'Cascais,' he advised. 'Get the train. A couple of nice beaches out there. You'd have seen them on our way in yesterday.'

Duggan followed his directions to the station at Cais do Sodré, following the road he had previously walked to get to the Irish Dominicans' church. He had already decided not to contact any of the people he had previously met. He couldn't keep up his pretence of trying to find out about Mr Aiken's visit now that the minister was back in Ireland. Besides, he already knew as much about it as he was ever likely to pin down.

The train was full of families with the same idea as him. Children shrieked and squabbled as they went along the busy riverfront and left the port activity behind and then sped through the exhibition of Portugal's colonial conquests at Belém. Flags and standards lined the tracks and everybody on Duggan's side stared at the Dome of the Discoveries, a huge half-globe with a band around it of what looked like semi-mythical figures from exotic places. Duggan caught sight as well of a three-masted frigate with a high stern moored beside the monument to the explorers. The passengers on the other side stared at the formal gardens of Imperial Square, stretching back to the rounded arches of Jerónimos Monastery and lined by exhibition buildings on a grand scale, with mock-ups of places from Macau to Brazil.

The families hurried away from the station at Cascais, spreading out to the various beaches. Duggan followed at a more leisurely pace to the nearest one, which was down a long ramp and bookmarked by rock outcrops. It was crowded and the sun sparkled off the sea, making it almost painful to look at it directly. The few shaded areas by one of the rock outcrops were all taken and he found a spot in the centre of the beach, undressed quickly and headed for the water, running quickly over the burning sand.

He dived into the water, the shock of its coolness taking his breath away for a moment, and swam quickly outwards with a steady breaststroke. He turned and trod water for a moment, looking back at the beach and the straggles of children at the water's edge. Then he rolled on to his back and floated with his eyes closed, feeling the waves rise and fall beneath him and the sun beating down on his face.

Afterwards he sat on the beach to dry off, the towel draped over his shoulders as protection against the sun, aware of how quickly his fair skin would burn. Nobody on the beach, as far as he could see, was as pale-skinned as him. He watched a young boy nearby building a castle with intense concentration, patting the sides of the circular cone to smooth it off, racing down to the water with a bucket to try and fill a moat which went dry again in seconds.

He forced himself to get dressed a while later, knowing how easily sunburn could sneak up. The agony would only come later, with raw and blistered skin. He wandered back into the town, recognising all the features of a seaside resort – the amusement arcades, the fairground, the old people on benches with faces up to the warming sun – and stopped at a canopied terrace for lunch. The war seemed further away than ever.

Back at the station he was waiting in a group gathered around a door to board the train when something made him glance towards the back of the train. A man in the group around the next door was staring at him and looked away quickly as Duggan caught his eye. He was about Duggan's height, a head taller than most of the Portuguese women and children around him, and also pale-faced, with sandy brown hair and blue eyes. Probably in his early thirties.

Duggan watched him as they both edged forward, memorising his firm profile, but the man kept his eyes fixed on the door ahead of him, as if getting into the train was his only concern. On board the train, Duggan took an aisle seat facing the carriage behind them.

Probably an American, he decided as the train's whistle blew and it began to edge forward. Or possibly a German, which would be more worrying. The Americans almost have to follow me, he thought, to make sure that I do actually deliver the Norden. In spite of his warning to Sullivan not to tell Linqvist how and when he was going to Lisbon, he knew it wouldn't have taken much effort for Linqvist to find out. The only routes between Ireland and Lisbon were by air, which was controlled by the British and Americans through PanAm, and by ship. And there were few ships on the route. They would have had plenty of time to put arrangements in place while he was on his way, and it would have been very easy to pick him up leaving the docks here in Lisbon.

Duggan cast his mind back over the day, trying to remember if he'd seen anyone like this man earlier, but he was sure he hadn't. He'd been the only pale-skinned person on the beach.

When the train drew into Cais do Sodré station, he walked slowly, not looking back, his towel rolled under his arm like any other casual visitor returning from the seaside. He crossed Duque da Terceira square into Rua do Arsenal, taking the shady side, and came to Largo Corpo Santo. On a sudden impulse, he crossed the road and went into the Irish Dominicans' church, thinking this could be a good opportunity to see if the man was still following him.

It was empty, the air still and heavy with the scent of candle wax. Duggan sat into the last pew, savouring the coolness, wondering if he could go through the sacristy and find another way out. But that would alert his tail that he had spotted him. Do I want to do that? He probably knows already but that would confirm it. And whoever is following me would be more careful the next time. Put someone else on to me.

The sacristan appeared inside the altar rails, glanced down the church and saw Duggan and then looked again as he recognised him. He went up the steps to the altar, took two candleholders, and glanced again at Duggan as he went back the way he had come, carrying the candlesticks like a one-man procession. I should go now, Duggan thought. The tail should be waiting outside, and easy to spot.

But he was still there, enjoying the coolness, when the sacristan reappeared and motioned to Duggan to approach the rails.

'Father Alphonsus wishes to see you,' the sacristan said, opening one side of the small gold gates in the rails for Duggan to step through.

Duggan followed him through the corridor behind the church and into the reception room where he'd waited before. He tried to work out a cover story in case the priest challenged his previous claims. But nothing came to mind. I'll have to stick to my story, brazen it out, he thought, if he spoke to Aiken on his return and challenges me.

'He won't be long,' the sacristan said with a thin smile and a hint of apology as if he was keeping him waiting.

The man's attitude was different: friendly instead of distant, helpful rather than suspicious.

Father Alphonsus's attitude had undergone a similar sea change when he arrived some moments later.

'Something came to my attention after your last visit,' the priest said after they shook hands. 'But I didn't know how to contact you.'

'I was back in Ireland,' Duggan said.

'You were enquiring about people showing an interest in Mr Aiken's talk?'

'Yes.' Duggan braced himself in case the priest was about to say Aiken knew nothing about any researcher from Dublin enquiring into his earlier visit.

'There was a man associated with the British legation who apparently discussed it with one of our parishioners.'

'Yes?' Duggan's interest perked up, overwhelming his relief.

'A Mr Hopkins,' Father Alphonsus said. 'I remember the name because of the poet. You know the poet? 'Glory be to God for dappled things'?'

'Not very well,' Duggan admitted, thinking instead of the MI5 man who'd come to his rescue at Pembroke.

'You should read him. A great poet. A good Catholic.'

Duggan gave a thoughtful nod before trying to get the conversation back on track. 'Did he have a first name? Mr Hopkins?'

'I don't know it.'

'Do you remember what he looked like?'

'I've never laid eyes on him,' Father Alphonsus admitted. 'He's an acquaintance of one of our parishioners. And associated with the British legation. Something to do with trade, I believe.'

'Is he still here?'

'I have no idea. The parishioner is involved in business. I suppose they may have some dealings about trade and so on. All those things have become complicated since the war.'

'Is he Irish? This parishioner?'

'I'd rather not say anything about him. It wouldn't be proper. I haven't discussed this matter with him. I came upon this information in a somewhat roundabout fashion,' Father Alphonsus said, shifting uncomfortably, uneasy at how he had learned of Hopkins's dealings with the parishioner.

Duggan decided not to press the matter. 'Thank you very much for the information. It's very helpful.'

'I thought I should tell you if you turned up again.'

'Yes, thanks. It'll be of great use to us.' He clearly didn't meet Aiken on his way back to Ireland, he was thinking.

'I'm delighted, by the way, to hear you're opening a legation here,' the priest said. 'It's badly needed, as I told you the last time.'

'It certainly is,' Duggan agreed. It was news to him that Ireland was opening a legation in Portugal but he suddenly realised that that was why the priest had changed his tune. *Maybe he thinks I was influential in the decision.*

'Will you be staying here then?' Father Alphonsus said, confirming Duggan's conjecture.

'I'd love to,' Duggan said. 'But I'm too far down the pecking order, I'm afraid.'

'I see you're enjoying some of the local amenities,' Father Alphonsus said, nodding at the rolled towel Duggan was still holding in his hand.

'Yes, I had some time off this morning and decided I needed to cool down.'

'This heat takes some time to adjust to,' the priest said, leading him along the corridor and stopping at a door before they reached the sacristy. 'I don't think I would survive the Irish climate now if I had to go back.'

He opened the door on to the side street and Duggan thanked him again and walked back to the right. So, Hopkins just happening to be near Pembroke was a lie, he thought. And what about his interest in understanding Ireland's neutrality? General curiosity? Or, more likely, a belated attempt to understand the background of Aiken's comments. After he'd made a stab at interpreting them himself? And sent his stab back to London for forwarding on to Washington. To make sure that Aiken's mission to get American weapons would fail.

Jesus, he was thinking, as he turned the corner to the front of the church, it was frighteningly easy for people and governments to make big decisions on the basis of badly understood information. Aiken's views on neutrality had none of the subtleties and nuances of Mr de Valera's policy towards the war. Why had the Taoiseach sent him on that mission to America? Duggan wondered again. It never made any sense to send one of the least diplomatic of his ministers.

He had almost forgotten about the man who had followed him on to the train when he saw him standing at the tram stop in the centre of the small square, his eyes on the door of the church. He almost did a double take as he spotted Duggan come around the corner. Duggan hesitated, considering whether to approach him. A Number 28 tram bound for Estrela came from the city centre and stopped between them.

The man had no choice but to get on board, and he remained standing with his back towards Duggan, hanging on to a ceiling strap although there were plenty of empty seats. The tram moved off with a clang of its bell and passed by Duggan, close enough for him to have reached through the open windows and touch him.

Duggan smiled to himself as he walked off in the opposite direction to Rua do Arsenal. Whoever he is, he thought, he's not very good at this. He really fucked that up.

Fritz Wiedermeyer was already sitting at the back of the terrace of the Metropole Hotel in Praça do Rossio when Duggan arrived five minutes early. There was a glass with some clear liquid on the table in front of him.

'*Guten tag*,' he said, holding out his hand as Duggan sat down. '*Wie geht es Ihnen?*'

'Hello.' Duggan shook his hand, pretending he didn't understand the German greeting and wondering why Wiedermeyer kept throwing German phrases into their conversation.

Wiedermeyer raised a finger to a passing waiter, and gave Duggan an enquiring look. 'Beer,' Duggan said to the waiter almost adding '*bitte*'. Be careful, he warned himself again. Be very careful with this man. '*Por favor.*'

'You're learning some Portuguese,' Wiedermeyer said, giving him a faint smile and taking a sip of his drink.

'That was about the extent of it.'

'"Please" is always a useful word,' Wiedermeyer said, seeming very relaxed. Duggan wondered if he made a habit of sitting here with a drink at this time every afternoon, knowing that whoever he met or talked to would be spotted by the British and by PIDE, the Portuguese security agency. And if he did, why did he want to show off his contact with the IRA?

The waiter came back and poured half a bottle of Sagres into a glass. Duggan scanned the area while he did so. Most of the customers on the terrace had their backs to them, facing the square. A steady stream of people passed by on the pavement. He didn't recognise anyone.

On his way here he hadn't bothered trying to spot his tail. If he was a German, he knew where he was going. If he was American, this was what they wanted to see.

The waiter finished and was leaving the bill on the table when Wiedermeyer shook his head. The waiter took it away. So, Duggan thought, he has an account here. Maybe he lives in this hotel.

'You have something for us,' Wiedermeyer said after the waiter had gone, more a statement than a question.

'A Norden bombsight,' Duggan said, raising his glass to him and taking a drink.

Wiedermeyer stared at him, a flicker of surprise in his eyes, and raised his glass to him in what could have been a compliment as well as a response to his own gesture. 'On your ship?' he asked after taking a drink.

Duggan nodded as though he approved of the beer, and put the glass back on the table. Anyone watching would have assumed they were politely toasting each other.

'Who knows it's there?'

'Nobody.'

'Nobody on the ship?'

'No,' Duggan said. 'Only one person knows where it is, but not what it is.'

'What size is it?'

Duggan showed him the rough dimensions with his hands.

'You didn't tell us you were bringing it.'

'Hadn't time. It was all a last-minute rush. We didn't expect to get it as quickly as we did. And then the ship was sailing. It all happened after our last message to you.'

'Somebody else could have sent us a message while you were on your way.'

'We wanted to keep the information about this as tight as possible. You don't want the Americans knowing about it.' Duggan desperately wanted a cigarette but he didn't want to display any sign of nervousness. He had no doubt this had turned into an interrogation, in spite of Wiedermeyer's pleasant tone. In plain sight, on a sunny afternoon, in the midst of women stretching out their coffees and businessmen beginning to arrive for post-work drinks.

'You have security concerns?' Wiedermeyer kept his tone casual.

'We're always concerned about informers,' Duggan said, holding his stare. 'We've had some trouble with loose talk recently. That's why we're trying to keep everything as tight as possible.'

'How much did it cost?'

'Nothing,' Duggan said. 'One of our volunteers heard that a black-marketeer had it. He gave it to us when its importance was pointed out to him. For the cause.'

'You got the money we sent you?'

Duggan shook his head. 'I haven't heard from the bank. We can send it back to you now it's not needed.'

'Leave it there for the moment.'

'OK.' They do have something in mind, Duggan thought. Something they want the IRA to do that'll cost money.

Wiedermeyer took another sip of his drink and put the glass down and ran his finger around the rim. 'Your last message,' he said in the same relaxed, pleasant voice, 'was not true.'

'What?'

'About the British planning to invade southern Ireland. It's not true.'

'That's the information we have. They're increasing their numbers in the North. Why else would they do that?'

Wiedermeyer shook his head as if he was disappointed, and ignored Duggan's question. 'Don't think you can fool us into fighting your battles for you.'

'What do you mean?' Duggan asked, trying to figure out what this sudden change of direction meant. Did the Germans have a source of information about British intentions? Was this why the British wanted that message sent to the Germans? To see how they would react? To confirm their own suspicions?

'You have to fight your own battles,' Wiedermeyer said with an air of patience. 'We will not be fooled into doing that for you.'

'I don't know what you mean,' Duggan protested. 'I thought we're on the same side.'

Wiedermeyer gave a slight nod that signalled little conviction. 'We will not come to your rescue just because you keep telling us that the British are about to reconquer Eire.'

Ah, Duggan realised, the IRA have probably been telling them this since the start of the war and the Germans are fed up hearing it. 'It's the information we have,' he said, letting the words sound lame. 'And the only reason for them to increase their forces in the Six Counties is because they're getting ready to come across the border and invade the South.'

'We will offer any assistance we can when it happens,' Wiedermeyer said, also making it sound less than convincing. Like a ritual restatement of positions that had lost meaning through repetition. 'But first you must do something yourselves. Something more than talk and warnings.'

'It's not easy,' Duggan offered. 'So many of our people have been interned. And confused by Free-State forces sowing dissent and causing confusion through their provocateurs. We're trying to regroup and build up an effective force.'

Wiedermeyer nodded, as if he had heard all that before too. He finished his drink and stood up and shook hands with Duggan. 'We will be in touch,' he said with a slight bow.

Duggan watched him go, threading his way between the tables and heading north towards the Avenida da Liberdade. He lit a cigarette when he had gone from his sight and took a hungry drag. The message was clear, a reassuring one for Ireland. The Germans had no intention of making the first move, however much the IRA might hope. This was probably reassuring for the British, too, he realised. They didn't need to keep half an eye on their back door, could even reduce their numbers in the North. Unless they had something else in mind, of course.

But why wasn't Wiedermeyer more interested in the Norden? He'd showed no interest in it other than some almost polite enquiries after that first flash of surprise. Said nothing about the handover.

Duggan took his time finishing the beer and his cigarette, keeping a close eye on everyone who passed by, and those near him. The terrace was filling up, the waiters moving about faster, their high trays fuller. Nobody paid him any attention. Nobody looked like they were there for any reason other than to meet friends and have a drink.

They arrived at Antonio's in high spirits, all wound up for another night's drinking. Duggan hadn't meant to go along but he'd been persuaded by his card-playing partners. They'd had another few rounds of Twenty-Five on the ship, the pennies moving from one to another, nobody ever seeming to win or lose much in the randomness of the good and bad hands. Then most of them had gone off to their cabins to tidy up and Jenkins had persuaded Duggan to come along to the bar too. He'd had no good reason to explain why he couldn't.

But I'm going to pace it properly tonight, he told himself as they entered. The bar was busy, a layer of smoke already becoming visible along the low ceiling. The guitar player was in his alcove plucking the strings but the notes were lost in the hubbub of conversation. They sidled their way towards the bar in single file and Strasser appeared from somewhere in front of Duggan and indicated that he should follow him.

Duggan turned to go after him and said to Jenkins behind him, 'Be back in a little while.'

'Business is business,' Jenkins said, giving a knowing wink. 'I'll order you a rum.'

'No,' Duggan said, passing him. 'Beer only tonight.'

Strasser, waiting by the door, said, 'We need to talk.'

Duggan nodded, assuming that he meant about delivery of the Norden, and followed him out on to the street. It was dark, and seemed darker now than it had before he'd gone into the bar because of the lights inside. 'There's a place we can talk in private,' Strasser said, leading him downhill.

Duggan thought he heard footsteps fall into place behind him and he realised that this might not be what he thought it was. He didn't look back, thinking, I don't like this. Should I just cut and run? He was fit and fast and could almost certainly outrun Strasser and whoever was behind him, if there was someone behind him. Race them down to the dock gates and through the checkpoint there. But that would blow his cover, put an end to the operation. His thoughts raced while his ears tried to pick out the sounds of footsteps behind him. What if he didn't deliver the Norden? Would Linqvist reactivate his threat against Gerda?

Strasser turned into a narrower street and Duggan stopped. 'Where're we going?' he asked.

'Just here,' Strasser said, stopping at the first door and ringing the bell.

Duggan glanced back the way they had come. A man had stopped about ten yards back. His face was in shadow but Duggan knew from his stance and shape that he wasn't the one who had followed him on the train. He was broader and not as tall.

The door opened while Duggan was still weighing up whether to wait or to run. He followed Strasser inside and the door closed after them, locking out the man behind. They were in a small square area and then a door in front of them was opened by a middle-aged woman with rows of pearls covering the lace top of her high-necked blouse.

Strasser nodded to her and she stepped aside to let them through. They were in a larger room where several girls sat on couches in various states of undress. Some of them stood up as the door opened and began to adopt provocative poses. They stopped and sank back on to the couches when they saw Strasser.

He ignored them and went through a doorway opposite and into a short hall. Duggan followed and waited while Strasser opened the door of the first room off the hallway with a key.

The room was small, made even smaller by the dark red wallpaper and a chaise longue which took up one wall in front of a faded gold-brocade curtain. A small table covered in the same material stood in the centre of the room, a red upholstered chair on either side. Strasser tossed his hat on to the chaise longue and pointed to a chair. Duggan sat down, remembering that the captain had told him on his first visit about the British claims that the Germans ran brothels in this area to gather intelligence from sailors.

Strasser sat down opposite him. 'You lied to me,' he said.

Duggan stared at him, every sense on high alert, not knowing what Strasser was talking about but aware that his response could spring a trap. He shook his head slowly.

'You said you were in contact with Herr Dr Goertz.'

'Yes,' Duggan said, and bowed his head in a gesture of contrition. He knows I'm not Goertz's messenger. A tripwire in the code? Or that trick mention of all being well in Mannheim in the first message? Or something that Henning Thomsen managed to communicate to Goertz without G2's knowledge during one of his visits? 'I should have told you. Our contact with Dr Goertz has been broken but we're confident of restoring it soon.'

Strasser said nothing, waiting for him to explain. Duggan looked him in the eye. 'The prison warder involved was dismissed. But we're trying to re-establish contact through someone else.'

'What's his name?'

'Who?'

'The warder who was arrested.'

'He wasn't arrested,' Duggan said, making it up as he went along. 'He was suspected of carrying messages in and out of the prison. They questioned him but couldn't prove anything, so they just fired him.'

'His name?' Strasser demanded.

'Seamus O Cathain,' Duggan said, staring back at him, unblinking.

'In English?'

'James Kane. But he doesn't use the English version.'

'Where does he live?'

Duggan shrugged. 'I don't know. I can find out.'

'When?'

'When I go back.'

'He's one of yours?'

Duggan shook his head. 'Not a volunteer. Just a man who helps out. Helped out.'

'Why didn't you tell us?'

'It wasn't that important,' Duggan said, looking apologetic. 'Because we've got the direct radio link established now.'

'That link was set up for our agent to communicate with us.'

'We thought Dr Goertz wanted it so you could communicate directly with us. Now that he's not free to act as an intermediary.' Duggan could feel the sweat running down his back and hoped it wasn't going to break out on his face too.

'If you have lost contact with Herr Dr Goertz then he did not code your messages.'

'No,' Duggan agreed. 'He gave us the code.'

'He gave you the code?' Strasser's voice rose with disbelief.

'Yes,' Duggan said, holding his sceptical gaze. 'O Cathain knew he was under suspicion and he told Dr Goertz, and Dr Goertz gave him the code for us. So we could continue communications with you if he was cut off. You know how much work he had put into getting a secure link to you. Even when he was free. He didn't want it to fail now that we've finally managed to establish it.'

Strasser sat back in his chair and studied him while he took out a packet of Lucky Strikes and tapped it on the table. Duggan held his stare, trying to look like he had nothing to fear. Strasser raised the pack to his mouth and withdrew a cigarette with his lips, keeping his eyes on Duggan. After a moment, he offered the pack to Duggan.

'No, thanks,' Duggan said, taking out his cigarette case and selecting an Afton. 'I prefer the Irish ones.'

Strasser lit his cigarette and then leaned across the table with the lighter still lit and put it to the end of Duggan's cigarette. He kept his eyes on Duggan all the time. Duggan managed to stop the cigarette or his hand shaking. Nothing to fear, he kept telling himself. Nothing to fear. I'm telling the truth.

'Thanks,' he nodded as he got the cigarette going and inhaled, grateful for the second time that day for the rush of nicotine. 'The other reason we didn't tell you is because we're sure we'll be able to re-establish contact with Dr Goertz. There's another warder we're talking to. He's a little nervous at the moment but will probably help when things quieten down again.'

Strasser inhaled and exhaled heavily, almost a sigh. 'Keep us informed in future. Of every detail.'

Duggan gave a solemn nod, trying not to let his relief show. 'Yes,' he said. 'Yes, we will.'

They smoked in silence for a time. There was no sound from the rest of the house other than occasional footsteps on the corridor outside. Eventually Duggan asked about arrangements for collecting the package he had brought with him.

'That's being worked out,' Strasser said, finishing his cigarette and standing up. He held the door open for Duggan to leave. 'Take your pick,' he said, flicking his eyes towards the reception room. 'On the house, as you say in English.'

'Thanks,' Duggan said. 'Some other time maybe.'

He stepped out on to the side street and pulled the door closed behind him and took a deep breath of the soft night air. There was no sign of the man who had followed them to the brothel. He thought about going back to the ship but he was too tense to do that. What he needed was a stiff drink. He turned back towards Antonio's, hoping that Jenkins had ignored his instruction and lined up a glass of rum for him.

Eighteen

Duggan had a sleepless night, the dark of the cabin magnifying his worries. Jenkins snored in a drunken stupor in the other bunk, but Duggan felt stone-cold sober. All he had drunk had unknotted the tension in his stomach and calmed the shake in his hand after he had left the brothel. The bar and the banter had stilled his thoughts but they had all rushed back as soon as he lay down in the darkness.

He got up after a while, pulled on his trousers and shirt and went barefooted on deck. The quiet of the city was broken by the barking of dogs and the sounds of a ship being loaded or unloaded somewhere downriver: a dull thudding interspersed with an engine of some kind. He sat down with his back to the ship's bridge, on the river side, and watched the water flow towards the sea with the ebbing tide.

He thought back over his conversations with Strasser and Wiedermeyer. The Germans were clearly suspicious, but was it of him or of the IRA? If it was of the IRA and its capabilities and its usefulness to them, that was fine. But if it was of him, that was a different matter. Was there anything to indicate that they suspected him of double-dealing? Not really. They were suspicious in general. Cautious, maybe. They didn't have proof of anything. Or, if they had, they hadn't shown their hand. If their suspicions were confirmed the consequences could be nasty.

He shivered at the thought and lit a cigarette, aware that he was smoking too much. I have an excuse, he told himself, leaning his head back against the cold metal of the bridge, feeling the slow strain of the ship against its moorings and the creaking of its restricted movements on the tide.

There were so many things that could wrong. Tip their suspicions into certainty. If one of the sailors used their whorehouse and mentioned Duggan's arrest in Pembroke and their surprise at his reappearance. If their legation in Dublin managed to check with Goertz on whether he had given the key to their code to anyone. If any one of many things were to happen to expose the growing pile of lies he was telling them. If, if, if.

Maybe McClure was right, he thought. We shouldn't be playing in this league. Especially when we're not altogether sure what the game is.

Hold your nerve, he told himself. That's all that's required. Believe the cover story. Act like you're telling the truth. Don't over-explain.

He finished his cigarette and flicked the butt over the side. He pulled up his knees and rested his head on his arms and drifted off to sleep.

He woke with a crewman looking down at him and saying, 'Jaysus, I thought we'd got a stowaway there for a minute.'

Duggan yawned as he raised himself up against the wall. 'It was very stuffy inside.'

'You mean Jenkins'd wake the dead with a feed of drink on him,' the crewman laughed. 'Why do you think you got bunked in with him?'

'I know now.' Duggan gave him a rueful grin.

The sun was just above the horizon and he stretched himself and breathed in the fresh air of a new day.

Later the captain took him aside and told him he'd be going ashore for the day if he needed his package.

'You better give it to me then,' Duggan said. He had to give it to the Germans today whether they were ready to receive it or not: the ship was due to sail the next morning.

He waited on deck while the captain went down into the vessel and brought up the Norden. Duggan took it down to his cabin, pulled the clothes from his kitbag and forced the box into it. It was a tight squeeze, and all too obvious that the bag contained a square box. But he had nowhere else to put it. He shoved some dirty clothes back into the bag and pushed it under his bunk, hoping it would be safe there.

I need to get rid of it as soon as possible, he thought. Maybe bring it along to Strasser and just hand it over. Or even leave it at his brothel. But that would raise the Germans' suspicions, if he seemed desperate to get rid of it. On the other hand, he had an excuse: their departure time was fixed.

He checked his watch: it wasn't quite nine o'clock. Another two hours before he could see Strasser in Antonio's. He lay on the bunk but was too restless to stay there. He decided to go for a walk instead, burn off some of the nervous energy created by the tension and uncertainty.

The Greek freighter behind them was casting off as he went by, churning up the filthy water at the dockside as it angled out into the river. Beyond it, bales of some material were being swung by a crane on board another freighter and disappearing into its hold. The port was busy everywhere with trucks and carts being loaded and unloaded.

He emerged from the docks into the expanse of Praça do Comércio and took shelter from the blazing sun under the arcade running along its nearest side. Most of the buildings were offices, interspersed here and there with cafés. A queue of dark-clothed people waited along the wall outside one doorway and Duggan realised when he neared them that they were refugees from German-occupied countries queuing outside a shipping office. Some were old couples, some parents with children, a few on their own. Most of them looked pale and drawn and over-dressed for the climate.

As he went by he thought of Gerda and how wise her father had been to get his family out of Austria in time. And he wondered if any of these people might be her relations who'd been caught in Vienna by the *Anschluss*. Her presence in New York would be a help in getting them American visas.

He came to the end of the arcade and was about to step into the sunshine when a man came around the corner and brushed against him as he went by. Duggan felt the man's hand on his before he registered who he was and, like a newborn baby grasping a finger, he took the piece of paper pressed into his hand without thinking. The man was past him in an instant. Duggan restrained an instinct to turn and look after him. He knew who he was, had recognised him in the brief moment when he registered the face under the hat, the eyes staring straight ahead, not looking at him.

He continued across the tram tracks to Rua Augusta and went under its triumphal arch, heading for the city centre. He hadn't bothered to check if his tail was with him this morning, not caring, as he wasn't going anywhere in particular. But now that Tom Hopkins had made contact with him, he wondered if he was being followed, and if the follower had seen Hopkins pass the note to him. He doubted it. It had happened so fast that anyone not expecting it was unlikely to have noticed it. Unless, of course, his follower the previous day had been one of Hopkins's colleagues, a possibility that hadn't occurred to him before.

He walked up Rua Augusta until he came to its second café, then stopped suddenly and took a seat outside facing back the way he had come. There was no sign of his tail from the previous day.

He ordered a *café branco* and a roll and the waiter brought him a large cup of coffee and a small jug of warm milk. He broke open the round bread roll and buttered it and put a dab of jam on one side. He took his time eating and drinking, all the time wondering what Hopkins was doing here and keeping an eye on the street back to the square. He didn't recognise anyone or see anyone who looked out of place.

When he'd finished eating, he took the note from his pocket and unfolded it. There was a number on it, a telephone number he presumed. Nothing else.

He strolled up the street to Praça do Rossio and went by the Metropole Hotel. A man with a cigar in his mouth and the *Diário de Lisboa* open in his hands sat at a front table, seemingly unaware of the small boy polishing his shoes under his table. He went on into Praça Restauradores, stopping to look at the cinema posters but not recognising any of the stars' names, and up to Avenida da Liberdade.

He went into the post office he had used before and found a row of phone cabins in a corridor. There was a short queue of people waiting ahead of him and he joined the end of it, listening to the rumble of rapid-fire conversations of those on the phones. When his turn came he closed the door tight and dialled the number on the piece of paper.

A woman with a crisp voice said, 'Hello?' He asked to speak to Tom Hopkins, his hand around the mouthpiece to keep the sound down.

'Mr Hopkins is not here at present,' she said. 'Please call back in half an hour.'

He continued his stroll up the avenue, as if he was a visitor seeing the sights. That phone number was no trade office in the British legation, he knew. No query about who was calling. No offer to take a message. The real questions were why Hopkins was here in Lisbon and why he had made contact. And, for that matter, how he knew Duggan was there and how he knew he was walking up that arcade at that time. There was someone else keeping an eye on him.

He tried to figure out if anyone was following him now but it was impossible to know here. The streets were busy and the multiple lanes of traffic were separated by footpaths and the linear park with trees. A tail could be anywhere, easily keeping out of sight even if you knew where to look. He stopped at a news kiosk and joined some other men reading the newspapers pinned on a board at its side. The headlines were about Russia but he couldn't make out much beyond that.

The sports pages, pinned on the other side of the kiosk, had a bigger readership and meant even less to him. He used the kiosk to turn around and go back the way he had come, trying to spot anyone stopping or changing direction, but nobody did anything that called attention to themselves.

He rejoined the queue for the phones in the post office and dialled the number again when his turn came.

'Do you know the Tivoli Hotel?' the same crisp English voice asked.

'Yes.' He had just passed it on the Avenida da Liberdade.

'Go in the main entrance. Walk through the bar and the residents' lounge and go out the door on to the side street. There is a small bar fifty yards down the street on the other side. It has an old sign advertising Sagres beer beside the door. Clear?'

'Yes,' he said. 'When?'

'Now.' She hung up.

He followed the instructions, taking his time, as if he was still meandering around the city without any specific purpose. The terrace of the Tivoli Hotel was beginning to get busy with mid-morning customers, apart from one or two tables occupied by people with the lost air of refugees. Inside, it was quiet, the residents' lounge empty, and he went out the side door on to a narrow street.

The bar was tiny, marked as far as he could see only by a black-and-white aluminium sign nailed to the wall by the door showing a Sagres bottle with the lid off and a slogan saying '*A sede que se deseja*'. There was no one inside except Hopkins.

Duggan sat down beside him on a wooden chair. The place was tiny: there were only two tables, a small bar set into a corner, and faded photos of football teams on the walls. He realised Hopkins was seated at an angle which gave him a view through the single window of the side door to the hotel. 'You like a drink?' he asked, his eyes still on the window. He hadn't looked at Duggan at all.

'No thanks.' There was nothing on the table in front of Hopkins and no sign of a barman. Duggan took out a cigarette and lit it.

'There's a kind of gentlemen's agreement here,' Hopkins said, still watching the window. 'Leave each other alone for the most part. Keep an eye on each other of course. Compete for the favours of the Portuguese. Buy up their wolfram, that sort of thing. But no rough stuff, by and large. Although things can get out of hand now and then. Regrettable excesses of zeal. Usually involving the flash boys of Naval Intelligence. People like that.'

'Somebody's been following me,' Duggan said.

'Now?' Hopkins flicked his eyes from the window to him.

'I don't know. Yesterday. From Cascais.'

'Ah.' Hopkins gave a faint smile as if that was understandable. 'The new boy in town.' He turned his attention to Duggan.

'Me or him?'

'You. Everybody gets interested when some fresh blood comes on the scene.'

'How'd you know I was here?'

'Word gets around,' Hopkins said, giving him a slight grin which could have been an apology, and changing the subject. 'How's Fritz?'

'Gave me a lecture. About how the IRA would have to fight its own battles. The Germans aren't going to be fooled into doing it for them by scare stories about British invasions.'

'That's good news. For both of us.'

Duggan nodded. 'That the answer you wanted from the message we sent them for you?'

'Could be,' Hopkins shrugged. 'But nobody explained to me the purpose of the message. Ours not to reason why, you know.'

'That can be frustrating.'

'Only if you think too much about it,' Hopkins said, as if he was happy being a messenger. Duggan didn't believe it for a moment. 'He doesn't suspect you, does he?'

'I don't think so. But I'm not certain.' Duggan told him about Strasser's questioning and his visit to the brothel.

'Ah, Pausch.' Hopkins nodded, as if this answered a question that had troubled him, 'Heinrich Pausch is the man you call "Strasser". Their whoremaster. Looks like an overgrown schoolboy who can't believe he's been left in charge of the tuck shop.'

Duggan recognised the description of Strasser when he was in a good mood or being pleasant.

'I hope you haven't partaken of any of Herr Pausch's goodies,' Hopkins was saying. 'You might catch more than some poisonous politics.'

'Was that why you wanted to see me?' Duggan kept the question casual, wondering if he should upset this cosy chat, challenge Hopkins about the Aiken speech. If an opening presented itself.

'Concerned about your welfare,' Hopkins replied in kind. 'When you turned up without notice.'

'Should I have told you I was coming?'

'No, of course not. No need.' Hopkins brushed aside the idea, a ludicrous suggestion, with a wave of his hand. 'Just thought we should touch base. And give you the number. In case of any difficulties. Give Belinda a call any time.'

'You think there might be?' Duggan probed.

Hopkins shook his head. 'Unlikely. Live and let live, as I said.'

'Why does Wiedermeyer keeping meeting me at the Metrolpole? So you people can see me?'

Hopkins nodded. 'One of Fritz's little games. Likes to meet innocent civilians there. Ties us up trying to check them out and maybe upsets them if we step on their toes. Now and then he throws in someone who might be of genuine interest to keep us coming back for more. Like Sean McCarthy.'

'Interesting,' Duggan said. 'So the IRA is nothing to them but a minor bait.'

'Precisely,' Hopkins said, giving him a questioning look. 'Unless he's been whispering meaningful somethings in your ear?'

'Only giving me an earful about the IRA having to fight its own battles,' Duggan said.

Hopkins pushed back his chair and they both stood up. Nobody had appeared behind the bar in the time they'd been there. They stepped out into the street. 'I'm in luck,' Hopkins said, raising his hand at a taxi coming down the road. 'Take care. Never hurts to be careful. And call Belinda if you need anything.'

'OK,' Duggan said as the taxi stopped. 'Thanks.'

Hopkins opened the passenger door and told the driver where he was going. The driver didn't catch it and Hopkins sat in, telling the driver again where he was going as he pulled the door shut, raising his voice as he did so. Duggan was walking away and almost stopped in surprise. But he kept going, hoping Hopkins hadn't noticed his hesitation. He recognised that address.

Nineteen

Strasser was waiting for him in Antonio's by the time he got there, slightly out of breath from hurrying. 'Sorry,' he said as he sat down. 'I was wandering around the city and didn't realise how long it would take me to get back here.'

'Sightseeing,' Strasser said as if he was trying out the phrase. 'See any interesting sights?'

'Just wandering about. It's a nice city.'

'They're improving it. A lot of work going on these days.' Strasser was in a pleasant mood this morning, more like Hopkins's description of him than he had been the previous night.

'You been here a long time?' Duggan dared to ask, playing the innocent abroad. The woman came from behind the bar with a coffee and a glass of water for him without being asked.

Strasser had already emptied his small cup. 'Long enough.'

'I'd like to stay longer. But my ship sails tomorrow.' Duggan took a sip of his coffee. 'So I need to deliver the item I brought from Ireland today.'

Strasser studied him with an unblinking stare. Duggan held it for a moment, then turned his attention back to his coffee to avoid creating the impression that he was getting into a competition. 'He hasn't given you any instructions?' Strasser asked at last, his neutral tone failing to conceal his surprise.

Duggan shook his head. Strasser didn't know anything about the Norden, he decided.

'You'll have to ask him.'

'I could leave it for you,' Duggan offered. 'Around the corner. In that house.'

Strasser shook his head. 'You have to ask him.'

'I'm running out of time.'

'Meet him at the usual place this afternoon.'

'Should I bring it with me? That might be the handiest thing to do.'

Strasser shook his head again. 'Talk to him first.' He stood up and left some coins on the table.

'Please tell him I'm running out of time,' Duggan said up to him.

Strasser nodded, picked up his hat and said goodbye to the woman behind the counter.

Duggan sat back in his chair and closed his eyes as a wave of tiredness broke over him. He'd had hardly any sleep and the day already felt long, although it wasn't yet noon. The uncertainty of the last few days, Strasser's suspicions, the man who'd been ineptly tailing him, and trying to figure out Hopkins's game were all taking their toll.

He thought about going back to the ship and lying down for a while but knew that his mind was too active to allow sleep. Maybe he should go back to Cascais or Estoril for another swim, take his mind off all of this. But he knew it wouldn't.

Fresh blood, he thought. The phrase Hopkins had used. That's what I am. Which created a less-than-reassuring image of sharks circling in the water, moving in for the kill. Don't be overly dramatic, he told himself, opening his eyes and lighting a cigarette.

The woman was sitting behind the bar, reading a magazine, and there was no sound in the café, only the distant rumble from the docks and some construction work somewhere, and the occasional grind of a nearby tram slowing its descent down the hill.

Hopkins. His thoughts kept coming back to him. What was he up to? Friendly Hopkins. Helpful to the new kid on the block. Offering assistance if needed. Just call Belinda. Which, he had to admit, was a reassurance. Not feeling completely isolated, completely on his own. No one to back him up if things went very wrong. No legation in which to seek sanctuary.

But Hopkins was clearly a liar behind the pleasantries. He wasn't an occasional visitor to Lisbon as he'd said on their journey through Wales. He hadn't just happened to be near Pembroke when someone was needed to bail Duggan out. And he was the one who'd made sure that Aiken's visit to the US was a disaster. With some assistance from Aiken, of course. He's working a case. And I'm it, thought Duggan. Fresh blood.

But he couldn't see what the operation was. Maybe just to exploit this supposed IRA radio link to feed disinformation to the Germans. Another game, like Wiedermeyer's ploy of afternoon drinks with innocent bystanders. Maybe that's what all the spies spent their time doing in Lisbon. Playing mind games with one another. It was hard to see how any of it could make a difference to the real war. But he wouldn't know, he told himself. He was already long enough in the business to know that small things could mount up and have consequences out of all proportion to their apparent significance. Like the interpretation of Aiken's after-lunch comments.

He stood up and left a couple more coins on the table and said '*Obrigado, senhora*' to the woman and went out into the blinding sunlight.

He climbed up the remainder of the hill of Alfama, walked around the Castelo de São Jorge, continuing his random rambling, followed the tram tracks down the other side through steep narrow streets of faded houses, and found himself in Praça da Figueira, the square beside Rossio. He went on into Rossio and crossed between the cars parked in its centre to the Metropole Hotel, and checked its terrace for Wiedermeyer. There was no sign of him among the lunch crowd. There was one seat free at the back and he took it, ordering something off the chalked slate the harassed waiter handed him.

All around were suited businessmen having lunch. The refugees who usually occupied a few of the tables were absent. The waiter left a plate of large prawns in their shells in front of him and carried three more plates to another table. Duggan stared at the prawns, not sure what to do with them. He tried using the knife and fork to pry off their shells, then gave up and used his fingers instead, but with little more success.

The waiter offered coffee as he took the half-finished plate away, and Duggan nodded. The terrace was beginning to empty out fast as the lunch hour ended. A family speaking French took an empty table close by: the first of the refugees moving in for another afternoon of whiling away the time. Presumably they weren't among the lucky ones with places on the Portuguese liner still in the harbour.

A small grubby boy appeared in front of him and, before Duggan could say no, dropped to his knees and began polishing his shoes. He tried to pull his foot away but the boy had a hold of his heel and wouldn't let go. Duggan gave up and left him to it as the waiter brought his coffee. No one paid any attention to the shoeshine boy; they were almost as common as pigeons seeking pickings among the terrace tables.

The boy stood up and Duggan left a few coins on the table in front of him, not sure how much he should give him. The boy counted them with a serious expression and appeared satisfied. He nodded and smiled and placed a postcard on the table and wandered off. Duggan hadn't noticed that before, hadn't seen the shoeshiners giving their customers postcards, but maybe they did. Part of the trade for some reason.

The card was a black-and-white photo of Praça do Rossio, the same view he had sent Gerda the last time. Maybe I should send her another one, he thought, smiling to himself at an image of her surprise that he was back here. He picked up the card and tapped its side on the table. On the other hand, it had been foolish to send it to her, a breach of security undermining his cover story, never mind what difficulties it could have posed for her if it had stirred suspicions in the mind of some American censor. Even more so if Linqvist were to activate his threat against her.

He turned it over, still in two minds. There was an address, handwritten, in the area for the message: a number on Rua da Condessa.

He looked up quickly to find the shoe-shine boy but there was no sign of him. He scanned the terrace with greater care, to see if he was hidden by any tables, at work on someone else's shoes. He wasn't.

Somebody's been following me all along, he thought. Although Hopkins didn't think so when I met him. Unless, of course, the British are the ones following me. Or did someone pick me up from Antonio's, after meeting Strasser?

Maybe Strasser's henchman from last night? Or was it the Americans?

He looked at the address on the card again. He had no idea where Rua da Condessa was. Not anywhere where he'd been, as far as he knew. The handwriting had the telltale Continental way of writing the number '1' in the address. The Germans, he thought. A new rendezvous for Wiedermeyer. Strasser knew more than he pretended to.

He took his time before leaving the terrace, smoking a cigarette, deciding what to do, and trying to memorise all the faces of likely followers within sight. He had to go back to the ship first, to consult the street map he hadn't bothered bringing with him. He could ask someone for directions but it would be better to work out a route and how he might figure out if anyone followed him.

On board the ship he checked that the Norden was still in his kitbag, tossed out the dirty clothes, and left it out ready to bring with him. This was it, he had decided, the rendezvous that Wiedermeyer had been hinting at. He spread out the street map on his bunk and figured out how to get to Rua da Condessa. It was in Bairro Alto, another of the city's high hills, but an area he hadn't visited before. There were three *elevadors* serving it: it was just a question of which one to use.

He picked the only one he already knew and set off with the kitbag, crossing the open space of Praça do Comércio diagonally. The sun beat down, unhindered by any clouds or buildings, and bounced off the tiles. His shirt was wet with sweat from the heat and the weight of the Norden before he got to the shade of Rua Áurea and went up by its shops and banks to the Santa Justa *elevador* shaft. He joined a short queue, mainly of women with shopping baskets, to wait for the next car up the tower, which looked like six storeys of glassless church windows on top of one another.

This would be ideal to check if he was being followed, he thought. But he didn't mind being followed, if it was the Americans. This was what they wanted to see, the delivery of the Norden to the Germans. It was their own fault if they didn't witness the handover. He'd done nothing to throw them off this time.

But nobody who looked like a tail followed him into the *elevador* car as the operator took his money and shut the metal gates. On top a young couple who looked like they were on their honeymoon, climbed up the circular stairs to the viewing platform, but he followed the old women along the bridge over the canyon of city streets below and past the skeletal ruin of Carmo Convent. They came out into a small dusty square dotted with crabbed trees around an old fountain, and he went by the front of the ruin and a military barracks with striped guard huts outside and into Rua da Condessa.

The houses were high, five storeys, blocking out the sunshine from the narrow street as it climbed away from him around a left-hand bend. The buildings seemed to be holding themselves back from toppling downhill. Some had low doors, hardly five feet high, as if they too were digging in to resist the pull of gravity. Small balconies were draped here and there with drying clothes. He walked up the street's cobbled centre, passing the number he wanted with a sideways glance. It had a front wall of faded blue tiles in a flower pattern and its lower windows were shuttered behind bars. The bland exterior told him nothing.

He stopped at the top of the street, where steep steps led back down to the city centre and, on the other side, climbed farther up the hill into the distance. He turned back and checked the street. Nobody had followed him all the way up. The only person in sight was an old woman, all in black, who had paused for breath, one hand against a wall, the other holding a basket.

He made his way back down to the blue-tiled house and took a deep breath and rapped on the small door with his knuckles.

A bolt was shot back after a moment and the door moved inward. It was so low he could only see at first that it was a woman from her sandals and bare legs and he had to bend down to see her face.

'What ... ?' he began to say, but Gerda pulled him towards her by his shirt and he stepped down into the house and she put her finger across his lips and closed the door and then replaced her finger with her lips.

He responded to her deep kiss in kind, all the tumbling questions banished in the warmth and press of her body. She pulled back after a few moments to look at him, laughter twinkling her dark eyes. He found it hard to believe what he was seeing and went to say something again but she shook her head and put her finger over her own lips and took his hand and led him up the stairs.

He lost count of the number of flights until they came to a small room at the top of the building. A single bed against one wall took up half the space and there was a washstand at one end, with a big ceramic jug and bowl. A suitcase lay flat on the floor beneath the open window and he shrugged the kitbag off his shoulder and left it down.

She began unbuttoning his shirt and he started opening the buttons on the front of her dress and he unbuckled the narrow belt around her waist as she unbuckled his, all the time looking into each other's eyes. When they were naked they lay down on the narrow bed and made love without a word.

Afterwards, they held each other as their bodies cooled and he ran his finger over the round of her shoulder, feeling the firm texture of her skin and inhaling the scent of her black hair. All the questions had gone, no longer of any consequence in the here and now of her presence and the release of all the tensions of the last few days and the voyage before that.

They stayed unmoving for what seemed a long time and then Gerda moved back against the wall and propped her head on her hand. 'I've been dreaming about this,' she whispered.

'Me too,' he whispered back.

'About making love in a bed,' she grinned.

'That too.'

'Liar.'

'Well, not so much about the bed.'

'You preferred the cold floor of Mr Montague's office?'

'Hmm. Lino still reminds me of you.'

She leaned forward to kiss him again and all the months of stilted letters slipped away and it seemed that no time at all had passed since they had last made love on the floor of her former boss's office as snow drifted down on a freezing Dublin. They made love again and he dozed afterwards, to the distant sound of workmen's voices and the rumble of rubble being poured into wheelbarrows.

He woke with a start and she was lying on him, resting her weight on her elbows. 'We don't have much time,' she said in a quiet voice.

He made an effort to come back to reality. 'What time is it?'

'Nearly three. I have to be somewhere soon.'

'And then?' He put his arms around her and ran one hand down her spine.

'Then I'll come back. You can wait here.'

He sighed with relief. 'I have to be somewhere at five. Then I'll come back too.'

'Good,' she said and leaned down to kiss him. 'But I leave tomorrow.'

'Me too.' He searched her eyes, not wanting to bring up the present and future, but it was unavoidable. 'You're working for them. The OSS?'

She gave a slow blink of her eyes in silent confirmation.

'You're going back to America?' he asked, knowing the answer was no.

'Later,' she said, and kissed him again. 'I have to get dressed.'

He released her and she got up, trailing her hand along his arm as he let her go. She dressed quickly and he watched her, taking in all the details of her body, her quick movements, finding it hard to believe this was really happening. She sat on the side of the bed and brushed her black hair with firm strokes, and then kissed him goodbye. Her foot touched against his kitbag as she stood up and she said, 'Is that the secret you're giving the Nazis?'

'How do you know?' he asked automatically, taking her hand to delay her departure and pulling her towards him for another kiss.

She leaned in to him and dropped her voice even lower than the quiet voices they had been using. 'It's a trap.'

'I know.'

She searched his eyes. 'Then why are you doing it?'

He searched hers. 'What do you mean?'

'Why are you walking into the trap?'

'It's a trap for the Germans,' he said, a sudden sinking feeling in his stomach.

'It's a trap for you,' she said. 'For Ireland. So they can use it against you if the British invade.'

Duggan stared at her, instantly recognising the neatness of it. Ireland consorting with the Nazis as the Americans had suspected all along, handing over one of America's most important military secrets to the enemies of democracy. He could even imagine the presidential statements, the headlines. More in sorrow than in anger. 'People we always looked upon as our friends ... to whom we gave sanctuary over the centuries ... fully support the British invasion ... totally justified in taking military action in all the circumstances.'

'Oh, God,' she said, reading his realisation.

His mind was whirling, already a million miles away from their lovemaking.

She bent down to give him a gentle kiss. 'I'll see you later,' she said, half statement, half question.

He nodded, his eyes half seeing.

'I love you,' she added, and kissed him again.

She gave him a worried look as she went out the door.

Twenty

He lay where she had left him, naked, feeling like he might throw up, trying to get his racing thoughts under control and figure out the meaning of what Gerda had told him. Max Linqvist is one devious fucker if this is his scheme, Duggan thought. Was it all a lie? All just to create a compromising situation for Ireland? Or is the plan to trap the Germans' spy ring in America genuine? Does it make any difference? We have to get out of their trap. I have to get out of it. Now.

He lit a cigarette and blew smoke at the ceiling, becoming aware in the silence that there was movement elsewhere in the house. Was it an OSS house or just a guest house? He had no idea. Think, he told himself, inhaling another deep lungful of smoke.

The easiest option was not to give the Norden to anyone. Take it back to the ship, drop it overboard on the voyage back to Ireland. Now that he knew Gerda was working for the OSS, Linqvist's threats against her were meaningless.

I could even leave it here and walk away. Let her give it back to the Americans. But then she'd have questions to answer. How did I know to give it back? What had she told me? A smidgen of suspicion crossed his mind. Was Gerda part of the Americans' plot? But he dismissed the thought, refusing to believe it for a moment.

And then there were the Germans. What'll Wiedermeyer think if I fail to deliver what I promised? he wondered. They're already suspicious. It'll confirm their suspicions if I don't do it. Break the radio link we've got with them. And at a time when they're clearly planning something, if the money they've deposited into the supposed IRA account is anything to go by. Something that we certainly need to know about.

He got up to stub out the cigarette on the sill through the open window. The tiled roofs of other houses fell away below him into the valley of Baixa between the two hills and he looked across at the Castelo de São Jorge squatting on top of Alfama. It seemed like an age since he'd been there a few hours ago, rambling around like a tourist. His mind hopped about the events of the morning and something struck him. That could be a plan, he thought, trying to calm his thoughts into order, looking at things from several angles. He flicked the dead butt out the window, not caring where it fell.

He got dressed and swung the heavy kitbag over his shoulder and made his way down the stairs. There were sounds behind the doors on some floors; it seemed the house was divided into apartments. It would make sense for the OSS to have numerous pieds-à-terre around a city like Lisbon.

He walked quickly down the Rua da Condessa, hurrying with the hill past the Largo do Carmo, down towards the river, until he came to Rua Garrett and found a taxi leaving a well-dressed woman outside an expensive clothes shop. He got in and gave the driver the same address in Lapa that Hopkins had given his taxi after their conversation in the bar earlier.

Maisie Figueras opened the door herself this time and stepped back to pull it wider. 'Well, well,' she said. 'This is a nice surprise.'

'Can't get rid of a bad penny,' he grinned, encouraged by her reaction. This was going to work, though he didn't know how yet.

'Straight off the boat.' She eyed his kitbag. 'You brought me a present?'

'Only a token,' he said, taking his unopened spare packet of Sweet Afton from his pocket.

'It's the thought that counts,' she said, taking it. 'Come on in.'

He followed her along the cool hallway to the reception room they'd been in the last time. 'Rosario's having a siesta,' she said. 'So no Russian tea today unless you insist I make it myself.'

'Certainly not,' he said, leaving his bag down.

'Then gin it is.'

She opened the latticed door of a wooden cabinet and took out a bottle of gin and a siphon of tonic and two glasses. He watched her pouring large shots into each glass, wondering if she knew her husband had been the one who had shopped Aiken to Hopkins. Almost certainly, he had already decided. In fact he suspected she was as likely to be the British spy as her husband. Or both of them were. Hopkins hadn't been coming round here in the middle of the morning to meet her husband. And her performance last time had been perfectly pitched to deflect suspicion from them: the hints that she was an Aiken supporter from the civil-war days; the criticism of Britain's treatment of its old ally Portugal in the past; the casting of suspicion on the patrician Maud Browne.

'Say when,' she turned to him, finger on the trigger of the siphon.

'Fill it up please.'

She dropped one eyelid at him in a disappointed gesture but did as he asked and then gave her own glass a short squirt of tonic. She handed him his glass and raised hers to his and said '*Sláinte.*' She gestured at the couch and asked as they sat down how things were in Dublin.

'Not getting any easier,' Duggan said. 'Supplies are drying up. No petrol any more and lot of worries about coal shortages next winter.'

'You should come here for the winter.'

'If I'm lucky,' he said. 'I don't know if you've heard that we're opening a legation here.'

She nodded. 'That's why you're here?'

'Looking at some details,' he said, keeping it vague. 'You know Mr Kirwan in the Madrid legation?'

Duggan sipped at his drink as if he was trying to place him. 'I don't think we've met.' He had no idea who she was talking about.

'He was here about ten days ago or so.'

'Did you meet him?'

'Just heard about it on the grapevine. He was meeting the Foreign Ministry about the arrangements.'

'I hope nobody there is going to cause difficulties,' he said, giving her a knowing look, hinting at Maud Browne's Anglophile husband.

'Indeed,' she said, taking the hint and going to open the packet of Afton. He interrupted her, holding out his open cigarette case. 'Have one of these,' he said. 'Keep those for later.'

She took one and touched his hand as he leaned over to light it for her. 'Did you talk to Madam Maud?'

Duggan nodded. 'She wasn't very helpful.'

'Surprise, surprise,' Maisie said in a contented tone. 'Did you get to the bottom of that whole business about General Aiken?'

'Not really. Came to a dead end.'

'Bit of a storm in a teacup,' Maisie said, giving an airy wave of her cigarette, leaving a faint question mark of smoke in the still air. In the courtyard outside, the sun sparkled through the small plume of water from the fountain.

'Like a lot of political and diplomatic things.'

'You'll be able to keep a closer eye on the likes of Maud Browne when you're based here.'

'Not much chance of me being posted here, unfortunately.'

'You still saying you're a researcher?' She gave him a coy smile.

He smiled back as he nodded, injecting an air of ambiguity into his words. 'I just do the low-level stuff the diplomatic types can't be bothered with.'

'Low … level,' she repeated, separating the words as if to examine them individually. 'You mean underhand?'

'God, no. That's for the diplomatic types.'

'So what low-level things are you doing this time?'

'Looking around for possible accommodation. That sort of thing.'

'Well, this is the area to look,' she said. 'Most of the embassies are around here. But you'd want to be careful. You don't want to end up next door to the wrong people. Or even in the same street. You can be judged just by your neighbours these days.'

'That was one of the things I was hoping you would be able to help me with,' he said, seizing on the opening she'd given him.

'Only one?'

'I was also hoping we could have that lunch you mentioned last time,' he said, holding her gaze.

'That's a nice idea,' she said. 'What do you like to eat?'

'I'll try anything.'

'The adventurous type. That's good.' She finished her drink and held up the glass. 'Another?'

'No thanks.' His glass was still half full. 'I'll have to go. I actually have to meet someone near here about accommodation.'

She gave him an inquisitive look as she got up and went back to the cabinet and poured herself another gin and a splash of tonic.

'An auctioneer who's to advise us on property.' He searched his memory for some landmark, hoping she wouldn't ask who the auctioneer was, though he'd memorised the name off a sign on a building he'd passed on the way in case she did. 'I'm meeting him at that big cathedral.'

'The Basilica da Estrela,' she said as she came back with her drink and sat down.

'That's it,' he agreed. 'I'd like to get your opinion afterwards on whatever he has to say. To make sure we don't make any mistakes. Get in with the wrong crowd.'

'I'll be going out in an hour.'

'We could do it over lunch tomorrow.'

'Where would you like to go?'

'I'm in your hands,' Duggan said, spreading his hands.

'You could just come here. I'll try and think of something nice.'

'That'd be great.' He finished his gin and tonic in one long swallow and stood up. 'Thanks for the drink.'

He picked up his kitbag and she led him down the hall, her drink in her hand. 'Would you mind,' he hesitated when they got to the hall door, 'if I left this here while I meet this man? Don't want to be carrying it around. Looking like I'm straight off the boat.'

'Of course,' she said. 'I'll probably be gone when you get back but I'll tell Rosario you'll be picking it up.'

'Thanks,' he said, leaving the bag behind the door.

She raised her cheeks to be kissed: first one, then the other. 'Great to see you again,' he said.

'And you,' she said.

He went down the hill, heading for the tram tracks, checking his watch and thinking that the meeting had gone perfectly. He suppressed a sliver of doubt, suggesting that he might be wrong. She might be completely innocent, not know what her Portuguese businessman husband was up to. Maybe she was just having an affair with Hopkins, nothing political in it at all. But then she'd hardly be flirting with me.

Doesn't matter, he told himself. What matters is that she and her husband know Hopkins. And one or the other will tell him about the package I left there and never came back to collect. Especially after they look into the kitbag and see what it is. And let Hopkins handle it. Let him give it to the Germans if the British know about the spy ring in America. Or give it back to the Americans.

He came to a steep street with tram tracks and crossed to the down line and looked for the nearest stop. A Number 28 came almost immediately and he got a single seat on the right and took out his notebook and jotted down Maisie's address and tore out the page. Then he leaned his elbow on the open window, savouring the breeze as the tram careered downhill to the level ground by the church in Largo Corpo Santo.

He got off at the stop by Rua Augusta and hurried up to Praça do Rossio, thinking of getting back to Gerda as he went by the Santa Justa *elevador* again. Wiedermeyer was in his usual place at the back of the Metropole's terrace, looking relaxed as always behind his glass of clear liquid. Duggan weaved his way between the tables and sank into the wicker chair beside him, perspiring heavily. Wiedermeyer gave him a look that mixed curiosity with disdain.

'Someone's following me,' Duggan said, looking back the way he had come.

'Who?' Wiedermeyer asked, keeping his attention on Duggan, careful not to follow his gaze.

'Fucking Brits.'

'You saw them?'

Duggan nodded.

'You see them now?'

'No. I think I gave him the slip. Jumped off the tram and ran.'

Wiedermeyer took a sip of his drink and asked the passing waiter for a Sagres. 'What did he look like?'

Duggan gave him a description based on the man who had followed him from Cascais, but nothing precise enough to identify him. 'Do they have many spies here?' he added.

'Of course,' Wiedermeyer said. 'They think this is part of their territory. But it's not any more.'

'Should we be meeting in such a public place?' Duggan couldn't resist asking, casting a nervous eye around their surroundings.

'We're just having a drink,' Wiedermeyer said as the waiter came with the Sagres. 'Calm down.'

'There's another thing,' Duggan said when the waiter had finished pouring half the bottle. 'We've got a tip-off that they're going to search our ship.'

'Who?' Wiedermeyer's interest was piqued. 'The British?'

'The Portuguese. Their Special Branch or whatever they call it. The captain got a tip-off from one of his friends in the harbour office. The British are behind it.'

'He told him that?'

'It's obvious.'

'Why?'

'Why are they following me? They know I've got something for you.'

'How would they know that?'

'Fuckers have spies and informers everywhere.'

'You suspect some of the ship's crew?'

'Jesus, I don't know.' Duggan took a long drink and followed it with a cigarette, like a man at the end of his tether. Don't overdo it, he warned himself. 'But it's okay,' he said, breathing out a calming stream of smoke and lowering his voice. 'I got the bombsight off the ship. To a safe place.'

Wiedermeyer said nothing. His demeanour hadn't changed. He still looked relaxed, with neither a care nor a suspicion in his mind. 'Where's this safe place?' he asked at last.

'With a friend of ours here. A sympathiser.'

'You can trust him?' Wiedermeyer asked, a hint of interest creeping into his voice at finding someone else in Lisbon who might turn out to be useful.

'Her.' Duggan corrected him. 'Yes. She's reliable.'

'Were you followed there?'

'No.'

'You are sure?'

'Yes. I took precautions. That's why I noticed him later, but he didn't follow me there. I'm sure of that.' He took the note with Maisie's address from his pocket and held it under the table. Wiedermeyer disappeared it into his fist with scarcely a movement. 'If you ask her for the bag I left, she'll give it to you.'

'When does your ship sail?'

'Tomorrow morning.' Duggan poured the remainder of his beer into the glass and drank some of it. 'We have to call at one of the British ports on the way back. I'm fucked if they know anything.'

They lapsed into silence again, Duggan drinking and smoking in a display of nerves, hoping that Wiedermeyer would attribute them to the fears he had articulated. But Wiedermeyer was the real source of his nervousness. It was impossible to tell how much he believed, if any, of the story Duggan had spun him.

'It's good to be careful,' Wiedermeyer said at last. 'But not to the point where it stops us from doing what's necessary.'

Duggan nodded as if he knew what that meant, and finished his drink. He took some coins from his pocket but

Wiedermeyer waved them away. 'I'll take care of this,' he said. 'You be careful.'

'I will,' Duggan said. 'I'll send a message when I get home.'

'And remember what I said,' Wiedermeyer added. 'Keep us informed of everything. And not only what suits your own aims.'

'I understand,' Duggan said as he stood up.

There was a queue for the Santa Justa *elevador* this time and he had to wait near the top of the line for a second car. He watched it fill up behind him, looking for any possible tails. Most of the people getting in looked like office workers, and they all looked like they were Portuguese. Though, he realised, that didn't mean anything. Gerda could easily pass for a Portuguese woman too with her black hair and dark eyes.

He dawdled along after they got off on the top, and stopped to light a cigarette until everybody on the *elevador* had passed him by, hurrying home after work. He took his time following them and did a half-circuit of Largo da Carmo, cutting back through the park and pausing to circle its old fountain as if he was examining it. Satisfied that nobody was following him, he made his way up Rua da Condessa and knocked on the door.

Gerda opened it and gave him a worried look and whispered, 'Go upstairs.' She disappeared into a room off the small hallway as he climbed up to the top of the building to the room they'd been in before. He pushed off his shoes without unlacing them and took off his shirt and stood at the open window, feeling the cool air on his skin and looking at the stacked rooftops on Alfama mellowed by the sinking sun.

He lay down on the bed after a while and tried to figure out the possible consequences of what he had done. With a bit of luck it would upset everybody's apple carts. So much the better if Wiedermeyer sent someone to collect the Norden from Maisie's. Hopkins would surely hear about it from her, and MI6 would tell the OSS. And I can tell Linqvist I've delivered it to the Germans, Duggan thought. But they can't use it against us, say we've given American secrets to the Germans, when the conduit was actually a British spy.

And it sent the British a message too: 'We know who's working for you in Lisbon, helping you poison our relations with the Americans.'

If the Germans did call to collect the Norden, that would add to the confusion. Would they try and recruit Maisie, thinking she was an IRA sympathiser? That'd get Hopkins interested. On the other hand, what if the Germans realised, or even knew, she was a British agent? That would not be good for Sean McCarthy, though he could still bluff his way through it. 'We've been misled too by this traitorous Irish woman,' he could say.

Gerda pushed open the door with her foot and came in carrying a tray with bread and cheeses and cold meats, and a bottle of wine and two glasses. 'You look happier,' she said as he moved sideways to make room for the tray and she sat down on the edge of the bed.

'Why wouldn't I be happy? Alone with you at last.'

'I was worried when I left. You looked so sick.'

'I'm fine now.' He pulled her closer to him and dropped his voice. 'Thanks for telling me.' He kissed her closed eyelids. 'I love you.'

She smiled and poured him a glass of wine. 'You like red wine?'

'What I'd really like would be a nice cup of tea.' He took the glass.

'Ah,' she said, exaggerating her Cork accent, 'a nice cup of Barry's tea.'

'Proper Irish tea,' he corrected her.

'That's Barry's.'

'Never heard of it.' He sipped the wine. 'But this'll do for the moment.'

She broke off a piece of bread and held it up. 'What would you like on it?'

'I'll try that,' he said, pointing to a lump of solid-looking cheese.

She cut some pieces off it and put it on the bread and handed it to him and watched him eat.

'Aren't you hungry?' he asked, his mouth full.

She shook her head. 'We have to build up your strength.'

He drank some wine to wash down the food. 'Is that a promise or a threat?'

'It's a precaution.'

'It's not needed at the moment.'

'In that case … ' she said, lifting the tray and putting it down on the floor. She stood up and took the wine glass from his hand and began unbuttoning her shirtwaister.

The darkness settled unnoticed around them, leavened by the glow on the ceiling from the bright lights of the city down below. Muted sounds travelled up as well, a mumble of traffic and faint clangs of tram bells interspersed with dog barks and occasional closer sounds, shouts in nearby streets, doors banging. The building itself remained quiet, no sound of any other inhabitants, although Duggan now knew there were others there.

'You upset Chuck yesterday,' Gerda said during one of their interludes. 'With that trick on him at the church.'

'It wasn't deliberate,' Duggan admitted.

'I wouldn't say that if I were you. Forcing him on to a tram going the wrong way was brilliant.'

'Of course it was all planned,' Duggan added with a laugh. 'I had figured it all out. That the wrong tram would arrive the exact moment he caught sight of me.'

'He was mortified,' she giggled. 'He's just out of training. A big brainbox. Got a string of degrees from Harvard. And you trapped him into exposing himself on his first job. He's afraid they'll send him back to a desk job now.'

'Maybe he'd be better off.'

'He wants to be in the action. Live up to his father, who won medals in the last war.'

'And you?' Duggan asked, shifting his weight on to his left elbow so he could look down at her. 'You want to be in the action too.'

'I have no choice,' she said.

He nodded, knowing better than to argue with her about her need to fight the Nazis. 'I wish you weren't.'

'I know,' she said, pulling his head down to kiss him. 'But you know I have to.'

He kissed her again and held her tightly. 'You're going back to Vienna, aren't you?' he whispered into her ear.

She said nothing but he felt her head nod beside his.

'That's very dangerous,' he whispered, still holding her. 'Suppose someone recognises you?'

'They won't,' she whispered back. 'I was only a schoolgirl when I left.'

'It's still a big risk. You haven't changed that much.'

'How do you know? You didn't know me then.'

'People don't change that much in five or six years.'

'I have,' she said. 'Anyway, that's the reason I'm going. To contact people I know. Who'll trust me.'

'What if they've changed?' he said. 'Gone over to the Nazis since you knew them before. That's not impossible.'

'That's a risk I have to take.'

He shook his head in disagreement and tightened his hold.

'Ah,' she said, 'I can't breathe.'

'Sorry,' he said, releasing her and moving back to look into her eyes. 'Someone could recognise you on the street, inform the Gestapo. You wouldn't even know about it until they picked you up.'

'I'm an American,' she said. 'We're not at war with them.'

'That's no protection,' he said. 'You're an Austrian Jew.'

'Nobody knows that.'

'People you were at school with in Vienna know that. Having an American passport won't protect you. If they catch you they'll shoot you. Or worse.'

'Shhh.' She tried to rock him back and forth as though she was soothing a child troubled by a bad dream, but he refused to let himself be moved. 'I love you and I love it that you love me enough to be so worried, but this is something I have to do,' she said. 'You know that. You know I don't have a choice.'

They lapsed into silence, entwined in each other's arms and legs. Yes, he thought, I know from everything she's ever said and done that she has no choice. He thought too about Strasser and Wiedermeyer: there was no doubt about the steel behind their usually urbane exteriors. Nor, for that matter, of the willingness of Linqvist or Hopkins to do whatever they or their masters decided had to be done.

'Thanks,' he repeated, 'for telling me about the trap.'

'Can you escape it?'

'I think so.' He hesitated, not wanting to involve her in his plots, but unable to resist the temptation to find out more. 'Do you know whose idea it was?'

'No,' she said. 'Someone was briefing Chuck on why he was to follow you, what he was to look out for.'

'Do they know about us?'

'Probably.' She stifled a yawn. 'They've never said anything. But I don't mind. It won't change anything between us.'

Later he woke with a start, moulded to her back. He reached an arm over her, not sure whether she was awake or asleep, and cupped her breast. Her hand came up and moved along his arm with a light touch that barely ruffled the hairs on it.

'What time is it?'

'Late,' she replied. 'Or early.'

The light in the room had dulled and the sounds of the city had died. The night air was cooler and she had pulled a sheet over them. 'Was I asleep for long?'

'Not too long.'

'You should've woken me. I don't want the night to pass in sleep.'

She turned over to face him and huddled into his shoulder and he ran his hand down her back and over the hump of her hip.

'Come with me,' he said. 'Back to Ireland.'

She planted a series of kisses around his neck and said nothing. But he knew the answer anyway.

She pulled herself up a little to face him and searched his eyes. 'Come to America,' she said.

He kissed her on the lips and then said, 'I can't be a deserter.'

'You wouldn't be. You could get involved properly. Really fighting the Nazis. The OSS will take you. They're looking for anybody with experience.'

He closed his eyes, knowing that he couldn't do it, couldn't desert the country whose independence his father had fought for. Couldn't stomach the hurt he knew his father would feel even if he never said a word. Which he probably wouldn't.

'There's a liner in the port now,' she said.

'Where's it going?' he asked, playing for time, every sense in his body telling him to do it. Not to be trapped by the past. To look to the future in America with her.

'Rio de Janeiro. Then on to Philadelphia.'

'I can't take the place of some refugee,' he stalled.

'Then on the PanAm Clipper,' she beseeched him with her eyes. 'It can be done.'

He looked into the pleading depth of her eyes. 'If you come with me.'

She shook her head with a hint of irritation. 'Don't do that,' she said. 'Don't make it a test.'

'I'm not doing that,' he said. 'I don't want to go to America if you're not there.'

'I'll be there when I'm finished.'

'When will that be?'

She paused. 'I don't know.'

'When the war's over,' he sighed, as if that was a distant possibility, as distant as being old.

'It'll end sometime.'

'You told me before that it'd never end.'

'I know now it will. The Americans will fight. They're just looking for an excuse. And we'll beat the Nazi bastards.'

'I want to be where you are,' he said after a moment. 'I'll go to Vienna with you.'

She shook her head with a loving smile. 'Don't be silly. It's too dangerous.'

'We're not at war with them either.'

'It'd be too dangerous for me,' she amended. 'Having to mind you.'

'You think I can't mind myself?'

'Yes, but you know what I mean. I'd be more worried about you.'

Which would make it more dangerous for her, he knew. It wasn't the past or the future that was the problem, he thought. It was the present. The war. And all the lives that it had taken and the millions more it had disrupted. In that context it seemed the height of selfishness to complain of the difficulties they had in being together.

They stayed awake, talking little, as the murky predawn light gave way to the first tentative rays of the rising sun and the sky outside went from purple through shades of brighter and brighter blue. They made love one last time, more an emotional act than a physical one. Then they got up and dressed in silence. Duggan ate the last crust of bread with a slice of cold meat on it while he watched her brush her hair in front of a handheld mirror. She caught his eye in the mirror and gave him a slow wink.

'You leave first,' she said when she had finished.

He put his arms around her and they held each other tight for a moment, then parted.

'Write to me,' she added. 'At the same address. I'll let you know as soon as I'm back.'

'The moment you are,' he said, knowing that the coming weeks, even months, were going to be an agony of uncertainty. 'Be careful.'

'You too.'

He stopped at the door for a last look at her, silhouetted against the brightening window, her hair curling up just short of her shoulders, her face in shadow.

Twenty-One

He walked down the hill towards the port, his long strides speeded by the steep incline, feeling happy and desolate at the same time.

The city was waking up, the air still fresh from the cool of the night, early risers moving with purpose and the promise of the new day. The port was back in full swing, trucks and carts lined up by vessels, cranes swinging back and forth, hauling cargos in and out of holds. There was no activity at his ship but a steady plume of smoke came from its funnel and a crewman pulled in the gangway behind him as he came on board.

'Just in time,' the captain said when he climbed up to the bridge.

'Did I delay you?'

'Another few minutes and you would have.' The captain turned away to give an instruction to the engine room.

Duggan left him to it and went down to the galley as the steel plates of the ship began to vibrate with the growing rumble of the engine. 'The cure?' the cook offered with a pale grin.

'Just a cup of tea, please.'

Duggan took the mug of strong tea back on deck and leaned against the bridge as the ship edged away from the quay and a couple of crewmen winched in the mooring ropes. The ship began a turn around the stern of another coaster anchored in midstream. It already had steam up and he could see its anchor chain being hauled in as it prepared to take the berth they had vacated.

He lit a cigarette and watched the city glide away, the tiers of roofs bright and peaceful under the growing sun, and thought about Gerda, feeling her body against his, the tickle of her hair against his face, the touch of her cool palm on his shoulder, and seeing the slow dreamy smile grow and fill her dark eyes as if it came from the depths of her being.

The crewmen who had coiled the mooring ropes came by him, one singing 'We'll Meet Again'. He nodded back at the other and said to Duggan, 'He's in love. Can't wait to get back, though she won't even remember him.'

'Fuck off,' his colleague said. 'You couldn't even get pissed in a brewery.'

Duggan gave them a benign smile. 'I know how he feels,' he said to the first man.

'I didn't see you last night. Where'd you go?'

'Somewhere else.' Duggan left it vague.

'You got lucky too,' the second crewman said.

'I did,' Duggan agreed.

'He's just jealous,' the second crewman nodded towards his colleague.

They sailed slowly passed the *Serpa Pinto*, a thin column of grey smoke rising from its black funnel, and he could see some people strolling along its upper deck beneath a line of lifeboats. No point in regrets, he thought. I couldn't have done it.

The ship glided by the explorers' monument and the tower at Belém, picking up speed with the ebbing tide as the engines settled into their cruising rhythm. They were passing by Estoril and Cascais when his cabin-mate

Jenkins joined him and lit a cigarette. 'Your friend was looking for you in Antonio's last night,' he said as he inhaled the smoke.

'Yeah?' Duggan was mildly surprised that Strasser would have turned up again.

'He gave me a bag of stuff for you.'

'What?' Duggan felt his blood go cold.

'The usual stuff, he said,' Jenkins added, giving him a sharp look, taken aback at his tone.

'What kind of bag?'

'Suitcase.'

'Did he say what was in it?'

'Usual stuff,' Jenkins repeated.

'Did he show it to you?'

'The suitcase?'

'What was in it.'

'No.'

'Fuck,' Duggan said to himself, thinking, I didn't fool them at all. They've just planted a bomb on the ship.

'What is it?' Jenkins asked.

'Where is it?' Duggan asked. 'In the cabin?'

'No. I put it in a safe place. Assumed you wouldn't want it found if anyone was to look around.'

'You better get it back,' Duggan said.

'Now?'

Duggan nodded. 'And be careful. It could be dangerous.'

Jenkins gave a half-laugh and stared at him but the look on Duggan's face told him it was no joke. 'Fuck,' he said. 'It's a bomb?'

'Maybe,' Duggan said, trying to figure out what to do. If it was a bomb it was probably designed to go off when they were at sea, to sink the ship far from land. Which meant it had to be on a long timer: a day or even more. It couldn't be too sensitive to movement or it could've gone off before it even got to the ship. And there'd be no point in that. 'But probably not that dangerous at the moment.'

'You want me to get it?' Jenkins sounded unenthusiastic.

'No.' Duggan took a deep breath. 'Tell me where it is. I'll get it.'

'You'll never find it. I'll show you.'

'I better talk to the captain first.'

'Christ almighty!' the captain exploded when Duggan told him of his suspicions. 'How often have I told them not to bring stuff on board unless they know what it is?'

'It's entirely my fault,' Duggan said. 'To do with my mission here. And whether or not I've been compromised. It's all my fault.'

They were standing on the platform outside the bridge, feeling the wind rise as they came to the mouth of the Tagus and the river rolled out into the open Atlantic before them, the horizon as clear as an inked line.

'What do you think we should do?' the captain asked.

Duggan explained his thinking, that if it was a bomb it wasn't set to go off any time soon. 'We could just toss it overboard when we get away from land,' he suggested.

'We'd have to sink it,' the captain said. 'Otherwise it could just drift ashore and injure someone else. We'd have to weight it down, make sure it sank.'

'You have a rifle on board?'

'A .303. You a good shot?'

'I could hit a suitcase at a hundred yards.' And a bullet might explode it. Which would answer the question of whether it was a bomb or not. I need to know that, he thought. I need to know whether my cover has been exposed. Whether the Germans know we're double-crossing them. We can't go on communicating with them unless we know that.

***

Jenkins led him down into the ship, down below the water-line, near the engine room where the noise and the heavy air seemed to vibrate along with the metal floor and walls. He stopped at an alcove with a fire extinguisher on the wall and Duggan waited as he removed it and unscrewed a metal panel behind it, feeling sweat break out on his body and the first nauseous hints of seasickness. Please God, not now, he thought, trying to relax and go with the movement of the ship as it rose and fell and wallowed from side to side.

Jenkins lifted out a grey suitcase with both hands, careful not to knock it against anything. Duggan took it by the handle, his other hand against a wall to steady himself, while Jenkins sealed up the hiding place again and went ahead of him back up towards the deck. Duggan took his time, trying not to let the suitcase bang off the wall as the ship tilted and shifted with every step. He was covered in a sickly sweat and holding back nausea by the time he got back on deck and gulped in lungfuls of cold air.

There was no sign of Jenkins but the captain looked down at him from the edge of the bridge. Duggan shivered as the wind cooled his sodden shirt, and he looked back at the coastline, still close enough behind them that he could make out details of buildings and the marker buoys on the river channel. He made his way up towards the bow of the ship, which they had decided was the safest place to leave the suitcase until they had moved further away from land. If it was a bomb, its blast would dissipate in the open air and it would be too high up to hole the ship's sides. He tied it to a ring meant for lashing down cargo, making sure it didn't hit anything as it swung from side to side with the motion of the ship.

He stood up and made his way back to the bridge, examining the sea. It wasn't rough but the swell was increasing, leaving trails of bubbles here and there on the heaving water. He had no doubt he could hit a suitcase at a hundred yards if it was static and he was too. But this wouldn't be an easy shot, hitting a moving grey target on the blue-grey water from the shifting base of the ship. And there wouldn't be much time to get it right. To let the suitcase go far enough away that it wouldn't damage the ship if it exploded. And to keep it in sight long enough to hit it.

'Is it heavy?' the captain enquired.

'Not particularly,' Duggan said. 'May be a false alarm.'

'Better safe than sorry.'

The captain led him down to his cabin and unlocked a narrow cabinet beside his bookshelf. There were two Lee Enfield rifles in it and an unopened box of ammunition. Duggan picked one and worked the bolt. It felt a bit stiff and he tried the other one. It moved more smoothly. But he was thinking that his plan wouldn't work. It wouldn't necessarily answer the question.

If they've seen through our deception it's not just me who's a target, he realised. It's this ship and everyone on it. They may well look on it as a belligerent act. And make the ship a legitimate target for their U-boats and planes if the bomb doesn't sink it.

'You've fired one of these before?' the captain asked, seeking reassurance as he noticed Duggan's hesitation.

Duggan nodded, working the bolt forward and back again without realising it. If the ship was a legitimate target in German eyes, he was thinking, then everyone on board was at risk. Not just now but possibly on future voyages as well. We can't let them sail this route again if they are, he thought. It would only be a matter of time before they came into someone's sights. I have to know.

'You think you can hit it?' the captain asked.

'I don't think it'll work,' Duggan said, making a decision. 'It won't necessarily set off the explosives. If there are any,' he added.

Joe Joyce

'We only want to sink it.'

'I don't want to put your ship at risk. But I have to know what's in it.'

The captain shook his head, about to assert his authority.

'It's vital for my mission,' Duggan added, before he could order him to do something. 'Whatever is in that suitcase will answer an important question. A matter of life or death.'

The captain gave him a sceptical look and took out his pipe and gripped it between his teeth. 'What do you want to do?' he asked at last.

'Take a look inside it. If I can get a sharp knife.'

'You know how to defuse a bomb?'

Duggan shook his head.

The captain chewed on the pipe, making it bob up and down. 'Life and death,' he muttered.

'I'm not trying to sound dramatic.' Duggan gave an apologetic shrug. 'But it's important.'

'Your funeral,' the captain said at last.

'Thanks,' Duggan said without irony, in gratitude that the captain hadn't simply ordered him to toss the suitcase overboard. 'Would you have a sheet of paper?'

The captain opened the drawer underneath the top of his tiny desk and took out a sheet. Duggan realised he was still holding the Lee Enfield and he propped it back in its cabinet.

'It might be no harm,' Duggan said, remembering the conversation with the two crewmen earlier and his suspicion that one might have been in Strasser's brothel, 'to make sure nobody else brought any unopened presents on board. Just in case.'

'And you want a knife,' the captain nodded.

Duggan sat at the captain's desk and wrote a quick report for Commandant McClure on the main points of what had happened in Lisbon: his discovery about Hopkins and Maisie, his conversations with Wiedermeyer and Strasser, his delivery of the Norden. He paused before explaining the last of these, keeping Gerda out of the story, but describing his delivery system as a retaliation for Maisie's and Hopkins's roles in reporting Aiken's speeches in Lisbon to the Americans.

He didn't know how to end it. If you are reading this, he thought, I'm dead. Which was unreal. Melodramatic. Laughable. But possible. Even probable, now that he looked back on the demeanours and the reactions of the Germans. They hadn't been convinced by anything he'd told them. They know, he thought. Why did I think otherwise, even for a moment?

'Please inform Grace Matthews,' he wrote at last, giving Gerda's New York address. He signed the report 'Paul' and found an envelope in the captain's drawer and addressed it to Commandant George McClure, adding 'To be delivered in person'.

On the bridge he handed the sealed letter to the captain and the captain gave him a thin stiletto blade with a mother-of-pearl handle. Duggan took it with a look of surprise, wondering which of the crewmen had had that. It was perfect for his purposes.

He walked up the deck, rolling with the ship, the wind cutting through his shirt, now dry again, chilling him. The bow rose and dipped as he approached, rising towards the bright blue sky and then dipping to reveal a line of grey clouds beginning to gather on the horizon. Back behind them the coast was receding, its details smudging with distance.

He knelt behind the suitcase and examined it visually as it swung gently from side to side. It was made of grey cardboard with reinforced corners of a dark red material that were probably more for show than to provide any real protection. There were two tin catches with small keyholes on the front, which were also as much for show as for security. He leaned down to listen along the top but could hear nothing over the wind and the creaking of the ship and the slough of the water passing by.

Would they bother booby-trapping something like this? he wondered. Probably. As a matter of course. Opening the catches would probably set it off. But how would it be protected against someone doing what he was going to do. He had no idea.

He took a deep breath of the salty air and began reciting a Hail Mary under his breath: 'Pray for us sinners now and at the hour of our death … ' He pushed the sharp point of the knife into the centre of the lid and sweat broke out on his forehead. The lid dipped under the pressure and then stopped. He raised the knife again, not wanting to press against anything in the suitcase.

He picked another spot, about an inch in from the edge of the lid, and pressed down on it. The point of the knife broke through the cardboard. He began to pull it slowly towards him, careful to let nothing more than the tip of the knife into the suitcase. It was difficult to cut the cardboard with just the tip of the knife but he worked at it slowly until there was an incision about two inches long.

He tried to raise one side of it with the knife and peer in but there was little space and the interior was dark against the sunlight on deck. He knelt back on his heels for a moment, breathing slowly, raising his face to the sun, seeking its warmth as the cold wind chilled the sweat on his brow. Then he made a careful cut at a ninety-degree angle to the first one, and about the same length, and raised the cut patch to peer in.

The capped sailor in a circular buoy on the front of a packet of Player's Navy Cut cigarettes stared upside down at him, and he laughed as relief surged through him. Careful, he ordered himself. That doesn't mean there isn't something nasty inside. But there wasn't.

He made several more quick cuts near the front edge of the lid before he was confident enough to snap the catches and open the suitcase. It was packed with cartons of Player's and Gold Flake cigarettes and bags of coffee and four bottles of port. He opened a bag of coffee at random and let the beans pour out and rattle away down the deck. He also sliced open a couple of the cigarette cartons and opened an individual packet from each to make sure they were what they seemed. Finally, he stood up and turned towards the bridge and held aloft a bottle of port in each hand. The captain gave him a thumbs up and a big smile.

I did it, he thought as he carried the suitcase in both hands, staggering down the deck to the bridge in a wide-legged walk. I fooled them.

The captain came down to greet him and Duggan put the suitcase on the deck and presented him with two bottles of port. 'Everyone help themselves,' he said, throwing back the torn-up lid as some of the crew gathered around.

The captain clapped him on the back and handed him back his letter to McClure. Duggan took one of the packs of Player's he had already opened and lit a cigarette in the shelter of the bridge and went back to the stern. He leaned on the railing and felt the adrenalin drain away and the tension in his shoulders fade. He tore the letter into tiny pieces and tossed them, like a handful of confetti, into the ship's wake. The receding continent was now little more than a suggestion of land, a darker haze on the bright horizon, less tangible than the band of clouds building up ahead of them.

Epilogue

The marine at the gate to the American legation in the Phoenix Park raised the barrier and Duggan drove up to the building and parked to one side. Linqvist came out to meet him. Duggan rolled down the window and picked up the copy of *Life* magazine off the passenger seat and handed it to Linqvist.

'What's this?' Linqvist asked in surprise.

'Page 24,' Duggan said.

Linqvist found the double-page spread: mugshots of thirty-two people, three of them women, under the headline 'Greatest Spy Roundup in US History Produces a Great Gallery of Faces'. Almost all had German names. Linqvist gave him an enquiring look.

'Look at Hermann Lang,' Duggan said.

Lang's was the first mugshot on the second page of the spread. He had a strong-looking face with kiss-curls above a large forehead. The caption described him as a German-born American who had worked for Carl I. Norden Inc. 'as inspector of the famed super-secret Norden bombsights'.

'You lied to me,' Duggan said as Linqvist read it. The magazine was dated a couple of days after he had left for Lisbon and referred to FBI arrests the previous week.

'Nobody told me about this at the time,' Linqvist said, shrugging and handing the magazine back to Duggan. 'Forgot to keep us in the loop.'

'Bollocks,' Duggan said. 'I did what you asked me to do. Took the Norden to the Germans. What was it all really about?'

'What I told you at the time,' Linqvist said, nodding at the magazine on the passenger seat. 'Building a case against those guys.'

Duggan shook his head in disgust. He knew what it was really about but he was here to play the innocent, to protect Gerda. 'I took a lot of risks,' he said. 'Meeting the Germans in Lisbon. Giving them the Norden for you. All for nothing.'

'It wasn't all for nothing.'

'It was a load of lies,' Duggan said, nodding at the magazine, noting that Linqvist didn't dispute his statement that he had given the Germans the Norden. Maybe they had collected it from Maisie's house. They had made no further mention of it in their radio messages to him. He knew nothing about the fallout from his last-minute manoeuvre with the bombsight in Lisbon. There was no word from the British either about what had happened. But that didn't surprise him. Hopefully they were all still trying to work out what was going on, who was playing whom. 'Those guys were under arrest before I even got to Lisbon.'

'You got to meet Grace again.'

'Leave her out of it,' Duggan exploded. 'Don't fucking threaten her again.'

'No, no,' Linqvist raised his hands in surrender and took a half-step back. 'I'm not threatening her. She's one of ours, you know that.'

'And you knew it before, when you forced me to do your bidding.'

'No, I didn't,' Linqvist protested.

'Jesus. That makes it worse. You really were threatening her.'

'Look,' Linqvist said, trying to take a metaphorical step backwards, to calm the discussion. 'None of this is personal. It was just a fuck-up. Lack of communications. Nobody knows what the FBI is up to. Probably Hoover doesn't even tell himself.'

'You made it personal.'

'OK. That was a mistake. Obviously, it won't happen again.'

Duggan rubbed his eyes and sighed. 'Any word of her?' he asked in a quiet voice, in two minds about revealing his concern, letting Linqvist know that he still had leverage over him. But there was little point pretending otherwise. Besides, he wanted to know anything he could find out about her whereabouts – had she returned from Vienna, was she safe – to have some link with her, however tenuous. And Linqvist was his only possible conduit.

Linqvist shook his head. 'I'll let you know if I hear anything.'

Duggan nodded his thanks.

'By the way, we've talked to people about those ships your government wants to buy. The logjam should be shifted soon.'

'Thanks,' Duggan said.

'Look,' Linqvist added, 'as I said to you before, we've got to keep in touch. Try and keep communications clear so that our bosses don't hunker down into their corners.'

'Then we've got to be straight with each other,' Duggan said, conscious of his hypocrisy but not doubting for a moment that Linqvist was being just as hypocritical. It went with the job.

'Totally.' Linqvist held out his hand and Duggan reached through the window to shake it.

He drove back to the office, passing the growing clamp of turf, now eight feet high, as a sudden cloudburst sent rain hammering down. The turf workers scattered for shelter under the side of an army lorry and he slowed down: the wipers made little impact on the volume of water hammering on the windscreen. The rain stopped as quickly as it had begun and the sun came out again, raising little wisps of steam from the bonnet when he parked outside the Red House and went inside.

Author's Note

Like the other novels in the 'Echoland' series this is a work of fiction set against a background of real events, in this case in June and July 1941. The political, diplomatic and military backgrounds are broadly accurate, but the plot and the main characters are fictitious.

Once again I'm indebted to my friend and unpaid researcher Maurice Byrne for his assistance with period details and, especially, for introducing me to the Norden bombsight, which was the most expensive piece of military hardware developed by the United States before the Manhattan Project.

My thanks also to Sam Tranum, who edited this book, and to Dan Bolger and all at New Island for this edition.